Also by Nancy Frederick

Hungry for Love
Touring the Afterlife
A Change of Heart
Starstruck
The Sportin' Life

The Astro Tutor
Love and Sex Under the Stars
The Lover's Dream
Love Games: Psychic Paths to Love
Palmistry: All Lines Lead to Love
Tarot: Love is in the Cards

Copyright 2013 by Nancy Frederick
ISBN-13:
978-0615859408 (Heart and Soul Press)
ISBN-10:
0615859402

This is a work of fiction. Names, characters, places and incidents either are the product of this author's imagination or are used fictitiously, and any resemblance to any actual persons, living or dead, events, or locales is entirely coincidental.

Heart & Soul Press

Dawn Any Minute

Nancy Frederick

Being no stranger to the sort of shipwreck that involves no boats, but nevertheless leaves you capsized and gasping for breath, Alice long ago had formulated the one philosophy that to this day she attempted to uphold — remain in shallow waters, in hazardless spaces that could harbor no threats to life, limb, or more importantly, peace of mind. Take no risks, make no sudden moves, never let a whim or a passion provoke the sort of spectacular foolhardiness that could ultimately result in utter and unrecoverable misery. There were powerful forces below the surface, that Alice knew only too well, but in the right environment, with the proper degree of orchestrated serenity, no threats of that sort would be there at the ready to rise from murky depths and forever change the course of her destiny.

At this moment, watery calamities were nowhere on Alice's mind, although there was a shipwreck of sorts claiming her attention. Her sister, who was supposed to dress up as Princess Cupcake, had begged off at the last minute — again. And now Alice stood face to face with this clown named Julian, who appeared young enough to be a high school student, yet he claimed to be a friend of Alice's twenty-two year old daughter. He smiled up at her, and Alice was by no means tall. His hair, sandy and limp, was rather shaggy, and as Alice gazed at him, he stepped even closer. She had the sense that this was some learned behavior, designed to draw her in. But to what?

"Skye wanted me to let you know she'll be here in time to fill in as Miss Cupcake."

"It's Princess Cupcake," Alice corrected, feeling silly. Who was this clown, Alice wondered.

"I'm an actor," he confided, smiling cinematically. "Skye thought I could help you with the entertainment— I've been on the stage many times—and even on TV— commercials—you probably saw some." Once again he unleashed what Alice was sure he believed was an irresistible smile.

Alice glanced toward the kitchen. The big mixer, a barely functioning relic, was making a worrisome noise, and the cook preparing the pizza dough needed some help. Today she had three parties running, a tea for pre-teens who would arrive in dresses and flower-adorned hats; a cupcake decorating party for little girls; and a pirate pizza party, which should start in less than an hour. And the pizza dough in the kitchen was barely rising. It was the sort of day that made Alice wish for the millionth time that she'd had the nerve to break free from this place and open a little bakery with a few tables. She could see the cases filled with beautiful baked goods, the soups bubbling at the back and a choice of salads, maybe a cheese platter with artisanal bread. It would be a wonderful, far less stressful place to work, and Alice could see it all, but she could also see her aunt, and her uncle, their legacy, her own history, and the haven provided for her when she really needed it. Once she had been a rebel, and look how that had turned out.

Julian, sensing her momentary lapse, coughed subtly, then twitched a bit and scratched at his neck, where the ruffle of his clown suit had created a red streak. In his hand was a satchel, which Alice imagined contained brightly colored scarves, balloons, and other tricks of the clowning trade.

Alice took only a second to muse. "The boys' party has a pirate theme, and we do have a pirate costume, but I don't think it'll fit you. My uncle used to wear it, and he was very large."

Julian—were babies still named Julian—blushed. He tugged at the polka dotted sleeves of his costume, which floated over his wrists. "Oh don't worry. I have many skits right here," he said, pointing sagely to his head. "The thing is this—use your instrument, flow into the moment and the moment will adapt all around you."

One of the cooks emerged from the kitchen to pull Alice back into another problem, so she nodded toward Julian.

"The costume closet is right there," said Alice, pointing, "In case you need any props or—um—accessories. Check it out, then come into the kitchen for something to eat before the party starts."

Apparently Julian had the gift of improvisation, and it was that which today he bestowed on the birthday boy, dragging him up before the group of his schoolmates and into a little skit, which would have been fine, had it not somehow been lifted from *GoodFellas* or some other violent crime drama. He'd remained in his clown suit, but had added an eye patch, a fedora, a sash holding a rustic looking sword, and a revolver from the Dillinger era. He paced across the room as though upon a stage, each step more threatening, each expression more intimidating. "You," he shouted menacingly, pointing to one of the guests, "I know all about that sleazebag stunt you pulled. And now you're gonna pay for it. When I get done with you, you'll beg to die! Get over here, get on your knees, and start praying!"

When the boy blushed and remained seated, Julian strode up behind him and strong-armed him, saying, "Your time is up, mother—um—sucker." He fondled the revolver and glared at the child, saying, "Soon you'll be begging me to shoot you. But then I'd have to collect for the bullet too!" Julian put an arm lock around the child, elevating him from his seat, while the group of boys, jaws agape, watched stunned.

"Wait a minute," squeaked the guest, but Julian had pressed his hand to the boy's mouth, and seemed to be manhandling him down to the floor quite violently, as the other boys gasped. Then Julian bent over, his back to the boys, and appeared to be pummeling their friend into bloody oblivion. "Scream," he whispered into the ear of his supposed victim, and the boy obliged rather convincingly, causing more gasps from the crowd.

"Bobby!" Julian shouted to the birthday boy, "Kick him. Get him in the nuts!"

"His name is Colton," said one of the kids.

Colton, who lacked Julian's appreciation for the dramatic, grew hysterical and began weeping. "Nuts," he cried, "They have nuts here. Somebody could die!" Everyone at school knew how dangerous nuts were and no nuts were allowed there. Nuts were poison, everyone knew that.

Alice, who had been in the kitchen filling squeeze decorating bottles with a rainbow of buttercreams, emerged to see an angry young mother walking toward her. She was the sort of quasi-anorexic California blonde who didn't function well around food anyway, and the smell of pizza, hamburgers and the other food on the *Party Party Party* menu probably had made her even angrier, because she no doubt had never consumed any of these foods not only recently, but since before puberty.

"That deranged clown ruined my son's party. Never mind the party, Colton's been traumatized. Tonight he'll probably have clown nightmares. We didn't even order a clown, and certainly not a homicidal, violent clown. How dare you hire a psycho to menace children."

Alice looked toward the center of the vast space, designed by her uncle to host several parties at once. Less a restaurant than an empty room which could be filled with anything the host desired, it provided food from a decent kitchen and a total party experience for children. Today a play area had been filled with a bouncy house, a sliding board, and a large jungle gym. Colton was inside the jungle gym, running down the ramps and laughing.

"I'm terribly sorry," said Alice. "I'm sure he won't have nightmares—look—he seems okay now. Julian just didn't realize what he was supposed to do."

"That interests me how?"

Alice knew she was completely in the wrong, and although it wasn't her fault, it was her responsibility, but something about this woman irked her, reminded her of someone she'd despised long ago, and her inclination was to do nothing to make amends. Her eyes narrowed, and she reached protectively up to her forehead as she often did when meeting strangers, so that she could cover the scars there. But her bangs hid them, Alice knew that, except for a little area at her temple, which her hand now shielded. She glanced toward a nice looking older man who'd walked up and gently wrapped his arm around the blonde's shoulder. Funny, though, the man didn't look the sort to need a trophy wife. He looked—well—human—that was the way Alice described him to herself.

"I'm really sorry about this mix-up with the entertainment for your son's party," said Alice sincerely. "He's a friend of my daughter's and just came along today—he wasn't actually booked. I know that's no excuse. He's a drama student and apparently not used to entertaining children. I really do apologize."

"Colton is severely traumatized. Are you going to pay his therapy bills?" asked the woman.

"My daughter is just worried about my grandson," said the man, smiling. "Though he doesn't exactly look any worse for wear." He glanced to where the boys were playing and laughing happily.

"I tell you what," said Alice, relaxing a bit on hearing this, "We'll take care of the charges. I really am sorry, and I know you've been here before. And I'll pack up some extra cupcakes for you to take home with you."

"That's very kind of you," said the man. Inexplicably, he extended a hand toward Alice and said, "Tom Angelico."

Alice shook his hand and replied, "Alice Catson."

"I appreciate your sense of honor," he answered, leading his seething daughter away.

Julian by then had retreated into the prop closet, and quickly emerged with the too-large jacket of a Prince Charming costume over his clown suit, which he belted with a tight sash. Alice pictured some insane romantic skit in which his pants fell to his ankles, revealing baggy clown underwear — or worse — his 'instrument.'

"Listen," she said somberly, "No more violence, okay? These are children, birthday parties, you get it, right?"

"Once art is dictated by its observers, it stops being art," he said, as though reciting from a text book or, thought Alice, reading a fortune cookie.

"We're serving cupcakes, burgers, pizza, tea sandwiches here. Not art. It's children's birthdays not — um — um — dinner theater."

"But now little Bobby has something to remember about his birthday, a story he can always tell."

"Who?" asked Alice.

"Little Bobby, the birthday kid."

Alice sighed. "Why don't I pay you for your work today. I appreciate you filling in." She looked toward the door hopefully, imagining him walking through it and out of her way, before he could instigate any further kamikaze clown stunts, forcing her to start paying the customers instead of the other way around.

"Don't be silly," he said, cinching his waist just a bit more tightly, "I'm happy to help you out. I couldn't possibly take your money. And besides, Skye and I will be doing a skit together later for the cupcake thing. She told me to wait here for her."

"Nothing violent," Alice said, "No bad language. Skye knows what to do."

"She's very talented," he said implausibly.

Alice, briefly contemplating his assessment of Skye's talents, wondered was he a patient at the dental office where Skye was a hygienist. Alice looked toward the door again, but then the group of girls had arrived for their tea party, and she had to greet them and lead them to the patio, which had already been set up.

It was a beautiful June day, and by now the Santa Monica marine layer had burned off and there was a sunny spot out in the back garden, which was a favorite location for tea parties, bridal and baby showers, and other girly gatherings. She'd set up a long table outside, and there were lace doilies on the flowered table cloth, silver candelabras, and two bouquets of beautiful pink and white flowers. Alice greeted the mom in charge, Mrs. McMurtry, and her adult friend, and watched as the girls seated themselves at the table.

Wait staff brought out several pots of tea in antique flowered china tea pots, as well as tiered servers with dainty sandwiches, scones, small muffins, pots of clotted cream, jam, and flavored butters. Each place was set with a different antique china plate, and in front of them were tiny baskets of chocolates. The napkins were tied with grosgrain bows. It was a paradise of sweet innocence.

Everything was going very well, and when she saw Julian distributing party favors from a basket of roses provided by the mother of the birthday girl, which actually were hair clips with glittered silk flowers glued on, it seemed that he had understood her, so Alice returned to the kitchen to set up the trays of cupcakes for the next group.

Rising over the normal chatter of the kitchen staff, came a shrill scream from the patio, prompting Alice to race out there. Julian, who'd been making the rounds of the table, offering each girl her rose hairpiece, had with each delivery spoken a few lines from Shakespeare, something that did in fact seem appropriate. By the time he approached the eighteen year old sister of the guest of honor, he knelt with a flourish, took her hand in his and gazed deeply into her eyes, causing the younger girls to giggle. He summoned all his actor's majesty, and with deep import, intoned, "They do not love that do not show their love. The course of true love never did run smooth. Love is a familiar. Love is a devil. There is no evil angel but Love."

Oddly, the teen shrieked, then sniffled and rose from her seat, her hand over her mouth, and she dashed toward the ladies' room with her mother running behind her. Alice followed them both, baffled at what could be wrong, and she found them jammed into one of the stalls with the girl throwing up.

Mrs. McMurtry turned toward Alice and said, "What was in those sandwiches? My daughter has food poisoning."

Alice shook her head. "No, of course not. They were all made just minutes ago."

"Love is an evil angel-devil," said the girl, walking to the sink to rinse out her mouth, as both Alice and her mother turned to look at her.

"Love?" asked Mrs. McMurtry.

"Love!" said Alice.

"Love," repeated Mrs. McMurtry glumly, comprehending something she did not want to know. "Jocelyn, is there something you want to tell me?"

Jocelyn shook her head despondently, indicating she'd rather die than tell her mother. "Charley got down on his knee like that, and he gave me a rose. And then what did I see? He was kissing puke face." Jocelyn glanced toward the stall where she herself was a puke face just seconds ago.

"I should give you some privacy," said Alice respectfully.

Mrs. McMurtry said, "And your stomach is upset," although she knew it wasn't.

"Show your love," said Jocelyn wretchedly, as Alice inched toward the door.

Mrs. McMurtry took her daughter by the shoulders and shook her. "I'm going to kill you. What were you thinking? Eighteen years old."

"It can't happen the first time, everyone knows that."

"Yes it can," said Alice and Mrs. McMurtry simultaneously.

Alice saw her own reflection in the mirror along with that of the two other women. Her brown hair was smooth and silky, and her face still pretty and unlined—in fact she was prettier now at forty than she ever was in her thirties. Her blue eyes still sparkled as merrily as they always had. Her figure was rounded, but not too rounded, and she didn't look bad in her old-fashioned apron. Then she saw the faces morph into images from her past, the girl before her transformed into her own earlier self, the mother into her own mom, one scared and humiliated, the other enraged and disappointed. How odd to feel it being relived, to have it all come back.

"You've ruined your life," said Mrs. McMurtry, just as Alice's mother, ever the stern high school principal, had said to her. Then Great Aunt Kitty had stepped in and said that no, of course it wasn't ruined, it was just changed.

"Maybe it's just a change in plans," said Alice, "But eventually…"

Mrs. McMurtry turned angrily toward Alice, saying, "Why are you still here?"

"Of course," said Alice. "Let me know if you need anything." She was speaking to the mother, but her eyes locked on the daughter, and she hoped the girl saw her, saw that she wasn't as lost as she feared.

By this time, the cupcake decorating party had begun, and apparently Skye had been there and done a good job as Princess Cupcake, and whatever extra skit she'd planned with Julian had been completed without tears, and they'd both taken off without waiting to chat with Alice.

Before she could begin showing the girls how to decorate cupcakes, she was accosted by the irate mother of the guest of honor. "Nobody was watching these children, did you know that? And one of them squirted frosting onto my daughter's dress. What would've happened if I hadn't come back in to attend to her?"

Alice looked toward the table, where several of the girls were at this moment frosting their fingernails. "Where were you?" Alice asked calmly.

"Not that it's your business, but I had to make a phone call, and went outside."

"Parents are required to stay with the children. We don't provide babysitters. We teach how to frost cupcakes yes, but someone isn't at your table every moment of the party. We did let you know that."

"Not that you would understand this," said the woman huffily, "But I have a very important job."

"Next time get your assistant to keep track of the children," said Alice, refusing to be brow beaten any longer. The woman looked sheepish, and she said nothing as Alice turned and began demonstrating how to frost a cupcake.

Once the partygoers had gone, Alice was left alone to review the stack of repair estimates on her desk. *Party Party Party*, or P3, as it was called by the family, was in trouble. Alice wondered, as she often did, how Aunt Kitty and Uncle Henry had managed this place so adeptly, but of course there were two of them, a seamless unit. There were supposed to be two of her as well; her sister Totsie pretended to be her partner, but only on days when checks were issued. She looked toward the ceiling for a moment, recalling something, what was it—a joke—or a saying—*the faster I goes the behinder I gets*. Was that it? Wait, she thought, no, wasn't it Lewis Carroll, *the hurrier I go, the behinder I get*. She sighed, thinking that about summed it up.

Alice slumped into the house, and sighing with exhaustion, set down a collection of boxes containing party leftovers. There, in the booth built into one end of the old-fashioned kitchen, sat her sixteen year old nephew Cooper, who'd been crashing with her for a few weeks, and her future son-in-law, Greg.

"Skye's missing," said Cooper, with a glance toward the back door.

"No, she's not," answered Alice. "She filled in for your mother as Princess Cupcake this afternoon."

Greg slouched visibly in his seat. Alice could read relief on his face but also something else, concern.

"She hasn't been home in days," said Cooper.

"What?" said Alice.

Greg nodded glumly. Alice wondered why he had said nothing about this, but she was used to his shyness and his silence.

Alice stepped to the back door and peered through the kitchen window. Beyond the house in which she'd lived for quite some years was a two-story strip of apartments that inhabited what might have been a nice back yard were they not there. She smiled, thinking of Uncle Henry and his practical nature. Once upon a time she'd moved into one of those apartments with her new baby, her joy marred by trauma and tragedy, back when Great Aunt Kitty and Uncle Henry had lived here in the house. Now, she tried to glance toward where Skye lived with Greg, but of course she couldn't see her daughter's car, for the building blocked her view of the street where Skye normally parked.

"Car's not there," said Greg.

"She left P3 a couple hours ago," said Alice, "I assumed to come home. We didn't really have time to talk—it was a crazy day. Is something wrong? I mean have you been fighting?"

A look of insecurity crossed Greg's face.

"Did she take any clothes with her?" Alice asked, reaching for her cell phone.

Cooper immediately clicked his own phone, then said, obviously to voice mail, "Yo Skye, enough with the bunk-off. You better bounce back home like yesterday...."

Hearing all this, Alice walked toward Cooper, shook her head and took the phone from him, speaking into it, "Hon, we're a little worried. Greg says you haven't been home. Could you give me a call, please."

Alice handed the phone back to Cooper and asked, "Did you check with Aunt Kitty? Both boys shook their heads, so Alice grabbed one of the boxes she'd brought home, and stepped out into the courtyard beyond her kitchen door. It was the open area that lay between her house and the L-shaped row of apartments which now she owned, small units that were constructed like one side of a parenthesis on the edge of the property. Alice tapped on Kitty's door. Inside she could hear the sounds of the television.

Kitty beamed, "Oh you brought a tea party, and just in the nick of time. I'm dying for you to see this. It's always on. They don't seem to have any other programs any more, but it's worth it."

Alice followed her aunt into the living room placing the box filled with leftover tea sandwiches and cupcakes on a coffee table, then reached for the remote to lower the volume of the television.

"Look," said Kitty, beaming, "Meet my new boyfriend. Doesn't he just remind you of Reymundo?" Kitty laughed. "Henry was so jealous of the way he flirted with me. Made our marriage even more fun. Drive a man wild — it's worth it every time."

Alice glanced at the screen. There was a tall, handsome chef dicing peppers elegantly, and briefly Alice admired his excellent knife skills. He spoke confidently and comfortably, as though he were at home with friends, rather than in front of a camera, and somehow to Alice his New Orleans accent sounded like liquid sex. He didn't look like the typically doughy cook, but was chiseled and well-muscled, as though he worked out at least as much as he ate. He had dark brown hair and eyes which looked a bit dramatic against his fair skin, and teeth that were so spectacularly white and sparkling, he might have been cast in a toothpaste commercial. Immediately she was drawn into the show, and all thoughts of querying her aunt about missing programming flew out of her head. Something happened deep inside her, a sort of squirminess she'd long ago thought was under control. Then he grinned, and Alice felt herself almost lose her balance.

A smile crossed Aunt Kitty's weathered face. Her blue eyes, still flinty, gleamed. "He's as hot as his food, isn't he, Ally?"

Alice blushed.

Aunt Kitty bit into one of Alice's sandwiches. "Mmm," she said, "Salmon spread. We never did that back in the day. That's right up Mr. Wonderful's alley. He's some kind of badass, that's what they call him, badass chef, so naughty! Don't you love the way his eyes sparkle?"

Alice was indeed mesmerized by the chef's sparkling eyes, and she remained silent until they cut to commercial, which finally snapped her out of her trance, restoring to mind the reason for her visit, so she asked her aunt, "Have you seen Skye?"

"Not today. Isn't she off with her hands in somebody's mouth? Teeth," she shuddered, "What a way to make a living. Opposite of parties, that's for sure."

"The office isn't open on weekends any more," said Alice. "She was Princess Cupcake today, though. Brought some clown with her."

"Shaggy little guy. Yeah I've seen him. Those little terriers never appealed to me. Give me a *man*, like Reymundo here, or your Uncle Henry. Or Skye's dad, what's his name, poor guy."

"Harvey Itzkin," said Alice softly.

"That's not it," disagreed Kitty. "That's not what you called him."

"Itch," sighed Alice, wondering was she being pulled into some odd sort of time warp. The thought of this did not please her, for she had tried all her adult life to avoid the past and to put its memory behind her. Why was it floating back so insistently today?

"These little ham and cheese biscuits are wonderful. You can make these when you finally go on *You're Cooked*. Oh wait, it's not on any more."

Alice shielded her temple with her palm. "You know that was just a fantasy. But the show's on. Weeknight, Tuesday maybe?"

"I don't think so," sang Kitty with certainty, as she dug around in the box of leftovers to locate her next nibble.

Alice took a moment to explain to her aunt how the online guide worked, and how to watch live or recorded television, but almost immediately she interrupted.

"Don't lose Reymundo," Kitty crowed.

"It's right here, don't worry," said Alice soothingly. "But if you want to watch something else, just click this."

Yearning to lie on her couch and nap for a while, Alice kissed her aunt and walked back to her own door. She melted down into the booth with the boys, wishing only to breathe, and not deal with any more dopey problems or annoying people.

Cooper lowered his voice to a whisper that was still clearly audible. "Bird brain alert."

Robin, Skye's step-dad, strode into the kitchen holding up several pairs of socks with the tags still attached. His sandy hair was neatly clipped, and his eyes were lined due to many hours on the golf course. He was a small man, barely taller than Alice herself, and his demeanor was of an expectation of the privilege and respect due to someone in the medical field, yet under it was a shadowing of disappointment and resentment that the hoped-for respect remained permanently beyond his grasp.

"What's this?" he said irately.

"Aren't they jazzy," said Alice, "Harrison Ford wore some like them in a movie."

"Since when do I need million dollar socks?" He snapped the bands on the socks suspiciously, as though he were investigating were they imposters, shoddy goods that in short order would not prove their worth.

"They're so nice," said Alice, sighing. "I thought you'd enjoy wearing them."

Cooper, long weary of this man he considered a blight on Alice's life, started to rise from the booth, saying, "Yo, Cheapy Cheaperson, didn't your mother teach you to say thanks when you get a gift?" When Alice put her hand on his to quiet him, Cooper sat back down, but his eyes flashed angrily.

Robin glared at the boy, saying, "You know they have laws about dumping kids off at the fire station. Doesn't have to be an infant — any kid you want to get rid of."

"I know so many lawyers," said Cooper, "I'd be an emancipated minor before you could say sock puppet."

Alice laughed, trying to diffuse the tension. "What, you're Stanley Kowalski now with a lawyer acquaintance? What an imagination."

"Why are you still in my house?" queried Robin, quarreling as though with an equal. Alice cocked her head and looked at him imploringly. Somebody had to be the grownup.

"No," said Cooper with utter confidence and not the slightest degree of fear, "You're in my aunts' house. This house belongs to Kitty and Ally, not you."

"Some day you might grow up a little," said Robin, seething, "And then maybe you'll be a decent person."

"Yeah, at least there's hope for *me*," said Cooper, looking Robin up and down with a sneer.

"Lord almighty!" Alice's patience broke, and she rapped her fist on the table. "Enough. I can return the socks. I've been dealing with aggravations all day." Alice rose from the booth, raised her hand in a gesture demanding silence, and walked to the kitchen door.

"Sorry, Aunt Ally Cat," said Cooper.

"This is dinner?" asked Robin, opening the boxes and shoving them aside.

"We don't have to eat this if you don't want. Let's go out," said Alice. "It's Saturday night. We'll have a nice dinner and relax."

"What—is it somebody's birthday?" scowled Robin.

"In my world it's somebody's birthday every day. We could go try that new fish place."

"Fish? That's like thirty bucks a plate." Robin looked toward the boxes of leftover pizzas and then up toward the ceiling. "I work hard, you know. Doesn't mean I want to spend it all on flounder."

Alice shook her head with frustration. "What exactly do you want then, Robin?"

"I want my wife to cook me dinner like she's supposed to. And not because you're playing some stupid version of a TV cooking show."

Greg had shrunk down, trying to be invisible long enough so that he could make a dash for the door and exit the strife. Cooper, who was already over six feet tall, scowled and rose from the bench, protectively striding over to Alice and stepping between her and Robin, who immediately took a pace back as Cooper encircled Alice's shoulders with his arm. "I'll take you out to dinner, Aunt Ally—anywhere you want to go." He patted his jeans pocket and said, "I'm loaded. Want a flounder or a halibut—or both. It would be my pleasure."

Alice smiled and shook her head while Robin glared at the boy.

"You're so loaded maybe you should start paying rent around here. Or go home where you belong," sneered Robin.

Alice glanced at Robin, remembering back to the day when five-year old Skye had looked up at her, saying 'I think Robin's my daddy.' Alice had just said 'You know your daddy. He's in the hospital. He's resting—you know—he's like Sleeping Beauty.' Then Skye had squinted with determination and said 'I hate to tell you this Mommy, but real daddies wake up. They're not Sleeping Beauty—that's just a story. Real daddies wake up in the morning—they're not make believe like Sleeping Beauty.' Alice had blinked back tears then and hugged Skye for a long time.

"Well," said Alice, "I'm going out. To the fish place. C'mon boys, let's get some dinner. You coming?" she asked Robin.

"I'll be damned if I'll treat these freeloaders to a meal. Where's Skye, anyway?"

"I'll go check if she's back, you go without me," said Greg, beating the retreat he'd been praying for.

Robin harumphed and shuffled out of the room, leaving Alice and Cooper to walk to the car without him. "How'd you get to be such a Sir Galahad?" Alice asked Cooper.

"What, for my favorite aunt? That's dinner, not chivalry."

"You're just too smart."

Cooper laughed. "Nope, I'm just smart enough. And I really do know some lawyers. Anytime you want to skeet shoot." Cooper made a gesture of someone lifting his rifle, looking toward the sky for the clay pigeon to appear, and then he pulled the trigger with a loud rushing noise. He looked toward Alice and began humming *Bye Bye Birdie*.

"You kill me," laughed Alice.

After dinner, they drove toward Beverly Hills, where Alice's sister lived with her much-older husband.

"Oh no," said Cooper, grimacing. "Nobody wants to see *Dumb and Dumber* right after dinner. We could be puking up that expensive fish."

Alice continued driving toward Totsie's house, knowing she should check on her, and also wondering if she could be counted on for the parties they were doing in the next couple of days. She felt disloyal every time she considered hiring someone to replace her sister, because Totsie made such a big deal of their supposed partnership, but more often than not she was absent when Alice needed her most, and she had no real stake in the business except an imaginary one.

"She begged me to bring you over," said Alice.

"You're dumping me back there?" Cooper blanched, and Alice saw his bravado evaporate. "I just can't be part of that, you know it."

Alice patted his shoulder. "Hon, you can stay with me as long as you want. Nobody's dumping you anywhere. I just think we should check on them."

"Way to give a growing kid a heart attack."

Alice smiled at Cooper, "You'll always have me. Good aunts run in our family."

Cooper took a deep breath, and Alice saw the tension leave his face. Then his normal impudence returned, and he said, "So last night I saw this really old movie about some bad kitty with a wangsta husband she hated, and this himbo she sassered into icing the dude."

"Coop, have you ever heard of a decoder ring?" asked Alice.

"Lotta funny stuff in the movie, you woulda liked it," he answered.

"I had a decoder ring, well it was an old one, probably belonged to my dad actually. Each letter was in code, and you put in one for another and finally spelled out the word."

"Totally," said Cooper, smiling at her in the way kids did at uncool people they loved anyway. "Shoot your eye out, I remember. Red Ryder. Soap poisoning. *A Christmas Story*. You want to watch that after we referee the pezzas?"

Alice shook her head. She knew he was teasing her. "I don't have that decoder ring any more. You think maybe there's an app for all this slang you keep inflicting on me?"

Cooper gave her a glance, a sort of audacious scowl with a downturn of his lip and a flip up of his eyelid. He'd been doing it since he was a little boy. He pulled his phone from his pocket and typed in something as he read aloud, "App for wiseass aunts to decode handsome nephew's lingo, wait, wait, wait, it's scrolling, searching. Sorry Aunt Ally Cat, they say you're not ready for this cool stuff."

Alice laughed. "If you only knew," she said.

"See now," that's the sort of dope line I'm talking about. Really old movie. Guy falls for the booth babe and they have this great banter."

Alice turned down Totsie's street, but a Porsche was hogging the middle of Totsie's two lane driveway, so she parked on the street.

"Blargh," said Cooper, "Astronaut's Wife alert. C'mon, let's go in through the garage."

"We'll have to see them eventually—I mean we're here to visit, so we could just knock on the door," said Alice, but by then Cooper had already opened the door at the side of the garage, and so she followed him in.

"Watch it," he said as Alice nearly tripped over some faded For Sale signs from a defunct real estate agency. The lights came on automatically and Alice jumped. A mouse darted out of a case of decades old herbal diet drink canisters and disappeared.

"At least it's not a boathouse rigged to explode," said Cooper.

"There was no boathouse in *Double Indemnity,*" said Alice, as she squeezed between Totsie's VW Rabbit convertible and a pile of boxes containing out of style shades of Lucy L'Amour lipsticks.

"What?" Cooper asked, moving aside a couple of boxes holding unpacked waterless cooking sets. On top of that he stacked some boxes labeled *Cooper's baby clothes.* "I just wonder which of them is gonna scam some doorknocker into offing the other. Like in that old movie. It's bound to come to that, sooner or later."

"Yeah," said Alice, "*Double Indemnity.*"

Finally they got to the interior door, and Cooper opened it, saying softly, "C'mon to my room 'til that aviation blonde pulls a ghost. Bad enough dealing with the two of them."

"Aviation?" asked Alice, stepping past a guest bathroom which was so crammed with giant packs of paper goods the door would no longer close.

"You don't want to know, it's crude," said Cooper. He crept up the back staircase, and Alice had no choice but to follow him, because how was she going to march into the living room, where Totsie had a guest, and interrupt while Cooper was with her but not with her.

They walked past the long hallway, which was littered with boxes of every sort, into Cooper's room. "So, he's trying to pick up this—ahem—*woman*—" said Cooper, "And he tells her how he wants to love someone, hold someone, how he needs it. It's touching and romantic."

Alice stopped folding up a bunch of laundry mixed in with new clothes piled on the bed, and just looked at Cooper, who was smiling as he told the story. She couldn't help but return his smile and give him her full attention.

"And she, all unconcerned, says, 'So get married.'"

"Um, hmm," said Alice, totally up to speed, but she didn't want to give away that she knew the movie.

"And then he says 'but I only need it for tonight.' And she spits out Italian ice all over her white shirt."

Alice laughed.

"So you saw it."

She nodded. "I've seen them all. Maybe sometime you'll see *Double Indemnity*—it's the movie *Body Heat* was based on. Very risqué for its day."

"I'm so glad you're here!" A booming voice came from the doorway, as Mitchell Briarwood stepped into the room and hugged first his son then Alice. "I've had these in my pocket for days," he said, handing checks both to Cooper and Alice.

"Wow, ten K," said Cooper. "Thanks, Pops," then he hugged his dad again.

"I can't take this," said Alice, pressing it back into Mitchell's hand. "Why," she said, "What were you thinking?"

"And here we go," said Cooper, pocketing the check.

"It's just a matter of time," said Mitchell despondently. He was tall and robust, like his son, and even though he was close to seventy, he glowed and looked as though he could move an armoire without even panting.

"Until what?" asked Alice.

"The end. Of course, the end," said Mitchell.

"End of what?" asked Alice.

"Me," said Mitchell dourly, "Of my life. Nothing lasts forever."

"You're sick?" asked Alice. Cooper had pulled a couple of duffel bags from his closet and was packing some clothing, remaining silent as he worked.

"I'm so sorry." Alice stretched out her hand and laid it gently on Mitchell's arm. "I didn't know. What's wrong exactly, if you don't mind my asking."

Mitchell slumped down onto the bed, where Cooper had recently removed the collection of new clothes. "They won't tell me. I had a check up, and they said nothing's wrong. For all I know it's my pancreas."

"Oh," said Alice, "I'm sorry. But you look so totally healthy and well."

Mitchell scowled as though he'd just been given a death sentence instead of a compliment.

Cooper turned from the closet and said, "Pops, you're not sick. I'm happy to take your money, but you're not sick. Not one but three doctors told you you're fine."

"Conspirators," Mitchell answered. "Well I can give away my money now, before I die, it's my call, nevermind the lying medicos on your mother's payroll."

"Look, Pops, you're old, super old, I give you that. But what you're not is dying. At least not now. Somebody could find you blown up in a boat house one day, but that's got nothing to do with a perfectly good pancreas."

"A boat!" said Mitchell. "Now you're home, we'll get a boat. What do you think — speed boat or sail boat —

maybe both. Let's enjoy the summer, what I have left of it."

"Thank God!" exclaimed Totsie, walking into the room carrying several heavy shopping bags. "I thought my idiot husband was now talking to himself, giving more money away, but to imaginary people, well that would be better, wouldn't it." She shoved some bags already waiting in Cooper's closet aside and deposited the new ones in front.

Totsie wrapped her arms around Cooper and shrieked, "My baby is home!" Her hair this week was a bright red, almost orange really, and she wore a tank top and designer jeans that came from the junior department. Although she was Alice's younger sister, she was only two years younger, but she'd never stopped acting like a teenager.

Mitchell turned toward his wife, and said in a stern and punitive tone, "I made your sister a little present," holding the check out for Totsie to see. "But she won't take it. Yet." Then he smiled at Alice as though he expected to change her mind.

"I need an aspirin," said Cooper.

"What're we going to do when you've given all our money away, and we can't pay property taxes on this place?" asked Totsie, enraged. "If you think I plan to move into a refrigerator box with you, think again."

"You've been spending my money like a Vegas hooker since we got married," said Mitchell, "And now you're bitching when I do the same."

"I get stuff we need," said Totsie, as though it were true. "I'm not some delusional crazy psycho, pretending he's dying and giving away money."

"Delusional and crazy," said Cooper, "Don't need a slang app to translate that into parents." He grabbed the bags he'd packed, and turned to go out the door. "I'll be in the car."

"Wait," said Mitchell, "Let me give you some dough."

Totsie pulled on Alice and said, "Come downstairs for a bit. We have to talk."

Alice sat on one sofa in the living room facing Totsie on another. There were several bubble-wrapped, oversized paintings stacked on the floor in the corner, and on a large table at the end of the room, several pieces of antique silver from a vintage tea set were also cocooned.

"You're actually getting rid of some stuff," noted Alice.

"What?" exclaimed Totsie, glancing around desperately to determine what was going missing. "I just got these. Anyway never mind that. You know who was just here, right?"

"Some aviator?" asked Alice.

"That's disgusting," said Totsie. "I can't believe you'd use a word like that."

"I'm losing track here. It was a killer day," sighed Alice.

"My life coach, that's who, and I'm sure she's a natural blonde, for your information. And neatly waxed."

Alice squinted all around the room without seeing much, as she was trying to understand what was being said. There was a blonde life coach who flew planes and polished furniture seemed to be the answer, but it still made little sense. Wow, did she need a nap.

"I had a fantastic breakthrough, just a few minutes ago, right on this couch. You want to know what I learned?"

"Okay," said Alice.

"This is the only moment we're in," said Totsie.

"Okay?"

"That's it," said Totsie. "That's *it*. Take some time and really think about it. This is the only moment we're in."

"Okay," said Alice, thinking about the couch in her den, and wishing she were lying on it.

"I'm no time traveler," explained Totsie. "I'm not in yesterday any more. *This* is the only moment I'm in."

"Um, okay," said Alice.

"So you understand," said Totsie, smiling happily. "I was so worried this would be harder. But you're on board. You're on my side. Oh, Ally, this means so much to me." Totsie leapt from the couch and reached out to Alice and hugged her tightly.

Alice looked off into the distance for a moment, growing more exhausted by the second. "What am I on board with?"

"With my big decision of course." Totsie reached into her skin-tight jeans and struggled briefly, then finally extracted a now-wrinkled business card, which she presented to Alice as though it were an award. "Tatiana Briarwood, Certified Life Coach," she intoned majestically, just as she had when she'd become a licensed real estate broker, a cosmetics distributor, and an interior decorator.

"Oh geez," said Alice.

"Don't worry Ally, it's only a thirty-minute course online. I can do it. I know you believe in me."

Alice remained silent, smiling wanly and realizing that she now would have to hire someone to fill in for Totsie, until she got sick of this new career and stored whatever paraphernalia was attached to it in the garage.

"I love you so much," said Totsie, hugging Alice again. "And I'm here for you. Don't you worry, I'm here to offer you my help and wisdom any time you need me."

After embracing Totsie, and refusing yet again the check from Mitchell, Alice slowly walked back outside to her car. She'd been awake for at least twenty-two hours, and she needed to sleep.

Alice sighed and said, "Don't suppose you want to be Princess Cupcake for a while."

Cooper laughed and launched into a Julia Child imitation, as he began typing on his cell phone. He asked her a few questions, still in the infamous falsetto, then said, "Okay, you have an ad running, and you can either select a free intern or pay some chick to be Princess Cupcake."

"What would I do without you," Alice said, her mind on tomorrow's cakes and cupcakes she had yet to bake tonight, but she knew a nap, even just an hour, was absolutely necessary, so the moment she entered the house, she walked into her den, which was completely unchanged from when it was Uncle Henry's, and she flopped onto the scuffed green leather couch. Then she saw Robin, seated at her desk, some bills in his hand and her laptop in front of him.

"Want to tell me how you plan to pay all these bills? A new roof for that stupid *Party Party Party*, a new walk-in. The place is falling apart, and you're barely making ends meet." Robin glared at her, then thrust her laptop at her with a spreadsheet on it. "When is it going to be my turn, that's what I want to know, our turn."

Alice glared back at Robin. "I'm not doing this now."

"At least you didn't spring for an expensive dinner. Finally that brat is good for something." He grasped several pencils, and began inserting them into the battery operated sharpener on the desk.

"Are you kidding me? You think I'm going to let a child buy me dinner? Of course I paid. He's my nephew."

"I just don't want you expecting me to foot the bill for all this folly. We should sell P3. Sell this falling down dump too. It could fund a very nice retirement. Buy a nice little condo. Take the pressure off."

Alice grew more irritated and asked, "Who's the pressure on? Does the money for any of this come out of your pocket? You've lived here rent free since you moved in with us when Skye was six. You think it's some big sacrifice that you spring for utilities and groceries? You know what—you're poring over my finances—maybe tomorrow I'll go over yours." Alice looked defiantly at Robin, who had blanched, and in fact appeared quite terrified. He *was* a Cheapy Cheaperson, she thought; Cooper was right. Then her exhaustion increased, rage set in and Alice said, "Maybe I should start charging *you* rent."

"This is not the life I signed on for."

"This is exactly the life you signed on for. Now let me rest before I have to start all over again."

Robin glared at Alice then stormed out of the den, and although she knew she could shut her eyes and be deep asleep in seconds, she rose from the couch and locked the door. Then she returned to the couch and clicked on the laptop, typing *badass chef* into the search bar. She didn't expect it to work, but there, immediately, was a link for Johnny Badass, and links to watch full episodes. Alice clicked the link, and the episode started, and she watched and listened, and something inside her relaxed, something opened up, and she melted into the vision on the screen. Another part of her, a stern, ironclad part, nudged her, pushed her to turn off the episode, to turn off the show, to stop watching, that watching was a very bad idea, but Alice wasn't in the mood to be ironclad, that squirminess inside her was at this moment too strong, and when she relaxed she also let go, and was lulled into a state of peacefulness, which only increased when her eyes closed, and she could just hear that liquid voice—or was it smoky, she couldn't decide. And then she nodded off, plunged at last into sleep, but it wasn't dreamless, and she was taken back in her dream to when she was eighteen and madly in love with a wild football player named Itch, and he'd said she was the bread to his peanut butter and Skye would be the jelly.

It wasn't the sunlight washing across her face that awakened Alice, but the smell of cakes baking. She sat up abruptly on the old, sagging couch and heard the vertebrae in her back crack. In the kitchen, inexplicably, Skye was baking, and she had managed to produce most of what Alice should have made by now, which was a good thing, because it was nine in the morning, and she had to be at P3 before eleven.

"Sweetheart," said Alice, hugging her daughter tightly. "Thank you so much. I can't believe I passed out like that."

Skye was wearing one of Alice's old-fashioned aprons, and she looked so pretty with her long dark hair tied up in a pony tail. She glanced at Alice nervously, then looked away, then two pairs of blue eyes met across a counter filled with cakes and cupcakes.

"Something wrong, hon?" asked Alice.

"Everything's great," said Skye, "Dad around?"

Alice cocked her head. She had no idea where Robin was. "Did you look upstairs or call out when you came in? He might be playing golf already."

"I might be and I should be, but I'm not," said Robin, entering the kitchen in his slippers and robe. "Not 'til breakfast anyway." He hugged Skye and she kissed him on the cheek and it seemed like a normal morning.

"I made popovers and a frittata, so let's eat," she said.

"Isn't Greg coming?" asked Alice.

"Um, no," said Skye.

Alice looked at her daughter, who sat in the booth next to her, as Robin shoveled the food into his mouth opposite them both. "I'm starving," he said accusingly, "Nobody made me dinner last night."

"I don't want you to get upset, Daddy," Skye said, glancing anxiously at Robin, twisting the engagement ring on her finger. His eyes rose from the food and locked on Skye, but he kept chewing vigorously.

"What's wrong?" asked Alice.

"I quit my job last Friday," said Skye. Robin's mouth hung open and the food in it tumbled back onto his plate. "I realized something important," she continued, "This wasn't what I wanted to do with my life."

"What!" exclaimed Robin. "You're in a dental office, what's better than that?" He glared at the sweets on the counter and scowled. "You're not giving up a real profession to run stupid kids' parties with your mother are you?"

Alice was about to speak up and give him something to think about, when she realized that another fight with him would solve nothing at this moment, so she remained silent and reined in her temper.

"Now, Daddy, I know it was your dream, and you spent all that time in dental school only to end up still working in that lab instead of being a dentist, but maybe you could take that test again. I believe in you, and I know you'd pass it and then you'd have your dream. But, I realized it's not my dream."

"But we talked about this for years," said Robin. "You'd work in my dental office."

Alice shook her head at Robin. He'd been talking about passing the dental boards since she met him in the hospital when Skye was born — and he'd never passed; he always froze during tests. But he still talked about it as though it were an option. She turned to her daughter and asked, "So what is your dream? You could go back to college. That would be wonderful."

"Julian says the theater of life is the best school."

"Who?" demanded Robin.

"That clown," said Alice.

"Now I know you don't like him," said Skye softly to Alice, "But he's amazing, you'll see. Brilliant and super talented."

"Who said I dislike him? So what is it you plan to do?" asked Alice.

"It's not all worked out quite yet. I just know I don't plan to go back to what I was doing. I might take some classes with Julian—you know—audit."

"In the school of life?" asked Robin sarcastically. He clutched a popover in his hand and tore it to pieces, dropping the shards onto his plate.

"USC," said Skye. "I've been with him at school this past week. It's been amazing."

"This is not how we raised you, shacking up in some dorm," said Robin, "When you have a fine fiancé who's a dentist."

"I haven't been shacking up," said Skye in a tremulous voice. "I've been right here every night."

"But Greg said you'd been gone for days," said Alice.

"I've been sleeping here in my room. Then when he's gone off to work, I go home to shower and change."

"You've been sleeping here, and I didn't even know it?" asked Alice. "It's the weekend and he's not at work. So you're hiding out in the kitchen?"

Skye shrugged. It was clear by her eyes that she was feeling rather tortured. She gazed imploringly at Robin and said, "Greg will still help you get your dental license if you want it."

"So are you breaking up with Greg?" Alice asked.

"I don't know." Skye sounded truly miserable.

Alice felt a wave of terror wash over her. Her stomach clenched and her heart raced. A throbbing pain pierced her skull right between her eyes. She clutched Skye's hand. Here was her kind, sane, solid daughter racing out into unknown waters, and perhaps everything would go wrong. Her whole life could be capsized and then what? Disaster could strike. Disasters did strike. It happened all the time. Alice couldn't see herself delivering a stern lecture as her mother had done to her, but how could she shrug and say *go for it* or something else equally absurd. Then it would be her fault when Skye was swallowed up in a tidal wave.

"Well, hon, I don't know," said Alice, haltingly. "Maybe you should give it all a little more thought? Maybe don't make any final decisions immediately."

Skye jumped up and pushed her way out of the booth in front of Alice. "I knew you'd never understand," she said irately, and slammed out the door.

Robin yelled with a full mouth, "I can't even recognize you any more."

Alice rose and followed Skye out the back door and toward her apartment, but before she could knock on the door, she was accosted by her newest tenant, Layla, who was, as usual, wearing as little as possible. Her legs extended so far beyond the shortest of shorts it seemed a physical impossibility, and her inflated breasts were challenged by a bikini top which seemed by comparison to have been designed for a toddler. What was she, thirty, wondered Alice, feeling about a thousand herself, plus her actual forty.

Layla clutched a piece of paper in her hand and seethed visibly. "What is this?" she asked Alice, although clearly she had read it. "You can't legislate my smoking in my own home."

"Normally before anyone new wants to move in we ask if they smoke, and if so we don't rent to them. Nobody here likes smoke."

"This is because of that old fart Alan, isn't it," she asked. "He knocks on my door every day to bitch about something, even when I'm not smoking. He's just... just... just... pervy."

"Look," said Alice as placidly as possible, "Tenants have complained, and that's because there's no smoking here. This just makes it official."

Layla lit a cigarette. "I'm outside now, so I can smoke here, outside."

"You can smoke outside but not in this courtyard. Not in any part of this property. This is a no-smoking building, as it says on that paper. You'd have to go out to the sidewalk, beyond this building."

"I have rights. You have no right to demand I don't smoke in my own home. Robin never said a word about this crap to me when I moved in."

"Well I'm sorry about that—he rarely deals with tenants, so it was an oversight. But you'll have to follow these rules."

"I'm going to talk to Robin about this," said Layla, blowing a puff of smoke in Alice's face.

"He knows," answered Alice, extricating herself from the conversation by stepping around Layla and knocking on Skye's door, which was open, so she walked inside to find Greg and Cooper staring out the window.

"Gosh she's cheap," said Greg.

"I love that about her," said Cooper, grinning.

"Where's Skye?" asked Alice.

Greg shook his head miserably.

"Oh geez," mumbled Alice, "You didn't realize she was baking in my kitchen all this time? Okay I'll call her from the car."

By the time she was on the way to P3, Alice had left three messages for Skye, the last one suggesting they have dinner together and talk some more. She didn't know if her daughter was avoiding her or just unable to talk at the moment, but at least this gave Alice some time to consider what she should say and what she should do. What would be best for Skye, Alice wondered, but she was unable to come to a reliable conclusion. Normally people search for themselves at a younger age, then they settle down, but Skye had settled down too soon, or so it seemed. Maybe she just believed she had settled; Alice hoped this was not the case. Had she allowed Robin to have too much input into Skye's choices? Obviously she had, but how could she tell her daughter, who for whatever reason had always loved Robin, not to pay attention to him. Maybe this was a good thing, and maybe it meant that Skye was in fact her own person, and that she would make a choice for herself that would make her happy; that's what Alice hoped. If only Alice could look at it from Skye's perspective and not see disaster at every turn — maybe she could find the faith to believe that Skye would remain the sensible girl she always had been. How could she say a prayer for that to be the case, Alice wondered.

Then she was at work and the clock was ticking and soon a collection of partygoers would expect good food and a good time. The first party was due at one, which was late, but it was a Sunday, and when someone knocked at the still-locked door at noon, Alice assumed maybe it was Skye, come to talk to her in private.

Instead, it was a girl about Skye's age, with russet hair and strikingly luminous green eyes. "You're Alice?" she asked, and when Alice nodded, she said, "Your son told me you'd be here."

"My nephew," said Alice smiling and accepting the tin of cookies handed to her.

"My mom always said if you arrive with homemade cookies, no matter what, people will be happy to see you." Despite talking about cookies and happiness, the girl was obviously nervous and even distraught, which made little sense to Alice, who observed her picking at her nails and biting on her lip.

"Oh I'm definitely happy to see you," said Alice. "And you look like just the right size. Come on in the kitchen and let's talk. "What's your name?"

A look of surprise and a little confusion crossed the girl's face, but she answered smoothly, "I'm Emma Delamere."

"So Emma, how long have you been cooking?"

Once again the girl looked a little bewildered, but she answered, "I love to cook. I've always cooked. My mom taught me."

"Fantastic," said Alice, "Here, frost these cupcakes." Alice set three cupcakes in front of Emma and several squeeze bottles, which Emma seemed to hesitate to tackle, but then she finally began as Alice watched and assessed — she had skill and speed. "Like kids?"

"I don't have any kids yet," said Emma. "My dad died and my mom got sick, and that kind of took up the last few years of my life."

Alice wondered why the girl was so forthcoming, but she was refreshingly sweet, and she seemed intelligent and competent. "I'm so sorry. And now she's all right?"

Emma shook her head. "They're both gone now. That's why I came up here."

"I see," said Alice. "And do you think you could manage a group of kids, even though you don't have any? Teach them to frost cupcakes, make sure they don't frost each other?"

Emma's eyes opened wide as she considered this possibility, but she still looked baffled. She reached in her purse, but Alice stopped her. "I don't really want to see a résumé. Not too many places like this anyway. Here, come with me and let's try this costume on you."

"But," said Emma, as Alice walked her into the prop closet.

"Come back into the kitchen once you're dressed," said Alice, looking at her watch. "The invasion is about to begin."

It didn't really matter that Emma looked a bit sheepish returning in the Princess Cupcake costume, because the doors were open and kids were bouncing in. "Here's what we'll do," said Alice, "You greet the parties, see the kids are seated, be charming, you know like Billie Burke in *The Wizard of Oz*, that sort of fairy godmother thing. And I'll let you teach the first group to frost the cupcakes. I'll be right here though, so don't worry, I'm sure you can do it. The other groups really you just act as a hostess, think you can do that?"

"Umm, well, I mean…." mumbled Emma, tugging at the skirt of her costume.

"I'll be right here, in and out of the kitchen, so don't worry. Just pretend you're hosting a party, and be sweet to the kids."

"And we'll talk later?"

"We'll work out all the other details when the parties are over, by four or five. I'm sure you'll be great, and I'm really happy to have you here."

Alice was enchanted. Emma worked hard, and it made a huge difference in the day. She seemed to know exactly how to handle the kids, and everyone was happy. Just the fact that Alice didn't have to comp anyone's party was good news enough; this girl was her savior. Eventually the kids were gone and the kitchen was clean again, and all the staff had left, and Emma had changed back into her own clothes.

"You've done really well," said Alice, "I was happy to have you here. There's one more test, but I'll go easy on you." She ducked into the walk-in, grabbed some fresh asparagus, some goat cheese, a couple of lemons, an orange, and some smoked salmon. "You can use anything else in the pantry or fridge. Go ahead, cook something."

Emma's eyes opened wide, "Oh my gosh! This is just like *You're Cooked*, my favorite show."

Alice smiled. "Mine too. We always play this game at home. The whole family teases me 'cause I'm too chicken to try out for the show."

Emma thought for a moment, then she heated a grill pan for crostini. Soon they were sitting and talking while eating salmon and goat cheese appetizers and arugula salads with orange segments.

"This is fantastic," said Alice, "Great job."

"I always wanted to go on *You're Cooked* too," said Emma, smiling. "But of course I'm not a chef."

"It was a madhouse here yesterday," said Alice. "I can't tell you how happy I am you answered the ad. So you're not an intern, you want this as a job, but that's fine. It's not really a kitchen job anyway, so a chef wouldn't get that sort of experience, but at least I know you can cook in case you ever had to pitch in and help. Would fifteen dollars an hour be enough? When Emma looked a bit stressed, Alice said, "Okay look, I can pay eighteen. And you can be an assistant manager, which would be good on your résumé, right?"

Emma seemed to be nodding, then she shook her head, causing Alice to panic and say, "Okay twenty, but I really can't pay more than that."

Emma reached into her purse and pulled out what Alice still assumed to be a résumé, then said haltingly, "I didn't come in answer to any ad. I came because of this." Then she handed Alice a piece of paper with the logo of the hospital where Skye was born.

Alice scanned the paper, her eyes growing wider and wider. "How is this possible," she asked, "It's dated fourteen years ago."

"After my mom died, I went through her things and found this paper. I mean I knew I was adopted, but this says there was a mix-up of babies in the hospital, and it lists the numbers of everyone with a baby born the same week. You'd think there would be confidentiality issues, but I guess they figured full disclosure."

"I never got anything like this," said Alice.

"Maybe when my parents got it, they figured it didn't matter, since I wasn't their birth child anyway, but I was their child."

At that moment, Totsie walked into the kitchen and sat down at the table next to Alice. "I had horrible news today," she murmured.

"Emma, this is my sister Totsie, who used to do what you did today," said Alice.

"Oh hi," said Totsie, distractedly, nibbling from Alice's plate. "Mmm," she said, "Better than anything on the menu. Meanwhile, back to me. Know what I learned today?"

"What?" asked Alice, looking sympathetically toward Emma, hoping she didn't feel displaced by this new mini-drama.

"That certification course for being a life coach that was supposed to be thirty minutes, well it's not, it's thirty *days*. I had no idea it took so long to become a life coach."

"So you're not doing it?" asked Alice.

"No, I'm committed. It just seems an awfully long, long time, doesn't it? I was a head cheerleader, I know this stuff."

Alice shrugged, then asked Emma, "Would you mind if I showed this to my sister?" When Emma acquiesced, Alice handed the paper to Totsie.

"Holy crap!" said Totsie. "I guess that's what happens when they leave babies lying around in hospital rooms instead of keeping them in a central nursery."

Alice felt quite dizzy. "You know," she said, "It was a new program. The babies were right in the room with the mothers. There was this girl Misty in the other bed — actually she was someone I knew in high school." Alice didn't say knew and hated, although that was the phrase in her head. "She planned to give her baby up for adoption, and she and her boyfriend kept arguing about it. But I was in the middle of a huge crisis and couldn't think straight. The day after giving birth, I left the room to visit someone who'd been in a bad accident — the nurse said it was fine 'cause of all the monitors — and came back and Misty was in the shower, and it was time for me to leave, and I looked down and saw the babies' name tags were gone, and my daughter was in the wrong bed, so I picked her up and went home with my aunt and uncle."

"Holy double crap," said Totsie, "Maybe you switched the babies yourself. Not like you were in your right mind for years after all that happened."

"Misty Philpotts?" asked Emma. "Her name is on this list."

Alice held her hand to her head and closed her eyes briefly, envisioning everything that had happened, seeing the faces, the babies, remembering it exactly as it was. She knew her own baby, didn't she? Didn't everyone say how Skye looked just like her? Wasn't that what Alice was worried about right this moment? That

Skye would fall for some wild guy and end up in a mess, or worse, a tragedy?

"You know," said Totsie, "Didn't Itch have green eyes like hers?" Emma looked at Alice quizzically. Neither said anything, there was just a penetrating stare, and suddenly Alice was plunged into a state of both panic and recollection. She and Itch were secretly eloping, and he had fixed that mesmerizing gaze on her, and Alice had smiled and said, 'What is it about your eyes? How can you do that to me with your eyes? You fix that liquid green on me and I start to drown.' Itch had laughed and once again gazed deeply at Alice, 'It's my super power,' he'd joked. 'I know,' she'd said, 'That's what got us into this situation.' And Itch had laughed, and said 'If my eyes were what did it, they'd really be a super power.' And then they rode on Itch's motorcycle to the house of a boy who'd gotten a mail order minister license from some crazy faraway newspaper called the *Village Voice.*

Alice pulled her mind back from the past, and gazed once again at the girl in front of her. The eyes were so similar, but didn't many people have green eyes? Many people had dark hair and blue eyes too, she thought next, but that was an idea she wouldn't allow herself to sustain for very long—it was just too frightening. At least nobody could come now and take Skye away from her, could they? Of course not—Skye was an adult, Alice thought, breathing only a touch more easily.

"I don't really know why I'm following up on this now," Emma said. "I mean all the babies are grown—it's not like some toddler is in the wrong home."

"So were you planning to visit everyone on this list?" asked Totsie. "That's like ten babies. By now most of those people would have had those tests, you know cheek swab tests."

"I didn't really have a plan, it just seemed like something I should do."

Alice reached out her hand and enveloped Emma's. "How long since your mom died?"

"Only two months."

"Oh you poor thing," said Alice, "You're still in shock."

"I closed up the house, came up here and rented a furnished place. Figured I'd look into this, clear my head, think about what to do now that I'm on my own. I didn't want to go back to nursing, at least not right away."

"Well it's a good thing you're here working with Ally. If anyone can help you cope and sort things out, she can," said Totsie. "And of course as you heard, I'm a life coach."

Emma hesitated for a while, then said, "Well okay, I guess, life is strange isn't it? So I guess I'll see you tomorrow?"

Alice smiled and nodded, rising to clean away the mess as Emma was leaving, when Totsie piped up and said, "Oh don't throw these leftovers away. I'll take them with me."

The difference between absolute certainty and the tiniest whisper of a doubt was a vast chasm Alice didn't want to plumb. She drove home, her head pounding, reliving in her mind all the events at the hospital where Skye was born, the look of her baby, the look of odious Misty's soon-to-be-adopted baby. Did that baby look like Skye? Did she look like Emma? This was one of those moments when Alice wished she had the power of total recall, in fact the first moment ever, because it had always been her preference to set aside as much as possible, and ease her mind of the pain from the past. But now the past had returned, well a small piece of it, well not so small, was it? There was a girl wanting to find the truth of her origin, and that truth could threaten Alice's forever after.

She raced into the house and dragged Robin into Uncle Henry's den, closing the door behind them. "Look at this," she demanded, thrusting at him the Xerox she'd made of the hospital's letter.

Robin scanned the paper and blanched. Then his eyes shaded over, and he looked at her with fury. "You went through my files?" he asked, enraged. "How dare you."

"What," said Alice, almost shouting, "You know about this? You've seen this?"

"Where did you get this?" he asked, with the tone of a district attorney or irate cop.

"A girl came to P3 today, that's where, but apparently you've seen this. You got this letter and didn't show it to me? For all these years?"

"Stop interrogating me," he said, his eyes flashing, but behind them Alice saw fear.

"Why wouldn't you show this to me? I had a right to see it, more a right than you—in fact it would have been addressed to me, not you. You stole my mail, very important mail, and hid it from me. Why?"

"To protect Skye of course. And you. I think we know our own daughter."

"It's great how you love her and all, how you befriended us after the tragedy and all, but she's not actually your daughter. And you certainly have no right to withhold my own mail from me, not even if we were married, which we aren't."

"Get your eye on the big picture," Robin said, clenching his teeth, "The important thing now is to get Skye back on the right path, to snap her out of this insanity, so she's back in her career and with her fiancé."

Alice's temper rose, and her voice grew louder, her comments more heated, "Obviously I'm worried about Skye, but not that she isn't turning into someone you wanted to be, but couldn't get it together to become. I want her to be happy, not to be the stand-in for you and your unfulfilled dreams."

Robin shoved Alice aside then said, "You can be a real bitch, you know."

Alice glowered at him, thinking of Misty and how they met, and answered, "Yeah, good thing you have a type."

Alice slumped down onto the couch to think, as Robin stomped out of the den. Skye was her daughter—that was one thing that would never change—but could it in any way be a possibility that Skye was not her baby? It was an unthinkable possibility, but one Alice could not avoid considering, as much as she wished she could banish the suggestion.

She sat there mired in apprehension for what seemed like an endless stretch of time, until Skye stuck her head into the den. "So where's this dinner I was promised?" Alice leapt up at the sight of her, and enveloped her in a hug and refused to let go.

"Mom, Mom," said Skye, smiling. "You've been crazy tired and all emotional every time I see you, and I know what's wrong."

"You do?" whispered Alice.

"You're pregnant," said Skye. "About time you gave me that baby sibling."

"No," she said softly, "I'm not pregnant."

"Ah, Mom," said Skye, holding Alice's hand, "Well don't let it get you down. I'm sure if you keep trying, it'll happen."

Alice looked for a moment toward the couch, her solitary napping spot, then back into the eyes of her daughter, eyes that had always seemed a mirror image of her own, and she asked, "Are you pregnant?"

"Of course not," said Skye, "What are you thinking?"

Alice murmured somberly, "I'm just so worried about you."

"Well, you're my mom. That's your job. Like keeping me from starving to death."

Alice rose and said, "Okay, we'll talk more at dinner. Pasta primavera sound good—with shrimp maybe? Or I could make a jambalaya if you'd rather. I have shrimp, sausages, scallops."

"Molten lava cakes?"

"Done," said Alice, smiling. "Go ask Cooper to see if Aunt Kitty wants to come eat." Had she been crazy? Everything was normal again, wasn't it? But when she entered the kitchen, there was that clown, doing a crazy headstand in the booth, while Cooper watched.

"I figured this would give you a chance to know Julian better," whispered Skye.

The batter for the desserts took minutes, then Alice made the salad, some garlic bread, and the jambalaya. She felt a little guilty, because she'd planned to go to the market and get a roast, but after everything that had happened, dinner wasn't exactly on her mind.

"Where's Dad?" Skye asked Alice, who shrugged, but Skye set a place for him in the dining room anyway.

Kitty took her usual seat at the head of the table, with Alice and Cooper to one side of her and Skye and Julian to the other, when Robin appeared with Greg. "Look who I found," he said, "Oh set another plate, we seem to have some extra mouths here."

Skye blushed, but she rose to get a plate, saying, "Greg, this is my friend Julian." The two boys glared at each other, as Alice and Cooper watched. Skye set Greg across from her, next to Cooper, and returned to her seat next to Julian.

"Let me serve you," said Julian, reaching for Skye's plate. "Skye's been starving for hours and she loves shrimp, even if they are insects of the sea."

"You know," said Aunt Kitty, "I tried to go to work today, but this crazy woman dropped in to visit me, and I just couldn't get her to leave."

"She's your..." Cooper was about to say *babysitter*, when Alice covered his hand with hers, and he stopped talking.

"You love Mrs. Lopez," said Alice gently, smiling at her aunt. "She visits you every day. You know how lonely she is. I don't know what she'd do without you."

"This is really delicious," said Julian. "Skye said your food was good, but I had no idea." He lifted his plate and took a big, dramatic whiff of the food.

"What," said Robin, scowling, "Nobody ever fed you at home? Have you met Greg, Skye's fiancé?"

Greg blushed, as Julian looked quizzically toward Skye, when Kitty said, "I saw something like this in a movie—three people stranded on a desert island. One big hut, one little hut, gal had to—um—switch hit."

"I'm in a play this summer," said Julian, "I hope you'll all come. Skye will be working on it too." He reached across the table to the basket of garlic bread and grabbed a piece, which he then placed on Skye's plate.

"You are?" asked Alice, scrutinizing Skye for any evidence of what her real plans were, then looking to Greg, who sat glumly eating in silence.

"I don't know how I'll be working," said Kitty. "With me always stuck at home with this lonely woman, how am I supposed to be making a living, that's what I want to know. Why doesn't she hang out with some of her other friends? I could use a day off."

"Aunt Kitty Cat, you're retired now. You don't have to work any more," said Cooper, with a mouth full of jambalaya. "Wowza this is good."

"Hankie, don't be ridiculous. You want to go to college, don't you? Well that takes money," said Kitty.

"No, no Aunt Kitty, I'm Cooper, not Grampa Hank."

"So, Greg, tell Skye about everything she's missing at the office," said Robin, his disgusted expression meant to indicate that any further nonsense from Alice's aunt should be ignored.

"Um... um... um..." said Greg, "Mrs. Allenton was asking for you. She doesn't like Sophia at all."

"It's hard for people to accept change sometimes," said Julian, "But life is better when they do. Skye is a very special person, and she's going to do great things."

"I might have to start working at night," said Kitty. "How else will I get all those cakes baked? I'm telling you this woman never stops talking. I can't think clearly enough to measure out the flour."

"I bake the cakes here at night," said Alice. "You can help me tonight if you want to."

"I should probably go to P3 and check on things," said Aunt Kitty. "I never got there at all today. Things were fine yesterday, though."

"I was there yesterday," said Julian. "What a cool place. There was a birthday kid with a nut hysteria. Did you see the amazing skit Skye and I did?" he asked Alice.

"We don't do skits at P3," said Kitty. "You must have been at a different place, because if you were there I would have seen you." Kitty took a bite of her garlic bread then said to Alice, "Did you know they did skits at a dental office? That could take the edge off for sure."

"I'll be right back," said Alice, "Gotta put those molten lava cakes in the oven. Skye, want to help me?"

Skye followed Alice into the kitchen, and watched as her mother scooped the chilled batter into the ramekins. "Okay, so what do you want to know?" asked Skye.

"What's going on exactly?" asked Alice.

"I'm just spending time with someone interesting, I guess."

"Are you breaking up with Greg? If so, you probably ought to tell him. He's been pretty upset," said Alice.

"So you're saying I should go back to Greg?" Skye's eyes clouded over.

Panic floated over Alice like the fog rolling in. She grasped tightly to the edge of the counter for a moment and tried just to hold on. Did she think Skye should return to Greg? Not really—he was pretty dull. Did she think Skye was in any danger with Julian? She didn't know. She couldn't speak for a moment because she had nothing formulated in her mind as a response, so she just shook her head.

"I really don't want to disappoint you," said Skye, "I just want to live my life."

"You could never disappoint me," said Alice, thinking unless you turn out to be someone else's baby. Then she popped the tray of ramekins into the oven and hugged her daughter.

They walked back into the dining room to hear a loud electronic voice saying *Super Cooper, Super Cooper* over and over.

Cooper grabbed his phone off the table, punched something into it that stopped the voice, and said, "See, I can always find it cause if I say, "My phone's lost. Where's my phone?" it answers me. "Gimme yours," he said to Skye, who handed him her phone, watched as he typed something into it, spoke into the phone on demand, then waited until he said, "Ok say it now."

Skye said, "My phone's lost. Where's my phone?" Everyone looked up and around anticipatorily.

Then her phone spoke in a loud, squeaky, parrot-like voice, *Pie in the Skye, Pie in the Skye*, and everyone laughed.

"Oh, cool," said Alice, "I'm always losing mine. Do mine." She grabbed her purse, wrangled the phone free, and handed it to Cooper. Then she repeated the steps Skye had taken, and soon enough her phone was playing *Alley Cat* and saying *time to make the donuts.*

"My phone is back in my apartment," said Kitty. "It's on the wall. If I pulled it off to put it in my purse, it wouldn't work any more. Would it?"

"I'll get you a cell phone if you want it, Aunt Kitty Cat," said Cooper.

While Cooper was programming everyone's phones, Alice returned to the kitchen to serve the desserts. Skye cleared the table and seemed in a good mood, which Alice didn't want to disturb. Maybe she could just wait this phase out. When the cream was whipped, she mounded some on each plate to the side of the lava cakes, and tossed on a few berries.

"This looks like a restaurant dessert," said Julian, whose phone was playing *Send in the Clowns*, and he said, "Coopy, c'mon, stop toying with me. I told you to make it say *Action!*"

"Coopy?" said Cooper, raising one eyebrow.

"Your brownies didn't cook all the way through, dear," said Kitty, "But this could catch on, really yum."

"You drove here separately in your own car, young man?" asked Robin. "Because of course Skye will be staying here after dinner. It's late. And she lives here with Greg." Greg glanced up hopefully, as Julian looked challenged.

"She's not staying here," Julian said, "Skye loves going to the after hour clubs."

"As much as we appreciate all the information about our daughter you so proprietarily are sharing," said Robin sternly, "We know all about Skye, thank you very much."

Julian sat up straight and said, "Maybe you don't know her as well as you think."

"Stop it, stop it," yelled Skye. "I'm not going to be in the middle of all this." She leapt up, grimaced toward Alice, and bolted toward the door, with Julian trotting at her heels.

"Thanks for dinner," he yelled back from the front door, "Skye and I really enjoyed it."

"Why don't you *do* something," said Robin to Greg, who stood and lumbered toward the front door, disappearing only briefly, until he returned to his place at the table. "Couldn't catch them," he said.

"Don't you worry," said Robin, "She'll come to her senses. We dentists have to stick together."

Alice walked into the kitchen to clean up, glancing at the clock on the wall. She'd have a few hours to nap, then she had to start baking again. She felt a little calmer thinking about Skye, because despite her exit, she didn't seem to be planning anything too extreme, so maybe it was just some little youthful folly, nothing that would lead to anything terrible. That's what Alice wanted to believe, and she tried to breathe deeply and just let that idea take hold in her mind, when Cooper came into the kitchen looking worried.

"I was about to go to Ben's for a while, but I saw Kitty driving off in your car. Is she allowed to drive?"

"What!" said Alice, rushing into the dining room where her purse lay open on the table. "You let Kitty take my car keys and said nothing?" Alice asked Robin, who shrugged his shoulders.

"How should I know what she's up to," he said nonchalantly.

"Did she say anything about where she was going?"

"Do I listen when she speaks?"

"P3!" said Alice and Cooper simultaneously. "Let's go," said Alice to Robin.

"It's late," he answered. "I get up early. I can't go joy riding with you now."

"C'mon, Ally, I'll drive you," said Cooper.

"You stay awake in case she comes back," said Alice angrily. "And call me immediately if she does."

"No way this kid is driving my car. You drive," he admonished.

Alice shook her head at Robin, too disgusted even to answer him, then she and Cooper walked out to the garage. "Here, Ally, c'mon," said Cooper, pointing to a little car parked on the street.

Alice climbed into the Mini-Cooper, saying, "When'd you get this?"

"Six months ago," said Cooper, driving as fast as possible but not fast enough to upset his aunt.

"You've only had your license for three months," said Alice, and then Cooper gave her that wry glance she usually found so cute.

"I needed it for work," he said cryptically.

"Work is now slang for the beach?" Alice asked distractedly. Then they pulled into the P3 parking lot, and there was Alice's car, sitting open, with not even the front door closed. Likewise the front door of P3 was open, and Alice yelled, "Kitty, Kitty, are you here," but of course she was in the kitchen, baking cupcakes.

"I don't have enough ovens at home to do all this," Kitty said calmly.

"You scared me to death," said Alice. "You know you're not allowed to drive any more."

"What do you mean, since when?" asked Kitty, turning the big mixer up to high and making it clank noisily, reminding Alice of yet another thing she'd soon have to replace.

"Since Nixon was president probably," said Cooper, taking a spatula off the counter and licking it.

"That criminal?" asked Kitty, "Is he coming here? It's not his birthday, is it? I didn't make a cake."

Alice led Kitty to the small kitchen table and seated her calmly. "Kitty, please listen to me, okay? You're retired now. You don't work any more. I work here, not you. But look around, the place is fine, isn't it? I wouldn't let you down. Everything's okay. We're all fine."

"Of course it's fine," said Kitty, her eyes coming into focus again. "You do a great job, Ally. I'm so proud of you. And you dragged me here just to see everything is fine? I know it is. I know you have everything under control. But I have a problem."

"What's wrong?" asked Alice.

"It's past my bedtime. I'm pretty tired. Being retired is hard work." Kitty smiled at Alice and laughed at her own joke.

"Let's go home and get you to bed," said Alice kindly, turning off the oven and surveying the mess. She could come in early tomorrow and clean it up before the staff arrived or worse, just leave it for them. They'd understand.

During the drive home, Alice was relieved that Kitty's senior moment had subsided and that she was able to converse coherently. She saw her aunt safely into her own apartment and that she'd locked the door and was ready for bed, so it seemed permissible to lock herself in the den so she could nap for a while. She turned on her laptop, and watched briefly as Johnny Badass cooked something amazing, then her eyes fluttered shut as his sexy voice washed over her, and soon she was napping, her mind at rest.

Before the morning light, Alice was awake and in the kitchen baking. The summer was always the busiest, but fall was no better, and then the holiday season followed, so she'd long ago come to accept that this was her life, sweetness in the night, the silence and the solitude, the scent of bourbon vanilla, the creaminess of melting chocolate, swirls upon a birthday cake. It was a pleasure to bake, and a good time to dream of this and that. By now it was like clockwork—hours of what felt like choreographed action, no gesture or movement wasted, and then there were counters filled with whatever baked goods were expected in a few hours.

Alice exited the spacious walk-in pantry to the side of the kitchen. She carried several large cardboard boxes, which soon would be assembled and filled with the cakes and cupcakes for the celebrations of the day. The kitchen seemed rather bright, and the old musical streaming from her iPad was quiet enough not to muffle the hopeful sound of the morning birds about to begin their wake up call. But no, there was a dagger of light on the floor, yet beyond the window no birds sang, and not even a hint of sunrise had yet emerged.

It was the back door—and it sat open with lights from the courtyard streaming in—although Alice knew that moments ago it had been shut fast. Nothing worrisome lay beyond that door, and Alice was more curious than concerned as she stepped outside, breathing in the honey-scented air of the California night; it was as sweet as the aroma of the baked goods cooling on her counters.

At first she gasped, then she jumped. There on the patio was Kitty, frail and reedy in her cotton nightgown, an umbrella raised as though it were a weaponized baseball bat, her eyes steely and her jaw clenched.

"Henry is cheating on me," she said through time-aged yellow teeth, "He didn't come home last night. You know her. Damn half-naked floozy."

"Oh Kitty," sighed Alice, concern mingled with sorrow, and she wrapped her arm around those ancient, beloved shoulders, drawing her close, while disengaging the weapon and lowering it down in her hand. "Come inside. Let's have some tea."

"Don't let the whistle on the kettle blow — it'll wake up the baby."

Alice steered her aunt to a seat at the table and said, "You know Skye's all grown up now. You saw her at dinner, remember?"

Aunt Kitty rose stealthily from her seat, saying, "Let me just check things out," and tiptoed toward the front of the house, holding her finger to her mouth and making shushing noises toward Alice, who smiled.

Alice reached for a canister of oatmeal, knowing that it made a good vehicle for the coconut oil she'd read could be helpful in cases like this, when a scream came from upstairs. It sounded as though a teenage girl had witnessed an indescribable atrocity.

Alice shook her head and walked toward her bedroom, to find Robin standing by his side of their bed, covers pulled up to his chin, as Kitty lay there snoring.

"She actually groped me," he said. "Groped."

Alice laughed. "This was her room for a lot of years before it was mine — ours," she said.

Kitty suddenly sat straight up, her knobby hand outstretched, fingers pointed toward Robin as she accused, "Imposter! You can't pretend to be my husband. I know my Henry."

Alice walked over to the bed, sat down and took Kitty's hand in hers. "Uncle Henry died a long time ago. That's when you moved into my apartment outside and we moved in here, remember?"

"Who is this guy, Alice? Itch is going to kill you. And I'm going to kill Henry. Wait…. What? Did I kill Henry? It that why he's dead? What? No that can't be."

"Nobody killed anybody," said Alice calmly.

"Not yet," added Robin, looking toward the window. "Pitch dark out. Some of us have work in the morning."

"You're not Henry and you're not Itch," scowled Kitty. "You can't fool me."

"You know Robin," said Alice.

"Bird brain," sneered Kitty.

"Come watch me pack up all the cupcakes and we'll talk about today's parties." Alice helped her aunt out of the bed, and began to lead her back toward the kitchen.

"I'm locking the door," said Robin.

Alice shrugged.

"I'll be damned if I'm going to allow you to drag me into this psychotic witch hunt," said Robin furiously.

Alice held the DNA test kit she'd ordered, and was determined to swab everyone. She'd thought it would be most difficult to swab Skye, because she wanted her to know nothing about this hospital mix-up now while her life was up in the air, and hopefully this would prove that nothing need ever be said about it. But as Skye was sleeping at home now, Alice had managed to creep into her room in the middle of the night, swabbing her cheek without even disturbing her slumber. Instead, it was Robin causing the problem.

"But what if Emma is your daughter?" asked Alice reasonably. "You were so miserable when Misty insisted on putting your baby up for adoption—you fought so hard for Misty to keep her. This could be your chance to get to know her—she's a really sweet girl."

"This is ridiculous. Do you know how insane you sound? Are we in a telenovela?"

Alice leaned in toward Robin. "Just open your mouth and let me do this. Once and for all we'll confirm the truth, and can then resume our lives. Do you really think I don't believe Skye is my daughter?"

"And what then," he said ominously, "You discover Skye isn't who you think she is, and then what—off to the dog pound with her?" Robin shoved his way past

Alice and out the door. "I'm not participating in this. It's wrong."

"What's wrong?" asked Skye, startling Alice as she came down the stairs.

"Oh nothing," said Alice, quickly pocketing the swab vial. "He's just being a drama queen." Alice walked into the kitchen with Skye behind her.

"I was doing some research," said Skye. "Take a look at this." She handed Alice her iPad with a list of places in Los Angeles to have children's parties. "They all have entertainment. Magic tricks or plays or other things."

"We teach kids to frost cupcakes, and we have Princess Cupcake. Were you thinking you wanted to be Princess Cupcake now?" Alice gulped, thinking of Emma and how mean it would be to fire her after just having hired her. She'd assume it was about the hospital mix-up. Alice pulled a couple of plates down, and began making breakfast.

"Well, no..." said Skye, musing. "I was thinking maybe Julian and I could do a little theater group or skits or something there. Part-time. When we're not doing this play."

"Really?" asked Alice, thinking how wonderful it would be to have Skye working alongside her.

"You just seem so tired," said Skye kindly, "And I feel so bad for letting you down."

Alice hugged Skye, saying, "Honey, all my life I've tried not to let my family down, after, well, you know. I'd never want you to feel that way. You'd never let me down. I just want you to be safe. And happy, of course."

Skye smiled, and looked as though a weight had lifted. "I felt so guilty for quitting my job," she said, munching on the food Alice had just set before her.

"So are you thinking you want to be an actress?" asked Alice.

"I really don't know."

"Well, you know what? It's summer. Take the summer off and think about it."

Skye clung to Alice, "Thanks, Mom. Maybe that's a good idea."

Alice laughed, "Well you already did it, so it's your idea."

Alice's relief was rapidly transformed into concern, as Aunt Kitty's caretaker, Mrs. Lopez, walked through the back door into the kitchen, calling, "Kitty, Kitty, are you here?"

"Oh God," said Alice.

"I was in the bathroom just a minute, and then she was gone," said terrified Mrs. Lopez.

"She's not here," said Alice, reaching for her purse, which still contained her car keys. "Skye, Run upstairs and see if she's there."

"Not up here," yelled Skye.

"How far could she get on foot," said Alice, grabbing her purse and racing out the door. She looked up and down the street, but there was no sign of her aunt. Could she have gotten to the corner and stepped onto a bus? Alice jumped into her car and drove toward the corner and yes, there were buses, but going in opposite directions. Which way to go? She turned in the direction of P3, thinking perhaps Kitty had done the same thing twice. Could she be there now?

Alice looked at her watch. It was ten in the morning and nobody would be there yet, but of course Kitty wouldn't use that logic, so Alice drove toward P3, praying she'd see her aunt. Several times the buses stopped, and Alice pulled to the curb and waited, but Kitty wasn't one of the passengers who disembarked. What if something had happened to her? Alice's heart started racing.

She got to P3, but there was no sign of her aunt. She unlocked the door, but it was empty, as expected. Alice gulped, and dialed the police. She was promptly put on hold, and while she was waiting, her cell phone rang.

"She's at the Santa Monica mall," said Skye. "Security just called. They're holding her."

"Thank goodness," said Alice. "I'm on my way."

"I'll pack up these cupcakes and take them into P3," said Skye. "Take your time."

"Thanks, honey," said Alice, her heart still racing. She arrived at the mall in no time, and parked the car. She hadn't been there in ages—the place had been totally renovated and had really changed. It took three different people to point her toward security, and she arrived out of breath, to find Kitty sitting there chatting with the officer.

"Ally!" she said, "Where did you get to? I told this nice man you were lost. We've been looking forward to this shopping day for so long—but I don't know where anything is any more. Robinson's is totally gone—did you know that—and I was so worried about you. I know how you always get lost."

Alice hugged her aunt tightly. "You scared me to death," she said.

Kitty hugged her back, and stroked Alice's hair. "Oh honey, don't worry. I wouldn't let you stay lost for long. See—this nice man found you, and now we can shop and have lunch like we planned."

When Alice was younger, P3 was always be closed on Mondays and Tuesdays, and often in the mornings Kitty and Alice would visit a mall and have lunch out, either with Skye in her stroller or later alone while Skye was in school. They hadn't done that in ages, because now some weeks there wasn't even one day off. Alice tried so hard to spend as much time now with Kitty as she could, but maybe her aunt just missed the old days when life was simpler.

Alice smiled and took a deep breath. "Okay Kitty, let's walk and see the mall." She turned a relieved glance toward the security guy, and said, "Thank you so much for calling. I'm glad she knew the number." The officer gave Alice a sympathetic glance in return, and noted something on a log as they left.

"So," said Alice, "It's pretty early for lunch, but we can look in some stores I guess."

"Yeah I want to spend some of this money before they take it back."

"What?" asked Alice.

"More money keeps getting dumped into my checking account. Social Security gave me a raise maybe. Mad money!" said Kitty.

Alice laughed, thinking nothing of it. "You're the first person to get rich on Social Security," she said.

"Let's go look at some new clothes. How about something new for you?"

Alice looked down at herself. She was wearing the ratty jeans she'd changed into after work yesterday and a batter stained t-shirt. She really had to stop napping on the couch instead of actually sleeping. "Gee, I dunno," said Alice, looking around. "This mall sure has changed. Looks to me like the stuff they sell here now is too youthful even for Skye, let alone us."

"Speak for yourself," said Kitty, laughing like her old self, and then she said, "I have a hot young boyfriend now, so I have to look the part." Alice put her arm around her aunt's shoulders and smiled.

By the time she'd dropped Kitty back home and raced over to P3, it was already late in the afternoon, and the parties were over. Alice still had food orders to put in, and a call to place to the bank about a loan for new refrigeration and roofing. When she walked in the door, she was surprised to see her sister, her mother, and Skye waiting for her. They all looked deeply concerned. "You're staging an intervention," quipped Alice. "I suddenly have a drug problem nobody ever heard of before?"

She hugged her mother and sister, and took a seat between Skye and Totsie. "Everybody gone for the day?" she asked, and Skye nodded. There were tea cups on the table and pots of tea and coffee and a pitcher of lemonade. Emma's half emptied tin of cookies sat next to them.

"We have to discuss your aunt," said Pauline Catson. It was summer, but she was dressed in a suit, her professional uniform. She always looked as though she were ready to lower the boom on someone.

"What about her, Mom?"

"It's just not safe for her to live there all alone." Pauline had a stern voice and even the casual comments she made sounded as though she were delivering an edict to one of her students. She took a deep gulp of the tea in her cup, reached for a cookie, thought better of it, then dropped it back into the tin.

"How do you even know about this?" asked Alice, taking a cookie and eating it.

Skye gave Alice an apologetic glance, "I called everyone in the family when she went missing," she said.

"We were terrified she could be out there alone and all confused," said Totsie, pushing the tin of cookies beyond her own reach.

"This was just a crazy mix-up," said Alice more calmly than she felt. "She has a caretaker, you know. She's just been feeling a little antsy lately, and I'm going to spend more time with her, so when she's home with Mrs. Lopez she doesn't mind." Alice poured herself a glass of lemonade and sipped it quietly, hoping this meeting would soon end.

"Alice, Alice, Alice," said her mother, "Must you always opt for self-delusion as your go-to solution?"

"Grandma!" said Skye, "Don't be mean."

"What are your goals for the future, Ally," said Totsie, trying on her life coach persona.

"I just told you," said Alice, "Spend more time with Kitty."

"And what happens when she wanders off in the middle of the night?" asked Pauline.

"Do they have microchips for people like they do for pets?" asked Totsie, as the three other women glared at her. "What! It's a good idea."

"She needs to go to a home," said Pauline. "It's that simple. There are places that care for people with brain issues."

"You don't say," responded Alice with sarcasm, reaching into the tin of cookies and grabbing a handful, which she stacked on the table in front of her, as though they were poker chips.

"Exactly," replied her mother, ignoring the meaning behind Alice's comment, and pushing the tin of cookies away from Alice. "The Wellman Center has a facility for

Alzheimer's' patients as well as that long-term care wing. Like a rest home."

"Maybe it could be like a two-fer," said Totsie, as Alice looked at her imploringly, hoping that she would just be quiet.

"Life is more complicated than that," said Alice defiantly.

"No, dementia is more complicated than you can handle," said Pauline, clinking her tea cup down against its saucer.

"You just always hated Kitty," said Alice, knowing she sounded childish.

"Your father's aunt has always been a thorn in my side, that's true," said Pauline. "But that doesn't mean I'm unconcerned about her welfare.... I resent your tone."

"What else is new," said Alice, feeling her hackles rise.

"Wouldn't we all have more power if we stopped trying to rob each other of it?" asked Totsie.

Alice rose from the table. "I'll give it some thought."

"Remember," said Totsie, "Success and failure are different outcomes from the same process."

Alice's eyes rose involuntarily to the ceiling, causing her sister to scowl at her, but Alice was too annoyed to care. "Yeah," she said, "And life is always fatal."

"Exactly!" exclaimed Totsie, "It's just about what we do in the middle."

Alice completed the day's work in relative peace after the others departed, but as she sat there at the desk in Uncle Henry's small office, her mind floated back in time to the hours after Skye was born. She lay rather drugged up in a hospital bed, her forehead in bandages, while Itch was attached to a million tubes in intensive care. It was the first time she'd experienced any sense of foreboding, although she'd always been a worrier, and what she most needed was someone to hold her hand and tell her everything would work out just fine.

Then someone was wheeled into the room, another young mother, which would have been all right with Alice, until she got a glimpse of the worst person on earth, that bitch Misty, the dumber than fleas cheerleader who constantly—and insultingly—tried to steal Itch away from her. And now she was enthroned in the bed beside Alice, some horrid monkey offspring next to her. And toadying beside her was the dental student who'd thankfully taken her mind off Itch.

She expected to hear something nasty from Misty, but before the assault could begin, as Alice was fuzzily contemplating the various comebacks she could hurl at the beast, Robert or Roger or Rowan, no wasn't it Robin, pulled the curtain between the two beds, creating a divider in the room that was more symbolic than actual, because Alice could hear every word being said. And suddenly she realized that Misty didn't even have a clue she was there.

"Look," said Misty, "There's nothing more to say about this. I made the decision and it's mine to make. I'm nineteen and I'm nobody's mother. I'm going to New York and I'm gonna be a star. I don't even know why the baby is in the room. She's somebody else's baby. Face it."

"She's not anybody else's," Robin stammered. "She's my baby. Your baby."

"So, you take her," said Misty.

"What? By myself? I study like twenty-seven hours a day. But you can keep her. Your parents'll help you take care of her 'til I graduate. I'll come over when I can. Your parents have plenty of money and that guesthouse out back. It's not like you'll be trapped in your room in the house. They can hire a nanny for you."

"What part of me going on Broadway sounds like my parents' guesthouse?"

Alice was thinking how lucky that monkey baby was to be getting out from Misty's clutches, when she heard her mother's voice outside the door, "I hear one of my girls is in here," she said, and of course Alice knew what that meant. Her mother had two daughters, but neither was one of her girls.

Pauline Catson walked past Alice, touching her bandaged head lightly, and running a finger down the baby's tiny arm, then she parted the curtain and said, "Misty, how are you feeling?"

"Principal Catson, I can't believe you came to see me. How nice."

Alice heard her mother sit down in a chair beside Misty's bed. "So, how are you doing," she asked gently.

"Adoption," Misty said quickly. "It's the only choice."

"That's very brave of you," said Pauline.

Alice watched as Robin strode out of the room, obviously distraught, and she wondered would he be able to change Misty's mind, but there wasn't time to contemplate that soap opera, because her little sister Totsie bound into the room along with her Great Aunt Kitty and Uncle Henry.

"Is this him?" asked Totsie, staring at the baby.

"No," laughed Alice, "That's some rentababy. They give you this one to practice on 'til you get the hang of it."

From beyond the curtain Alice could hear her mother saying, "I know what it's like to be a single parent. My husband was lost at sea, you know."

"Only metaphorically," said Aunt Kitty softly, glancing wryly at Alice, as she sat gently on the side of the bed, squeezing Alice's hand and gazing adoringly at

Skye. "Ohhhhh so sweet, the most beautiful baby ever. I never saw a prettier one."

"What," said Totsie, "What about me?"

"We got married tonight," whispered Alice. "Before the accident."

"And you're going to be okay? You seem okay," said Kitty.

Alice nodded. "Maybe a scar or two under my bangs."

"Itch?"

Alice shook her head. "Not sure," she said painfully, "Have to wait and see. I'm so terrified."

"Oh honey, don't you worry," said Kitty, squeezing Alice's hand. "A big, strong guy like that—he's young and solid, and he'll be up and at 'em before you know it."

Alice took a deep breath. Itch would be fine. She would be fine. It would all work out, just like Kitty had said.

"We'll throw you a party as soon as you're sprung from here," said Uncle Henry. "You can invite everyone you know. It'll be a blast."

"Did I hear married?" said Pauline, sweeping the curtain aside and standing over Alice's bed. "Do you really think one mistake heals another? Just think about that brave girl over there, doing what's right for her baby, for herself. And what are your plans? No college, a too-young marriage, what next, a truck stop waitress? Alice, I'm ashamed of you. It's like your brains got scrambled in some horror movie."

Aunt Kitty stood up between the bed and Pauline, and said, "Stop it Pauline, stop it right now. We have a new baby in the family, a new marriage, and to people who don't live on a steady diet of prunes, this is happy news. Sometimes I can't even believe we're related."

"We're not related," said Pauline, "Only by marriage. And if you'd had any kids of your own, you'd not be so busy interfering with mine. Now I have a daughter who belongs in college, hasn't a clue, and a baby I'll have to raise."

"What's his name?" asked Totsie.

"She's a girl," said Alice, "And her name is Skye."

"Figures," said Pauline, "More head in the clouds."

By then the baby starting screaming, a nurse came in, and thankfully waved everyone out, but not before Aunt Kitty could lean down toward Alice and say, "You can move into one of our apartments out back if you want. I'll help you with everything, and you can work at P3 sometimes. If it's not too truck stop waitress for you." Then she winked at Alice, set a box of cookies on the nightstand, and left.

It was Aunt Kitty who'd helped her when everything seemed utterly hopeless. Kitty who'd gotten her through it, who cheered her up, who propped her up, who kept her up, Aunt Kitty who'd made it all seem all right. And now she would return the favor. She wouldn't let her aunt down. Maybe she couldn't rescue Itch in time, no matter how many times she'd dived into the frigid water, but she wouldn't send Kitty away.

"What are we, the G-d *Waltons*," groused Robin, stepping into the kitchen, where Alice was making breakfast.

"Hold your water, John Boy," said Alice, grinning into the open fridge, whose contents she was surveying.

Robin poured himself a cup of coffee, and made huffing and puffing sounds as he blew on it while speaking intermittently. "I just don't see why I had to give up my room so your aunt could sleep in it..... Huff.... She doesn't have a clue where she is most of the time.... Puff.... I go to work and come home and all my stuff is in another room.... Huff.... And she's queening it up in my room. And you've got that brat sleeping in my office where all my important files are.... Puff.... And speaking of holding water, we have to share a bathroom now. I liked the master with the master bath." Then he took a giant swig of the coffee, with the attitude that another tirade would be forthcoming as soon as he swallowed.

"Don't worry about me," said Cooper, sticking his head into the kitchen, and offering a guileless grin he knew Robin would hate. He didn't even bother to speak in slang. "I'm used to living in a place filled with hoarded crap from the past. Won't bother me in the slightest. Besides all I do is sleep there." He walked over to the fridge, and gazed into it along with Alice. "Is there a TV in there now?" he joked, removing a jug of orange juice.

"You could have kept your files in Uncle Henry's office, and then we'd have a proper guest room," said Alice, as she pulled some bacon and eggs from the fridge.

"We have a guest room," said Robin, "And now we're in it." He clonked his empty coffee cup down on the counter for emphasis.

"Well I'm happy to be *The Waltons*," said Alice. "I like having my family right here. I might even make waffles right now to celebrate. And bacon." She reached to the side of one of the cabinets, where her apron always hung and slipped it over her head, then tied it around her waist.

"Bacon isn't going to repair the crick in my back from sleeping in some weird bed," said Robin, who bent backwards a bit to produce an ominous crack from his spine.

"Well let's go shopping," said Alice, "We'll get a new bed, one of those cool ones with the remote controls and the numbers. Maybe after work tonight? Got your credit card?"

Alice paused for a moment to think. She actually would like to shop for a new bed, so needling Robin wasn't the only benefit to this line of conversation. She could picture herself sinking down into a bed perfectly attuned for her comfort—how much better that would be than always grabbing a few hours here and there on the couch.

Robin, who was about to level more complaints, clamped his mouth shut then and just scowled and stomped out the front door.

"Hmm," said Cooper, grinning, "I've seen it before. Bet he's having some credit card troubles."

"Why would you say that," asked Alice, mixing the batter for waffles.

"No reason," said Cooper, walking to the back door. "Hey look, Miss Las Vegas is out there."

Alice peered out the kitchen door. For some reason her least favorite tenant had decided the courtyard was her personal lounging area, and daily she set up a chaise and lay there soaking up the sun in a microscopic bikini. Alice shook her head. "She's the skin cancer poster girl." Just as she turned to walk back to the stove, Alice saw Kitty watering the plants. Well, that was safe enough, wasn't it? She'd have to get some guys in to install locks high and low, as well as other safety precautions she'd read about recently. As she heard Cooper begin to laugh, Alice turned back toward the door, and watched only in partial horror as Kitty began soaking Layla with the hose.

"You trashy floozy," she said sternly. "You think you can fool around with my Henry? I'll wash you back down the gutter where you belong!"

Layla struggled against the stream of water to rise from the rickety chaise and evade the flood, yelling, "Stop it, stop it you crazy old witch."

"Witch!" shrieked Kitty, "I'm not the one trying to put a spell on a decent man. I've seen women like you before. Guttersnipe!"

Just as Layla was about to storm Kitty and remove the hose from her hand, Alice ran out the door and turned off the water. "Gracious," she said, only partly sincerely, "Are you all right?"

Layla just glared at her as Alice took the hose from her aunt's hands. "I showed her who's boss around here," said Kitty, cheerfully following Alice back into the house.

Cooper was still laughing, and when they walked in the door, he kissed Kitty on the cheek. "Way to start the day out with some entertainment," he said.

Alice felt the day may have begun amusingly enough, but she was far less happy when yet another bank refused her request for a loan for the necessary refrigeration and new roof for P3. She sat in the office at P3, going over spreadsheets and sighing. There was no question that there were far fewer profits than in the old days. Everything cost more, and people were willing to pay only so much for the chance to eat relatively simple food. Alice assumed that due to the economy, people who used to hold parties out were now celebrating at home to save money. She'd taken over a business, really two businesses, counting the apartments out back, and where before there were no liens or loans, now she had a mortgage she could barely cover, and loans for equipment repairs from a few years ago, when she redid the kitchen at home to add more ovens, and replaced all the plumbing everywhere. Alice sighed—the numbers didn't lie. It was like being on a treadmill, and although she kept running faster, it made no difference, because she always remained right where she'd started. Alice felt like a complete failure, and constantly asked herself what Uncle Henry would have done. He would have cut corners to keep things in balance, but in those days maintaining financial balance was easier. And Henry didn't have the bills she did.

She looked at her own checkbook. Every month she paid thousands for Itch's care to the Wellman Center, whose bills were tremendous, but she didn't resent it at all. Itch's parents paid for as much as they could. After the accident, her mother had been determined to force Alice to sign an annulment. They'd been married only a few hours when it happened, and Pauline said that if she didn't sign, Alice would be liable for so many bills her head would spin. Well, her head was spinning, but as usual Alice didn't regret standing up to her mother, although at the time she just stood fast with Itch's parents in refusing to believe that he wouldn't recover. And when the tubes were disconnected and he didn't die, they were overjoyed and optimistic, not thinking about decades of maintenance. Marie Itzkin would never give up on her son and neither would Alice, so together they agreed to the feeding tubes and the stay at that expensive clinic, and together they prayed that a new drug would be developed or that a miracle would occur.

Alice was about to call yet another bank, when she thought of her sister. They had a ton of money, and she'd never asked Totsie to kick in anything for the business, which of course wasn't unfair since it was all left to Alice, but she did share profits with Totsie when she worked there, much more than she actually earned or deserved. Alice dialed her sister's number and without even a hello, Totsie said, "I was just about to call you."

"I could really use your help," said Alice. "You know we need a new roof and walk-in, and it's really hard to get a loan now. Think you could kick some money into the business?" She clicked on the computer, and watched the dismal spread sheets float by as she spoke.

"I was about to call and say I never got a check this week, and now you're asking me for money?" The sound grew muffled, and Totsie said, "No that one. No *that* one," but Alice realized Totsie was talking to someone else.

"What check?"

"From you of course," said Totsie. In the background was the noise of a department store cash register, and then Totsie said, "Yes, both of them, no, you know what, I'll take all three."

"You know the business is in trouble, you stopped working with no notice, and you still expect to be paid?

Are you kidding me? I did give out your check—to the person who is actually doing your job."

"You say we're partners, even though that place is technically yours, not mine, but then I get nothing out of it. And my husband is flushing money."

"No, *you* say we're partners.... Well maybe I should have accepted that check Mitch kept pressing on me. Come winter when there are floods inside here, what will we do then?"

"Without getting paid, I can't really consider kicking money in, now can I? That wouldn't be good business at all."

"Remind me never to need a kidney," said Alice crossly. She hung up the phone feeling a little guilty for her rudeness, but knowing that Totsie didn't even have a clue she'd been abruptly disconnected, because she was shopping as usual.

"Yoo hoo, mail call," said Emma, sticking her head in the office door, and making a little grimace, indicating what she held in her hand. Alice had sent in the swabs she did on herself and Skye, and had given Emma the one she'd taken from Robin while he slept.

Alice accepted the envelope from Emma, and gazed into the girl's eyes. "Well, we won't know everything, or maybe we will," she said nervously. At the same moment they tore the envelopes open. Alice smiled, then looked at Emma's downcast face.

"It says here Robin is no relation to me," said Emma.

"Oh gee, I'm sorry hon," answered Alice, relieved but not surprised to see that in fact Skye was her daughter. "How many more people do you have to contact?"

Emma sighed, "Only four. And I can't locate Misty Philpotts."

"Maybe you don't have to locate her," said Alice. "She was dating Robin at the time, so I guess if he's not your birth father, she's not your birth mother. She's probably still in New York." Alice reached for her laptop and typed Misty's name into a search engine, and some listings did come up, but they were more than ten years old. "Nothing recent here," she said.

"It's so strange," said Emma, "How you ended up with the guy whose girlfriend was giving birth right next to you."

"We just kept bumping into him for years here and there—it was very odd—and Skye really loved him, and he was a good dad, so one thing led to another."

"Life is strange for sure," said Emma. "And you never wanted more kids?"

"I do, er I did," said Alice. "Robin thought we couldn't afford more, and he and I, well…." she said, blushing.

"Okay, I'll keep you posted," said Emma, glancing at her watch, and rising to dress in her costume before the partygoers arrived.

"I know how much you miss having a family," said Alice kindly, "But you can be part of my family if you want—I'd love to have another nice daughter like you. You can come to family and holiday dinners, and just hang out if you want. I don't want you to be sad."

Emma walked around the desk and touched Alice kindly on the arm. "Ah thanks, Ally. I'd love that."

As Emma went off to change, Alice returned her focus to the computer, typing in a search for business loans, reading the information, and filling out the online application forms. She glanced upward briefly, examining the ceiling and wondering if the roof would hold for another winter. Even more serious was the walk-in—if the refrigeration went, they'd lose a ton of money on food, and worse, it could disrupt the parties for a day or two, and that would be so unfair to the children whose birthdays were ruined. Maybe she should buy an emergency fridge for P3, just in case. Alice pressed her hand to her head and just stopped to breathe for a moment.

It was an early day, and Alice decided, as she had now and then, to stop into the financial office at the Wellman Center to discuss money and ask if there were any new programs for which Itch possibly qualified. The news was seldom good, but it seemed worthwhile to check into it. Then she did what she allowed herself to do no more than once a month, walk down the long corridor to Itch's room.

Years ago, when all this started, Alice had visited him daily, often bringing Skye, who almost never wanted to go once she was old enough to express a preference. After Robin moved in with them, Alice tried, she really did, to make him her priority, so she began limiting her visits to once a week, but every time she saw Itch, it was so hard to go back to the life she was trying to build.

Now she walked along, immersed in a cloud of melancholy, weighted down even more with financial worry. Her mind floated back to the days they'd had together and all the things they'd shared. They'd sit in the movies, her small hand resting inside his big one, and Alice would take his hand and write in it with her finger, *I*, and she would draw a heart, and then write the letter *U*. Then Itch would take her hand, and write the same *I* and *U*, but in the middle, he'd draw a fatter heart, meant to be lips, and she knew it meant he wanted to kiss her, which he then would do, because even though you shouldn't talk in the movies, nobody cared about kissing.

After she arrived at the desk by his room and had greeted Mrs. Lewis, the nurse who'd looked after Itch for at least eight years, she asked as usual, "How's he doing?"

"Been a little restless this week," answered Mrs. Lewis, happily accepting the box of cupcakes Alice always brought for the nurses.

"Oh," said Alice, "No discomfort or bed sores or anything?" Alice almost hoped there was something wrong, because it would mean Itch was inside there somehow, feeling something, but the nurse shook her head in the way she always did, signaling that things were as they were.

Alice smiled softly at her, glad a nice person was there to look after him, and then walked into the room.

There Itch lay, silent and still, his face smooth and free of lines. It was as though he were deeply asleep, peacefully asleep, as though not only was nothing wrong, but as though nothing had ever been wrong. He was thinner than he used to be, but he still appeared sturdy, big and strong with clean, rugged features and dark hair. For more than half his life he lay there, lost in slumber. Alice pulled a chair over to his bedside, and took Itch's hand in hers sitting quietly for a moment, just breathing him in. She raised her hand and brushed his hair lightly. It was only a little thinner. She remembered back to years ago when she'd always kiss him deeply when she first arrived, and in her mind she'd think, wake up, Itch, wake up, as though it were some sort of fairy tale in which true love's kiss could break the evil spell. His lips were soft, but it was nothing like really kissing him, not so different than if she'd kissed her own hand. She was kissing lips that didn't pucker back, and it was heartrending.

Then she graduated to sitting and talking to him, sometimes to reading to him. For years she read him the sports news, none of which did she understand or care about, but she knew he'd like that better than hearing the actual news, which was far less cheerful since news is usually bad news.

Today she just sat there, Itch's hand in hers, and she thought of life and how terribly sad it all was. She wondered what might have happened if.... She pictured him awake and vital and them together, still in love, although really she was picturing Aunt Kitty and Uncle Henry, because that was the only happy union she'd experienced first hand.

Alice sighed, then took his hand and wrote *I heart U*, as she had done so many times long ago. And then she jumped. He had squeezed her hand. Had he squeezed her hand? It seemed he had squeezed her hand.

Alice reached for the bell and rang for the nurse. Once again she wrote *I heart U* in Itch's palm, but nothing happened. She looked at his face, and it seemed his eyes were moving. She stood and leaned in toward him, her palm against his cheek, and she said, "Itch, can you hear me, it's Ally." And then she waited. But nothing happened. The nurse looked in, and Alice asked her was it possible that Itch had squeezed her hand, and the nurse just shrugged, indicating who knew what was possible. Alice wrote in Itch's hand several more times and waited, but nothing happened.

This was the trouble with trips down memory lane, thought Alice, as she trudged back down the long corridor and out to the parking lot. What did Scarlett O'Hara say—that it tugged at your heart, and if you looked back too much, eventually all you could do was look back. Alice could envision herself becoming the sort of person who did little but lie on the couch and imagine the life she wished she'd had, who dreamed of a reality better than the one she lived—if she let herself. That was why she had to take control, why she couldn't just let go. She needed Spanx, well yes she needed them on her thighs, but that wasn't what she meant at all. She needed them emotionally, and Alice was determined to maintain control, to hold it all in.

Although there was a sense of security in this philosophy, there was little pleasure, but Alice didn't care. She would think about the reality with which she had to deal on a daily basis, for no matter how difficult it became, it was better than thinking about what she'd lost and how her heart had never stopped aching. This was what was on her mind as she drove up to the house and saw in front of it a parked police car, and Cooper standing on the sidewalk talking to a cop who was a head shorter than he was.

Alice's heart sank, and she leapt from the car and ran over, terrified that something had happened to Kitty. Tears poured from her eyes, and she knew they were tears long stored up, mingling with tears of apprehension. Before she could inquire what was going on, one of the officers shook Cooper's hand, and they both got back into their car and started the engine.

"What happened?" asked Alice, sobbing and unable to control her tears. "Is Kitty all right?"

"Whoa, dude," said Cooper, taken off balance, and wrapping his arms around Alice. "Kitty's inside watching TV with Mrs. Lopez. Take a breath, will you. Nothing's wrong."

Alice stood there panting, and wiping the tears from her eyes with the tail of her shirt. "But why were the police here?" She wheezed a few times, and her breath almost returned to normal.

"They're friends of mine," said Cooper. "I do some tech stuff for the cops."

Alice rooted around in her purse, located a rumpled tissue, uncrumpled it and blew her nose. "You do? Like what?"

"Tracking apps to help them catch crooks, computer stuff to wrangle money from deadbeat dads, lots of stuff."

Alice's eyes opened wide. "Kiddo, you amaze me. I want to hear all about this. You're like one of those cool spies on USA network."

Cooper steered her toward the house and gave her that rye grin, saying, "You already know too much."

She smiled and shook her head. "Nope, usually I know less than half of what I should."

After checking that everything was indeed all right, Alice found herself walking through a mall with Robin, something they hadn't done in a long time.

"Many dentists are doing it," he said, "Labs right in the office, all porcelain crowns, no metal underneath. Faster for the patient, more profit for them."

"So basically you're saying teeth are now made of the same stuff as dishes? Corningware teeth? What happens when people bite down on something hard, like an ice cube?"

Robin looked at her with what Alice thought seemed like gratitude for her display of interest, then he grinned. "Hopefully they break, and the patient is back for another crown." He stopped for a moment in front of a men's store, and said, "Hey look, my socks." There in the window were the socks they'd fought over a few days ago. He held up his leg and pulled his pants up to show Alice he was wearing them. "Actually very comfortable," he said.

Alice smiled. "I'm glad you like them. Look, here it is."

They walked into the mattress store and examined the beds. "This is the cheapest," said Robin. "Maybe start here and work our way up?"

"I'm thinking start with the most expensive and work our way down," said Alice, and she sat down on a very nice model, thinking it had been quite some time since she'd experienced a mattress at all. She kicked off her shoes and lay back, accepting the remote control from the salesman. She pressed the buttons, and felt the mattress grow alternately more firm and more soft, depending. "This is so cool!"

Robin walked to a much less expensive model and lay down, adjusting it precisely. "It's like an amusement park ride for the geriatric," he said.

"Don't call a perpetually sleep-deprived woman in the prime of her life geriatric."

Alice got up and walked slowly over to where he lay, taking her place on the other side of the bed. She could feel herself blushing. Then she put her head down, adjusted the remote, and watched the numbers flashing by. "Wow," she said. "This is great," and as she spoke, her voice grew fainter and fainter.

"Ally! Ally!" She heard Robin's voice from a distance, then she opened her eyes and saw him standing next to the bed. "The store is closing."

Alice sat up. "You just let me sleep? Here in the store—like what—a homeless person? With people going in and out shopping? Did you fall asleep too?"

Robin laughed. "I went to Nordstrom. Got some slacks for work. Figured you'd call me if you woke up and I was gone."

Alice shook her head at him. "Can we still get this one?" she asked the salesman. "How long for delivery?"

"We can have one like this delivered and set up tomorrow," the astonished salesman said. Clearly he assumed he'd make no sales off the crazy lady who Rip Van Winkled herself in his store. "Credit card or our financing?" he asked.

"Perfect," she said. "I'll be home all day tomorrow." She waved her hand at Robin, indicating that he should take care of it and steeled herself for an argument, but something floated across his eyes, she didn't know what, and for some reason he just went and signed the papers.

They walked out of the store, and Robin asked, "So does this mean you might actually be sleeping in the bed, hogging all the covers and snoring like you used to?"

Alice sighed and looked at him — it had been so long since she thought of him as more than just an annoyance. She smiled and squeezed his arm. "It could happen," she said coyly.

Robin wrapped his arm around Alice and said, "C'mon, I'll buy you a burger. Think the Apple Pan is still open?"

Alice smiled and said, "And pie?"

"It could happen."

After their pleasant night out, Alice felt more relaxed than she had in a long while. Or maybe it was the three hour nap in the mattress store. Then she walked into the living room, and was happy to see Kitty there watching an old movie and Cooper playing some game on his iPad. Skye and Julian sat on the floor going over some notes.

"Mom!" said Skye, "We have something exciting to show you. Julian's been working on this for hours. It's a whole entertainment concept."

"Well!" said Alice, smiling more because she was relieved that no crisis was afoot than interested in Julian's concept. She kissed her aunt and sat down on a chair near Skye. "I'm all yours."

Julian leapt up from the floor, flourishing the sheaf of papers and said, "It's the world of the clown. You know Chaplin?"

Alice nodded.

"Chaplin had his little tramp—I have my little clown—the clown is at the heart and soul of everything. Many skits, one character. And what makes it different, is that it's a clown. Like for example, I'm sitting there in a chair, and I'm talking. And I say something like this 'Just when I think I'm out, they pull me back in.' And then you see a rope around my neck, pulling me down, down, down. And the chair collapses. And I'm in a kiddy pool—all wet."

"Hmm," said Alice.

"I'm always in the clown costume—because I'm the *clown*," he said with much emphasis. "It's as though the clown suit is my skin. And sometimes the clown is playing a part, so elements of that costume go over the clown suit—like what I did the other day. So I could walk in wearing a sea captain's hat and holding binoculars or something, and we hear the famous *Jaws* music. And I'm distraught, really capturing their attention. Pacing, you know. And I say, 'You know the thing about a shark, he's got lifeless eyes. Black eyes like a doll's eyes. When he comes at ya, he doesn't seem to be living until he bites ya and … ah, then you hear that terrible high-pitch screaming." Julian reached into his pocket and pulled out a plastic shark that was about three inches long and as he continued speaking, he began menacing himself with the toy. "' The ocean turns red and despite all the pounding and hollering, they all come in and they rip you to pieces.'" His hand holding the toy shark was whipping around in front of his face, as Julian grimaced and projected terror to the far corners of the living room. Closer and closer to his face the toy came, and then Julian let out a shriek and collapsed onto the floor, reaching into his pocket and unfurling a red scarf to simulate blood. He lay there mock-dead for a long moment, and finally rose and looked at Alice.

"Notice how small the shark was? And the scarf for the blood is an old trick from ancient theater. See—I remembered what you said about violence."

"Well…" said Alice.

"Or I could walk in with a blazer over my clown suit—but you always still see the suit—that's the real pathos—and I grab a girl from one of the tables and whirl her around—or maybe Skye plays that part—if she wants to." He leapt up then, grabbed Skye and whirled her around in a mock dance, shouting "Who-ha, Who-ha!" He took several deep whiffs of Skye, breathing in her *scent* then continued, "And then I'd say 'If I were the man I was five years ago, I'd take a flame thrower to this place!'"

Alice sighed. "I had the urge to take a flame thrower to it myself today."

Julian had worked himself up to a state of visible excitement and couldn't stand still, so he paced a bit, then said to Alice, "So you see where I'm going with this?"

Alice said, straight-faced, "It's about the clown."

Julian's eyes opened wide. "Yes! Exactly."

"I told you she'd get it," said Skye. "Mom's a huge movie buff."

"And the thing that's so brilliant is that other characters can be played by puppets or toys. Or Skye of course."

Alice nodded with mock seriousness that only she knew was mocking, "Like Kevin Kline's one man Hamlet in *Soapdish*."

Julian stared at her blankly, but continued, "And the great thing is the clown becomes the central attraction because you never know what sort of skit he'll be in."

"Get it, Mom," interjected Skye, "the clown is a metaphor for everyman. It's really very deep, yet charming and funny. Brilliant, isn't it?" Skye gazed hopefully at Alice, who wished she could remain silent, but picturing more debacles like those Julian had already inflicted on P3, she had to speak up.

"Well," said Alice, "I can't really see how people will want to watch monologues from movies enacted like that, not to mention that we can't legally infringe on the rights of those scripts. Or talk about such intense stuff. People are eating. And most of them are children, as you saw. There's a reason why clowns stick to a certain program. Plus of course I have no budget for entertainment unless someone actually books a clown. Then I could hire you, but you'd have to do more traditional stuff. I can't exactly hire a clown and have you enact the suicide scene from *Sayonara*."

"O-M-G," said Julian, "What a fantastic example to use. Imagine the clown putting on the Kabuki makeup over his clown makeup. In front of a mirror. That's powerful."

"Maybe," said Alice, "But the point is not that it's powerful, but that it's what we can't do, not something we could do. Or even should do. Maybe as a drama thesis, but not exactly in the real world."

"What if we did it as a free trial run? Then when it takes off and you're raking in the dough, we can negotiate."

"I don't see how," said Alice, looking imploringly at Skye. "I had to comp that party the other day. Profits are dwindling fast enough without me paying for people to have free parties."

Julian sank down into a chair in a manner that appeared so deflated, Alice couldn't tell if he were still acting or truly upset.

"Mom!" said Skye out of the corner of her mouth, bobbing her head repeatedly toward the kitchen, so Alice took the hint and followed her out of the room.

"I can't believe you said all that—poor Julian—he worked so hard and you practically eviscerated him. He's totally emasculated."

"Well, I'm sorry," said Alice quietly, "But nobody'll want to watch that."

"But you said we could do skits."

"I never said we could have something wacko like that. It's a business. I have irate parents yelling at me over all kinds of stuff. I have to be responsible."

"You're responsible all right," groused Skye, "Responsible for hurting a brilliant artist's feelings."

"Look hon, I'm sorry, really, but maybe he's just too avant garde for children." Then Alice held back her smile but added, "Or adults."

Before Skye could continue her tirade, Kitty walked into the kitchen, hugged Alice, and said, "I have to go home now to meet my boyfriend."

"Kitty you live here now, remember," said Alice gently.

"But how will he find me here? This isn't where I live."

"Cooper put your chef on the TV schedule in the living room and on the TV upstairs in your room. Remember your old room upstairs? You sleep there again now."

"I don't think so," sang Kitty. "Look, here's the door. It's right out here. My room is right outside this door."

Alice put her arm around her aunt, saying, "Come on, let's go in here and see if we can find him."

"No, no," said Kitty, twisting out of Alice's grasp and going for the door.

"Cooper," yelled Alice. "Cooper!" When he didn't appear, she said, "Kitty could you help me find Cooper? I think he's wearing earbuds and doesn't hear me."

"What," she said, "Flowers in his ears? Is it the prom?"

Alice once again tried to lead her aunt back into the living room, and this time Kitty walked alongside her. Alice grabbed the remote, clicked it, and then the opener played for Johnny Badass.

"Julian!" said Skye, looking at Cooper, who made a gesture indicating that he'd gone out the door. "Mom!" she said, "You humiliated him so much he left."

"Well, I'm sorry," said Alice, "But if he's going to audition, people are going to say no, well some will. It's just part of the process when you work with people."

Skye scowled at Alice, grabbed her purse, and ran out the door.

"This isn't him!" shrieked Kitty, snatching the remote out of Alice's hands and clicking it so much that the DVR box froze, then began rebooting, and nothing appeared but a blue screen and a wait message.

"That was the guy you showed me," said Alice. "Remember we had a tea party and watched him cook jambalaya, and then later in the week I made it?"

"He wasn't cooking jambalaya just now. It wasn't him. He cooks the jambalaya. That guy was cooking crawfish. Like bugs. Snapping off bug heads." Aunt Kitty kept clicking on the remote and before the picture could return, the system kept rebooting.

"Maybe Cooper can fix it," said Alice kindly, handing the remote to Cooper and giving him an imploring glance. "Can't you get the same episode over here?"

"I could swap out the box there and the one here or the one upstairs," said Cooper.

"I'll just go home—I can go where I want you know—I'm not some baby," said Kitty, stomping her foot.

Cooper stood up, then spoke softly, "Now, Aunt Kitty Cat, if I stomped around like that, you'd yell at me. Here, look, here are all the episodes of the show. Here's the one with the jambalaya." He handed Kitty the iPad with the show running. Then he led her back to where she was sitting and helped her sit down.

"How'd he get inside this Etch A Sketch?" Kitty asked, shaking the iPad, and scowling when there were no flecks of gray showering down inside it. "He's always at home. Oh boy this isn't good, not good at all. The knobs are broken off." Kitty watched the show for a moment, then tried to toss the iPad away onto the floor but Cooper reached out and grabbed it before it fell.

"Badass, Badass, Badass!" yelled Kitty.

Alice and Cooper glanced at each other, both plainly worried.

"I tell you what," said Alice. "Maybe just for tonight we can go over there to where you used to live so you can watch your chef. I'll stay with you. Then tomorrow we can bring your machine and TV over here. Do you think that would be okay with Johnny? He could visit you here then, couldn't he?"

"How am I supposed to speak for him," said Kitty.

"I can go sleep there if you need to bake," said Cooper.

Alice touched him on the arm and smiled; he was such a nice boy. "Closed tomorrow," said Alice, "So it's no problem. I'll be fine on the couch over there."

"Someone stole all my clothes," said Kitty. "I have no pajamas. No nightgowns. I'm nightgownless."

"They're all here now, right upstairs in your old room. C'mon, let's go up there, get into a comfy nightgown or pj's, and then we can go watch your chef, okay?"

"What kind of criminal steals your stuff and moves it into another room? Do you think they're still up there? Vandals!"

"Tell you what," said Alice. "Cooper will go up there and make sure no criminals are hiding, then we can go get you into whatever you want to wear, and you and I will go have a party watching your chef."

Kitty seemed to have calmed down a little and she said, "You know I love parties. That's how I make my living."

"Hold your end up, dammit." Robin's voice came from beyond Kitty's door. Alice shook her head, and sat up on the couch. The television was on, but the sound was so low it was barely audible.

"I'll hold up my end when you start holding up yours," said Cooper, with sarcasm that obviously meant something beyond the immediate subject.

Alice crept to the window and peered out, squinting into the sunlight. She looked at her watch; it was only eight in the morning. For some reason Robin and Cooper were wrangling the old bed through the courtyard. Alice opened the door and leaned out. "What're you doing?" she asked. "The delivery guys will take that away. You can't just leave it by the dumpster."

"One of the tenants wanted it," said Robin. "Poor kid's been sleeping on a futon." Alice was about to shrug, when Cooper's expression alerted her that the 'kid' to whom Robin was referring was Layla. Briefly Alice wished she had bedbugs, then she shuddered and closed the door.

"Kitty?" she said softly, walking into her aunt's kitchen. There were dishes in the sink, which struck Alice as very odd, because her aunt normally washed the dishes almost before they were used. Alice crept down the hallway into Kitty's bedroom, but the bed was made, and nobody was in it. She looked into the second bedroom, which still contained Skye's old crib as well as a daybed. It was all spotless but unoccupied.

Alice dashed out the door, calling, "Kitty, Kitty?" Robin and Cooper had disappeared by then, presumably into Layla's bedless apartment. She ran into the house, calling for her aunt, who wasn't in the living room. Maybe she was upstairs napping, thought Alice, but before she could move up the stairs, the doorbell rang. The mattress, she thought, walking to the door but yelling "Kitty, Kitty."

She opened the door, but it wasn't the mattress; it was two police officers. Of course, she thought, the friends of Cooper's. "Oh, hi," she said, "Cooper's out back helping move a mattress, but you're welcome to come in. He'll be back in a moment."

"What?" said the young officer.

"We're getting a new mattress delivered," she explained, thinking she didn't have time for this until she could locate her aunt. "Cooper's helping move the old one. But he'll be right back if you want to visit with him."

The young police officer continued to look bewildered, causing Alice to cast her mind back in an attempt to recall what those pals of Cooper's actually looked like. Then he spoke, "Excuse me, ma'am, I think we have your aunt here."

"Oh my God!" said Alice, bursting out the door, and looking all around. There was Kitty in the back of the police car, wearing an old cheerleading costume of Skye's. Alice ran to the car and tried to open the door, but the other officer did it for her. "Kitty! Are you all right?"

Kitty looked a bit dirty and confused, as the officer who'd knocked on Alice's door said, "We found her stumbling along on Cloverfield. Her knee is pretty badly scraped."

Alice helped Kitty out of the car, and looked down at her knee. It was rubbed raw and caked with dried blood. "Oh my goodness, I can't believe you got past me, and I didn't wake up." She turned to the policeman and explained, "I slept on her couch last night to make sure she'd be safe."

"Enough with this lollygagging," said Kitty. She reached into her purse and pulled out two five dollar bills, attempting to give one to each of the policemen. "Can't forget to tip the taxi driver," she said.

"You're in a cheerleading outfit," said Alice. What was worse, having her aunt wandering the streets in a nightgown, or like this? Her heart clenched at either thought.

"All my clothes were stolen," said Kitty, limping a bit as she exited the police car. She continued, "We have to get back to P3 and put out the fire. I couldn't do it by myself."

Alice hugged her aunt, feeling utterly distraught. "There's no crisis today, Kitty, P3 is closed. Let's get you inside and clean up that knee. Did you fall?"

"I scraped my knees when I was kneeling, trying to hook up that hose—can't bend over for a long time like I used to." Aunt Kitty held out her knee to examine the scrape, and nodded when she observed that it matched what she was talking about. "We can take your car, can't we? I know I'm not supposed to drive because of Watergate." Kitty pulled on Alice urgently. "We really have to put out that fire."

"I have to wait for the new mattress," Alice said gently, but soon as it comes we can go make sure the doors at P3 are locked. Then I think we should see your doctor."

"A fireman would be better," sang Kitty. Alice led her toward the front door, and nodded thanks to the policemen, who had returned the money, and were about to drive away.

"I don't think you can lock a door once it's burned down," said Kitty, who turned and looked with interest, as the mattress truck pulled up. "Princess and the Pea," she chortled.

Alice guided two small men wearing back supporting belts to the bedroom upstairs, and they carried the parts of the new bed into the house, as Kitty grabbed the phone, saying, "I better make this call."

"Don't go outside, okay Kitty?" Alice said seriously, gazing deeply into her aunt's eyes, and feeling that she was heard. She dashed upstairs for long enough to see that the bed was installed in the right place, then raced back down again to find Kitty watching TV in the living room.

"Ally! I think you should see this," said her aunt.

Alice signed a paper on a clipboard, tipped the delivery guys, and waved them out of the house. Then she made an appointment with Kitty's specialist. "Come on, Kitty, we can see Chef Johnny later. Your doctor is squeezing us in. Let's get you showered and dressed."

Kitty shook her head, saying, "It's not broken. I don't need a cast on it. This is more important."

Alice glanced at the television, but there was a commercial on, so she managed to get her aunt up and moving toward the stairs. "Your clothes are upstairs, remember."

"I don't think so," sang Kitty.

Alice kept steering her aunt up the stairs, and said, "You like a little wager, don't you? Well I'll bet you five dollars that all your clothes are right up here."

Kitty shook her head at Alice. "We have a fire to put out. We can't play slot machines now. Sometimes I worry about you, Ally. We must focus. This isn't Vegas, you know."

Alice had maneuvered Kitty into the bedroom, opening the door to the walk-in closet, and pointing at all her clothes, neatly arranged inside it, as Kitty shrugged and squinted in amazement. "Good trick," she said.

"How about a nice shower," said Alice, "Then we can spritz your knee with Bactine and zip off to visit the doctor." Kitty let Alice help her out of the cheerleading costume, and laughed as Alice said, "See, I could never fit into this. But you're as thin as you ever were."

"Don't be silly," Kitty answered. "This thing is way small—it must have shrunk. I never wear skirts this short." She pulled the heavy sweater over her head, revealing the zipper that was inches from being able to close beneath it. "No wonder you think we're in Vegas—I look like a cocktail waitress."

Alice took a deep breath and changed into something decent looking, as Kitty managed to shower and dress herself in neat slacks and a nice blouse. Then she led Kitty to the car. "You know," said Alice, "We can go for a nice lunch after we see the doctor. Would you like that?'

Kitty grimaced, and said ruefully, "I hope you weren't planning to eat at P3."

"I told you," said Alice softly, "It's closed today." Alice drove the couple of miles to the doctor's office, and sat as he did cognitive testing on her aunt, after having taken samples for blood and urinalysis.

"We have a fire to put out, and he hasn't even looked at my knee," said Kitty, scowling with disgust toward Alice, then whispering, "Good thing you did the Bactine yourself. Doctors!"

After what seemed like a thorough exam, a nurse led Kitty off to wait, while Alice talked with Dr. Goldman.

"She's much worse," he said, "But you knew that didn't you?"

Alice nodded glumly.

"You're going to have to make a decision very soon," he said kindly. "No one person can keep track of her every minute, even with your caretaker. And it's not safe for her to wander off, even if she still remembers where you live."

"But how could I send her away because she's sick? She would never have done that to me."

"And if she wanders off and gets hit by a car, what then? This isn't a punishment, it's a matter of her safety."

"How long do you think she has at this level of lucidity?" Alice asked.

"The problem is not so much lucidity, but if she's putting you or the family—or herself—at risk." He looked into Alice's tortured face, and smiled gently. "Not long," he said, "Not long at all. It's a difficult process for everyone, I know."

Alice nodded and rose, shaking the doctor's hand. "Could you bring her a Band-Aid," she asked, "Then at least she'll know you looked at her knee." The doctor smiled and followed Alice out to the waiting room, after stopping into one of his exam rooms and grabbing a Band-Aid.

Kitty stood as they approached her in the waiting room. "Finally ready for me?" she asked the doctor. "I've been waiting for a very long time." She accepted the bandage and made no fuss as they exited the office. Whispering to Alice, she said, "They keep you waiting for an hour, then all they do is hand you a Band-Aid. Not like we don't have them at home."

"Hungry?" Alice asked as they walked to the car.

"I burned plenty of burgers in my day, but nothing like what I saw today."

"Johnny burned burgers?" asked Alice.

Before she could answer, Kitty had leaned her head against the car door, and was snoring. Alice patted her hand. She'd had a hard day. Thinking it might be easier on her aunt just to have a fruit salad and some grilled cheese sandwiches at home, Alice turned the car toward the house, but then she remembered her promise to check the locks at P3, so she drove in that direction. When she was two blocks away, she could see a plume of smoke in the sky, and she could smell a fire. The street was blocked off, so she couldn't drive down it, but she could see well enough to realize that all that talk about a fire wasn't fanciful. Alice gasped in horror. Kitty had set P3 on fire!

Just then Kitty's hand shot out and clenched Alice's arm. "Look, P3 is on fire," she shrieked. "Oh my God! You think anyone is in there? Park the car, quick!"

Alice pulled over to the curb, her heart pounding. "Were you baking today at P3?" she asked her aunt.

Kitty yanked vigorously on her seatbelt, then finally unclicked it. "Hurry up," she said.

"Wait," said Alice, "Were you baking today at P3?"

"I was too busy trying to put out the fire to get anything baked," said Kitty, and she sounded lucid enough. She wrenched her door open, and stepped outside, forcing Alice to do the same. There were fire trucks showering the place with streams of water, and the blaze seemed to be diminishing, but Alice didn't want her aunt to be at risk.

"We shouldn't be here," Alice said. "Why don't I take you home, and then come back and see what's going on."

"Good thing I called the firemen," said Kitty.

Alice looked at her aunt. She seemed coherent now, but had she set that fire? "How did the fire start?" she asked, craning her neck toward the scene.

Kitty shrugged. "How should I know? I haven't worked here in years."

Alice gripped her aunt's hand tightly, and they walked toward the barricade erected by the police.

"Ma'am, you'll need to vacate this area," said the officer standing guard.

"We own this business," said Alice, peering toward the fire and the streams of water that didn't seem to be putting it out.

"It's a serious fire," said the officer. "Nothing you can do here now. I'm sure they'll call you once it's out."

"I'd like to speak to a fire chief first," said Alice, pointing in the direction of the firemen, some of whom seemed to be doing nothing.

"I can't let you inside this barrier. I'm sorry."

Kitty wrenched loose from Alice for a moment and dug around in her purse, pulling out a whistle and blowing vigorously on it. When the fire marshal looked toward them, she waved and blew some more. "Can't browbeat us," she said sternly, wagging her finger at the officer. "Silly taxi driver."

The fire marshal walked over, and said, "Can I help you?"

"This is our business," said Alice.

"It's a bad fire," he said, "But doesn't seem to be anyone in there."

"No, we were closed today," said Alice.

"Any paints or solvents inside?"

Alice shook her head, "No, nothing like that. Just food, chairs, tables, linens. Any idea how and when this started?"

"We were called a couple hours ago."

"Will the building be okay?"

The marshal shook his head at Alice. "Lucky if even the outer walls'll be left. Call your insurer."

Alice felt dazed. She thought of a million things at once, and then of all the parties she'd have to cancel. "I just can't believe this," she said softly.

"Nobody ever can," said the fire marshal. "I've got to go back now."

"Thank you for everything," said Alice, "Please be careful — you and your men."

Kitty held out the whistle to the fire chief, and said, "Looks like you need this more than I do."

The man smiled and said, "Oh no thanks, ma'am, I have one of my own."

Alice wrapped her arm around her aunt's shoulder and led Kitty back to the car. "Lot of calls to make," she said softly.

"Henry!" said Kitty, "Call Henry right away. He'll know what to do."

Alice opened the car door and helped Kitty into the front seat. "Uncle Henry died a long time ago, remember?" she asked. Aunt Kitty said nothing, but began sobbing. "Oh Kitty," said Alice, "I'm so sorry."

"Henry burned up in the fire," Kitty said gasping between sobs. "Henry burned up in the fire. Henry burned up in the fire."

Alice's heart ached as she looked at Kitty, whose eyes were glazed over now, and her voice was hollow as she kept repeating that phrase. She reached out and took Kitty's hand in hers. "Look at me Kitty," she said softly, "Henry died a long time ago. He wasn't in the fire." She gazed at her aunt, hoping for an answer, for something helpful and healing to say, but nothing worked, and Kitty kept repeating that phrase over and over all the way home.

They were in the house in no time, and Alice futilely made her aunt some oatmeal with coconut oil mixed in. Then she began making calls to notify people that P3 would be closed for a while, and that their parties would have to be scheduled elsewhere. She thought of the deposits she'd have to refund, but that was the least of her worries. Wondering how long it would take for an insurance check to appear, Alice dialed her agent, who already knew about the fire. She was picturing him arriving at the door with a check as they did in the commercials, when he said that there would be a lengthy investigation; life wasn't always like TV commercials. Alice sighed, then called the staff and Emma to let them know what had happened. She took a deep breath; she was completely exhausted. It had been such a long day, then Alice glanced at the kitchen clock and saw that it was barely noon.

As she turned, Alice noticed an acrid smell in the room and smoke coming from the oven. She dashed to it, opened the door and saw a roast inside, still sitting on its styrofoam tray, still wrapped in plastic, the heat set to five hundred degrees, and the plastic melting inside the oven. She quickly turned off the oven, grabbed a cutting board and some tongs, and pulled the roast out.

"What're you doing?" asked Kitty, "That can't be ready yet. I just put it in. Henry doesn't like really rare meat."

Alice turned on the exhaust fan, opened the back door, then, in deep despair, she turned back and wrapped her arms around her aunt, saying "Oh Kitty, I'm so sorry," over and over again.

There were at least ten people in the waiting room, most of them younger than Alice, eager and fancy free candidates who nevertheless certainly had better résumés. Instead of being apprehensive, she told herself to relax, because it was obvious that nobody would choose her, so there was nothing to worry about. An assistant had collected all the résumés and everyone sat, flicking their phones, tapping their toes, and glancing at their watches. This must be what it was like to be an actor, lining up outside a room, waiting to be rejected.

Alice had expected by now to hear something definitive, and to receive an insurance check, but the investigation lumbered along, resolving nothing on any front, so when Cooper had shown her the ad for this job, she hesitated, but decided to apply. With money going in only a negative direction and no abatement of expenses, Alice lacked the luxury of remaining unproductive. Luckily, Kitty had enough money flowing into her accounts to cover her expenses at the Wellman Center. Alice's heart ached each morning when she awoke and realized she didn't have to go immediately to check on her aunt. There was little relief, much guilt, and even more pain. Daily she visited, and daily her heart grew more shredded.

"Alice Catson," said the assistant, leaning back into the waiting area from the doorway. Alice jumped up. Was this like jury duty, where they called the ones to be dismissed first? "Follow me, please," she said, and Alice was led inside the studio, where various styles of kitchens had been built, one of which she even recognized from a late-night infomercial about steam cleaners. After a bit of a walk, she arrived at the nicest kitchen set, one that looked like a copy from a very famous TV show. It had seats for an audience and several areas which could be used for different segments.

A familiar looking man walked up to Alice and shook her hand, "Ms. Catson," he said warmly.

"My goodness, hello," said Alice. He was the nice grandfather from that party she'd had to comp because of Julian's wacko skit.

"I was so sorry to hear about the fire," he said kindly. "You'll be rebuilding?"

Alice nodded. "Everything's in a holding pattern at the moment, insurance delays, you know." Alice wracked her brain to recall his name, but it wouldn't float back into her memory.

"Tom Angelico," he said, as though he were reading her mind.

"Of course," she said, smiling. "Grandson okay?"

Tom laughed and said, "My daughter's a little high strung. No damage at all. Boys will be boys, and so on."

"So you produce cooking shows? This is a beautiful set." Alice looked all around with admiration. They'd really done an excellent job creating a domestic world.

"I produce infomercials," he said honestly, smiling a bit at himself, "But my wife was in the theater, and she's determined to have a cooking show, so you know, new marriage, want her to be happy, figured why not." Tom walked through the set, Alice beside him, as he led her to the prep kitchen behind the scenes. "This would be your domain. Slicing and dicing, I guess," he said with an expression that indicated he didn't have a clue, but was willing to see what happened.

Alice looked at the prep kitchen and smiled. It was top notch. "Great," she said, nodding. "Your wife is a chef?"

Tom laughed and shook his head. "Not that I've ever seen." He paused for a moment as he pondered, and Alice waited for him to continue. "The thing is I don't know how long my wife will really want to do this."

"I see," said Alice.

"But I have some great studios here, and it might be profitable to do some other cooking shows too, well we'll see. I'm always thinking about the future. Meanwhile, we'll just start with this." He reached out and shook Alice's hand again, saying, "Welcome to the company."

"Oh," she said, rather astonished, "But what about all those other people waiting outside?"

"I had my girl—oops not supposed to say that—my assistant—send them home when I saw your résumé."

"Wow," said Alice.

"Come on, come meet my shining star."

Alice thought how sweet it was that he was so in love and doing all this for his wife, even though she didn't sound like much of a cook. But even if it was just a vanity production, it would give her something to do and some money, so Alice was thrilled. She walked along beside Tom, making small talk until he turned into a nicely appointed office and said "Here she is," and then Alice once again came face to face with the worst person on earth.

"Misty Philpotts," said Alice, wondering how this nice man had produced a self-involved daughter, and then married the world's most loathsome female. Poor guy—he must have a terrible curse on him.

"Ally Catson," said Misty, glancing up and down Alice's form as though she were a car up for auction.

"Fabulous!" said Tom. "You girls already know each other—how amazing." He wrapped an arm around Misty's shoulders and hugged her, smiling down at her adoringly.

Misty batted her eyes at Tom briefly, smiling sweetly and causing Alice to speculate how many millions he'd made producing those infomercials; it had to be quite a few. Alice wondered how much older than Misty she appeared, although she knew at forty neither of them looked old at all. It was just that Misty had this pampered air, like one of those show dogs who are taken weekly to a groomer. Her hair was perfectly bleached and coiffed, her nails long and manicured, and her face looked as though she'd had Botox or other injectables that thwarted all visible human expression, which Alice figured wouldn't matter in this case, because she couldn't imagine Misty offering her so much as the tiniest grin. In fact, Alice was wondering how long it would take Misty to fire her.

"So you're a cook?" Misty asked, with what Alice assumed was disdain, but Tom didn't react adversely, so maybe she was being overly sensitive.

"She went to culinary *and* pastry school," said Tom, as though somehow it meant Alice was a Rhodes scholar. "She's a double whammy." He beamed at his wife.

Misty's eyes, the only part of her face that betrayed the faintest emotion, clouded over slightly, and she asked, "You seem to know each other. How?"

"You remember—I told you about Colton's party, and the nice woman who took care of everything."

Misty nodded. Alice could imagine Misty's rodent-sized brain struggling to come up with a way not to hire her, and soon enough she said, "But we can't take you away from your family business. You've been working there all these years, huh, never gone anywhere, amazing."

"Yes," said Alice as placidly as she could manage, "From that perspective I guess you could say it's a blessing it burned down."

"And what happened here?" asked Misty, waving her arm around Alice's face.

"An accident," said Alice, seeing no reason to go into details about that now.

"Scary," said Misty, with what Alice assumed was feigned sympathy. "Ever see Tiffany?"

"Who?" answered Alice, although she recalled Tiffany very well as Misty's equally rancid other half, but believing nothing good could come of a discussion about that, it seemed easier to pretend to have forgotten.

"C'mon girls, you can reminisce and giggle later. Let's sit down and discuss the show." Tom took a seat behind his desk, indicating that they should sit on the couch, so there was Alice, the other bookend opposite her long-time nemesis. "We're calling it Angel Food," he said smiling.

"Oh, a baking show," said Alice.

Misty tried to scowl, but the most she could produce was a sour looking expression, as she said, "Why on earth would you say that?"

"Angel food cake," said Alice.

"As if that's a real thing," said Misty.

"Sorry, of course, Angelico," said Alice quickly.

Tom nodded, as Misty continued, "Why should I limit myself to baking? I plan to teach my audience about style, and cooking is part of style. And I really see this taking off. We could do a whole series, other hosts too maybe, eventually start our own network all about cooking."

"Like the Food Network?" Alice asked.

"Somebody stole my idea!" gasped Misty.

"They've been around maybe twenty years," said Alice.

Misty tried to cut her eyes at Alice, but they wouldn't squint, so she had to be contented grunting out a harrumph, as Tom said, "See it was great we hired Alice. She's our resident expert. She's going to make us both look good."

"Speaking of looking good," said Misty, once again taking stock of Alice, "I'll have to order you some of the custom chef outfits I designed for the show—well you won't really be on camera, but I still want my staff to have a certain look—anyway—what size are you? Large? Extra Large?" Then she produced a self-satisfied simper, the way starving women do when they confront someone who actually eats.

"Medium," said Alice, with no expression at all.

"Really?" asked Misty, as though she were at any minute ready to attach a lie detector to Alice, who just glanced at her without replying. "Okay then," she continued sternly, "But these are custom so I can't return them." Alice pictured Misty pricked and bleeding, as she sat in a closet helplessly wielding a seam ripper, pulling out labels marked size extra small and gluing—because of course she couldn't sew—new labels marked medium, all in the interest of torturing Alice.

As Misty continued talking about her plans for the show, and what in her vision Alice's job would entail, Alice listened vaguely, her mind wandering to the past and all the moments of her life for which Misty had been around. All Alice had to do was endure a crisis, and somehow this odious female managed to become part of it, so what Alice was now wondering was something quite frightening—namely—what next? Would they discover that ridiculous, absurd, psycho clown was actually Misty's son, and Skye would marry him, eternally linking Misty to them all? Alice envisioned her daughter, not as a traditional bride, but in some kind of white clown garb, probably with white-on-white polka dots. She cringed inwardly, while maintaining a sedate outer appearance, and continuing to consider all the other potential Misty-encumbered calamities that could now befall her, on top of what had just happened. Maybe this was some sort of sign, an indication that Alice should rise immediately and walk, no flee, from this scene, aborting any further future in which Misty would play a part. That idea appealed to her tremendously. She could shout 'You're the worst person in the world, and couldn't cook canned spaghetti for a dead 'possum, and then she could stomp out of there, leaving Misty to explain to her doting husband why anyone would hold that opinion of her. Alice ran various versions of this scenario back and forth in her mind for some time, changing them slightly and challenging herself to maintain a serene countenance when she wanted either to scowl or laugh.

"So you're clear on all this," Misty said, and Alice nodded, rising and wishing the stomping could commence. "We'll do trial runs this week, and shoot for real next, right darling?" Tom nodded, leaving Alice relieved, because in no way did she want to graduate from former nemesis to 'darling.' "I'll walk you out to your car," said Misty inexplicably, "Tom has some work to do, anyway."

"See you tomorrow, Alice, um Ally," he said pleasantly, and Alice followed Misty out of earshot. They walked along at a brisk pace in silence, Misty holding one finger to her mouth, so that Alice would say nothing, then when they exited the building, she began speaking.

"I know you know," said Misty, causing Alice to assume Misty meant that Alice knew she couldn't cook.

"Many people cooking on TV are far from expert cooks," said Alice, baffled at why she was being so placating.

Misty clenched her teeth together, producing an almost scowl. "How dare you," she protested. Then she repeated, as if the second time her unaltered message would actually be clear, "I know you know."

"What do I know?" asked Alice, looking toward her car, and thinking that soon she would be away from Misty, but that tomorrow it would all begin again. Could she really have agreed to take this job? Alice's head began to pound.

"About the baby. The baby I gave up for adoption." Even though they were outside with nobody around, Misty spoke in a whisper.

"Of course I know. I was right in the same hospital room as you." Alice stopped walking for a moment, and scrutinized Misty's face.

"That was you?" asked Misty, in a way that made Alice ponder if she were actually pretending not to know.

"I was going to mention this to you anyway," said Alice. "A few weeks back, a girl came to see me with some letter from the hospital about babies being switched. Her adopted parents were dead, and she sort of wondered about her birth parents."

Misty blanched, and almost lost her balance. She flailed out, grasped onto Alice's arm, then righted herself. "And what did you tell her?"

"We took a test—no relation. She's a really nice girl, though. Would you maybe like to meet her? She's not after anything, just sort of felt like solving the mystery of the letter from the hospital."

Misty's hand flew up and covered her mouth. Her eyes grew wide. "How am I supposed to tell my husband about this? He has no idea. I can't be having adopted babies appearing out of nowhere. What would he think of me? I can't risk that."

"He's a really great guy, and he loves you so much—why would you worry about that? Besides you could meet her in confidence. She's very nice."

Misty looked truly tortured, which Alice naturally found quite enjoyable. "This can't be happening, now that everything is going so well. Besides my baby was adopted by some nice people in San Diego, last name began with a D, can't hmm can't remember."

"Delamere?" asked Alice.

She cringed, then said "No, don't think so. They sent me an occasional picture for a while…." Misty's voice grew more and more quiet.

"Maybe it's not Emma," said Alice. "You could take a DNA test, and then you'd be out of the picture once and for all."

"I'm out of the picture. Always was," said Misty, her voice growing irritated. "Are we going to have a problem about this?"

Alice paused for a moment to think. How easy it would be to annoy Misty enough so that she would fire her, and then Alice would no longer be forced to breathe her air.

"Look," said Misty, "I know what the salary for the job is—I'll double it, okay? Tom won't mind. And you won't mention this again."

Alice stepped back and stared at Misty. "Maybe this is all a bad idea," she said firmly. Her car was fifteen feet away; she could be in it in seconds and speeding away. She was pretty sure she could trust herself just to drive off, without actually driving over Misty. Alice paused for a moment to envision the feel of the ka-thump as the wheels drove over Misty, the sound of her going splat; the goriness didn't bother her at all.

Misty grew more and more terrified, and decided to play on Alice's good side. "Look," she said softly, "We were friends once, weren't we?"

Alice could hear voices from *Gone With The Wind* playing in her mind, and Scarlett O'Hara saying to the odious overseer, 'When were we ever friends with the likes of you,' but she remained silent, looking into the anxious eyes of a woman who would need a double dose of Botox after today.

"What exactly are you planning?" Misty asked tremulously, fanning her flushed face with her hand.

"I'm not planning anything," said Alice. "I was just informing you, figured you'd want to know is all."

"And you really are a size Medium?"

Alice laughed, shook her head, and walked to her car. As she drove the few miles toward home, movies played in her mind of the many reprehensible things Misty had done. Itch had taken her to some football rally, and Misty shoved herself between him and Alice, saying, 'Thank God you came alone — that Ally is the world's fattest downer.' They were at a party, and Itch had bent down to kiss Alice, then Misty leaned in and said, 'Hey Itch, once you get tired of Miss Muffin Top, give me a call.' Alice could picture the photo of her butt crack circulated by Misty, after she'd snapped it when Alice was bent over in the girls' locker room. It takes a really centered teenager not to feel the sting of that sort of abuse, and Alice was no more able to manage it than any other girl of sixteen. Itch always laughed about it, and said she should have a sense of humor, but to Alice, Misty was like a nasty little wasp buzzing around her, perpetually trying to steal Itch away from her, and leaving irritating welts in the process.

To amuse herself, Alice turned the tables, and pictured scenes in which she could torture Misty with mentions of Emma, with meetings with Emma, with accidentally dropped hints of her past. She enjoyed envisioning all the mean things she could do, but Alice knew she would not be doing them. What point was there in turning herself into someone like the person she most despised? And, she thought rationally, her anger was a residue decades old. They weren't teens any more, so perhaps she should release this memory, and the sense of Misty as being so vicious, and therefore powerful. At this moment, wasn't she now no worse than a typical bimbo? People grew up, didn't they? Even nasty little vipers, so perhaps this was Alice's chance to defeat old memories and replace them with peace of mind.

Alice pulled into her garage and let herself into the house, surprised to see Robin sitting in the living room, having margaritas with a man she'd never met. "Ally," he said far too jovially, "Come and meet Dennis. He's a real go getter." Dennis was a guy who'd probably been investing heavily in hair gel for about a decade, because he'd been moussed into oblivion, his hair standing pretty much on end. He wore neatly pressed slacks and a business shirt, under what Alice was certain was a polyester sports coat.

Alice smiled and extended her hand to the stranger, who'd risen to greet her, and was once again surprised when Robin offered her a drink. She wondered how many paper umbrellas it would take to dull the thought of Misty. Alice sat in her favorite chair, and was even more astonished to notice that Robin, who could barely pour milk over cereal, had set out cheese and crackers.

"I'm very excited to meet you," said Dennis, smiling deeply with some rather intimidating dimples. "And to know that those bus bench ads are working."

Something clicked in Alice's brain and she said, "Oh?"

"I'm going to do a fabulous job for you," Dennis continued, "The more money you make, the more I make."

Alice thought about how little he would surely be making if that were his equation, and she decided to have some fun with him, and perhaps to strike a little fear into Robin. "I will be working on a TV show," she said nonchalantly, "But I really don't need an agent."

Robin momentarily looked joyful at the sound of the word *work*, but then his jaw clenched because he quickly caught onto Alice's ploy. He signaled her with his eyes, but she ignored him.

"Although, hmm, could you get me into red carpet events, with like, swag bags? That would be worth ten percent. Do agents still charge ten percent?" Alice reached out and helped herself to a chunk of cheese and some crackers, batting her eyes at Dennis. Robin had even set out napkins; that whole raised by wolves rumor must have been a lie.

Taking a cue from Alice, Dennis also took some crackers and cheese, attempting to keep his anticipation from being too visible, and he said with glistening eyes, "Ten percent is a very reasonable rate. And I will most certainly lay out the red carpet for any and all prospects. And—don't tell anyone—but when I've sold your property, it will be my pleasure—and I never do this—but since you're so nice and hospitable, it would be my pleasure—to present you with a very nice gift basket as we sign the contracts."

"Property?" asked Alice, rising and pouring herself another margarita. "Like a movie script? Oh no, I'm not a writer. I'm a chef. It's a cooking show." She took a deep sip of her drink and smiled. "Salty!" she said happily, feeling the hooch kick in.

"Why don't I get you a lemonade," offered Robin, as though he regularly served her. He attempted to pry the nearly emptied glass from Alice's hand, but she rose before he could, and helped herself to another margarita.

"Oh look," she said, "Dennis' glass is empty. Go make another batch, why don't you?" She beamed an insincere grin of adoration at Robin, then turned, grabbed more crackers and sat in her chair. As Robin feigned a smile and trooped back into the kitchen, Alice said, "And how much money do you see yourself getting for me?"

Dennis reached into his briefcase for a pad, took out a calculator, typed some numbers into it, pausing now and then to think. "The economy is terrible now, we know that," he began, "But I think we could realistically get this amount." Just like in a bad movie, he jotted down a number, which actually impressed Alice, who had no clue about the value of real estate, and held it out to her.

Alice nodded, slowly nibbled on her cheese and crackers, and asked, "Now, would that be weekly or annually?"

"What?" said Dennis.

"That seems a lot for a prep cook on a TV show. Are you saying you can get me that weekly or annually?"

Dennis squinted for a moment, then gazed at Alice as though she were just another dazed boozehound, but not wanting to lose the chance to make a commission double his usual, he said calmly, "It's the amount for selling your property of course."

Alice took a big swig of her margarita, saying, "But you're supposed to be an agent. We talked about the red carpet, didn't we? But you keep insisting you want to sell my property, but I told you I'm not a writer. I don't have any screenplays to sell."

Clearly, and rather hilariously in Alice's mind, Dennis endeavored to remain calm and said, "No, no, I'm a broker."

Alice ate another cracker and cooed, "Oh, so delicious!" She seemed to pause a moment to think for a bit, then said, "But I don't really need a stock broker. Well if you get me the salary you mentioned before, then I could probably invest. I never heard of a talent agent who's also a stock broker. You must be very smart."

Exasperated, Dennis said, "I'm an agent — a real estate agent. You want to sell a property, not a screenplay. And I'm not a stock broker."

"You're here to sell my house? On whose authority," demanded Alice irately, leaping from her chair, as Robin returned with the fresh pitcher of margaritas. Alice, as though infuriated, pointed a finger at Robin, and said, "Is this your doing?"

Dennis scrambled from his seat, hastily packing up his gear, saying, "If you want to sell that place that burned down, I could get you a good deal."

"If I ever get that screenplay written, I'll give you a call," said Alice, feeling incredibly mean and also incredibly good.

She listened as Robin walked the hapless guy to the door, and heard him whisper, "She's just going through a difficult phase. I'll talk to her and get back to you."

"Yeah, I'll be right by the phone, waiting for that call," said Dennis.

Alice heard the door close, and sank back into her chair, laughing. She imagined that Robin would now reconsider before attempting to inflict any more real estate agents on her. She could feel the rage building inside her, and knew that soon they'd be having a massive fight, when Totsie appeared at the door and followed Alice into the house.

"You having a party?" her sister asked, looking around the room.

"Cooper," yelled Alice, "Your mom is here." She looked all around. "I just got here so I don't actually know if Cooper is here." She walked toward the stairs and yelled up, "Coop, are you here?" Then she shrugged toward Totsie. "Not home yet I guess."

Totsie scowled at Alice on hearing the word *home*. "This isn't his home," she said crossly.

"Your sister is soused," said Robin.

Alice laughed. "I'm no drunker than I want to be." She reached for an empty glass, and poured Totsie a margarita.

"I'm driving," said Totsie, helping herself to the glass of untouched lemonade, and settling into the empty spot on the couch.

"So what about this job of yours," asked Robin, too greedy to wait even a moment to hear the details.

"That's what I'm here to talk about," said Totsie, eating a small chunk of cheese with no cracker.

"What do you mean," asked Alice, setting her margarita glass down. "How do you know about it already?"

"I'm a life coach," said Totsie, as though that explained anything.

Alice looked at her sister and raised her hands in the air in front of her, gesturing that she was baffled. "And what, you have a crystal ball now?"

"Misty called me, freaking out," said Totsie.

"My Misty?" asked Robin.

"How do you even know her?" asked Alice, wondering why there had been no mention of this during the discussion about the hospital letter that day with Emma. "How come you didn't mention…."

"We're friends on Facebook of course. And now she's my client," said Totsie.

"My Misty?" asked Robin more intently.

Alice said, "She's starting this lame cooking show, and her husband—a very nice guy—hired me to run the prep kitchen." Alice aimed this information at Robin, and waited for him to ask what she would earn.

Robin gasped, and all the blood drained from his face. His eyes opened wide, and he said, "How did she look?"

"Like somebody's pampered poodle," said Alice.

"She's terrified you plan to derail her life and her show, out of some twisted desire to get revenge for stuff you imagine happened in high school," said Totsie, sounding both serious and punitive. Alice smiled briefly, thinking for the first time ever that her sister reminded her of their mother.

"And you told her we're together?" asked Robin, gazing around the room desperately, as though some bit of crucial information might be hidden behind the drapes.

"I never said a word," said Totsie, unaware that the question had not been addressed to her.

"I didn't even know it was her show. Cooper found this ad, and as you might remember, P3 burned down and I'm jobless, so I went. Guy I knew from a party is there, he hires me, then I learn whose show it is. Like a joke from the great beyond. Or should I say the great behind."

"And you told her we're together?" Robin asked Alice.

"No, it didn't come up," said Alice. "She wanted to avoid the past, not revisit it."

Totsie shook her head. "You have to grant people's goals some respect, you know. She's detoxing her thoughts and her life. She's a Master Manifestor."

"Master something," said Alice sarcastically, rising and heading toward the kitchen, and hoping Totsie would take the hint and go home and make dinner for her husband. "How's Mitchell," Alice asked, when she realized that both Totsie and Robin were still on her heels.

"Very sick," said Totsie, sighing.

Alice turned toward her. "What? I thought he was fine."

"He is fine," said Totsie. "But he won't believe it. That's why he's sick."

"Maybe you should life coach him," said Alice, opening the fridge and peering inside, as Cooper walked in the back door.

"Every time I see you, your head is in that ice box," he said, laughing and allowing his mother to wrap him up in a smothering hug.

"At least it's not the oven," said Alice.

"Do you mind," said Totsie, "I need to talk to my son."

"Sit and be comfortable," said Alice, grabbing the phone and walking out of the room. "I'll go call that insurance agent again." Alice walked out of the kitchen with Robin still on her heels, and sat down in the living room to place the call. She had a brief conversation with her agent, and ended the call more stressed than she was before.

"They're pursuing an arson investigation," Alice said to Robin. She thought of her aunt, and wondered what would happen. Would they question and traumatize her, perhaps file charges? It didn't seem possible that such a thing could happen, considering her health. Alice walked back toward the kitchen, as Totsie and Cooper were still talking in hushed voices.

"That wasn't the deal we made," said Cooper sternly.

"But I need my credit cards," said Totsie, sounding more like the child than the parent.

"I put a halt to Dad's crazy giveaways, and you cut back the spending and hoarding. That was the deal."

"The *h* word, really?" said Totsie.

What on earth, wondered Alice. How could Cooper stop his dad's spending, and how could he be in charge of Totsie's credit cards? Maybe Alice was more tipsy than she realized, and hearing things incorrectly. She coughed loudly as she entered the kitchen, and sat down next to her sister in the booth. "Arson. They think it's arson. Long investigation."

Cooper glanced at Alice and their eyes locked; they each knew what the other was thinking. "Even if she did it, it was an accident," he said, "And they couldn't do anything to her even if it wasn't. I'll call Parakkat."

"Oh no," said Totsie fearfully, "Don't call him."

"For Ally," said Cooper, but as he spoke, he looked at his mother so seriously she blanched.

"Who?" asked Alice.

Cooper laughed. "A lawyer acquaintance," he said, grinning.

Totsie stood up, scowled, and said, "Just remember I'm your mother, and it's not the other way around."

Cooper frowned at her and said, "Ditto."

"I'm not finished discussing this with either of you," Totsie continued, walking toward the front door. "See you tomorrow," she said inexplicably to Alice, who was about to respond, when she noticed Skye pulling into the driveway and exiting her car.

"Horrid news," said Skye, "And I need your help."

Alice faced Skye on the couch, and reached out to hold her hand, thinking of the many frightening possibilities that could have materialized. Cooper sat on a chair, munching on some of the cheese and crackers, and

Robin stood by the couch, peering down worriedly at Skye.

"What's wrong?" asked Alice.

"It's all gone to hell," said Skye. As nobody said a word, but all eyes were still on her, she continued. "You remember the play we were working on?"

Alice breathed a huge sigh of relief. The play. No form of play-related hell could worry her all that much. "Yes," she said.

"They kicked Julian out. Artistic differences," she said miserably, as Alice tried not to allow her face to reflect her thoughts, which if articulated would simply have been 'there's a shock.' Cooper laughed, but Alice shook her head at him, and he retrained his focus on the snack he was eating.

"That clown again?" asked Robin disgustedly.

"They're doing this old Sam Shepard play, *A Lie of the Mind*, you've heard of him, right? The vet in *Baby Boom*...."

Alice nodded. "No clowns in that one, very sad story of abuse and family suffering."

Skye nodded intensely. "That's what they said. They didn't get it at all. The whole metaphor thing."

"They axed him 'cause he wanted to play a wife beater in a clown suit?" asked Cooper.

Skye nodded, looking miserable. "I felt so bad for him. So many disappointments in a row."

"Disappointment is precisely the word that comes to mind when I think of that clown," said Robin, sighing as though the weight of the world lay on his shoulders.

"Are you really saying that you think an intense drama set in the West would be improved with a clown costume?" Alice asked Skye, who shook her head.

Cooper said, "What are you doing with this Clowny Clownerson anyway? You're a rockin' babe. At least

Greg didn't turn left at the corner of funkdafied and freaky-deaky."

"Greg is a very fine dentist," said Robin, glaring at Cooper, mainly because he didn't feel comfortable being on the same side as Alice's nephew, whom he normally despised.

"Hey!" said Skye, about to rise and storm away, but Alice held her hand tightly.

"So what did you want me to do to help?" asked Alice, hoping it was something simple, like making a batch of cookies.

"I figured maybe you could say you were sorry for saying no to his plans to do shows at P3. I mean it's burned down, so it wouldn't be a problem for you, and it might make him feel better. And then he could have something to look forward to. And he wouldn't feel like he was evicted from the family. We're all he really has."

"Our family?" asked Cooper incredulously. "Don't we have enough wackos that come built-in? Why are you recruiting from clown college? What was he—left on their doorstep when he was a drooling junior jester?"

"I don't want to be mean, and maybe I could do this, but hon why are you with this guy? I mean what's going on here?" Alice tried to sound as understanding as possible, but anyone looking closely in her eyes would see that her thoughts were being expressed precisely by Cooper.

"I think he's interesting is all, isn't that allowed?" said Skye a little petulantly.

"No," said Cooper. "Guys like that get girls with braces and lopsided hair."

"Stop attacking me, Cooper. You're just a kid, and you don't know squat," said Skye furiously.

"I was complimenting you," said Cooper, shrugging and popping a whole cracker into his mouth with a resounding crunch.

"For once Cooper is right," said Robin, in a voice that unmistakably sounded astonished.

"It's official," said Cooper. "Armageddon is here. I guess the first sign of Armageddon isn't ravens or locusts, but clowns."

Alice ignored the previous comments and spoke up, "Just for a moment let's assume I do this. I say I was wrong, he's brilliant, and he can reenact movie scenarios as a clown when we rebuild. How does that help him?"

"I just don't want him to feel sad." Skye sighed deeply, as though something beyond dreadful had transpired.

"I love that you're sweet and kind," said Alice, "But we all have to deal with the real world at some point, and I'm not sure it's in his best interest to hear that he's on the right track." Alice paused and examined her daughter's face. She looked so tortured, and it just didn't make sense. "Do you think maybe he's a big distraction preventing you from considering your own life and choices? Just wondering," said Alice kindly.

"You just don't understand me," said Skye plaintively.

Alice smiled encouragingly and patted her daughter's hand. "Tell us what we're missing," she said.

"I just like his creativity. I'm not used to it, oh gee I don't know. Do I have to diagram it for you?" asked Skye.

"There's lots of creativity that goes into making a well fitting dental plate," said Robin, almost huffing with disgust.

"Jeezum!" said Cooper. "Look, it's simple. Are you in love with Clowny? That's what everyone wants to know."

"Maybe," said Skye.

"Oh, God," said Alice and Robin simultaneously.

"Thanks a lot for ganging up on me," said Skye, rising and wrenching her hand from her mother.

Alice sighed and said, "I just wish you'd gone through this in high school like most kids."

Skye moved toward the door, and said sullenly, "Well pardon me for doubly disappointing you." Then she bolted outside, leaving her mother shaking her head.

"I feel like Paul Dooley in *Breaking Away*," Alice said.

"Oh she'll snap out of it," said Cooper.

"Do you really think so?" asked Robin, as both Alice and Cooper stared at him.

After much more discussion about Skye and her future, an easy dinner, and Robin saying he was going up to bed, Alice did as she now did nightly—the same thing she'd done for years—she went into her uncle's den and reclined on the old leather couch. No longer was there any urgency for a nap, no baking to be done, and eventually she would tiptoe up the stairs and creep into bed next to a snoring Robin, able to sleep for all the hours she needed, but for now she would do the one thing that made her feel peaceful and relaxed.

Alice closed the door, turned on her laptop and clicked on one of the episodes of the badass chef. She didn't care what he cooked—it was all beautiful food, well made. Alice heard the sound of his voice, saw the image of his handsome face, and all the troubles that plagued her throughout the day melted away. For once she was in the moment, and she could do something just for herself.

On some level, Alice knew how foolish she was to feel this profound connection with someone she didn't know and never would meet. Unlike her aunt, she suffered from no mental confusion. She knew there were probably thousands of women watching the show and swooning. He was handsome and sexy, and seemed so nice. Of course women would fall in love with him.

Alice didn't think she was in love, but somehow this man she didn't know provided for her a conduit back to the past, not as it was, but as it might have been, a memory brought back to life of the way she once felt, and assumed she would feel for a lifetime. This is how she might be feeling right now, today, if not for an insane motorcycle accident that took away her future. And for a few hours every night she allowed herself to sink back into those feelings, as though into a whirling tub of soothing hot water. If things were as they should be, as she imagined now in her heart that they were, there would be someone else up those stairs, and he wouldn't be asleep, and she would run up there and fall into his arms, and life would be real and wonderful and true.

So this was how the rest of the world lived, Alice thought, after having plenty of time for a good night's sleep and even a breakfast date with Emma. It might as well have been a vacation, with so much time at her disposal, time enough to introduce Emma to someone at the Wellman Center about a nursing job, and to visit Kitty without feeling pressured. Alice knew this feeling of wellbeing could and likely would evaporate as soon as she actually began working alongside Misty, but for this moment she almost felt good.

Alice tapped a few times on her aunt's door, glancing at her watch and wondering if they'd already come to escort Kitty to breakfast. It was a safe facility, with many precautions so that Kitty couldn't take off, and there were social activities, games, art, and even exercise. Alice knew her aunt was safer and better off, and she prayed she wasn't sad or lonely. Kitty flung open the door and said, "You come earlier and earlier to drag me to breakfast. Must I keep farmer's hours just because of you?"

"It's me, Ally," Alice said, scrutinizing her aunt.

"Ally!" she said, "You look so old. Where's the baby?"

Alice hugged her aunt. "How are you doing, Kitty? Everything okay?" Alice looked around at the spotless room. On one side was a nicely made up bed, and on the other a little sitting area, furnished with a loveseat, easy chair, and coffee table. In a place where it could be seen from anywhere, sat the television, although Alice knew there was no warehousing of patients, and her aunt was seldom confined to her room. Kitty gestured toward the sitting area, and they both took a seat.

"Had a little accident," said Kitty, pointing below the waist. "They keep moving the bathroom. I think they're doing renovations."

Alice looked up. Kitty had a private bath to one side of the sleeping area. "There's the bathroom, near the bed," she said.

"Yeah, today," said Kitty. "Might be gone tomorrow."

"I could bring you some of those stretchy, padded undies, if you want." Alice was careful not to say adult diapers, or any of the other names for what she was describing. "And maybe we could hang a sign on the bathroom door?"

"That might work, unless they move the door again."

"Do you like the food here? Have you made any friends?" Alice asked kindly.

Kitty rose for a moment and walked to the window, which faced a pleasantly landscaped outdoor area, bordered by some rolling lawns. "I never see Henry out there," she answered. "He seems to really like it—he's always out playing golf. Most of the time he's not even here for meals. Does that seem odd to you?" Kitty peered out beyond the lawns, then turned her attention back to Alice. "They're so determined that I eat at a precise time. There's not even a coffee shop—it's a very strict resort—I mean who are they kidding with all these rules—don't they know we're on vacation? They don't even have room service, I don't think, but I keep calling anyway, just to let them know people want it. Does your room have room service?"

Kitty paused for a moment, then pointed toward some drawings that were hung on one wall. "They think I'm in third grade," she whispered, then she turned toward the door, which was being opened, and glanced at a caregiver who peeked inside, as Kitty continued, "See—I told you."

"Ready for our breakfast?" the young woman asked.

Kitty rolled her eyes and answered snidely, "I hope you're not expecting me to eat for two."

As Alice walked through the parking lot toward her car, thinking about how horrible it would be when Kitty no longer recognized her, she spotted Emma, waving at her.

"There was a job and I got it, thanks to you," said Emma.

"Oh, I imagine there are lots of jobs for good nurses like you." She hugged Emma, and said, "Congrats, Nurse Cupcake! At least the outfit is less itchy. When do you start?"

"Orientation later today," she answered. "Official start in a couple days."

"That's just great. I should make a celebration dinner for you or take you out to dinner."

Emma smiled brightly. "That would be lovely. Tonight I'm having dinner with Skye. But tomorrow or later in the week?"

"You are?" asked Alice. "I didn't know you girls had become friends. That's great."

"Yeah, ever since she came in that day your aunt wandered off to the mall, we've been hanging out."

Alice thought for a moment, then asked, "Does she ever mention Julian, and what she's doing with him? We're all so worried about her."

"Gee, I dunno," said Emma, obviously conflicted, and unwilling to betray any confidences. Then she brightened and said, "He's pretty nice to her, anyway."

"We don't think he's a bad person, but he does seem kind of crazy," answered Alice, knowing she shouldn't keep putting Emma on the spot, but unable to resist getting some answers. "It's like she's going through some delayed teenage rebellion."

Emma laughed, started to say something, then remained silent.

"You're a good friend," said Alice. "But if you learn something that I really should know, you'll tell me? I'm just praying this crazy phase of hers will end soon."

Emma hesitated and said, "Don't worry so much Ally — she's a smart, level-headed person. I think she was just bored. She's not going to pull a bank heist or anything."

"No, they'd all be in clown suits. Oh wait, there was a movie like that, Bill Murray. Geena Davis, I think. Geez, what am I babbling about — I have to go to work now." Alice hugged Emma, and said "We'll talk later about a dinner."

Alice was amazed to discover that she had been assigned a dressing room with her name on it, and inside were the custom chef whites Misty had mentioned, although these were pink, and made of dupioni silk trimmed in a gray and white stripped piping. Alice squinted at the label, marked medium, and it seemed to have been sewn in by the manufacturer. Alice shrugged, wondering how these would ever stay clean, and tried on one suit, which fit her perfectly. There was a lighted mirror all along one wall, which Alice couldn't imagine needing, being always off camera in a prep kitchen, and a counter below it, for the typical personal items and makeup.

Someone had placed several neatly typed sheets of paper on the counter, and they contained the notes for what Misty would be doing in the first five shows, as well as what Alice had to do in preparation. Although it all was clear, none of it actually made sense, but Alice took the list and walked into the prep kitchen, where she was happy to find an apron that would protect her silk getup, and went to work.

Tom's assistant peered into the kitchen, and said, "Meeting in the conference room, then we'll start shooting." Alice followed the girl into a large room with a central table, around which sat Tom, Misty, a number of people Alice hadn't met, but who looked like a possible film crew, and of all people Totsie, who waved happily at Alice. In front of each place sat a beautifully wrapped box. Alice took a seat and waited.

Misty rose and said, "This is it! We're all here to start something new and great, and soon our show will be a massive success. To help us each day before we begin, I've brought on board someone truly wise and special, Tatiana Briarwood, a life coach who will guide us in this amazing journey."

Alice noted the look of bemused acceptance on Tom Angelico's face, and tried to maintain a complete lack of expression on her own, as Totsie rose and began speaking.

"Hello, everyone!" she said particularly confidently, as though she had suddenly grasped in her hand the answer to all of life's mysteries, and the solution to all of its ills. "I know you can't wait, so before I start, go ahead, open those boxes." She stood, maintaining a beatified expression, as they all reached out and untied the ribbons, removed the glittery paper, and finally opened the box that lay in front of them, revealing the contents inside—nothing. A few members of the group groaned. A couple laughed. Some looked at their watches.

"This is a gift from me to you," said Totsie, as more people chortled, but unfazed, she continued, "The gift of today, right this minute. It's here, waiting for you to fill it up. Every day is empty—just like this box—and how we fill it up is our own choice. I'm here to help you embrace that choice, and to fill up your day with success."

Alice glanced about the room, noting everyone carefully trying to hide their natural expressions, although astonishingly, a few were smiling in agreement.

"Anyone here worried about anything?" asked Totsie, who looked around as a few people nodded. "It's natural to worry about something new, but what does that accomplish? We're not here to be paralyzed. We're here to hone our sense of focus, and to manifest our goals. What is the most important thing we're here to do?" asked Totsie, looking toward Misty.

"To win an Oscar!" said Misty. "No wait, an Emmy."

"I knew you'd say that," said Totsie, and she reached down into a satchel and extracted a miniature gold plastic Emmy, which she ceremoniously presented to Misty.

Misty leapt up as though it all were real, and launched into an acceptance speech with a long list of thank you's, gesturing toward people in the room who nodded pleasantly, but couldn't manage to alter expressions which implied that she'd gotten all their names wrong. As she spoke, Alice pondered Misty's attire, which in no way belonged in a kitchen. She sported a semi-formal cocktail dress that was so low cut that Alice prayed she wouldn't be bending over any food, but of course—she was dressed not to cook but to accept a fictional award.

"Now, remember that empty box, and how to fill it. Get out there and make that Emmy winning television show!" said Totsie with a huge, cheerleader finish.

Misty walked over to Totsie and hugged her like a long-lost relative, then everyone left the room. Alice returned to her place in the prep kitchen, and Misty took hers in front of the cooking island on her set, ready to go through a practice run for the cameras, but before beginning, Tom ducked his head into the prep kitchen and said, "Might need some fine tuning and advice today, Ally, want to come out and work with Misty?"

Alice followed Tom over to where Misty was about to begin. "If there's anything we need to change or fix, please speak right up," he said, as Misty gave him what seemed to be a rather perturbed glance. Alice could imagine her thinking, *how dare he.*

"Welcome to our Hollywood premiere," said Misty. "Today on our first show, it's all about the carbs. We all know they're bad, and today we're going to make delicious food without them. There'll be no bread in sight, but we'll be enjoying a fine dining experience." She smiled at the camera for a very long moment, then reached for a box of spaghetti. "First step in our carb-busting meal—spaghetti. It's delicious, don't you think!" Misty ducked her head beneath the counter, and pulled out a large skillet. "It's very important that the size of the pan match the contents. You don't want your maid working overtime cleaning up kitchen spills!" She dumped the box of spaghetti into the skillet, added a little water, then set it on a burner on high.

"Obviously we can't have plain spaghetti," said Misty, "And if we just douse it with oils and cheese, that fills it with carbs. So we're going to add some healthy and delicious vegetables. Look at the beautiful colors! That's what dining well is all about." Misty took a cleaver, and hacked away at an unpeeled onion, some tomatoes, and a few peppers. "Don't worry if you get some seeds in there," she said, "The hot pasta will just melt them." She tossed all the vegetables into the skillet with the pasta, fluttering her hands above the pan as though she were bringing up the amazing scent to her nostrils. "I wish you could smell this," she said, beaming again.

By this time, the water in the skillet had boiled away, and the mostly uncooked pasta was scorching in the pan, along with the vegetables, which hadn't yet released any liquid. "Look," she said, "It's getting nice and toasty brown. That's where the flavor comes from." Before she could finish that thought, the pan started to smoke and an acrid stench filled the studio.

"Hang on, sweetheart," said Tom to Misty. "Is there stuff we need to fix here, Ally? I don't think we're supposed to cook spaghetti that way."

"Um, well," said Alice, hesitantly, "You need to change a lot."

"What!" exclaimed Misty, and Alice could hear the unspoken *how dare you* again.

"Firstly, this is an all-carb meal," said Alice.

"It is not!" said Misty. "I told you there's no bread."

"Everything here is carbs. Pasta. Vegetables. The oil and cheese you mentioned are fats, not carbs."

"Don't be ridiculous," said Misty. "Carbs is a word that means stuff that's bad for you. Negative. That's what carbs is. A nickname."

"No," said Alice, explaining as patiently as she could manage.

"I think you're confused," said Misty. "I told you what carbs means — something bad for you. Like bread."

"Pasta and bread are the same thing," said Alice. "Flour and water. Carbs. Vegetables are carbs too, the good carbs. And you're supposed to put on a big pot of boiling water to cook spaghetti." She walked behind the counter and extracted a pasta pot with its colander insert and set in on the counter. "This," she said.

"Don't be absurd," said Misty. "We're not having lobster on this show."

Alice sighed and said, "You could use that pot for lobster, or maybe a bigger one. This really is a pasta pot." Then she explained everything else Misty was doing wrong as thoroughly as possible.

"What part of this is protein?" asked Misty, her eyes slanting, as though she knew she would be tripping Alice up.

"No part of it," said Alice, "Although there'd be some protein in the parmesan cheese if you used it. Protein is meat, eggs, fish—see? I thought you wanted the shrimp for the pasta—that's protein."

Misty scowled. "This is absurd. If that were true how could vegetarians be on an all-protein diet?"

"Vegetarians eat mainly carbs. They get protein from beans and nuts sometimes," said Alice.

"Oh, please," said Misty. "That diet doctor who got murdered by the schoolmarm—he was a famous vegetarian. Atkins, wasn't it."

Alice looked off to the side for a moment. Where to begin? "Why don't you just concentrate on making good food without the nutritional labels like carbs?" she suggested.

"That does make sense," said Tom, "And it gives you more flexibility, more ways to shine." On hearing this, Misty nodded grudgingly. Then Tom said, "Maybe Ally could show you how to chop those vegetables so it looks more cheffy on camera?"

Alice walked behind the island, looked in a drawer, removed a chef's knife, saying, "This is a better knife for what you're doing. More control."

"But it's not very dramatic," said Misty.

"So you want to do a pasta primavera?" asked Alice.

"Okay," said Misty, her teeth clenched together. "Wait, no, with shrimp."

Alice filled the pot with water, added salt, and set it to boil, then explained to Misty how to chop vegetables and use a knife.

"Whatever," said Misty. "You can certainly chop fast with those stubby little fingers."

"Go on, try chopping," said Alice, feeling like Princess Cupcake. She watched as Misty cut adequately well, until she sliced off one of her brightly painted fingernails. "It would probably be better to trim your nails," said Alice, knowing precisely what reaction she'd get.

Misty glared at Alice as she added the vegetables to the sauteuse pan, and eventually some white wine.

"Oh no," wailed Misty, glancing at the bowl of shrimp Alice had prepped. "You removed their backbones. Now they'll go all limp in the pan. You've paralyzed them." She held one hand to her mouth and opened her eyes as widely as she could manage. "This could be some sort of sign. Tatiana was talking about paralysis before. We can't have that." She squinted at Alice and whispered so Tom wouldn't overhear, "Don't you dare keep trying to sabotage me."

Alice looked at her as though at any moment someone would be wrapping her inside a straight jacket. "That line along the back isn't their spine—it's the sand vein—waste—the—um—shrimp—um—there's no nice way to say this—it's poop. Tastes nasty. You don't want to eat that."

"Fine," grumbled Misty, and then in another whisper, "I'm on to you."

Alice set out a nice platter, drained the spaghetti, then added it to the sauteuse pan along with some minced herbs. She tossed the contents with one smooth jerk of her wrist, then poured it all out onto the platter, placing the sautéed shrimp on top. "If we write down the quantities of everything we did, that's a recipe," said Alice.

"Of course it is," said Misty, tasting the spaghetti, and trying not to look approving. "It's not terrible," she said.

"Delicious," said Tom. "Now all our star has to do is repeat this process, and we'll have a show." Misty brightened on hearing this, or perhaps it was hearing the word star.

"Next I was planning to make pizza. Not that people actually make pizza. Of course I know they don't. You have the crackers?"

Alice nodded. "And what are they for?"

"For the crust of course," said Misty, rapping her nails on the counter.

"Pizza dough isn't made of crackers," said Alice, thinking no it's protein, made out of dried apple dolls.

"I don't like the doughy pizza," said Misty. "You wouldn't know this of course, since you've never been anywhere, but they have this amazing pizza in New York City, with very crispy crust. Crust," she repeated emphatically, "Not dough."

"Yes," said Alice, "And it's still made out of dough. It's just rolled out thinner."

"Since this is my show, why don't we try it my way," said Misty.

Alice put her hand to her head, wished she had an aspirin, and waited for the rest of what was coming.

Misty had dumped whole some unhusked tomatillos into the Cuisinart and, after several unsuccessful tries at closing the lid, managed to get it to run, and watched happily as they thumped around in the bowl. Then she removed her faux crust from the oven, which was simply pulverized crackers, dumped the chunky mixture from the Cuisinart on top, and attempted to sample it.

"Ick! What did you do to my recipe?" she said, glaring at Alice accusatorily.

Tom, who was beginning to look tired, said, "Let Alice help you, honey. That's why we hired her."

"Fine," said Misty. "Do you know Wolfgang Puck?"

"No," said Alice, "But I know how to make pizza."

"Of course you do," said Misty, heaving the pan she'd made into the sink.

"You have to make the dough and let it rise," said Alice, "And that takes several hours."

"It's a thirty minute show," said Misty, clenching her jaw.

"So you have a swap out. You make the dough, turn it out into a bowl, and then pull out the risen dough and say something cute."

Misty looked up. "I can do cute."

Alice walked to the prep kitchen and returned with a bowl of dough. "I made this earlier when I saw you had pizza on your list." She removed a small Cuisinart from below the island and quickly made pesto. "This is what Puck uses as sauce — pesto."

"I don't see what this has to do with shooting or why pistols are involved," said Misty, adjusting her cleavage.

"Pesto," said Alice, "For mortar and pestle, because they used to grind it." Quickly she made the pizza, and popped it into the oven. "We should really have a pizza stone in there. But this will still be good." After a few minutes Alice removed it from the oven, cut slices and everyone sampled.

"This isn't disgusting, but it's not as good as what I remember," said Misty.

"Here's what we're going to do," said Tom. "You girls will sit and discuss each show. Maybe you could come up with serving advice, because you have so much style and flair," he said to his wife. "And Ally will come up with the recipes. She'll work with you on how to cook everything and use all these gadgets. And we'll shoot it all and use what we can, and you can refer to what she's said if you need refreshers."

"That doesn't sound like my show at all," complained Misty.

"It's your show. We use consultants all the time. The more ideas the better," he said.

Alice worked with Misty for the rest of the day, discussing menus and techniques, then drove toward home, wondering how good she could possibly be in bed for someone like Tom to have married her. She arrived at her home to see Totsie there, walking out of the house with some suitcases, which she was loading in her already tightly packed car.

"What's happening?" asked Alice.

"I'm taking my son back," said Totsie. "And by the way, Misty told me all about what you're doing, and I think it stinks."

"What are you talking about?" asked Alice, looking around to see if Cooper was aware of his mother's plan. "Where's Cooper?"

"Cooper is about to be living at home where he belongs. And you know only too well what you're doing to Misty." Totsie bent down and hoisted the largest suitcase into the trunk, shoving it until it was nearly all the way inside.

"Why don't you tell me," said Alice, as Cooper drove up and parked his little car on the street.

"You're deliberately making her look dumb and incompetent in front of her husband. And he's not just her husband, but her producer. It's a lousy thing to do."

Alice laughed. "Trust me, nobody would have to try to make her look dumb. And I've been working like mad to teach her how to cook so she looks good. She has no business with a cooking show—she knows nothing at all about food."

"You have a crappy attitude, and I won't have you spreading negativity about me to my son the way you're doing at work. You might not need the exorbitant salary Misty is paying you—oh yeah she told me she doubled your salary out of the kindness of her heart. But I need that seven K a week. I have to work for my money now."

Alice grew enraged on so many levels, the least of which was that her sister was being paid many times her own salary for what—a few minutes of nonsense a day. She was about to say something extremely mean when Cooper walked over.

"What's going on here?" he asked, looking around at all the stuff in his mother's car.

"Get the rest of your things, young man," said Totsie in her sternest voice. "You're coming home with me immediately. I have almost everything right here."

Cooper glared at her. "This is my stuff? You took it upon yourself to come and snatch my stuff when I wasn't even here?"

"You're a teenager. You do what I say. I've been far too lenient for far too long. Summer camp is over." Totsie grabbed the smaller suitcase, and shoved it into the back seat on top of a laptop and some other devices. "I'm refusing to allow your aunt to be your enabler any longer. I'm in charge here, not you, not Ally."

"You helped her do this?" Cooper asked Alice.

"I just got here," Alice answered. She was conflicted, because on one hand she knew Cooper was right, and that his parents both behaved insanely most of the time, but she also knew that he probably did belong at home. He wasn't the victim of any genuine abuse, although it didn't seem like a very wholesome environment. She stood quietly for a moment, then realized Cooper was scanning her face as she pondered it all, and reading her expressions.

"So you're not kicking me out?" he asked Alice.

"Don't you dare respond to that," said Totsie, glaring at her sister, and wagging a finger in Alice's direction.

"Here's what's going to happen," said Cooper. "Either you're going to back off and let me snag my things from your car, or you're going to drive off with them. I'm not going back with you. If Ally says I can't stay here, I'll get an apartment. No way I'm going home to the crazy behavior, the screaming fights, and the cheating."

Totsie gasped and took a step back, as if in shock.

"You didn't think I knew? Well I know. As parents go you suck, and you're the worst role models ever. Plus, you don't have a clue who I am, and you never will."

"I know one thing," said Totsie, "You won't be very happy living with just the clothes on your back. So when you wake up, and realize I'm the adult and you're the kid, you can drive your ass home. And don't you ever— and I mean ever—speak to me like that again." She took a giant breath, but her face was raging red, and even a one-eyed person could see the steam rising from her head. "And you Miss," she said to Alice, "Get your act together. No way you could steal Tom from Misty."

Alice looked at her sister as though she'd completely gone insane, then began laughing. "I'm not discussing Misty with you any more. Maybe I should just talk to Tom about it," she said, deliberately looking devious, and the darker Totsie's face grew, the more Alice laughed.

Totsie glared at both Cooper and Alice, slammed the back door and tried to slam the trunk, but it wouldn't close, so she hopped behind the wheel and drove away, zig zagging across the road.

"What a day," said Alice and Cooper simultaneously.

"You wouldn't really kick me out would you?" asked Cooper.

"I hate to create a war in the family, but no of course I could never ask you to leave," said Alice. "But is it really that bad at home?"

"Compared to kids being burned with cigarettes and so on, no. I just got tired of the idiocy," said Cooper, looking at his watch.

"Do you think maybe this is just some teen phase?" asked Alice kindly. "I mean most kids your age think their parents are idiots."

Cooper laughed. "Yeah, but in this case everyone else thinks they're idiots too. Listen do you have anything to do now? Want to come shopping with me?"

"Maybe you're your mother's son after all," said Alice, smiling. "But wouldn't you really rather just go home and get your stuff back?"

"Screw her," he said.

"Oh hon," said Alice. "She's your mother, so let's not say mean things." Alice ducked her head into the house to let Robin know where she would be, but he didn't seem to be inside, although his car was in the garage, so she locked the door and walked back out.

"Can we take your car?" he asked. "Gonna need lotta trunk space."

At Cooper's direction, Alice drove toward the Century City Mall, as he typed some stuff into his phone. "Okay," he said, "At least that's taken care of. Ordered a new laptop, iPad and stuff. We'll just have to swing by Best Buy on the way home, so make sure we leave the mall with like twenty minutes to spare."

"Just like that you bought a computer?" asked Alice. "Where's the money for all this coming from? Are you spending that check your dad gave you? Oh hon, I don't know. You have so much stuff at home."

"My dad's checks are all rubber," said Cooper.

"What?" asked Alice. "Your dad is a rich guy."

"We set up a system, the account he thinks he has doesn't actually allow checks. Well his checks. The bank won't honor them. Someone there calls anyone he gives a check to and explains. The checks don't bounce, but they can't be cashed. This way he can be crazy if he wants, but if he ever snaps out of it, he won't be broke."

"We who?" asked Alice.

"Me and this lawyer. It's all legal. Um, yeah, this is legal," said Cooper, pointing toward a space, which Alice quickly pulled into.

"But don't people he gives these checks to come back and say, hey you gave me a bum check?"

"An assistant filters those calls. And we explain away anything that goes wrong. At least now he's mostly retired and giving money to strangers, so paths don't cross," said Cooper.

"And you're saying this is legal, as though some of things you do are sort of shady," said Alice with deep concern.

"No, not at all. Everything I do is right and good and just," said Cooper.

"You're sounding a little like a vigilante there, pal. Please don't go all Charles Bronson on me."

"Who?"

"So what did you do with your mother's credit cards?" asked Alice, remembering that tipsy day when Totsie and Cooper were discussing them.

"I cancelled some and lowered limits on others, no big deal. Part of the tech business I do."

Alice was amazed listening to all this. Maybe none of them actually knew Cooper—for a teenager, he sure seemed like a grown up. "But you're a kid," she said softly.

"I'm a kid who comes from money," he answered, laughing. "And you know I like the techy stuff. Easy enough to put the two together. And now let's go spend some of my hard earned money. This is like the first time I'm ever buying clothes for myself. I mean Mom always bought so much, I never bothered." Cooper blushed for a second, and Alice smiled at him.

"Maybe you're still a kid in some ways," she said. "Underwear and tee's first? Macy's maybe? Then some cool stores for guy stuff? This is your chance to express yourself through your clothes."

Cooper laughed. "Yeah for all we know Shopazilla totally missed the really dope stuff, and it's right here in the mall waiting for us to snag it." He opened the door to Macy's, and followed Alice into the store.

"Just don't buy any of those saggy pants that show your butt crack," said Alice.

Cooper laughed again. "Maybe I'll get some three piece suits with ties and button down shirts, and then everyone will think I need therapy as much as my parents."

After a few hours of what some people would call power shopping, Alice and Cooper staggered into the house carrying many bags each, and trying to balance some take-out Chinese food. Alice stopped for an instant, and breathed in the sweet scent of chocolate chip cookies—Skye must be baking. She set down the shopping bags by the stairs, and walked toward the kitchen with the food.

Julian was speaking, "Mmm, these are the best chocolate chip cookies in the history of cookies since the beginning of time."

Skye laughed happily, saying, "They're not even baked yet. You're eating dough."

Julian groaned with pleasure. "Now wait—why are you using a melon baller? Will there be melon in the cookies? There's so much that I don't know about baking, and nobody knows more than you."

Alice remained beyond the doorway, listening to the praise Julian heaped on Skye. He really did seem to care about her, and find every little thing she did enchanting. She could see how that would be attractive to her daughter; everyone liked being praised.

"This is an ice cream scoop," said Skye.

Julian laughed. "No, really, I mean like what, for pixies? Oh Thumbelina, come out, come out, wherever you are. Bring some of your teeny tiny ice cream cones."

"Look," said Skye, "Watch me."

"You do that so brilliantly, and so fast. You're like Mrs. Fields—but better—and more beautiful of course. And smarter," said Julian.

Alice sighed. How could she continue to dislike someone who was so kind and loving toward her daughter? She thought back to the moments where she'd seen Skye interacting with Greg, but there had never been any sparkle that she could recall, no playfulness, no joy, although she knew Greg was a decent guy, and that he loved Skye. Immediately, she resolved to be more supportive. Maybe there was more to Julian than a clown, and maybe Alice would discover a great guy in him.

Skye walked across the doorway to reach the wall oven and insert the cookie pan, and she spotted Alice, "Oh Mom, you're home."

"Take-out," said Alice brightly, setting the food on the counter. "Hi Julian, how are you? Nice to see you," she said.

He immediately brightened, and said, "Hello! We made cookies for everyone. Well, Skye did. She's a cookie genius."

Alice smiled and said, "Come sit and talk with me for a minute. You guys hungry?"

Skye shook her head no, so Alice left the food on the counter and walked to the booth, where Julian followed her. "I feel badly," said Alice. "Maybe we got off to a bad start."

She paused for a moment, and was actually touched to see a happy smile light up Julian's face. "I was going to talk to you a couple weeks ago," she continued, "To let you know that you could do your shows at P3, then of course you know what happened."

Julian gasped in a way that seemed genuinely disturbed. His eyes opened wide, his hand clasped across his mouth, then he mumbled, "Oh no. What a waste that fire was."

Alice grew instantly irritated to think that the destruction of her aunt and uncle's legacy came down to a waste of Julian's psycho dream, but she calmed herself down and just said, "No kidding." She took a moment to observe Julian's face, and he seemed so sad about the loss of P3 that she softened, and decided just to be a mom and to help him. She took a deep breath, then said, "Julian, I want to give you some advice. I hope you don't mind."

Skye turned around from the counter and started signaling her mother, but Alice continued. "I love Charlie Chaplin's movies, of course, well who doesn't."

Julian appeared to be listening, and he shrugged, indicating that he could offer no argument there. Skye continued to give Alice a worried look, and slowed down her cookie scooping as a result.

"Honey, check those cookies," said Alice, "They're about thirty seconds from done."

Julian looked toward the oven and said, "Wow, you're not even near the oven, how could you know?"

Alice tapped her nose, then continued. "So what I'm trying to say is this—you seem like a very talented actor to me."

"Wow, thank you so much," said Julian, biting into a warm cookie. "Oh my God, these are even more amazing than I said before. All the other cookies are crying right now." He sat chewing and moaning, as Alice continued.

"So I'm wondering if this whole clown metaphor is holding you back rather than helping you. I mean, the thing was, Chaplin's costume matched the character and the story. And maybe there are more stories you could embody in other clothes is all I'm saying here. Or if you want to be a clown, in clown attire, maybe do clown things. So it's all coherent. If you don't mind my opinion."

Julian looked at Alice rather darkly, she thought, so she tried another tack. "Do you like rice?" she asked, and as he nodded, she continued, "Well I like it too. Rice is great. But what if I never agreed to cook with anything but rice, or always insisted rice be in everything I cook. Do you think those cookies would be better with some rice? They'd be something different, wouldn't they? But would they be better?"

"I appreciate your advice," said Julian, rising, "But if I took it, I'd cease to exist as an artist."

"Wait," said Alice, hoping he wasn't about to bolt out the door, "Why, why would that be?"

"This is my métier," he said, "But thanks for the input. Gotta run now. Skye, are you coming?"

"We came in my car," said Skye, looking around guiltily at the mess she'd made but hadn't cleaned up.

"I hope I haven't offended you," said Alice. "I was just being a mom."

"Sure, thanks," said Julian, "It was nice to see what that was like." He didn't stop walking though, and Skye once again shook her head at Alice, and backed out of the door, following Julian.

"I see that went well," said Robin, entering the kitchen from the open back door.

"Where were you?" asked Alice.

"Oh, out walking," he said smoothly.

How was it possible that a child of eight could learn to frost an acceptably pretty cupcake in the span of a one-hour party, when for weeks Alice had been explaining to Misty how to use a Kitchen-Aid mixer, and which of the two different beaters did what. There were only two of them. Just two — not counting the dough hook. It almost seemed as though she had a grasp on it, when she insisted on making meatloaf with it and using the whisk.

"The whisk," she insisted, "That's what real chefs use."

"Yes we use it to whip eggs and cream, not meat. Meatloaf is just tossed gently with your hands or it'll get dense," answered Alice.

"Don't be absurd," said Misty. "I went over some of the footage, and you said the whisk puts in air. Nothing is less dense than air. But fine, since you're being so pissy, we'll just whisk up some meatballs." Misty glared at her pointedly, in her usual exasperated way, and Alice was certain Misty had this habit of lingering on the scar at her temple just to make her uncomfortable, which it did.

"Meatballs and meat loaf are basically the same thing," said Alice sighing quietly, "And they're made the same way — by hand."

"Some people don't want to get a manicure every day, you know. Some people don't have Jacuzzi tubs to swirl meat crap out from under their nails." Misty cut her eyes at Alice, looked around to see if Tom were watching, then said, "I've arranged for you to see a plastic surgeon. He can zap those unsightly scars off you one two three. My treat."

Alice pictured herself shoving Misty's face down into the meatloaf, then responded quietly, "No need, thanks anyway, I'm used to them."

"Oh you're going," said Misty adamantly. "You might enjoy being a fright, but there's no reason I should have to get used to them. We're dealing with food here, and the sight of that would take away people's appetites. I mean it's not a Halloween show, is it?" Misty glared at Alice, as she had so many times, years ago. "I put the card in your purse." As Alice glared back, she was about to insist that Misty respect her personal property, when Misty continued, "Oh yeah, I almost forgot—your phone rang, and I took a message. Itch is awake."

"What?" said Alice, hearing her own voice drift off into the distance, as she collapsed onto the floor into a dead faint. When she opened her eyes, she had no sense if a minute had passed or a year. The crew stood over her and in front of them was Misty, waving a cut onion in front of her watering eyes. Alice blinked, then turned her face from the onion. What had Misty said?

"Did I faint?" she asked. Then it came back to her, Misty had said Itch was awake. Of all the rotten things she'd done, this was certainly a new low, and Alice began to grow enraged. This was it. Enough was enough. As she was about to rise from the floor, Tom raced over and peered down at her.

"What happened here?" he asked. "Did you slip and fall? Are you all right?" He knelt down beside Alice and took her hand, checking her pulse.

"She just keeled over on her own," said Misty. "I gave her a phone message about someone we used to know in high school, and kaboom she was on the floor." She leaned down toward her husband, and whispered in his ear in a voice that nevertheless was more than quite audible, "No liability on our part I'm sure."

Alice sat up. "That was an actual message?"

"She's obviously loopy," said Misty.

Despite cautions to remain on the ground, Alice rose and said, "I have to leave."

"Don't forget the wrap party tonight," yelled Misty from what sounded to Alice like the span of a thousand years.

Alice stopped walking for a moment, and turned back toward the voice. Party? She'd forgotten that weeks ago they'd arranged for a wrap party, assuming the show would be recorded and ready. That was before anyone realized that their star couldn't operate anything more complex than a drinking straw. The only cooking Misty could do, even after all this time, was to remove an apple from the fridge and eat it. Now they were still in preparation, many hours of footage shot, none usable, but apparently nobody had postponed the party. All the people connected with the show—and their families— were invited back to the studio—and expected to attend. Alice held her hand to her head, then waved toward the group of people staring at her, and dashed out the door to her car.

Once she was seated behind the wheel, she took a moment to breathe deeply, and only then did she realize that she was still in her ridiculous chef silks, but what did that really matter. She needed to get to Itch.

Itch was awake? Itch was awake? Could it be possible? At last her life was about to begin. Her husband was awake, and their life together would finally start— they would have a honeymoon at last, a life at last, happiness at last. Alice's heart beat much too fast, but she didn't mind; it was a joyous thunder inside her chest. She thought of all the things they'd do together, the moments they'd share, the nights, the family dinners. A baby — she would have another baby — if she still could. They were getting a do over and it was just amazing.

So many happy possibilities flew across Alice's mind, it was like a montage of Christmas or another thrilling holiday. Then suddenly she saw a picture of Robin. Robin! She'd been cheating on her husband for over fifteen years. In her mind she tried to enumerate the occasions during which she'd had sex with Robin, knowing how silly it was because one was too many, and after that it was insult to injury — literally in this case. Would Itch forgive her? Alice cringed briefly, but thought to herself if things were reversed, and she'd been in a coma for decades, she wouldn't begrudge him whatever happiness he could find while she was unreachable.

Unreachable — that was the word for it — and now she could reach out and touch, reach out and kiss, and he would be there to reach back. Alice was tempted to pull the car over so she could really think, really feel all the amazing sensations floating across her mind and heart, but how silly would that be when soon enough her imagination wouldn't be needed at all. She wouldn't have to close her eyes and float into some sort of romantic trance to envision the life she desired but never would have. Her life was about to begin, and it all would be real and beautiful, just as she'd envisioned in innumerable sad moments of yearning.

Alice raced but it felt as though she were going in slow motion, as in one of those cartoons where the character is suddenly clawing up a giant hill drawn with impossibly steep perspective. Her feet carried her forward very swiftly, but it felt to Alice as though they were leaden and barely moving, and that never would she arrive at his room.

But arrive she did, and there was Mrs. Lewis, Itch's nurse, gazing excitedly at her. "I just got the message," gasped Alice, not really stopping, but walking past the nurse's station into Itch's room. She looked about, expecting his parents to be there, a collection of doctors and other astonished medical personnel to be performing exams, or at least taking photos for the news, but maybe they'd come and gone, because he lay there alone, just as always, perhaps a couple more pillows behind his head. Yes, he was sitting up. And his eyes were open!

Alice walked over to the bed, getting closer and closer, her smile bright enough to illuminate the darkest night. Gently she sat down on the side of the bed, not knowing if anything she could do would cause him pain, all the while wanting just to hurl herself into his arms, and she leaned in and hugged him. "What a miracle," she whispered. "What a blessing." She kissed him tenderly on the cheek, resting one hand on the other side of his face, as she so often had done in the past, the hollow of his cheek just the size of her hand. It seemed like the longest moment in the history of time, and also the shortest, and then Alice leaned back a bit so she could look into his eyes. Again she smiled joyously.

And then she noticed the expression on his face, along with a baffling mixture of fear and revulsion in his eyes. It was as though he were cringing in her arms, as though every part of him recoiled from her touch, and somehow he was simultaneously terrified and disgusted.

"Hi, Itch," Alice spoke softly. "I'm so happy you're awake. I've missed you so much." She smiled at him once again, hoping to put him at ease. She took his hand in hers and held it to her heart, but the moment it touched her chest, he twitched and seemed to be trying to pull free, so she set his arm back down on the bed.

"Can you understand me? Can you hear me?" she asked softly, watching as he attempted to nod. His finger moved a miniscule amount, and it seemed he pointed toward his throat, then he coughed a little, and swallowed hard. "It's all right," she said, "You don't have to talk right away. You've been asleep for a very long time." She just sat peacefully, looking into his eyes, smiling now and then, saying something soft and comforting here and there.

He seemed to be listening and looking at her, although there was at the back of his eyes a level of apprehension which Alice had never seen before. Her heart ached for him, for all he'd gone through, and for anything and everything he might now be feeling. She reached for his hand once again and said, "Can you squeeze my hand?" and he did give it the tiniest squeeze, which Alice couldn't help but believe was a very good sign. "Can you move your feet?" she asked, not having a clue if anything she was doing made sense, but she looked toward the end of the bed, and she was sure she saw the covers move just a little and she smiled.

"This is such a miracle, such an amazing miracle," Alice said, as much to herself as to Itch. Then she watched as he opened his mouth, made a couple of squeaky noises, and swallowed hard once more.

"It's all right, sweetheart, don't try to talk yet if it's difficult," she said, reaching for his hand once again, and once again the hand seemed to twitch in some sort of spasm, so again she set it back down on the bed.

Alice couldn't stop smiling. She grinned at Itch, and wished he could somehow grin back, but his face looked a bit wooden, but how silly was she to expect more. For years she'd done research online about what transpired when people wakened from comas, and the one thing that was consistent, other than that every case was different, was the long recovery period the patients had to endure, sometimes made shorter by sheer determination.

"You know I'm sorry—I was here a couple weeks ago and wrote in your hand, and it seemed you squeezed my hand back, but I couldn't believe it was true. But it was true, wasn't it? You were waking up and coming back to me. I just feel so blessed." And then she smiled some more, but Itch's eyes remained dark and shielded. Alice decided to look on the bright side—at least his eyes showed something, perhaps not the loving devotion she expected, but that would come once he was truly awake. Surely he felt groggy. Who wouldn't?

"I can't wait for you to meet Skye, your daughter," she said. "There's a whole lifetime you've missed, and now you're here for it. It's like you've been gone in a war or something. If I had an oak tree I would've covered it with yellow ribbons."

Alice once again squeezed Itch's arm, and once again she felt him tense. She kept looking into his eyes, waiting for the sparkle to return, for the glimmer to come back and to intoxicate her as it had so long ago. "Don't worry," she said confidently, her voice brimming with determination, "You'll be your old self in no time. You'll show everyone. I just wish I could crawl in there with you, and take you in my arms and hold you and never let go."

Alice smiled at Itch so tenderly, she was certain it would bring back his grin, just as all those years ago she was sure her true love's kiss would waken him, but her words this time seemed to have the opposite effect, for he tensed all over and tried to raise his hand as though he wanted to push her away. It didn't matter though, because Alice was willing to be patient and to wait. This miracle was nothing to criticize, no matter how it unfolded.

Mrs. Lewis walked softly into the room, smiling at Alice. "I know you have lots of catching up to do, but we don't want him overtired. There'll be more time tomorrow." She touched Alice gently on the shoulder.

Alice looked at her watch. It had been the best day of her life, well one of them, and even though only a short time had elapsed since she'd entered the room, everything on earth had changed. The day wasn't over though, and she had some unpleasant tasks to perform.

She leaned down to kiss Itch, but could feel him pressing himself back against the pillow, recoiling from her kiss even before she could reach his mouth, so she touched him lightly on the cheek with her lips and smiled again. "Everything is going to be fine now, just you wait and see. I'll be back tomorrow. You just get some rest…. Not too much rest, though—only eight hours."

It was nearly impossible to focus on the drive home after what had just happened. It was simply too thrilling a sensation to realize that tomorrow she would see and talk to Itch again, and at some point he would answer. She would kiss him, and he would be awake enough to kiss her back. She looked at the dashboard clock and calculated the hours until morning when she could return to the hospital and see Itch again. Life was amazing—it was a wonderful world—and then Alice stopped for a moment, realizing that never for years had she felt this anticipation of joy and wonder. Of course there had been moments of happiness, the pleasure of watching Skye grow up, and being a part of all her changes and triumphs, but this was the first time Alice had the sensation that now her life would be her own, that something at last would be about her and for her, and that it would be something good, better than good. It was a miracle — what an amazing gift — what a validation for the determination she shared with Itch's mom, the faith to believe that he would wake up and come back to the people who loved him.

As she pulled into the garage and saw Robin's car, she wondered what she would say to him, and how she could explain what had happened in the most gentle way possible. The words would come because they would have to come was all Alice could think. As she walked in the door, she saw Skye and Robin, both all dressed up, sitting and laughing together in the living room. A pang crossed her heart. How hurt would Skye be when she learned that Alice had asked Robin to leave? Would she at least want to get to know her father? Alice hoped so.

Alice walked into the room and glanced at Robin. He was nicely dressed in a suit, but somehow had gotten a peculiar sunburn. The right half of his face was blistered and red, glistening with some sort of aloe, and the rest was the usual color.

"Shades of *Close Encounters*," she said, holding back a giggle, "You look like Richard Dreyfus. Did aliens take you too?" Alice paused for a moment. Would it be that incomprehensible if aliens had arrived, considering everything that had already happened today? Surely that would be the lesser circumstance.

"Is that what you're wearing to the party?" Robin asked.

Once again she'd forgotten the stupid party. Could she beg off? They'd seen her faint, so it wouldn't exactly be inexcusable or as though she were capriciously avoiding the party. She sat down briefly on a chair, ready to share the news.

"Mom! Hurry up!" said Skye, smiling. "Let's go celebrate."

"But I wanted to tell you…" began Alice. "I really don't want to go to…"

"When do we ever get to go to a party?" asked Robin. "This is a new suit."

"We'll talk later," said Skye. She looked so happy and relaxed, and Alice assumed that things were going well for her, so it seemed reasonable to wait to share the news until after the party.

"Okay," said Alice, "Fifteen minutes." She walked up the stairs, thinking about Itch, and having no clue what she'd wear to a party she wouldn't want to attend even if the day hadn't turned out as it did. But she showered, dressed, and was back downstairs quickly, amazed to see even Cooper nicely dressed and waiting. Fervently she hoped he wouldn't participate in any scenes with his mother tonight, because surely Totsie would attend the party.

In short order they'd arrived, and were mingling with the other guests. Alice fielded so many touching inquiries from concerned witnesses of her earlier fainting spell, that she temporarily lost sight of where everyone was. She did see Cooper across the room, having a heated discussion with his parents, but at least it wasn't loud.

Alice looked around and didn't see Robin anywhere, but then she spotted him, talking to Misty. Not wanting him to hear about Itch from her, Alice walked toward them. Their voices were hushed but angry.

"I can't believe you stalked me to here," Misty said. "Are you nuts? We were over long ago. I have a life."

"I didn't stalk you, I was invited. I just wanted you to see what you missed." Robin looked around, not seeing Alice at all, but spying Skye talking to one of the cameramen, and he pointed toward her. "See that beautiful girl over there? That's the daughter you never had time for. I made sure to keep her. Had to switch some babies and track her down, but I've been her dad for all these years."

Misty gasped and remained silent.

Alice also gasped, and started walking closer to both of them.

"And now you know what? I have a woman—a phenomenal woman—a woman who adores me, who loves me passionately, who thinks I'm the greatest guy on earth. A woman who makes you look like a bleached old hag. I just wanted to make sure you knew it. I feel for her a million times what I ever felt for you. True love, that's something you'll never know 'cause you're just an empty shell. Enjoy your life, bitch. You lost out big time."

Robin turned to walk away from Misty, who was still struck silent, and crashed into Alice, who was enraged and astonished. He had switched those babies? He belonged in jail. And he and Alice had true love? Never once in all the years they'd shared had anyone said the word.

"You switched the babies? You tried to steal my daughter from me?" Alice asked, but Robin shoved her aside and walked toward the exit, and as she turned to confront him further, she saw Skye, her hand over her mouth and running toward the door.

Misty found her voice then, and said to Alice, "Well you showed me, didn't you. You brought that girl here after all. You lard ass, scarface piece of shit."

Alice gave Misty a single incinerating glance, then dashed after Skye, who somehow wasn't outside any longer. Were there cabs available that easily? She glanced around the parking lot, and saw Robin driving away. Was he going after her?

Alice stood outside for a bit, letting the cool night air wash over her. She dialed Skye's number, but Skye didn't pick up, so Alice was forced to leave a message asking Skye to call her so she could tell her something important, and she also said as completely as possible that there was nothing to worry about concerning her birth.

Then Alice stood and breathed deeply. She'd now be forced to ask Totsie for a ride home, but at this moment, she needed merely to stand still, be alone and just breathe. Unfortunately her solitude lasted but a nanosecond; Misty walked out the door and over to Alice.

"Thanks for everything," Misty said. "You ruined my party and my life."

"First of all, you're a nasty viper. And secondly, that was Skye, my daughter, not the girl I told you about. I told Emma you weren't ready to meet her. So your secret's safe. I think only we heard what happened. So your life isn't ruined. But cheer up, I'm sure you'll find a way to ruin it on your own — the sooner the better."

Alice brushed past Misty, who stood there dumfounded at what Alice assumed was her nerve in speaking like that, and she walked back into the party and up to her sister. "Robin drove away," she said simply. "I need a ride."

Totsie's face clouded over, but Mitchell smiled cheerfully and said, "Sure. Looks like this party is winding down. Lemme just tip some waiters and we'll go."

"There are no waiters," said Totsie, reaching for Mitchell's arm and dragging him toward the door.

After being dropped off, Alice sat in the kitchen, drinking lemonade with Cooper, who'd asked what had happened, and Alice had decided to tell him; he wasn't the sort of kid you could shield from the truth. Then they both sat quietly, trying not to think about the evening and Robin's astonishing confession. How many babies could he have switched, she wondered. Every time she remembered what Robin had said about true love, Alice experienced faint pangs of guilt about what she was about to do to him, but then, immediately she could hear him talking—not just talking but boasting—about switching the babies. No wonder he'd encountered them so many times by chance; it hadn't been inadvertent at all. He'd been stalking them so he could keep his baby— or the baby he thought was his. And if Skye hadn't responded to him as she had, Alice never would have connected with him at all. But how could that have turned into true love, and how could he have felt that way about her, and never in all the years they'd shared, given any indication of the depth of his devotion? Alice believed he would be shattered now, but also somehow that it was a less brutal punishment than he actually deserved. He was willing to steal from her the chance to raise her own child, and even after all these years felt no remorse, only justification—and apparently he'd swapped other babies as well, and created chaos and misery in other families with whom he'd had no connection at all. No degree of unspoken true love could outweigh that.

Every few minutes she dialed Skye's number, but the calls remained unanswered. Alice began to feel increasingly desperate, but attempted to maintain a calm timbre in her voice with each new but equally urgent message, which for now Skye refused to return.

"What a mess, what a colossal mess," said Alice, thinking that it was a shame that Itch's awakening was marred by this crazy turn of events.

"What'cha gonna do," said Cooper, trying to be comforting, all the while typing something into his cell phone. And they sat there like that for hours, both exhausted but unable to go to bed. Eventually morning came, Alice put on some coffee, and planned to go to the Wellman Center to see Itch again.

Cooper looked out the back window, saying, "You need to see this."

Alice walked to the window and glanced outside, spotting Layla, clad in little more than a light robe. The left side of her face—and her body, which was visible where the robe gaped open, was blistered and sunburned too—the opposite side from Robin's. Alice gasped, but only for a second, and then burst into a fit of giggles. Sunburns like that came about in only one manner—two people lying face to face, falling asleep in the sun. She knew she should be jealous, incensed perhaps, enraged maybe. But Alice was overjoyed to be guilt free; she could extricate Robin from her life and feel nothing. She just hoped that if Skye wanted to maintain a relationship with him, that he wouldn't say no. Maybe she wouldn't even bother to tell him the truth. What would it hurt if he kept believing Skye was his? It seemed wrong, didn't it, but maybe if it prevented her daughter from feeling any more pain, it would be a lesser evil.

Alice hugged Cooper. "Thanks, kid, I needed that."

Alice had dressed in something pretty and applied makeup, but she still looked like someone who had been awake all night. She grabbed her iPad, and drove to the Wellman Center. It was early and nobody had yet arrived, so once again she had Itch all to herself. She tiptoed in the room, but he was awake and sitting up in bed, trying to move his arms. He seemed to have made some progress and could raise them quite a bit, then they sort of tumbled back down to the bed. Alice smiled. "I knew you'd be an ace at recovery," she said encouragingly. She walked to Itch's bedside, sat down on the side of the bed and leaned in to kiss him, but this time he was able to raise his arm to block her kiss.

Alice felt a pang in her heart, but brushed off the sensation as silly. "I'm sorry," she said, "Am I hurting you?" She touched his arm gently, felt it tense, and then moved off the bed to sit facing Itch in a bedside chair. "How are you feeling?" she asked, and he made a slight sound, but couldn't yet articulate any words. "Don't worry," she said comfortingly, "I read all about this. It might take a little while, but the words will come."

Alice reached out to hold Itch's hand, which she managed to do, although it felt extremely rigid to her. Her heart was so wide open that she could imagine all the love inside floating out from her, washing over Itch, and healing him instantly. She could picture him leaping from the bed and wrapping her up in a long, tight hug. "You'll be up and at'em soon," she said, smiling brightly, "And leaping out of that bed and crushing me in your arms. We'll be waltzing in no time." Then as Itch looked troubled, Alice laughed, "Okay, you got me. We never waltzed before. But I was just saying that, oh you know. Twirling through life, arm in arm." Alice laughed some more. "I feel so silly. I'm giddy and goofy I know, it's just so much to take in, and I can't stop all these thoughts, but why should I, it's like the best kind of drunk."

She sat silently for a moment and gazed into Itch's eyes, imagining that he could see all the feelings she couldn't begin to articulate, and would feel them too. His eyes seemed so shaded and troubled though, so lacking in merriment, but what did she expect? "Don't worry," she said kindly, "I know it all feels strange and disorienting. If anyone has a right to be disoriented, it's you. But welcome to orientation—ha—here I am to show you and tell you everything you missed."

Alice reached in her bag for the iPad. "Look at this nifty little toy," she said, smiling. She tapped it a couple of times and brought up a slide show. "This is Skye when she was a baby," she said, pointing at the screen. Alice glanced at Itch, and it almost seemed he was smiling. She flicked the screen, the image changed, and Itch's eyes opened wide. "Cool, right. You missed a lot of technology." She kept flicking the screen and narrating when the image was taken until a current picture appeared. "This is how she looks now," said Alice.

Itch seemed to get quite excited, which Alice considered a good thing. He was responding, and his eyes did seem brighter and less sunken. "Beautiful, isn't she?" asked Alice.

Alice clicked on another folder and some of their old high school pictures came up. There was a shot of the prom, and at a sporting event, some casual pictures taken at a picnic, several from graduation. "Remember these," she asked him. "Those were the days." Itch's high school yearbook photo popped up next, and Alice was sure she saw him smile. Then she turned the iPad around, clicked it and turned it back toward Itch. "Look what this can do," she said, showing him the picture. "Here's a picture of you right now."

Itch's eyes opened wide, and he stared at the screen unbelievingly. "It's really a picture," Alice said, "These gadgets are amazing. Here, look." She aimed the screen at the television, which was on but muted, and snapped a picture, then showed Itch, who looked back and forth between the device and the television, and then back to her with a glance that could only be described as deeply suspicious. "It's a lot to take in, I'm sure," said Alice, "But don't worry, you'll be up to speed soon, and soon it will all feel normal again. And I'm right here for you, with you. So don't worry."

Itch's nurse peeked in the room, saying "I figured you'd be here first thing. But there'll be rounds shortly, and they asked me to send you to the finance office when you arrived."

Alice nodded and said, "Itch, have you met Mrs. Lewis? She's been taking care of you for a long time."

His face seemed to tense, he coughed a bit, emitted sort of a scratchy sound, coughed again, and clearly was trying to speak. Alice leaned in more closely, worried he would hurt his throat if it wasn't yet ready for speech, but not wanting to prevent him from sharing something he thought was important. Maybe he was hungry or needed something.

"Did you want to say something, sweetheart?" she asked. "Try not to strain your throat." She put the iPad away and leaned in again, brushing Itch's hand and watching him as he tried to articulate.

"Prin," Itch said, so quietly it was nearly inaudible. Alice's eyes opened wide, considering it a miracle he could say even a part of a word. She touched his arm gently and smiled. "Prince," he said. Alice thought for a while, remembering the old dog he'd had when they were kids. Was the dog's name Prince? She was certain not, but what was his name? Snoopy! The dog was named after the cartoon. Could he be remembering the name incorrectly?

"Are you talking about your dog?" she asked. He shook his head the tiniest amount and struggled again.

"Principal Cat," he said as Alice gasped. He was talking about her mother. But why?

"Principal Catson," she said, looking into his eyes, and this time he clearly nodded.

"Principal Catson," he whispered, "I'm not..." and he stopped, and once again swallowed hard before continuing, "I'm not faking," he said, "I'm really," and he stopped here to breathe deeply, his eyes watering, and once more he swallowed and continued, "I'm really sick."

Alice's heart almost stopped. He thought she was her mother. She looked deeply into Itch's eyes, and remembered the most romantic thing he'd ever said to her, something that had touched her profoundly, and had stayed with her ever since.

"I'm Ally," she said softly. "You've been asleep for twenty-two years. We're forty now." Alice wondered if she were pushing too much, if the doctors would have said to be gentle and not say anything designed to shock Itch. She couldn't even imagine how he must be feeling.

A strange look crossed Itch's face, one no longer of disgust but of suspicion. Alice assumed he somehow thought her mother was trying to manipulate him. No wonder he'd recoiled when she kissed and touched him.

"Remember we were watching that crazy old show *Soap* real late one night. And aliens had kidnapped the guy and placed a lookalike in the house with his wife, and she had no clue it wasn't the real guy?" Alice looked deeply into Itch's eyes and smiled, hoping he could see her in her eyes, the girl she'd always been, still hiding there inside her eyes. "And I said to you if aliens switched me would you know, and you said yes, without even thinking, you said yes. And I thought that was the most romantic thing anyone could ever say to me. And I still do."

Itch's eyes opened wide, as though he were trying to take it all in. But when she took his hand again, he twitched uncomfortably, so once again she set it down on the bed.

As Alice rose, and leaned in to kiss Itch, he spoke again, "Ally," he said. "Where's Ally?"

Alice smiled at him softly, and said, "I'm right here. I'm Ally. Aren't I Ally?" she asked the nurse, who nodded.

Itch swallowed hard, wrinkling his face into an almost scowl, and coughed out a couple of words, "Get real."

It had always been Uncle Henry's policy to raise rents only when a new tenant moved in. For those already in residence, the rents remained the same, sometimes for years and years. Alice, wanting to honor her uncle's choices, had stuck with this strategy, but with increasing bills for Itch's rehabilitation, and the assumption after the party that she once again was jobless, there seemed little alternative but to give all the tenants notices of rent increases. Most accepted them with grace, but ironically, those there longest seemed the most annoyed, which actually made Alice feel better for having made the choice to do it. She was under no legal constraints to maintain rents or even to raise them by only the small percentage mandated by the stabilization board. The rents she charged, and the increases she decreed, were at her own discretion, and that was why Alice decided to amuse herself a bit and triple Layla's rent. The discussion they had was not pretty, but her goal was to get Layla out of there, not to gouge her, and she hoped it provided the necessary motivation.

Her last stop was Greg's door, and he smiled as he opened it. Alice walked in and glanced around. She cringed at bit at seeing her daughter's things, for after all, this was Skye's apartment, but Alice, because she had no choice, steeled herself and was determined to do what was fiscally sane. On second glance, she cringed for another reason: the place was in extreme disarray. She could imagine Bette Davis sauntering through and uttering her infamous line, 'What a dump.' The little wastebasket by Skye's desk was overflowing with soda cans and beer bottles. The sink was equally challenged by a number of encrusted plates, precariously inserted as though in some sort of Tetris game. Alice could see into the bedroom, and there were masses of clothes and piles of sheets, and the unmade bed was partially covered with clothes as well, such that a collection of toddlers and canines could be hiding beneath them and nobody would be the wiser. The carpet looked more like a sandy beach than a floor covering. And the coffee table had literally become that—there were dark rings on the white, painted surface, a number of mugs so dried and crusty that it would require an archaeologist rather than a tea leaf reader to offer any predictions other than encroaching disease.

"You've heard from Skye?" he asked hopefully.

Alice shook her head. "You know Greg, why don't you call her and talk to her?"

"Oh, I've tried. She's on some let's go nuts sabbatical." Greg looked annoyed, then he gulped, never having been this frank with Alice before.

"I'm not actually here about Skye, though," she said, feeling guilty, but forcing herself to continue. "I know you guys never paid rent to live here before, but things are kind of dire right now, so I actually raised all the tenants' rents, and I'm asking you to pay rent now too." She handed Greg the official paper about the rent, and watched his jaw drop. "It's less than half of what other tenants are paying for this size apartment," she said softly.

Greg flopped down on the couch, which Alice noticed now was stained in quite a few places. It was good Skye had chosen a white slipcover, because by the time she returned home, it would need several bleachings, and perhaps the services of an exorcist.

"I thought you knew," he said hesitantly, "We're, um, I'm saving for a house."

Alice looked at him, and Robin's face flashed before her. He did resemble Robin, didn't he. Come to think of it, so did Julian! She felt evaporate any tenderness she might have had toward this schnook, who was previously to be her son-in-law, but now who knew what role he might or might not play in Skye's future. Alice was proud of herself. Despite her infamous temper, for too long she'd been much too nice.

"Greg, you're employed in a good career, and although saving for a house is a worthwhile goal, you can't expect me to foot the bill for that goal. Whether or not you and Skye get back together, you're going to have to start paying rent. I shouldn't have been so lax before, as I can see it did you little good."

Once again Greg's jaw dropped. "But this is Skye's apartment," he protested.

"Is she even here?" asked Alice, feeling mean.

Greg sighed. "That's a low blow," he said, flopping down onto the couch so violently the springs screeched.

"Look, hon, I'm sorry. I don't want to make you feel bad. I also don't want to end up in foreclosure. It's just that simple. You're an adult, and you have to pay rent." Alice looked at the television mounted on the wall, the one thing Greg had contributed to the apartment, and saw inches of dust. Didn't men at least watch TV when they were alone? Could anyone see through this dust, no matter what fancy resolution the gadget boasted?

Greg scowled, and continued, "This place doesn't even have a mortgage on it."

Alice realized that this was the longest conversation they'd ever had, and then became infuriated, and almost felt happy that Skye was rethinking their attachment. "First of all, that's none of your business," she said in her steeliest voice, "And secondly that's untrue. Remember all that plumbing I had to do? Do you think plumbers donate their services? They don't."

"This is unreal. I can't believe you're kicking me when I'm down."

"I'm not kicking you, Greg, I'm asking, no telling you to pull your own weight. This is your rent and it's due the first of the month, every month. And you know what? Clean up a little. You've got potato chips all over the couch."

Greg sighed deeply and looked down beside him, where crumbs were embedded into the seams of the piping. Alice felt his pain, and she truly was sorry for him, but she also realized that this was the right thing to do, not just for herself, but for him as well.

"Sitting around moping isn't the answer to anything," she said kindly. "Get off your butt—do something—you'll feel better if you do."

"I can't promise I'll stick around here," he said ominously.

"Well, you know, that's up to you. Go on Craig's List, and see if you can live better and more cheaply. You'll learn a thing or two." Alice turned to walk out the door, and then she turned back toward Greg. "Sometimes grownups have to do things they'd rather not do, but we do them because we have to. I don't have a choice here. So just keep that in mind."

"Yeah, whatever," he said morosely, reaching for one of the many filled glasses also occupying the coffee table, and attempting to determine which was fresh and which a relic from weeks ago.

Alice walked back to her kitchen door, feeling stressed. She'd been forced to make so many changes recently, and it seemed that every day brought something else, admittedly something wonderful in the case of Itch, but could she rely on herself to make the correct choices? For so long, all her adult life really, she'd tried to stay in-between the lines, to follow the course set by trustworthy others, to avoid that wild and reckless part in her own nature that could cause her to be harmed or to harm others, but it was getting more and more difficult to do so, because the rules and guidelines on which she'd counted for so many years seemed no longer to be relevant. Could she take a breath and have faith that she would know what to do in charting a new, previously unforeseen course? Could she be the grownup she'd just indicated she was? Alice prayed she could.

At least Kitty had a good excuse for clinging to a memory, for refusing to believe a reality decades true. What excuse did Alice have? Had anyone ever said to her that she must follow rules that worked for her aunt and uncle when she was a child, rules which no longer worked for her, and were they here in charge of the world they'd built and entrusted to Alice, rules which no longer would work for them. As far as she remembered, there was nothing inflexible about Henry, and certainly not in Kitty, so why was Alice so ossified? Why did she cling so to the rigors of the past?

Alice shook her head, but she knew the answer. She was just trying to avert her natural tendency toward disaster, to be safe. But now she had taken steps, she had changed the rules and had done what was necessary, and if she felt anything today, it was the approving hand of Uncle Henry on her shoulder, congratulating her for behaving as an adult, and not a minor ruling an adult's world.

Emboldened by a new sense of courage, Alice walked, no marched into the kitchen and sat at the island, her laptop in front of her, and she pulled up the website for *You're Cooked*, her favorite television show. Four chefs competed under extreme time constraints for a prize of thousands of dollars, making a meal from ingredients not of their choosing. Alice watched the show relentlessly, always knowing what could be made from those ever changing, odd, quirky, and sometimes revolting ingredients. Yes, it was always easier to imagine performing spectacularly at home than to be there under duress, and under hot lights attempting grace — and culinary excellence — but how would she know if her bravura were deserved, if she didn't take a chance?

Alice began typing, and in mere moments, she'd filled out the online application and made a little recording with her webcam, a required attachment. Who knew? Surely not everyone who applied made it to the show. Maybe there was some sort of audition. Maybe she'd be forced to attempt to teach the complexities of a potato peeler to a silicone-poisoned nitwit with absurdly long fingernails, but if so, her time with Misty had prepared her for that eventuality. Maybe. Perhaps it would be worse, and of course that was the fear.

Alice rooted around in her purse and finally located a tiny mirror which she held up in front of her face. Were her scars dire enough to frighten children on Halloween? Or on any day of the year? Alice glanced in the mirror. There was only one place at her temple where the scars were extreme. And it could be somewhat concealed with make up. Or maybe some pâté. She winced a little and laughed too.

Alice reached over to the keyboard, and clicked on the *send* icon. Triumphant, she looked around, wishing there were someone to tell, but she was completely alone at home, something rare these days. Soon Itch would be there, and never again would there be solitary joys or stresses, for she would live in a bubble of bliss and satisfaction, whether or not she'd won the big bucks on a cooking show.

Alice reached for her phone and dialed her daughter. For so long Skye had tried to get her to apply to *You're Cooked*, but Alice always refused. Wouldn't she be excited to know that at last the application had been submitted. But the phone rang and rang, no answer, nobody home, as people used to say in the days before we were all everlastingly tethered electronically. Alice sighed and left yet another message, as Cooper walked in the door and sat down on the stool next to hers.

Alice smiled at him. "Almost time for school, huh? Summer went fast."

Cooper nodded, "Always does. No word from Skye?"

Alice shook her head. She reached for a cookie jar sitting on the counter, opened it, took a cookie, and offered it to Cooper. "Know what?"

Cooper took a cookie, laughed and said, "Probably."

"Don't be so smug," said Alice. "I know something you don't know."

"I hope so, or you'd have wasted a lot of your million years older than me not paying attention." Cooper flashed his wry glance at Alice, then shoved not one but two cookies in his mouth.

"Hmm," teased Alice, "Maybe I should just keep this a secret. Maybe you're not on my need to know list."

Cooper shook his head sagely. He took quite a while eating several more cookies, assuming Alice would recognize the mood of suspense he was mounting. Then he said, "You know what the British say. Quid pro quo."

Alice laughed. She almost stopped, and then she laughed some more. "That's Latin hon. Many people say that. It's not British."

"No, no," answered Cooper, for once seeming his age. "Quid is English slang for money, pounds I guess."

"And that applies here how?" she asked. "You think I'm gaining many pounds from eating all these cookies, and you plan to pay me to gain self control instead?"

Cooper looked a bit less certain, an expression he almost never displayed, for he was nearly always an over-confident boy, then said, "Quid pro quo—means I pay you and you give me something. Or maybe at a discount. Or gunpoint?"

Alice refused to laugh again, and looked at her nephew as an adult always looks at a beloved child, not with condescension but with a desire to teach. "It means tit for tat—you scratch my back I scratch yours."

"Well they do have too many massage parlors down there."

"Where?" asked Alice.

"Where Skye is."

"Where is she? Did you take a message?"

A flash of guilt crossed Cooper's face, but it quickly was replaced with a look of justification. "I was worried maybe you wouldn't approve, so I didn't tell you this, but it seemed like a good idea at the time." Alice just stared at him, reading the emotions crossing his face and waiting, her hand tapping on the counter impatiently, as he finally continued. "That night you made jambalaya— remember?" Alice nodded, tapping louder, wanting to yell, hurry up, tell me. "And I was playing with everyone's phones?"

"Oh," she said, understanding what was coming.

"I put a tracing app on everyone's phone. Figured she was acting so nuts, you'd want it. But I was afraid you'd go all Constitutional on me and say it was an invasion of privacy, so I didn't tell you. But I guess by now you need to know."

Alice reached over and hugged Cooper tightly. "Yes," she said sternly, "That was totally wrong of you." She looked Cooper in the eye then smiled brightly, hugging him again, "But wow am I glad you're such a bad boy. Where is she?"

Cooper clicked on his own phone and held it out, and there was a map with several bright colors on it, simulating pins for everyone's location. Alice glanced at it and said, "I figured as much, just didn't know precisely where." She jumped down from her stool and said, "Will you come with me? I need a tour guide."

Cooper nodded, following Alice out to the car. "So where's my tat?"

"Huh?" she said, imagining all she had to tell Skye.

"Nobody is scratching my back," he continued, smiling.

Playing along, Alice stopped walking, reached behind him and scratched his back. "Where does it itch?" she asked.

"C'mon Ally, kids my age haven't developed the patience lobe in their brains yet. Spill it."

Alice locked the front door behind them and took her time in replying, then said painfully slowly, "I applied for *You're Cooked.*"

"Oh, I knew that," said Cooper, teasing her with his lopsided grin.

"How?"

"Your laptop was sitting open."

Alice shook her head. "Okay Sherlock Homeboy, you got me."

They drove for quite a while, and eventually Alice parked the car where Cooper directed, saying, "But I don't see her anywhere. You sure this thing works?"

Cooper snickered, reminding Alice that she was a person of another generation, then he said, "What—you want to charge up like the cavalry and give everything away? Then they can have someone who isn't as clueless as they are find the hidden app and remove it. You might want to find her again, you know." He looked so seriously at Alice that she just shrugged, waiting to be directed further.

"C'mon," he said. "USC—that way. Ice cream place—that way. Right down this path—the culprits, who we'll be very surprised to bump into after our nice tour of USC. I gotta have a higher education, ya know."

Alice laughed. "I'd certainly hope so. Something intellectual and not too useful, like literature or fine art. Otherwise you'll rule the world."

"I can't draw worth nothin' and geez Auntie, my readin' and writin' are jess so-so. Maybe I better just rule the country. Don't want to get too grandy-yose."

Alice laughed some more. "Nobody makes me laugh as much as you do."

"Look," he said.

Alice could see for herself. There, in the middle of the busy walking path, was Julian in his clown suit, stopping passersby to do little tricks and so on, probably with some sort of bizarre twist, and humiliatingly, Skye, passing a hat to scoop up the tips. Alice pressed her hand to her heart, and stopped for a moment just to breathe. Was this panhandling?

"Pretend we're talking," said Cooper, laughing at something imaginary, and pointing off in the distance, saying, loudly enough so that it all seemed quite natural, "Ice cream place is right over there," when Alice practically collided with Skye.

"Mom!" Skye flushed a deep crimson, and took a pace back. "What are you doing here?" she asked.

"Skye!" said Alice, reaching deep inside herself to locate any latent acting skills. "I can't believe it. I've been calling you for days. And now we bump into you while touring USC? How on earth?"

"No way," said Skye, indicating surprise, but not suspicion.

"I'm really angry with you. It's just not acceptable that you ignore my calls," Alice said, gazing sternly into her daughter's eyes.

"Oh, gee, I guess I didn't realize you'd called. My phone's lost." Skye looked genuinely remorseful until there was a ringing sound from her jeans pocket, and once again she flushed.

"Busted," said Cooper as Skye glared at him.

"And now you're lying to me as well as refusing my calls?" Alice shook her head, and looked deeply into her daughter's eyes. "Cooper and Julian can catch up for a bit while you come talk to me."

Skye glanced toward Julian, who waved gaily toward Alice as though nothing at all were wrong, and then turned her attention back to her mother.

"Now," said Alice.

There was a bench a little ways off, so they walked toward it and took a seat facing each other. "What's going on with you?" asked Alice. "I saw you run out of the party and needed to talk to you, and you've been AWOL ever since."

"Wouldn't you, if you heard what I heard? My dad is a criminal, and I might not be related to anyone. Then I get some insane message from you not to worry about it, that I am who I think I am. Well who's that, that's what I'm starting to wonder."

Skye listened as Alice explained to her about Emma's letter and the DNA test, and she seemed to be a bit calmer after realizing that Alice hadn't been offering idle assurances in all those phone messages. "You kicked Dad out. He's left me a trillion messages too."

Alice nodded. "I haven't seen him since the party, so I didn't actually get to kick him out, but I did send his things to storage. He thinks he's your dad, that you're his baby, the one he switched. But I was going to ask him to leave even before that bomb dropped. Itch is awake."

Skye's eyes opened wide. "Awake? Like awake, awake? He's awake—no more Sleeping Beauty?"

Alice nodded again. "Disoriented but awake. Improving daily—it's a blessing and a miracle—I can't believe it myself. I want you to come with me to see him in the hospital soon."

"Okay. I guess. Swap one dad for another. What the hell."

"Look, I know you and Robin are close, and you can stay close if you want. I don't mind."

"Yeah, I can visit him in jail."

Alice cocked her head for a moment, picturing that image, and almost wishing that's what would happen. "So what's going on here? You're panhandling? Are you broke?"

Skye tried to swallow, almost choked, and began to cough on her own saliva. Once she could speak again, she said, "Street art. What's wrong with you?"

"This has been going on for way too long," said Alice, becoming exasperated. "Summer's ending. Have you made any strides in deciding what you want to do with your own life? Because to me it looks like you've decided on becoming Julian's full time assistant or something."

"I really didn't want to have to say this to you, because it's too mean," said Skye, "But I realized I didn't want to be like you, living some dull life, with some guy you never loved, no excitement, no fun, no passion, just in it for the security."

"That's an interesting perspective on Robin and me," said Alice, tightening her jaw.

"Is there another perspective?"

Alice almost said nothing, but instead realized this was not the time for silence or subtlety. "There was a little girl who saw a man who wanted to be a father, and she said she thought Robin was her dad. And I gave her that dad. It was always about you, not about me."

Skye gasped. "That never happened!"

Alice nodded. "You were a little kid. Of course you don't remember, but that's precisely how Robin came into our lives. I just didn't know there was a motive on his part to insert himself there."

Alice watched as this information was absorbed. "Look," she said kindly, "I would never suggest that you live a dull life. A safe life yes, but a dull one no. What is it you want to do in your own life? For yourself?" Alice felt the tremors of worry float through her body, as she waited for Skye to answer. As usual, she pictured dire consequences, but she tried to control herself. "You know," she said softly, "Today I had a thought. Both Greg and Julian remind me of Robin — in different ways of course."

"What a creepy thing to say."

"Sometimes the truth is unpleasant. But back to my question. What are your plans?"

Skye shook her head. "No clue," she said despondently.

"Right now you're living Julian's life, not your own, you realize that?"

Skye nodded, and her face reflected the deep inner misery she obviously was feeling.

"I have a suggestion. How about you come home. Sign up for some college classes, anything that interests you, doesn't have to be for credit, just to give some structure to your life for a while. See Julian if you want.

Figure out if you're done with Greg. Focus on your own life instead of avoiding it."

Skye nodded, seemingly in agreement. "And you and my real dad are going to be together?"

Alice nodded happily. "He's the only man I ever loved."

Skye began to weep. "I'm so sorry. All those years with someone else because of me, and longing miserably for your true love."

Alice reached out and took Skye's hand. "Itch was never expected to recover, and Robin was a good dad. So at least we both have that." She paused for a moment and asked, "You two haven't been going hungry or anything? Who passes a hat for money if they don't need it?"

Skye laughed. "Us I guess."

"C'mon, let's all go get some dinner. And then you can drive yourself home?"

Skye nodded and rose with Alice, their arms around each other. They walked toward the boys and Alice said, "From now on when I call you, pick up the blasted phone," and Skye nodded again.

Then Alice smiled and said, "Hey—I applied for *You're Cooked.*"

"About time."

Alice was tired but happy after her dinner with the kids, and feeling so relieved that Skye would be back home and taking classes, that she decided to bake some muffins and quick breads. After weeks' hiatus from all the years of late night baking, it seemed so odd to be back in that routine, but it was comforting. As the date nut and apple walnut breads cooled on the counter, Alice tucked chocolate chip muffins into the oven, thinking to herself that she was deep into the land of overkill, but no, Cooper would eat what she and Skye didn't.

When the doorbell rang, Alice was astonished to see Tom Angelico outside, holding a giant gift basket filled with fruits, cheeses, and even some wine.

"Oh you're not in the hospital," he said, in a manner that sounded deeply relieved, which to Alice was even more perplexing than his late night visit.

"Visiting hours are over for the night," she answered.

Tom blanched oddly, saying, "I'm so sorry—I've come too late. I can leave, it's all right."

Alice grinned at him, and said, "I meant hospital visiting hours, not you. Please, come in, it's not too late at all—I've been baking." He followed her to the kitchen and sat in the bench opposite her, drinking tea and sampling slices of Alice's quick breads with some cream cheese and sliced pears from his basket.

"Wow, this is amazing," he said, smiling, then eating another bite. "I guess they don't hold people in the hospital for a concussion any more. They say what—don't bang your head around when you're making delicious treats?"

"Who has a concussion?" asked Alice.

"Misty said you weren't at work because you were being treated for a concussion from your fall." Tom took a deep drink from his tea cup and another hearty bite, then said, "I'm not here to pressure you or anything—I was just worried."

"I never had a concussion," she said, telling him briefly about Itch. "So I've been at the hospital more than usual, but not for myself," she finished.

"That's an amazing story," he said, "Leave it to Misty to get it wrong—she's so adorably daffy."

That was one way to put it, Alice thought, saying nothing.

"I know you girls haven't always been the best of friends," he said, causing Alice to wonder just how much he knew.

"What makes you say that?" she asked.

"Oh I don't know. Maybe I'm wrong, just feels like an old competitiveness there. But you do have very interesting chemistry. Take a look at this—when you get a chance." Tom handed Alice a DVD, which she immediately inserted into her laptop and watched.

"So she's Lucy and I'm Desi?" she asked, as Tom grinned.

"It's just so amusing the way you keep trying to get her to learn to cook, and she's so huggably hopeless at it. I think people might like to watch that—you know like those two British women on that comedy, but with actual cooking."

Alice sat silently for a moment, wanting desperately to extricate herself from the possibility of any further contact with Misty, but always at the back of her mind remained the image of the bills stacking up.

"I know it's not what you signed on for," said Tom.

"I thought Misty wanted to be the next Martha," said Alice, not mentioning how dumb the clips made her look.

Tom nodded, "I know. I tried to get her to co-star in some infomercials—she'd be great at that—you know the sidekick who oohs and aahs—but she didn't see herself that way."

"Hmm," said Alice, thinking how exhilarating it must be to make choices based on how you saw yourself, rather than what was necessary.

"Why don't we keep going as we are. You can reduce your hours if need be. Maybe do an intensive teaching Misty one thing, then you go attend to your hubby, and we'll record her attempts to do it. Eventually she'll get it—I mean we're not building Plutonium here, just food, right?"

Alice cocked her head to agree with his assessment, and raised her eyebrows to communicate that he might be wasting his money.

"You're very sweet to be so tactful and loyal. Misty has a good friend in you," said Tom kindly, smiling at Alice.

"She has a better one in you."

Tom rose then, and Alice saw him to the door, thanking him again for the gift basket, and promising to be at the studio in the morning. She watched him drive off in his SUV, and was about to close the door, when Robin pulled into the driveway and quickly stood face to face with her.

"Ally," he said, reaching out to hug her, which she managed to sidestep, "I've missed you so much." In the act of evading his hug, the door opened, and Robin slipped into the hallway before Alice could insist that he remain outside.

"What are you doing here?" she asked.

"I came to apologize about everything."

"Why—did the police track you down?" Alice wanted to blockade entry into the house, but Robin was on the wrong side of her, and he walked all the way back to the kitchen, where the timer was beeping, so Alice followed him and removed the muffins from the oven.

"Police," he said, blanching, and helping himself to a muffin, then yelling, "Ouch, hot," but he kept chewing and said with a full mouth, "You called the cops?"

"I didn't, no, but someone should inform them of what you did." Alice set the muffins on a cooling rack and removed it from Robin's reach.

"Look, it's been a crazy week, okay. I just need to come home."

"Listen to me Robin, this isn't your home any more. I was going to tell you that night, Itch is awake, but even if he weren't, after hearing what you did, do you really think I'd want you here?"

"But where am I supposed to go? This is my home."

"I heard what you said to Misty. If you think you have true love with Layla, then go be with her. Get yourself a place, and move in together. Marry her. Be happy." She watch Robin's face drain of color and was amused to see that he had no clue she knew about his affair.

Recovering far too speedily, Robin sighed, walked over to the fridge, took out a carton of milk and began swigging directly from it.

"Hey!" said Alice.

"I can't afford to get a place. And you tripled her rent, so she has to move. What am I supposed to do?" He finished the milk in the carton, tossed it into the trash, and began digging around in the fridge for something else, until Alice shoved him over a bit and closed the door.

"I imagine after all these years of freeloading, it does feel stressful to have to pay bills. Welcome to my world. You have a job, go get a place to live." Alice followed Robin to the other side of the room, where he was about to eat another muffin, and she said, "Enough. Leave the muffins alone. Go back to wherever you came from and leave me alone too. I've had enough. I wasted over fifteen years with you—I don't have to waste fifteen more minutes."

"I always knew you had a mean streak," he said morosely, "And I didn't want to tell you this, but I'm the victim here."

"You and whatever babies you switched."

"No, I mean of identity theft. So much of my money keeps getting sucked out of my bank accounts. Every month. And I can't say a word. My whole 401k is gone too."

"I suggest you tell the bank, not me."

"Someone is doing this to me," he said in a whisper, "Obscene things on my credit card statements from disgusting porn sites. Not mine of course, but how am I gonna call and say these aren't my charges."

Alice shrugged. "Let me walk you to the door. I had your mail forwarded to the office, but you can send it wherever you want when you get a place." She gestured toward Robin, who held his ground, and then she said, "Now," and dejectedly he followed her. "Good luck to you," she said, "And I hope you'll remain in touch with Skye. She does love you."

Robin gulped as though he were about to weep, then he crept back out the door.

Alice closed the door behind him and yelled for Cooper, who came down the stairs. "Need a taste tester?" he asked enthusiastically. "I couldn't wait much longer, but I knew that work guy was here."

Cooper walked into the kitchen, and began sampling everything, as Alice said, "I guess you wouldn't know anything about disappearing 401k accounts and slimy porn charges that look like identity theft, right?"

Cooper's face betrayed absolutely no emotion as he asked, "What?"

"Robin," said Alice. "Thinks he's the victim of identity theft."

"Well," said Cooper, as Alice stared at him apprehensively, terrified to learn that he somehow had perpetrated fraud, "I'm sorry," he said, worrying her even further, and then he finished, "For anyone stuck with that gronk's identity."

"Grand larceny and fraud are very big crimes," said Alice. "People go to jail for committing them."

Cooper nodded with his mouth very full and mumbled, "Good to know."

True to her word, Skye had spent the night in her room at home, and had agreed to visit Kitty and her father with Alice, but instead of smiling as they met in the parking lot of the Wellman Center, Skye scowled at Alice and complained, "Greg says you're gouging him for money."

"Oh?" asked Alice.

"He seemed terribly upset," said Skye.

"Are you kidding me?" asked Alice. "Are you planning to move back in with him?"

"I don't know," Skye said miserably. "I just feel bad that he feels hurt."

"So you're saying you think the cause of his anguish is me asking him to pull his own weight for a while, when I'm in a monster financial crunch?"

Skye sighed and looked downcast. "I shouldn't be at home, I'm costing you money. And Cooper eats like he's at a Chinese buffet."

"Honey," said Alice, "You're my daughter. And if you were in your apartment, well I might need some help, but I wouldn't press you because you're not working, but Greg is far from unemployed—he's just being cheap. Not to mention what he's done to all your stuff. It's like post-apocalyptic filth in there."

"I guess," mumbled Skye, "But he said you were asking a huge amount, and it sounded like he felt you were trying to evict him from the family."

"Did you actually talk to him?" asked Alice.

Skye shook her head. "He left a message."

Alice clenched her jaw in frustration. "I asked him to pay half what other tenants are paying. Half. And it's up to you to have a conversation with him about your future, not me."

"But what if I break up with him, and then I'm sorry?"

Alice put her arm around Skye and hugged her briefly. "Well, hon, you can't string two guys along—it's unfair. Do you love Julian? Do you love Greg? Maybe you don't really love either of them. When you're with the right one, you don't get distracted by other people."

"I don't think it's that simple," said Skye, stopping before they reached the door.

"Explain it to me then," said Alice.

"Oh I don't know. If I could explain things, maybe they'd make sense. I just think I could have a different life with each of them."

"What I'm worried about is you feeling you should define your life by the man you're with. That's why I keep saying take classes, so you can find your passion and get an idea of the life you want for yourself. Then you'd know who'd be the best one to share it with," said Alice, continuing, "Whew, I sound like a feminist, and they were before my time."

Skye laughed. "There are still feminists. But I want to go back to the times when women only had to worry about the garbage disposal, not the garbage in their lives."

"Good luck with that," said Alice, opening the door and walking toward Itch's room.

"I feel so nervous," whispered Skye as they entered the room. This time they weren't alone—Itch's brother Stanley was there with his son Ben, Cooper's best friend.

Itch was flexing his fingers and moving his arms, which Alice considered a good sign, and he said to Ben, "Bring my guitar in and we can play like we used to." His voice sounded pretty good to Alice—he was making progress.

"No, I'm Ben," said his nephew. "This is my dad, your brother. He's the one you played with."

Itch cocked his head in a disbelieving manner. "Don't kid a kidder," he said, grinning almost like his old self.

Stan sighed briefly, as though they'd had this discussion before, and he reached into his wallet, removed his driver's license, and handed it to Itch. "See—my name is right there. See my birth date."

Itch was able to hold the license, which to Alice was also good news, because it meant his motor skills were improving, and he held it to his eyes and squinted.

Stan laughed. "You might need glasses," he said, and removed his own and set them on Itch's nose.

"Since when do I wear these?" said Itch, but it was obvious that they did help his vision. He looked at the license, paused a long time, looked at his brother, looked back at the license then up at Ben. "Gotta love it. I'm in the hospital with mono, and you're here shining me on."

"You don't have mono," said Stan, "You just woke up from a coma. You're like Rip Van Winkle, remember him?"

Itch looked up then and spotted Skye, and his face lit up. "Ally! I've been calling for you," he said. "They gave me some sort of shot, and I can't get up, but it's starting to wear off. I wanted to go find you, but they won't let me move."

Alice walked up to Itch and took his hand, which he pulled away, his eyes maintaining their focus on Skye, who stood hesitantly a few paces from the bed. Alice gestured to Skye, who then approached and cautiously said, "Um, hi, wow, this is surreal."

Itch reached for Skye's hand, and she allowed him to hold it.

"Isn't she beautiful?" asked Alice, smiling proudly and sitting beside Itch on the bed, as he squirmed away from her and closer toward where Skye stood beside him.

"Did you tell her?" Itch asked Skye, who just looked perplexed.

"We're having a baby," he said to Alice, "And getting married. There. It's out."

Alice smiled at Itch and stroked his hand, which tensed with each movement she made. "We already did that. This is Skye, our baby—she's all grown up."

"You've been sleeping my whole life," said Skye, then smiling, "But now you're awake, and we can get to know each other."

"Okay," said Itch with a strained, uneven grin, "I get it." He moved his face side to side, scanning the room. "Where is it? I don't see it."

"See what?" asked Alice.

"The camera," said Itch. "Candid Camera. I get it."

"You were in an accident," said Stan, "Then a coma. You just woke up. It's been more than twenty years. We're all twenty years older."

"Twenty-two," said Skye.

"And you—Stan," said Itch, pointing to Ben, "You going along with this?"

Ben blushed. "I'm Ben, your nephew. I was born while you were sleeping. I'm seventeen. You just met me today."

"Quick," said Itch, "What year is it?" And when everyone answered immediately with the same number, he said, "You sure got your stories straight."

"It's a lot to take in," said Alice gently, "But don't worry, you'll be up to speed in no time."

Itch nodded. "I can't wait to get back on my bike. And the band, it'll be so good to play in the band again. It feels like it's been weeks since we practiced."

"Well, maybe," said Stan. "We sort of grew up though, but sure, I can try to get everyone back together once you're out of here."

"C'mon," said Itch, "Who gives up being a rock star? I mean I know I didn't make the majors, but I can still be a rock star." He squeezed Skye's hand, saying, "It's gonna be amazing."

Alice smiled, remembering how often he used to say just that. It was as though for a moment she'd been transported back in time, back to her former self, and her heart opened with the sensation of youthful promise. She leaned in to kiss Itch on the cheek, but the physical therapist entered the room, and everyone knew it was time to leave. As Alice rose from where she was sitting beside Itch, he made a gesture toward Skye, who leaned in closer, her ear to his mouth, then on hearing what he'd said, she wrenched her hand loose from his and jumped back.

"That's disgusting!" she shrieked, and swiftly stepped back toward the door.

Itch looked more baffled than embarrassed, but he blushed anyway, and Alice sighed, imagining what he might have said. "He thinks you're me," said Alice to Skye.

"I'm your daughter," said Skye with revulsion. "Act like it." Then she walked out of the room with Alice behind her.

Alice and Skye stood silently for a moment outside the door. "Geez," said Skye. "Ick."

"He's not himself yet, try to understand," said Alice.

Skye glanced toward the ceiling, shrugged, then said, "I understand. I just don't like it."

"I'm sorry," said Alice. "He thinks I'm Gram."

"Double ick," said Skye.

Alice glanced at her watch. She had to be at work shortly. "We still have time to see Kitty, I think."

"At least she won't be coming onto me. Creepy crazies. What a family."

"Oh hon, I don't see how it's the same thing. Nobody is crazy anyway. Just old. Or recovering."

Skye laughed. "What about you—fatally optimistic—that's a mental affliction, isn't it?"

Alice shook her head. "With the way I worry, nobody ever called me optimistic before." She led Skye toward Kitty's room, and her aunt opened the door, hugging them both. "I have something for you," she said, while Kitty watched with interest as she removed a box of twinkle lights from her tote.

"It's not Christmas, is it?" Kitty asked. "This is the longest vacation ever."

"It's for your bathroom door," said Alice. "I'm going to hang these around the door and then you can always see where it is."

"Do you want me to get Reymundo to put them up?" Kitty asked.

"Who?" said Skye.

Alice pulled out a packet of little adhesive plastic hooks and affixed them around the outside of the door frame. "I can do it," she answered.

"Reymundo is our chef, kitchen guy, big flirt," said Kitty to Skye. "You don't remember him? And they say *my* memory is going. He used to play with you all the time. Then he went away for a while. Now he's back. He's been here a couple times to see me." Kitty laughed.

"He likes to visit when Henry's golfing—I told you, big flirt."

Skye, not knowing what to make of all this, nodded, as Alice turned back toward her aunt and said, "What do you think? Where's the bathroom, Kitty?"

"Apparently right by the Christmas tree," answered Kitty, grinning almost like her old self. "I guess you're too old for a new doll," she asked Skye, who smiled and nodded. "Just teasing," said Kitty, "Maybe some clothes for the dolls you already have?" When Skye said nothing, Kitty began laughing. "Reymundo has given me a new lease on life," she confided. "Nice to be in a good mood."

Alice hugged her aunt. "I'm glad you're happy and feeling chipper," she said. She set some magazines on the table in Kitty's little sitting area. "Just in case you want something to read when you're not entertaining…. Have you been cold at all? The weather hasn't turned yet, but I wondered if you needed any more sweaters. You do have some right there in your dresser."

"You kids are a riot," said Kitty. "You act as though I'll be here forever. What is this—the vacation that never ends?"

After visiting a while longer, Alice and Skye walked back down the corridor to their cars. "She seems much worse, doesn't she?" asked Skye.

Alice sighed. "She actually seems more lucid, but she must be worse. She's living in a fictional world, but maybe that's a good thing, because at least it's keeping her brain active."

"And this Reymundo guy is make believe?"

"No, no," said Alice, "He was real, and he did play with you, but I think he went back to Mexico when you were six or seven. He did flirt with Kitty, and Henry was very jealous. Now, apparently every attractive guy she sees reminds her of Reymundo."

"It's so weird to think that old people actually had lives," said Skye, pulling her beeping phone from her purse and reading a text. "Julian is up for a big part," she added, smiling happily.

"Great," said Alice, hugging Skye, and entering her own car to drive to work. "See you later, hon. And please think about what we said."

"Maybe I could make up a husband and a couple of kids, and then my life would be simpler and happier too," said Skye.

"I think you could have real ones," said Alice, "Okay hon, see you later."

It had been only a few days since Alice had been at work, but it felt like ages, and when so many people approached her to inquire about how she was mending from the concussion, it seemed easier just to nod and say she was fine now. Then of course Misty appeared, scowling in her usual constantly-perturbed way, and said, "I have a bone to pick with you."

Alice looked at her, wondering if she would have to instruct Misty in how to pick that bone before the conversation could progress. "Oh?"

"I go out of my way to cover for you so you can keep this job and not piss Tom off, and you make it sound like I'm some kind of liar."

"Yeah, I have some nerve," said Alice, looking deeply into Misty's astonished eyes.

Misty gasped. "Well, you could at least apologize. And thank me for looking out for you."

"It's tragic I was so distracted by Itch coming out of a twenty-two year coma that I failed to celebrate your sainthood."

"So it's true?" Misty asked, choosing to ignore Alice's dig. "Did he mention me?"

"Yeah, your name was the first word out of his mouth."

Misty's eyes opened widely, "Really?" she said, in a near whisper.

Alice paused dramatically, enjoying torturing Misty, then said "Uh—no." She wondered why she didn't do what everyone else would do, namely quit this job.

"You know, you really have a mean streak," said Misty, looking improbably downcast, and toying with the diamond necklace she always wore.

"I've heard," said Alice.

Misty glanced up and down Alice's form, and sighed. "A padded bra would do wonders for you. You're so flat and square." Alice looked down at her natural C-cup and said nothing, thinking not everyone wanted a bustline that could provide shade for a kindergarten class. "Did you call that plastic surgeon yet?" Misty made a gesture toward Alice's face and grimaced as if in pain.

"Are we cooking today?"

"I've decided to throw a cocktail party, so we're going to make hors d'oeuvres. Today we'll make puff pastry and phyllo dough." Misty looked triumphantly at Alice. "See—I've been reading cookbooks and doing my homework, while you were off on your little vacay."

"It's possible to make puff pastry, but most home cooks would just buy it frozen, and virtually nobody would make phyllo at home. The one place that carried it fresh had to stop, because the baker committed suicide. But sure, if you want to try making phyllo, I'm all in favor of it," said Alice.

"Hey," said Misty, with more than the usual degree of outrage. "It's your lack of boobs that makes you so mean."

"Working with phyllo is difficult," said Alice, "So if you can master that and show how to make some fillings for it, that would be a good show."

"Fillings? I thought we baked it like a cake and cut it up."

Alice looked up at the ceiling for a moment, holding back her laughter, then asked, "You've had pigs in blankets, right? Everyone's had that."

Misty nodded, saying "You're just so smug, crushing all my inspirations. You can't help yourself, can you, and I know why—you resent me because I have a waistline."

Alice continued, "Most people use that canned croissant dough, but really it's puff pastry, so see—that's a pastry wrapped appetizer. There are many wrapped and filled apps, and people love them. Spanakopita, tyropita, samosas…."

"I know you're trying to intimidate me," said Misty, her eyes blazing, "But when you make up words, you just make yourself look foolish and desperate, and if I do say so myself, jealous."

"Those are real things," insisted Alice.

"Oh please. Green eggs and ham."

After they'd stumbled and argued through the making of a number of fillings while the doughs defrosted, Alice stood next to Misty, attempting to show her an easy way to make phyllo cups in a mini muffin tin. "I don't like all that melted butter," Misty complained, as Alice showed her how to brush each sheet. "It's too many carbs, um I mean, calories?" she mumbled.

"These doughs are filled with fats, yes; this isn't diet food," said Alice.

"It's not filled with fat—you're pouring on butter—it's your fault," Misty sighed. "If anyone thought I ate this stuff, I'd die."

"This was your idea."

Misty stomped her foot for a moment, then said petulantly, "But how was I supposed to know you'd add a bucket of butter? I never said do that. This isn't movie theater popcorn."

"The butter is necessary between the layers—it's a chemical thing," said Alice.

Misty shook her head. "What an imagination. And all to torture me. It almost makes me feel good that I'm so important to you that you can't stop trying to make me miserable." She glanced off into space for a bit, then smiled and said, "I do have that effect on people."

Alice paused for a moment, realizing there was no point in continuing the conversation, then said, "Okay here's a trick you might like." She took some of the squares she'd cut and spritzed them with an aerosol butter spray, then overlapped them in the wells of the muffin tin. "Easier, less calories, though not quite as good, I'd say."

Misty imitated Alice's every move, and nodded as she managed to make ragged phyllo cups alongside Alice's perfect ones. Then she sprinkled in the chopped ham, brie cubes, candied pecans and dried cranberries. "So this is like a cheese muffin?" Misty asked as she inserted the pan into the oven next to Alice's.

"It's a super easy appetizer anyone can make," said Alice. "Now we'll do a harder one." Alice cut the phyllo into long strips, brushed them with butter, added some of the spinach filling, and rolled them up into triangles the way color bearers do flags.

"Whoa, slow down," whined Misty, the dough impaled on her epically long fingernails. Alice made a second triangle, working deliberately, as Misty watched, then a third equally slowly, as Misty attempted to duplicate her smooth motions. "No, it sticks, it oozes, it tears. This is gross! It's like a horror movie."

"Try again," said Alice, demonstrating once more.

Misty shredded a few more attempts, then said, "This dough is broken—that's a cooking term, you know."

"Broken isn't dough—it's sauces that don't stay homogenized."

"Oh please," said Misty, "I know that means milk. Anyway the dough is broken, too thin, whatever—it's defective. We need to return it."

Alice laughed. "What, return it half used? It's not defective—this is what it's like. Try again. And consider cutting your nails."

Misty squinted angrily at Alice. "You would say that. You don't care what you look like. Well, I do."

After a few more hours of ineffectual appetizer making, Alice at last was liberated, and she visited Itch for a while, then drove home thinking about her day. She was surrounded by people who believed she was attempting some form of trickery. No matter how many times she told Itch she was herself, he refused to believe it. And Misty was, well Misty. How did someone grow up and learn nothing, Alice wondered. At least Itch had an excuse. It was so exhausting, though to be around people who felt she was trying to put something over on them. And there was Aunt Kitty and her problems, and Skye and a clown, not a metaphorical clown, the thing most parents consider any suitor for their daughter, but an actual clown. What was she to do about all of these preposterous situations? Alice had one idea about how to help Itch, and the rest she felt would remain a strain for as long as she could endure it, at least in the case of Misty. Surely Tom would snap out of it shortly, and stop pouring money down the drain.

Alice thought about her future. Soon the fire would be resolved, and then she would have to reopen the business. In her heart, Alice knew she didn't really want to rebuild P3. It was exhausting, and provided very little in the way of satisfaction, but how would she tell Kitty she'd opted to move on, and how could she betray the trust involved in putting that legacy into her hands. It was her obligation to keep it running, for her aunt and uncle, and also it was what kept her safe. If she made a different choice, who knew how it might work out in the end? She could open a new business and watch it tank, her aunt and uncle's money and legacy lost. That would be tragic, and a source of unending pain. There ultimately was no choice but to reopen P3. That was the plan for her life. The thoughts swirled around in her head as she sat at the desk in her den, a large roll of parchment paper unfurled before her. Once she finished what she was doing, she slept, but all night Alice tossed and turned, envisioning herself baking with Misty, or trying to tell Itch she was herself, and nobody believed her.

Early the next morning, Alice arrived at the hospital, and found Itch laughing and joking with his young physical therapist, a girl a few years older than Skye. While she pressed against his limbs and demanded he provide resistance, he obliged, making funny comments here and there. He sounded so happy and relaxed, but when Alice entered the room, he became silent.

"Oh, look," she said, "Great job, you're moving your legs. Can't keep number twenty-seven down, can they."

Itch appeared bewildered as he glanced at her, "I didn't know you knew my number," he said, then he squinted, tried to remember something, seemed confused, stopped talking and pushing, and his leg fell to the bed.

"I know everything about you," Alice said softly.

"We'll pick this up later, after you two have a nice visit," said the therapist.

"Thank you so much," said Alice.

"I'm Frankie," the therapist said, shaking Alice's hand. "And don't you worry, mister, we'll have you back up on that bike before you know it."

Itch smiled, "You know you will," he said, winking. Then he turned toward Alice and said, "Where's Ally?"

Alice sighed sadly, then immediately brightened for Itch's sake. She didn't want him to think he was disappointing her, or not recovering quickly enough. The time table had to be his, Alice knew this. "I know it's been very difficult for you to come to grips with everything that's happened since you were asleep, well why wouldn't it be? You weren't here, were you. You were asleep and had no idea of time passing. So I thought maybe this would help you."

First she withdrew a sticky name pad from her tote. It was the sort that people use at conventions or professional gatherings. She wrote *Ally* on the top sheet, tore it off, and affixed it to her shirt. "See, now you can see who I am, and soon you'll get used to me being me." She smiled kindly at him. "And everyone who comes in, we'll ask them to wear these too, so that way when Stan is here, you'll know him and you'll know Skye, and soon enough we won't need them any more because now you're awake, and you'll start being used to us all." Alice paused briefly, and just looked deeply into Itch's eyes. The storm clouds passed for a moment, and he seemed to relax. "I know you're trying really hard, working really hard to recover," she said softly, almost more for herself than for him. For the first time he smiled at her, a faint grin, and it gave Alice hope that she was on the right track.

Then from her tote she pulled last night's art project, and she unfurled it across Itch's lap. Alice laughed. "You know how much I like art and show and tell. Well, here it is. This is the history of you and me, and pretty much the world, our little piece of it anyway. See—it's a timeline and everything important is right here. Can you read it?"

Itch nodded. Apparently he hadn't forgotten how to read and the big letters she'd used were plainly visible, even if he did need glasses. He ran his finger across the long sheet of unbroken paper marked with notches for years, and illustrated with photos.

"See—here's your baby picture, and mine. And see how you're growing up, and see the matching pics of me?"

Itch nodded, smiling. "World series, 2008, 2009, 2010…" he said, shaking his head. "Super bowl year after year. Presidents. Best Picture Oscars."

Alice nodded, briefly touching his hand, and he looked up at her, saw the name tag on her shirt, and didn't pull away. "I knew you'd want to know the sports stuff. That this would make you realize time had passed."

"I missed so much," he said.

Alice squeezed his hand. "We missed so much, not having you with us. I missed so much." She smiled bravely at Itch, feeling his pain, and wishing things could be easier for him.

"And this little girl is Shy?" he asked.

Alice laughed. "Skye," she said. "Remember you chose the name when we were watching that old musical. Remember Sinatra and Brando?"

"Luck be a lady," Itch said.

Alice beamed, "Yes!"

"And this is you on Halloween?" he asked.

Alice laughed again, "No that's me in my chef whites. I went to cooking school so I could work with my aunt and uncle at P3, remember it?"

"This is amazing," Itch said softly. "It really does show time passing. I bet lots of people would like to have one of these. You're very talented."

Alice squeezed his hand, and this time he gripped her hand in return. "I don't know — many people wouldn't want to confront pictorial evidence of them getting older and older and older."

"Oh I think they would. Memories are worth keeping. I wish I had some."

"Oh honey," said Alice, "You're not old. You missed a lot, but you have the rest of your life now, the rest of our lives, and there will be memories, beautiful memories."

Itch strained to move a bit in the bed, hoisting himself up slightly, but he managed it successfully as Alice beamed, and then he said, "But your paper ends right here."

Alice took a marker out of her tote, leaned over and drew an arrow at the end of the time line. Then she wrote *this way to the future — it's gonna be amazing.*

A spark of recognition lit Itch's eyes this time, and he gazed at Alice in the way he used to. Without thinking, she rose and began kissing him. For the merest second he tensed, then Alice felt his lips relax against hers, and they floated along together in kisses that were so soft and tender, it was like the best sort of memory revisited.

Alice sat on the bed, leaning in against Itch, relaxing along his side, her arm around him, her head on his shoulder, and she sighed happily.

His voice grew raspy for a moment, and in an almost-whisper he said, "I used to dream you were here next to me like this."

"It wasn't a dream." Alice said.

Alice felt herself floating, rather than stepping on the ground, as she moved about the kitchen, making dinner for Emma and the kids. She pictured the future, and knew that one day soon Itch would be there with them, and he would be at the head of the dining table, where he belonged. There was no little voice in her head saying slow down, don't get ahead of yourself, because of course she knew he had much work to do before his recovery reached the point where he could leave the hospital and come home, but those were just the details, weren't they, the gears moving toward the joyous eventuality that at this moment she was picturing, and yearning to have as part of the blessed ho-hum of everyday. Everything in her longed for that moment, and it was as though it were a fact already, or so it seemed as she floated between the fridge and the stove, making sauce, rolling out pasta dough, and assembling a nice lasagna Bolognese.

When the phone rang, she jumped, and the first thought was that it was Itch, calling to chat with her, and how wonderful that was. She grabbed the phone, and answered it with a sing-songy, ultra cheerful "Hello!" Before she could continue and say something cute and flirty, she glanced at the little window in the phone, and could see by the caller I.D. that it was some sort of production company calling, not Itch at all. Was it Tom Angelico or his assistant?

"Ms. Catson?"

"I'm Alice Catson."

"This is Suzy Wilson at *You're Cooked*. We're booking the coming season, and wanted to include you in the show. You made it!"

"Wow! How fantastic!" Alice walked around the island, and sat at one of the stools, trying to catch her breath.

"We loved the little demo you filmed about how to use a Cuisinart. Usually people just have clips doing hobbies or at their restaurants."

"Oh thank you," said Alice, "I might have done that but it burned down."

"Yes," said Suzy, "We read that. Terrible. But dramatic, and a good story to tell."

Alice laughed. "Drama I have plenty of."

She listened as Suzy Wilson discussed their schedule. Alice scanned through her calendar as Suzy went over available dates, and they agreed on one not too far away, as Alice said, "I'm excited!"

"I'm sure you'll do great. We'll be in touch again the week before the show."

"Thanks so much. I'm super excited."

How about that! Alice had never really expected to be chosen for the show, and now she had a chance to compete — she would be competing. On camera. Against other chefs, chefs who cooked in restaurants every day. Suddenly Alice's mind raced, and her heart began to thunder. What had she done? She gazed off into space, terrified, then glanced at her watch, as though the timepiece would tell her how many days she had to prepare for what would likely be a humiliating debacle, then she looked once more out the window, and repeated the whole cycle. It seemed as though she were trapped in a time loop for quite a while, but after a relatively short time, she actually saw the watch, and realized that she had to complete the dinner, so in a semi-trance, Alice rose and did just that, wondering all the while would she be in a trance while on the show, and be one of those addlebrained chefs who fail and end up serving half-empty plates.

Skye and Julian arrived first. "I bumped into Dad outside," she said, "And he looked so miserable, I said he could come to dinner." Alice's brain, still out of focus, pictured Itch out there, magically recovered and arriving to claim his place at the table as she'd envisioned, then she quickly realized Skye meant Robin.

"What was he doing out there?" asked Alice, but Skye only shrugged. When the doorbell rang, Alice assumed it was Robin, and Skye went to let him in but came back with Emma instead. Alice barely had time to hug Emma before Cooper came bounding into the kitchen and instantly grew transfixed by her.

"Hello, you must be Cooper—I'm Emma," he said, blushing, then stumbled, mumbled, and tried to correct himself while both girls grinned at him. When Emma reached out and hugged him, he turned from mild pink to neon red.

"We spoke the first day I was here in town," Emma said, as Cooper flushed an even darker shade of red.

Alice smiled to witness this scene, never having observed her nephew flustered by a girl, but wanting to alleviate some of his agony, she said, "Let's all sit down in the dining room for a moment. Dinner will be ready shortly, but I have something to say." Alice observed each of the kids as a worried glance crossed all four faces. "Gee, we're not at war," she said. "I just got a phone call. I'm still in shock."

"Itch is dead?" asked Skye.

"Of course not," said Alice, "Geez."

"Is Kitty all right?" asked Cooper.

"What's wrong with you kids? Did you graduate from the college of gloom and doom?"

"Is there bad news about *Party Party Party*?" asked Julian

"It couldn't double burn down could it?" answered Alice. "No the news is about me. I got accepted for *You're Cooked*." Alice smiled, then clenched her teeth and grimaced, expressing her fear and nervousness.

"Wow, how amazing," said Emma, "You'll win it no question."

"Of course you will," said Skye.

"Who could outcook you," said Cooper.

"What's *You're Cooked?*" asked Julian.

Before anyone could fill him in, Robin, followed by Greg, entered the dining room. "Thanks for having us," said Robin improbably, staring down at the table, which had been set only for five.

Greg immediately sat in the empty chair next to Emma, offering her his hand, "I'm Greg. I'm a dentist."

Emma smiled, and shook his hand.

Greg then nodded curtly at Julian, gave Cooper a high-five, and looked at Skye with what seemed to be a combination of pain and annoyance.

"Let me help you," said Robin to Alice, and he followed her into the kitchen, as she mused that never before had those words come out of his mouth.

"What are you doing here?" she asked him, as she pulled two more place settings from the cabinet.

"Greg has been letting me sleep on his couch, you didn't know that?"

"You saw that girl at the table? She's Emma, one of the babies you switched. Or at least we think so."

Robin blanched. "She knows who I am?"

Alice pulled the heavy pan of lasagna from the oven and started walking toward the dining room. "Guess she's about to find out."

"Oh my God, I forgot, I have a meeting," Robin said, making a big show of glancing seriously at his watch. Tell Skye I'll call her later." Then he raced out of the kitchen and toward the front door, stopping only long enough to grab a couple of slices of garlic bread from the baskets on the counter.

Alice laughed to herself, thinking it was the only time she could remember him running away from a free dinner, and marveling that he lacked the hubris to ask her to pack him a to-go box. She entered the dining room as Greg was leaning toward Emma, saying, "How fascinating. You must make a huge difference in their lives."

Alice set the lasagna down, and returned to the kitchen for the salad and bread. When she took her seat, Greg was still talking to Emma, asking her many questions, which she answered as Skye looked on with a frown.

Alice grabbed the two antipasto platters that the kids had emptied and stacked them on a sideboard, then she turned and said, "All righty. Anyone hungry for dinner?"

"Skye loves lasagna," said Julian.

"Nobody doesn't love lasagna," said Emma, smiling.

"Where's Dad?" asked Skye.

"Said sorry, an urgent meeting," Alice answered with a mostly straight face, as she began to cut and serve the lasagna, handing each plate to Skye, who heaped some salad onto them and passed them down the table until everyone was served.

"Here," said Julian, "Don't forget the bread," and he set a slice on Skye's plate, and ignored everyone else.

"Let me help you," said Greg in an astonishing display of chivalry, and he served some garlic bread to Emma and himself, then handed the basket to Cooper, who was watching both him and Skye with interest.

"And you've been taking care of Skye's dad?" Greg asked Emma.

She briefly looked off toward where Robin had disappeared, then her focus snapped back and she realized he meant Itch, and she said, "No, I'm not in that wing yet. Maybe soon though."

"Where do you live?" he asked. "There's going to be a vacancy here soon."

Skye glared at Greg, as he blithely inserted a bite into his mouth. Julian stared at Skye with disbelief, and seemed to be reaching for her hand under the table.

"There is?" asked Alice. "Nobody told me that."

"Layla," said Greg. "Going back to Ontario."

"I didn't know you knew her well enough to know where she's from," said Skye frostily, as Julian put another piece of garlic bread on her plate. "Enough with the bread," she said crossly, then shook her head and said, "Sorry, geez."

"Canada, how lovely," said Emma. "It's so beautiful there, and the people are so nice. Wow, this is definitely prize winning lasagna."

Cooper, Greg and Skye laughed, as Alice said, "No they mean Ontario, California. A few miles inland."

After Alice had served chocolate cake with homemade strawberry gelato, Greg stood and leaned over Emma, smiling. "It was so nice to meet you. I hope to see you again soon. And be sure to call me if you need a cleaning or anything." Then he reached into his pocket and handed her a card, stopping first to write his cell phone number on the back. He smiled at Alice and said, "It was a wonderful dinner. Thanks for having me."

Who knew, thought Alice, Greg had game. Or did anyone call it that any more? Shortly thereafter Julian departed, perhaps after Skye whispered something to him, but what she said was unclear to Alice, who by this time was clearing the table with Emma's help. Skye walked back from seeing Julian to the front door, and scowled at Emma. "What was that all about?" she asked, enraged.

"Huh?" said Emma.

"You're trying to steal my fiancé. Why?"

"Skye!" said Alice, shocked at her daughter's nasty tone.

"I'm not trying to steal anyone," said Emma.

"Hey cuz, we're not Mormons. How many boyfriends can you have at one table?" quipped Cooper, finding his voice again for the first time of the evening.

"You know I'm going through a lot right now, and you're flirting all over him. I mean if flirt was slime, he'd be covered in ooze."

"Eww," said Alice, Emma, and Cooper simultaneously.

"So you're going back to Greg, and dropping Julian off at the clown depot?" asked Cooper.

"Shut up, Cooper," said Skye. "You smartass."

"I should go," said Emma. "Thanks for dinner. I'm sorry it didn't quite turn out as expected." Emma hugged Alice, then turned to Skye, "I'll talk to you in a few days when you calm down." Then she handed Greg's card to Skye, and walked toward the front door, with Alice following her.

When Alice returned, she looked at Skye and said, "That was really mean. I'm surprised at you."

"You ditched my dad, and I don't need you fixing up my fiancé."

"Are you nuts?" asked Alice, growing angry. "I didn't ask Greg here today. You did. Well you asked Robin, and he invited Greg. Are you going back to him?"

"Why are you so determined to define everything?" asked Skye, storming out of the kitchen and racing up the stairs.

"And you're sure that DNA test was correct?" asked Cooper, helping himself to another slice of cake.

"I'm beginning to wonder," answered Alice. "And you—how are you doing?" Alice smiled for a moment, then said softly, "You know Emma's the same age as Skye, right?"

"Once I marry her and we move to West Virginia, it won't matter at all that she's a few years older than me."

"West Virginia?"

"So it won't matter that she's my cousin."

Alice laughed. "Kid, you're one in a million."

Cooper nodded, shoved a giant piece of cake in his mouth, then mumbled through cake-encrusted teeth, "Yeah, that works in my favor, I figure."

"Everything going okay at school? Do they think you're here or at home?"

"Dunno. When it comes to school, the less anyone in charge thinks the better."

"What?" said Alice. "That's the opposite of true."

Cooper laughed. "You're a million years gone from school."

"I just figure *in loco parentis*, you know."

"The parents being loco is why I'm here."

Alice patted Cooper on the shoulder. "Just let me know if you need anything. And how you're doing at school, I guess. You're not failing anything, right? Or dealing drugs? Or doing drugs?"

Cooper took a long pause, looked up at the ceiling, squinted, and said, "What was that middle one?"

"Drugs aren't funny, Coop, I'm serious."

"Oh crapsky, Auntie, so you're saying I gotta stop dealing helium? What'll the kids do? They'll be so deflated."

Alice took Cooper's empty cake plate, loaded it in the dishwasher, and turned it on. "Early morning," she said, and headed toward the stairs. She stopped to look in on Skye on the way to her own room, and found her daughter hard at work making a list. "Wow," Alice said, "You're using pen and paper, not a device."

"Easier to destroy," said Skye, chewing on the end of her pencil. "Electronics are forever."

Alice entered the bedroom, sat on the end of Skye's bed, and looked around. It was still as charming as it was when Skye was in high school. The furniture was painted a Shabby Chic French blue with gray and green undertones, and the quilt on the double bed was an ethereal white. There were many pillows on the bed, some of them with little flowers, others with cottage stripes, some toile. The big bay window had cabinets below a charming window seat, padded with a cushion covered with a romantic cabbage rose print. For years Skye had sat in the window, talking on the phone with her girlfriends, and now the cushion, with its pale blue ground and deep pink flowers, was a little faded, making it even prettier. In the corner, sat an old wicker rocker in natural rattan. It was the sort of room nobody would ever want to leave, and when Skye moved inches away into the vacant apartment next to Kitty's, she all but duplicated the style of décor there. Baby steps, that's what Alice had called it. Now she felt like the old lady neighbor in *Breaking Away*, who looked at the bike-obsessed Dennis Christopher, and confided, 'He used to be as normal as apple pie.'

"So," she asked, "What do we have here?"

"Pros and cons," Skye answered, handing the list to Alice, who scanned it. At the top, she'd written *Julian* and *Greg* and below each name a plus and a minus and then there were a list of qualities.

"Let's see," said Alice, all the while wondering why her daughter wanted to be with either of the two boys. "Hmm, Julian. Creative. Affectionate. Sexy? Really?"

Skye nodded, looking miserable. "Don't go there," she said.

Alice continued, "And the negatives, a kid. Mommy issues. Clown obsessed." Alice laughed. "That's one way to say it."

"It all goes together," said Skye, her eyes shading over.

"What?"

"Okay, so if I tell you this, it's a secret. Nobody—and I mean nobody—can hear this. And he can never know I told you."

"Okay," said Alice, lowering her voice.

Skye jumped up, peered out the door, closed it tightly, and returned to her seat on the bed, as Alice, growing more and more apprehensive, scrutinized her daughter.

"Talk," said Alice, afraid of what she might hear, but then thinking how silly she was always to worry so much.

"So Julian's mom walked out on them when he was three."

Alice sighed, and felt a little corner of her heart open up toward Julian. "Oh, that's so sad."

"She gave Julian a bath and then she left. Not because of the bath." Skye looked down at her manicure for a moment, up toward her list, which Alice still held, then continued. "And she dressed him in his favorite clown pajamas."

A glimmer of light dawned, and Alice said, "Oh, no. Geez. Holy crap." She scrutinized her daughter for a moment. Was there any chance Skye was listening to herself?

"And one Halloween, maybe five years later," Skye continued, "Julian went as a clown. And he was sure he saw a glimpse of his mom, peering around from some bushes. And then he decided to be a clown every Halloween. And then, well, you know...."

Alice emitted a long, slow gust of air. "Good lord. That sounds like years of therapy needed. And I'm guessing no therapy actually performed."

Skye shook her head. "It's not like he's dangerous or anything."

"How old is Julian actually?"

"Twenty he says. College age. Not so much younger. I mean it's not like I'm anyone's idea of a mommy substitute. Right?" Skye looked imploringly at Alice.

Alice shook her head. "You're not a cougar, no, but you not being old enough to be his mom doesn't make him not crazy. Er sane. Or this relationship, whatever it is, a good idea. What is it exactly?"

"Who knows," said Skye. "Isn't that what I'm trying to figure out?"

"Well, I'm just saying those are pretty serious minuses. It's like you say plus: the guy is charming, sweet, rich, sexy, smart, and likes what you like, then you say negative: he's in jail for murder. Kind of negates the positives, don't you think?"

Skye snorted and scowled for a moment. "He's not in jail. Nobody's in jail, are they? So how is that even remotely the same?" She reached behind herself, grabbed several of her many pillows, vigorously punched a few to plump them up, and replaced them behind her back.

"In jail, insane. My point is, some negatives are so big they outweigh any number of very nice positives."

"Maybe this is a bad idea. You saying he's insane is just mean."

"Okay he's not insane, but he has issues, big issues."

Skye flicked her head to the side on hearing this, and answered, "Who doesn't have issues?"

"Quirks yes, eccentricities, yes, insecurities, yes, but issues like that, no. I just want you to see that this is serious. It's not something small like always wearing a baseball cap."

"I made the list, didn't I?" Skye's tone was filled with deepening resentment. "I'm considering both of them, aren't I?"

"Okay, let's see here. Greg. Plus: adult, good career, practical, reliable, stable, predictable. Sort of makes him sound like a good used car."

Skye nodded. "Exactly."

"And minus: dull, predictable." Alice gazed at her daughter. "Doubly predictable, huh? What about cheap?"

Skye nodded. "You came in as I was about to write that."

"Well hon, let me save you some time. The reason why you can't decide between these guys is they're both the same—Mr. Wrong. It's like you're shopping at Walmart for a wedding gown, and can't decide which one you like. It doesn't help to make a list about what are the pros—machine washable, sturdy plastic zipper, veil that can become a fishing net after."

Skye laughed. Alice watched her giggle, and started to feel relieved. Maybe she would come to her senses after this conversation.

"Silly," said Skye. "They don't sell wedding gowns at Walmart."

"There's a reason for that," said Alice. "You're in a hurry here. For no good reason. You haven't met anyone close to Mr. Right. Ever in your whole life. If you did, you wouldn't need a list, because you'd be madly in love, and you'd know you belonged with him, and that your whole life was meant to be shared with him. Not should you settle for a cheapskate like your step dad, or a clown with his color hair and eyes."

Skye gasped for a second, put her hand over her mouth, and her eyes opened wide. She looked toward the window, and gazed out. "So what—I dump them both, and then I'm all alone."

Alice took Skye's hand. "You're not alone. You have a family. You have friends. And you're young and gorgeous. You met them, didn't you? Give yourself time to meet the true love of your life. Stop trying to settle. You're still just a kid. Not to mention that this whole conundrum is just a smokescreen to help you avoid dealing with your own life."

Skye groaned deeply and said, "I'll think about it."

Alice rose from the bed and kissed her daughter on the cheek, hugging her tightly. "You're going to be just fine, I promise you."

"Maybe you're just too romantic," sighed Skye, "All these years dreaming about Itch."

"Dreams do come true, you'll see." Alice smiled as she left her daughter's room, hoping that Skye was now on a better track, and that she could worry less about her.

Alice slept well, and early the next morning still felt herself almost floating as she entered Itch's room. She beamed at Itch, who was out of the bed and sitting in a chair, trying to lift his legs up and down, mostly with success. "Oh wow, look at you," she said joyfully. "You're doing great!"

Itch squinted a bit as he looked at her, and Alice could see he was trying to make sure who she was, so she grabbed one of the name tags and scrawled *Ally* on it, then affixed it to her shirt as Itch nodded. She walked over to him, took his hand, and said softly, "You know, maybe they could get an eye doc to give you a checkup. You think?"

"More than just my eyes are fuzzy."

Alice smiled. "Yeah, you're right. It will all unkink soon. Go ahead, show me your leg lifts."

Itch raised his hand, and waved it at Alice's face. "What's all that? Ally doesn't have those wrinkles," he said. Alice could see his mind whirring, and she knew he was still wondering was she really herself.

"You don't remember the accident, I guess. They're not wrinkles, they're scars. But you know, I could have them fixed. Do you think I should?"

Itch strained to lift his leg to hip height, grunting, "Why," then he lowered the leg, lifted the other, and continued, "Not?"

"Okay then," said Alice, "I'll call the doctor." She blushed, and confided softly, "This is the first time in a long time I've cared what I look like."

Itch glanced down at himself, at the limbs whose muscles had been sleeping far too long to be the strong and robust version of the only self he could remember, and gave her a wry glance. "Doctors aren't so scary. I got doctors in and outta here all the time."

Alice smiled. "And they're helping you a lot. Look how great you're doing. They'll be writing you up in the medical journals."

"I'll tell you what's scary, I'll tell you."

Alice reached out, touching Itch gently on the shoulder. "What's scaring you, honey? Don't worry, you're going to be fine. The worst is behind you now. It's all sunshine ahead."

Once again Itch looked puzzled, and he said, "Stan, that's what scary."

"Your brother is playing tricks on you?" she asked, certain it was untrue.

"He says when I'm out of here, I'll go work with him. I told him I don't want a paper route. Day after day the same thing. It's like he's clueless. Money is all that matters to Stan." Itch by this time had stopped the leg lifts, and was lowering and raising his arms, which he could do and still speak fluently, something Alice considered a huge step forward.

"Stan hasn't had a paper route since he was a kid. He's an accountant. You'd have to go to school to do what he does. But maybe he wants you to help in his office until you're ready to make choices about what you want to do."

Itch looked terrified and truly despondent, and Alice didn't really know how to help him. It was just so much to assimilate, and she could imagine how difficult it all would be. "Look, honey, don't worry about that. You already have a job, right now, and your job is to get well. And I'm really proud of how hard you're working. And of what a good job you're doing."

Itch smiled. "You do sound like Ally. She always really believed in me."

"I still do," she whispered.

Later, Alice found herself at work, sitting at the conference table with Misty, Tom, and her sister Totsie. Her mind floated in and out of the conversation, because she was so consumed with thoughts about Itch and the future they would share.

"The thing we're going to work on today is what they call Brandy," said Totsie.

Tom looked at his watch, and Alice assumed he was wondering if they could get away with having cocktails way before noon.

"What?" said Misty, her eyes glazing over a bit.

"Brandy. How they decide what your message is and what you stand for."

Alice and Tom glanced at each other briefly as both at once said, "Branding."

"I'm not a cow you know," said Misty, adjusting her cleavage.

Tom smiled and said, "Your brand is your identity in the public. It's why people like you — what of you they're buying."

"Finally," said Misty. "I was afraid they still didn't know who I am."

"That's what we're here to change," said Totsie, turning a laptop toward Misty. "I have a couple food stars here for you to see. Look at this one — she's made a fortune. Cooking is super easy. She has everything already in little bags in the fridge."

Misty nodded, as Tom resumed focusing on his cell phone. Together she and Totsie watched the clip of the show, and Misty said, "That's a good idea. Simple food that starts in a baggie.

"They don't come that way," said Alice. "Someone has to do that prep work."

Totsie glared at Alice. "The point is success, not how chopped peppers get into a baggie."

"I could do this," said Misty, "And I don't have that annoying voice. That Robin Roberts better watch out. I'm taking her down."

"I think Robin Roberts is a newscaster," said Tom.

"Whoever," said Misty.

"Now check this out," said Totsie. She clicked the computer, and raptly they watched a woman making food that was mostly prefab, with an occasional added ingredient in order to simulate cooking.

Misty grew visibly excited. "That's it. That's IT!"

Totsie nodded. "She's brilliant, isn't she. And the boobs are first rate too."

"And that's why it's Angel Food," trilled Misty, animatedly. "Because the food is heaven sent. Nobody has time to cook. They need a cake now. The maid is too busy cleaning to go to a bakery. So we take a mix and throw in some carrot shreds, and it's homemade cake. Or guests pop in and the maid is gone, but there's some brie in the fridge, so you toss on some nuts and cranberries to make it special. Without all that greasy, butter soaked dough." She turned toward Alice, pointed accusatorially, and scowled.

Totsie jumped up from her seat, twirled around in a circle, and sat back down. "It's all just so thrilling, I'm so ecstatic for you. You're gonna be a huge star."

"I've been brandied," said Misty. "You got all this, right," she said to Alice, who nodded.

"You want to copy that TV blonde who doctors more than cooks," said Alice.

"How dare you!" said Misty. "She's just worried I won't need her with my new Brand. Brand? Or Brandy?"

"Brandy," said Totsie.

"Brand," said Alice and Tom.

"And by the way, now that we're all here, I have something urgent to discuss," said Misty, pointing her finger at Alice, "About you." Alice met Misty's gaze and Tom looked up worriedly from his phone. "We've discussed this a million times. I gave you the card.

You've got to fix all that, doesn't she Tots?" Misty wagged her finger toward Alice's forehead. "I could have young fans, and you'd scare them. You're going to my doctor this week, and we'll pay for it, right Tom? It's a necessary expense." Misty looked toward her husband, who was glancing at Alice in an embarrassed way.

Tom said, "Misty! I can't believe you'd say something like that. So caustic. It's not like you at all." Tom looked deeply disturbed as he gazed at his wife, who decided to hold her ground. Alice wondered how such an intelligent, savvy man could be so selectively blind.

"Tom. Tommy. Tommy sweetheart, you must be hearing me wrong. You know I'm crazy about Ally. I want what's best for her and the show is all. And I offered to pay, I mean like a present." She smiled sweetly at her husband, and stroked her cleavage as he watched, not at all mesmerized.

"We can't ask Ally to do that. It's not just wrong, it's illegal," he mumbled.

"You know what," said Alice, "It's fine. I'll go."

"About time," said Misty, attempting to simulate an expression of triumph on her frozen face. "And you can pay us back out of your salary."

Tom raised his hand a moment, saying, "Of course not. She's on our insurance anyway, and that'll probably cover it and if not, it's our gift. I'm really sorry, Ally. Please don't feel you have to do anything like this."

"She does too," said Misty, reaching under the table to nudge Tom with her foot. Then she raised her hand imperiously, clicked one button on her cell phone, and everyone listened as she insisted to the doctor's office manager that an immediate appointment was not only desired, but absolutely essential. "Perfect," she said, as though any other outcome were impossible, and rising from her seat, she turned toward Alice and said, "Let's go."

"Now? In the middle of work?" asked Alice.

"Now is always the best time for everything. Besides our meeting is over, brilliant work was done, and now you have to get laser-zapped or whatever he decides, and we can't have your face peeling off into the food, so there could be a delay of a couple days. So I might as well have a chem peel too."

Both Alice and Tom winced at this imagery, and Tom said, "You don't have to do this now or ever. Or you can take some time to think about it."

"No, I said it's fine," said Alice, smiling at Tom. "I really appreciate your sensitivity and generosity. You're always so nice and so understanding, and I really thank you so much."

"What about me?" said Misty, "I'm the one who's fixing your face and your life. Where's the thanks for my generousness?"

Tom said, "Her life isn't broken. Geez Misty, what's up with you today?"

Misty looked around for her purse, rooted in it for her car keys, and scowled at Tom as though he were severely out of the loop. "If someone's life is working, they don't have scars." She glared at him pointedly, conveying her disapproval of his entire reaction, then she snapped her fingers at Alice, saying, "Let's go, chop, chop." Then Misty emitted peals of laughter as everyone gazed at her a little perplexed. "Did you hear what I just said? Chop, chop. To Ally. Get it?"

Alice blanched, imagining Misty right there in a doctor's office beside her. Quickly she said, "You don't have to come with me. Besides, I'd need my car to get home."

Misty shook her head with frustration. "You know, sometimes you act like we're not even friends. I'm giving up my day to take you. What if they have to put you to sleep?" She waved her hands at everyone, "Oh calm down, not like a dog. Everyone—okay most everyone—wakes up. But ninety five year olds probably shouldn't have face lifts, now should they. That's on them."

Misty gave her cleavage one final shimmy to adjust it back into her bra, as though somehow she were dealing with runaway breasts, leaned over and planted a very slobbery kiss on Tom, then firmly took hold of Alice, and strong-armed her out the door, despite Alice's protests. "Oh for God's sake—I'll bring you back to your car." As they walked, she giggled now and then, occasionally saying, "Chop, chop."

It all had seemed so easy, and Alice marveled that she felt lighter after having had that laser procedure. Yes, it was possible she'd need one or more other treatments, but it felt as though something had changed inside her, as well as on her face. She walked cheerfully, gingerly touching the bandages on her forehead. Soon they'd be off, and she would be a new person, maybe not as young as her old self, but somehow less damaged. Wanting to thank Itch for encouraging her to take this step, her first stop after being dropped back at work by Misty was to drive to the hospital. She strolled the corridor gaily, her feet springing along, something she was becoming more and more accustomed to, now that her life finally was heading in a direction about which she could feel not just cheerful, not just optimistic, but overjoyed.

As she peeked into Itch's room, he was there leaning on Frankie, the therapist, who was helping him back down against the pillows in his bed. His hand slid and came to rest against Frankie's hip but instead of pulling it away, he seemed to be pulling her closer. Saying, "There you go, bud," Frankie stepped back and away from Itch, stopping only to pat his cheek with her hand.

Alice cringed for a moment, then dashed the ludicrously suspicious thoughts from her mind. "Anybody home?" she said cheerily. Frankie smiled at Alice, and waved at Itch on her way out the door.

Itch's eyes opened wide. He glared at Alice, not with a lack of recognition, but with a kind of fear. Did she look so hideous, Alice wondered, knowing that she hadn't looked that awful with the small bandages on her forehead and temple. Surely he wasn't having some horror movie flashback. "Don't worry, hon, it's me. Not the walking dead," she said, smiling. "I took your advice about the scars."

Itch began panting. He gasped for breath. His eyes opened and closed rapidly, as he attempted to regain his equilibrium. He began spitting out words in between deep gasps, as Alice was about to ring for a nurse. "We were on my bike, moonlight. Wedding. Brian and Lauren. Was it legal? He said it was." And he stopped to catch his breath, taking a sip of the water that Alice handed him. "And we drove up the coast on my bike, and I said, 'You're so pregnant now, should you be on this thing, we can borrow Stan's car,' and Ally said 'No, let's go up the coast. Look at this pier, let's go out and stand in the moonlight, and say some real vows.' And I laughed. Weren't the other ones real, and Ally said, 'Say some personal vows, things we would always remember,' and I said, 'What, you already forgot the wedding?' And Ally laughed, and I drove onto that pier.

It was too rickety, too old, but we slipped around that barricade, and just stopped near the end of the pier." Itch gasped, pausing for a moment just to breathe.

"Take it easy, honey, slow down and catch your breath. It's okay, we're both okay. Here, drink some more water." Alice touched his arm gently, holding the glass as he sipped from the straw.

"My foot was on the ground and the bike was fine, but Ally said 'Go closer to the water, let's be in the moonlight, it's more romantic,' so we went right up to the edge, but then the lights flashed and the pier jumped and bounced, and it all rippled, cracking with a loud noise like thunder, and Ally bounced on the back of the bike, and I thought what about the baby, but I couldn't say get off, or back up because the ground was shimmying."

"It was an earthquake," said Alice softly.

"Earthquake. I forgot, yeah I remember. And the water washed up, and the pier gave way, and my other foot was hooked to the pedal, and we went down into the water. And Ally went into the water, I saw blood, I was terrified, blood, was the baby being born in the water in the earthquake."

"My face scraped against the pier as we fell off it," said Alice.

"And I turned to push Ally free of the bike, hoped she'd float 'til I could turn around and grab her and pull us to shore. Freezing, it was freezing. But my foot was stuck, and the bike pulled me down. I yanked and yanked on my foot, but my boot was stuck. And I was swallowing water, I pushed against the bike, but it was heavy, and I was swallowing water. And then I couldn't see Ally, couldn't swim to save her."

Alice sighed, and said as calmly as possible, "I tried to free your foot. I dove down to where you were, and finally I did get your foot loose, and I shoved and you floated up with me, and I pulled you to shore, and there were sirens going off, someone called 911, someone had seen us. And the ambulance came, and they gave you oxygen, and they took us to the hospital, and I went into labor even though it was a couple weeks early. And you were in a coma." Tears ran down Alice's face as she looked into Itch's terrified eyes. "They said you'd never wake up. They wanted to turn off the breathing machines and they did, but you didn't die. They didn't know you like I did. I knew you'd wake up as soon as you could." She smiled softly and squeezed Itch's hand, pressing it to her heart.

He pulled his hand away, and scowled at Alice. "This is all your fault. I would've been a normal guy if we didn't take the bike on the rickety pier for some dopey romantic nonsense."

"I know," she said. "I'm sorry. I was just a kid."

"You should have known better," he answered.

"I know," said Alice, tears streaming down her cheeks. "Oh please say you forgive me, that you don't hate me."

"Stop crying," said Itch, still agitated. "You know I hate it when you cry."

Alice couldn't stop though, and as much as she tried to refocus her mind to other things, to suppress the tears pouring from her eyes, they came like a waterfall, her sobs uncontrollable, almost as though it was the first time she'd ever cried about this tragedy, the first time she really let go and let it out. "I'm a terrible person," she sobbed, "I know it. I can't be trusted with anything. I'm so sorry I ruined your life. I know you can never forgive me now."

"Oh, get over yourself. Do we need to be washed away in another tidal wave?"

Alice looked at Itch then. He seemed calmer. He'd made a joke, but it didn't feel like a joke. The front of her shirt was soaked with her tears. She shrugged. "Guess I lost a few pounds today."

"What'cha gonna do?" Itch said. "Eventually I'll be outta here, and my band will be running, and I'll be on tour, and there'll be money and traveling, just like I always dreamed. And when that Baba Wawa woman interviews me, I'll have a good story to tell. Not that I can remember any of it. Well, whatever. Like I always said, take a summer, go cross country. Nothing has to be different."

Alice thought for a moment about all her responsibilities. Once Itch was released, it would be a huge relief financially, but she had other bills to pay. She couldn't just go cross country for a summer. "Things don't feel different, but life is different. I had to be a grown up, pay bills, take care of things and people."

"So you're telling me to give up my dreams and go deliver papers with Stan?"

Alice squeezed Itch's arm. "No, of course not. All you have to do now is get well. And eventually things will feel different, more grown up and maybe you'll want different things than you did at eighteen. You'll catch up."

Itch laughed. "Keep thinking Ally, that's what you're good at."

Alice had prepared and prepared, making meals daily from an assortment of improbable ingredients suggested by everyone she knew. She'd committed to memory a collection of recipes she could use and adapt to a variety of ingredients. Her knife kit was complete with everything she could imagine needing, including shellfish crackers, lobster picks, a tweezers for fish bones, and a mallet. She had cheesecloth, parchment, twine, and even some rubber bands. Most of the chefs wore the jackets they normally used at their restaurants, but Alice decided to bring one of her old fashioned aprons—they were sweet and sort of chic.

Pulling smoothly into a spot of the studio parking lot, Alice took a deep breath. She was ready, as ready as she could hope to be. She glanced in the car mirror; her face looked good. The scars were barely visible and were now easily hidden by makeup. She wondered if there would be a TV makeup person, or would she be allowed to go on camera as she was. The show lasted only an hour, but Alice knew it took much longer to create, and she was told the taping would take all day. She exited the car, carrying her knife kit, a tote bag with not one but two aprons, and an actual chef's jacket.

Her feet pressed forward, as she followed signs with arrows labeled with the logo for *You're Cooked,* and in her mind began to play a series of hopes, prayers, and wishes, like a mantra. *Let them all be in a good mood…. No noisy wackos…. No offal…. Nothing I never heard of….*

Nothing alive I have to kill…. All be in a good mood…. And it kept repeating, changing only slightly, until she reached her destination, then she simply tried to keep in her head everything that she needed, and to shove the terror far to the back of her mind.

It all moved forward in a blur, then she was standing at her station, one chef to her right, two to her left, and the host was describing the ingredients they'd have to use to make an appetizer in twenty minutes. There was ground turkey, which most chefs hated because it easily dried out, rainbow chard, a package of pre-fab mac and cheese, and some marshmallow peeps. Alice grabbed a couple of bowls and dashed to fridge and pantry. It was as though she could hear the ticking of a giant clock, a clock bigger than Big Ben, a clock louder than a heartbeat, and she knew the time would be gone in what felt like twenty seconds rather than twenty minutes. But she was hearing something else, opera music. Now and then, the guy to her left would let loose with a bit of an aria, causing the other chefs to wince. Alice wished she'd brought that noise-blocking headset, but no, she'd just have to focus and block out the noise.

She scooped some boiling water into a sauce pot, and dropped in the macaroni. While two sauté pans heated, Alice chopped some onions, red peppers, and tomatoes, separated and chopped the stems from the chard, and emptied some sun dried tomatoes into a cheesecloth square and tied it. Then she began sautéing the onions and peppers in one pan, the turkey and the chard stems in another. Quickly she mixed up a dough, adding the cheese packet from the mac and cheese to it, and with a cutter from her knife kit, smoothly cut some biscuits and tucked them onto a sheet pan and into the oven.

That guy, that idiot opera guy, was walking through her station, singing "behind you," and continued singing until he returned.

"You," said Alice, "Be quiet." Then she almost fainted to think she'd done that.

The opera idiot laughed. "Bossy lady," he sang, even more loudly.

"I hope you can cook better than you sing," Alice said, as the other two chefs laughed.

She added the sun dried and fresh tomatoes to the onions and let it simmer. Then she dashed to grab some soup plates and set them on the counter in front of her. Everyone turned to stare at her then because nobody else was ready; Alice wasn't ready either but she wanted it all laid out. She checked the biscuits, cooking perfectly. She checked the mac, not quite done, but time to be drained, which she did and added some to the turkey along with some of the sauce, stirred it, then turned down the heat. She chopped up the marshmallow peeps, added them to the sauce skillet along with a dash of vinegar. Working more swiftly than she thought possible, she dunked the chard leaves into the giant pot of boiling water, then laid them neatly on the counter. Quickly she centered some of the ground turkey on each, and rolled them up into little packets. The clock, where was the clock? She had three minutes. Should she return them to the pan and risk it? Swiftly Alice set the stuffed chard rolls into the pan with the sauce and let the flavors infuse, even if only for a moment. She tasted everything, added a little more salt and pepper, then pulled the biscuits from the oven. She chopped a little mint for the sauce, tossed it in, reserving some for garnish, and then turned around and lifted the rolls back from the sauté pan into the serving plates, added some sauce on top and some mint, with a biscuit to the side of each, just as time was called. Everyone, including Alice, raised their hands.

Then she was standing in front of the judges as they were being introduced. She recognized three of them, a nice Mexican guy, a pregnant blonde, an Indian woman, and some new guy who looked familiar, but whose name she didn't quite catch. First was the singing freak, who had made a turkey burger with sautéed chard and mac and cheese. He put one peep on top of each.

The blonde judge said, "Maybe more of your creativity could have gone into repurposing these ingredients instead of singing."

The Indian woman said, "But mine isn't dry, and it's a pretty good burger, and you used the right amount of garlic in the chard sauté. It's not creative, but it tastes pretty good."

"What am I supposed to do with this, play rubber ducky?" asked the Mexican chef, holding up the marshmallow peep, as opera dude shrugged.

The familiar looking judge began to speak, and suddenly Alice felt her knees almost give way under her. It was Johnny Badass! But he was older, not the young barely-thirty-something guy on the TV show. He was her age.

The host, notoriously observant, spotted Alice and said, "Uh-oh, we have another one. It's that New Orleans accent, makes the women swoon."

Johnny laughed and said, "It's the *Fish Called Wanda* effect."

He's a movie buff, she thought, like me. He smiled rakishly toward Alice, who locked her knees in place, and tried to erase the memory of all those nights she'd fallen asleep on the couch with Johnny's voice in the background.

Next up was her dish. The Mexican chef said, "I love this. I can't believe you infused so much flavor so quickly. I'm going to steal that trick with the sun dried tomatoes."

The blonde said, "Clever the way you split up the mac and cheese, and that cheesy flavor really comes through in these biscuits."

The Indian woman said, "Maybe a touch more spice—some chili flakes in the sauce."

"Do you always dress like you escaped from *Downton Abbey*?" Johnny asked, as Alice just looked down at her quaint apron. "Is this cumin?" he continued. "Seems a little heavy to me. And the mac in the roll could be a little more cooked. Biscuit could be a little more flakey."

Alice was incensed. "I didn't use cumin," she said, thinking her biscuits were perfect.

"Maybe you should have," said Johnny.

Alice cocked her head at him, smiled just to be polite, and asked, "So which is it, too much cumin or not enough?"

Johnny grinned, saying in his twangiest voice, "Wow, you're tough as nails and twice as sharp!"

Then the blonde smiled, but she stood up for Alice, saying, "I could eat a million of these biscuits."

Johnny answered, saying, "Honey lamb, you're pregnant. To you everything tastes as good as a cold collard sandwich."

She looked bewildered for a moment, then said mischievously, "I'm not from down yonder and I don't speak country—I don't know if that's a compliment or an insult, but these are fantastic biscuits." Everyone laughed then, as the blonde leaned in very close to Johnny and took the unfinished biscuit off his plate. Alice hoped the chef's husband wasn't watching, because his pregnant wife was clearly enamored.

Next was the organic, natural, vegetarian chef, who worked at an ashram. She'd made a salad of the chard, with a slab of toasted sourdough and a thin turkey burger.

"Was it hard for you to use the turkey? I know you're a vegetarian," said the Mexican chef.

The woman nodded. "I haven't touched meat in twenty years."

"So I guess you didn't taste it?" asked Johnny. "If it were any dryer, it could be worn as a sandal."

"Sorry about that, chef," said the vegetarian, bowing toward Johnny with both hands together as though she were praying.

"I don't taste the peeps," said the Indian judge.

"I ran out of time, so sorry," said the vegetarian.

"Missing an ingredient doesn't automatically disqualify you," said the host, "It just depends if anyone else made worse errors."

The final candidate was up, and had made a pastitsio.

"This one of my favorite Greek dishes," said the Mexican chef. "Nice presentation to serve it like this in soufflé dishes."

"Mine's cold," said Johnny, holding up a forkful and then letting it fall back into the ramekin. "And where's the chard?"

"It was supposed to be a sauté on the side, but I kind of missed it. Sorry."

Then all the contestants were in the back, drinking bottled water and waiting to hear who'd been eliminated. Alice wagged her finger at opera dude, saying, "Stop trying to sabotage people by making noise. Do it with your food." The guy just sneered at her and began singing something from *Rigoletto*.

"I know it's me," said Maya, the vegetarian.

"No, they were down on me too," said the Greek chef. "We both missed ingredients."

"But yours didn't taste like shoes," said Maya.

Then they were back in front of the judges, and Maya was proven right and eliminated. The three remaining contestants returned to their stations again, as the entrée basket was unveiled. It contained hanger steak, dried blueberries, carrot juice, and bulgur wheat, not the whole grain kind from Bob's Red Mill but some paler, instant version from Trader Joe's, which looked more like couscous.

After setting the grill pan on two of the burners to heat, and dousing the blueberries with some boiling water, Alice poured the carrot juice into a skillet and put it on high, then dashed for some ingredients. Working quickly, she donned some gloves and began removing the silver skin from the meat and separating it into four portions, which she coated with a rub she'd made on the fly while gathering ingredients. To her left, the opera guy was banging on the meat, which he had sliced oddly, and the noise from the two pans he was using as a mallet was thunderous. Everyone looked toward him, he shrugged, grabbed two cleavers and began whacking away at it, not with the blade edge but the top, resulting in only marginally less noise.

Working quickly, with her body turned to the side so she could keep an eye on the rapidly boiling carrot juice, Alice mixed up some corn bread, added the drained blueberries and poured it into mini muffin tins and shoved them into the oven. Almost without thinking, she added bits of butter to the reduced carrot juice, and removing the boiling water from the stove top, added the wheat to a sauté pan with splashes of a couple different broths and a sprig of rosemary. She grabbed the carrot juice pan and set it to the side and she quickly peeled a few baby carrots and steamed them in a little water and butter. She checked the clock but a scream from the Greek chef drew her attention.

He'd portioned the meat into kabobs after making what looked like a tabouleh, but in cutting the steak, he'd cut his finger and blood spurted out all over the meat. He grabbed for some gloves, then went to rinse the meat, but as he kept working blood dripped into the tabouleh. Alice felt badly for him and said, "Gosh, are you okay?" The guy grimaced in pain, but kept working. Meanwhile Opera dude was singing and running his food processor, apparently grinding up the bulgur. Alice glanced at the clock again, set the steaks on the grill pan and dashed for some dinner plates. She turned the steaks and glanced at the clock. She had a minute to breathe. Flipping her board, she chopped some parsley, added it to the almost-done wheat, removing the stalk of rosemary. She pulled the corn muffins, nicely studded with blueberries, from the oven and began plating, finishing with maybe six seconds to spare.

A medic had attended to the Greek chef's cut, and he was bandaged as they stood before the judges for the second time. Opera dude was first, and had made chicken fried steak, dusted with the ground bulgur instead of flour, and a salad with carrot blueberry vinaigrette.

"Your steak is tough," said the Mexican judge. "You can't slice this meat with the grain, you should know that."

"I do know that," said Opera dude assertively, "But there wasn't time to butcher an anaconda sized piece of beef."

"The other two contestants did," said the blonde. "But this is a very nice salad, fresh and healthy."

"It's missing something," said Johnny. "There's no starch on the plate, just a sliver of meat and some greens. Is this chicken fried spa food?"

Next was the Greek chef, whose food looked good but the judges didn't want to eat it. "It's not just all this," said the blonde, pointing to her belly, "It's blood. We can't really taste food covered with your blood. We could get sick."

The Greek chef nodded apologetically. "I understand."

"And what did you make?" the host asked Alice.

"I made a grilled hanger steak with bulgur pilaf in a carrot butter drizzle with baby carrots and blueberry corn muffins," said Alice.

"I can't believe all you did in thirty minutes," said the Indian chef. "This is delicious."

Alice smiled at her, as Johnny interrupted. "I like my meat rare. This is quite a bit over."

"It's hanger steak, needs to be medium," said Alice, trying to be pleasant.

"We don't fruit up our corn muffins in the South," said Johnny.

"Maybe you should," said Alice, unable to resist a comeback, as Johnny looked up at her with that same devilish grin.

"I love these muffins," said the blonde.

It was obvious that the Greek chef would be eliminated and he was, so Alice was stuck going head to head with that noisy opera singing idiot. They stood at their stations again, as the dessert basket was unveiled. It contained an already baked small cheesecake, some pecans, frozen strawberries, and a jalapeno pepper. Once again Alice dashed for ingredients, racing first to the fridge so Opera dude couldn't snake away all the eggs.

She set a pan of sugar on the heat to caramelize with a sliver of jalapeno, then quickly chopped some pecans in the Cuisinart, dumping them back into a bowl. Without even taking a breath, she added sugar and butter to the food processor, whirled it, then added the eggs and dry ingredients and some of the pecans, pulsing them into a dough, which she portioned into a dozen cookies and popped into the oven. Then she yanked the jalapeno and dumped the rest of the pecans into the caramel and poured it onto a sheet pan to cool.

Working as swiftly as possible, Alice separated some eggs, added milk and cream and began making a custard for ice cream. She swapped out the Cuisinart bowl for a clean one and chopped some strawberries in it. She stirred the custard, which wasn't quite hot enough to worry about and chopped up the cheesecake into some chunks. Then she stood at the stove, stirring the custard as it came to a simmer and strained it into a pitcher. Just as she was ready to take it to the ice cream machine, she saw Opera dude dash over there with a bunch of stuff. He hadn't even made a custard, not that Alice saw, but he was now ladling ingredients into the ice cream machine. She raced to the blast chiller and inserted her custard.

Alice looked at the clock. She checked the cookies, which needed maybe nine more minutes. Shaking her head, she dumped the defrosted strawberries from the Cuisinart and added more frozen ones to the bowl, pulsing quickly, then she ran for the now cool custard and added it, incorporating air as she whirled it, but knowing it was far from ice cream. Grabbing the cut cheesecake and a sheet pan, she ran for the cold plate, looking at the ice cream machine, as Opera dude struggled with it. What poured out was a gloppy, wet mess, so he inserted it again.

Alice shook her head again, set the sheet pan on the cold plate with the cheesecake chunks to one side and the partially whipped strawberry custard to the other. Then she looked around for a hand mixer, which she couldn't see, but managed to grab an immersion blender. Working across the mixture, Alice whirled and stirred with the hand blender, hoping to gain as much silkiness as possible, but knowing it would never be true ice cream. It seemed to be working somewhat, though. It was chilled and it was airy. Stirring the now-frozen cheesecake chunks into the almost-ice cream, Alice removed the pan from the cold plate and shoved it into the blast chiller.

She had five minutes left, and the cookies were now cooling on the counter. She grabbed her mallet, whacked away at the candied pecans, breaking them up into manageable pieces, then ran with the cookies to the blast chiller and back for some plates. Four minutes. She removed everything from the blast chiller, tasting her ice cream and thinking it wasn't bad but not her best. Quickly she assembled ice cream sandwiches between the cookies, rolling each edge in the candied pecans and setting them back on the cold sheet pan. Would it melt in the remaining ninety seconds? Alice was unsure. She had to plate, though, so she sprinkled some candied pecans on each plate and added an ice cream sandwich. She was done.

She first took a breath when standing before the judges. Opera dude had made strawberry jalapeno mousse cheesecake with pecans. After all that subterfuge—his ice cream was a mousse? And he just smeared it over the cheesecake? Alice began to feel positive about the game. Maybe she actually could have won.

"So was that a strategy, bogarting the ice cream machine to produce this mousse?" asked the Mexican judge, as Opera dude smiled, but said nothing.

"The taste isn't bad, but wow that jalapeno packs a punch," said the Indian chef.

"You didn't really do anything with the cheesecake," said the blonde, inserting a big forkful into her mouth.

"Sometimes an ingredient is good enough on its own," said Johnny. "Is that the case here?"

"I put out great taste and pure flavors," said Opera dude. "Nothing prissy or pretentious." He glared at Alice.

Then it was her turn, and she described her ice cream sandwich.

"Do I have any cheesecake in here?" asked the Indian chef.

"There are chunks of it in the ice cream," said the blonde.

"This isn't really what I'd call ice cream," said Johnny. "It's just not airy enough." He was about to say something more, but he took another bite and his eyes opened wide. "I think I cracked a tooth on these nuts," he said, holding his mouth. "You must have left a shell in your pecans."

"Oh my goodness, I'm so sorry. I did it quickly—I didn't even think of shells," said Alice, mortified. Her pecans came from the farmer's market and were always perfectly clean.

Then she was in the break room, waiting with that idiot, who spent the time boasting about what he would do with the prize money. And then he actually won. Alice wasn't that surprised; if you crack a judge's tooth, can you really win a cooking competition?

She drove home quietly, thinking about Johnny and how they got the ass part of his name correct. What a jerk! What a total pig. Johnny Badass? Should be Johnny Big Ass. Had she really cracked his tooth? Alice smiled. Maybe it was worth it. She cast her thoughts back, trying to envision those pecans, to recall any stray bits of shell, but in her mind they appeared pristine. He just had it out for her, for no reason she could identify. Maybe she should have put some cumin in the ice cream. That smug jerk! You just never know, Alice thought. Someone can seem so appealing on TV, and then in person he turns out to be the world's biggest jerk, sexy accent or not. Maybe she should make that brittle again for more of the people who annoyed her. Alice chuckled some more, feeling less badly than she'd expected. At least she made it through to the end of the contest, and she'd produced pretty good food. And it wasn't as terrifying as she'd anticipated, just fraught with idiots.

Alice pulled into her driveway, grabbed her stuff, and walked toward the door; but a man was standing there, about to ring the bell. "Can I help you?" she asked.

"Cooper Briarwood live here?" he asked.

"And you are?" Alice felt the adrenalin still pumping from the show, but in her heart, she began to cringe. He looked official, but he wasn't wearing any uniform, so that was good news. Oh dear, was he from the school? Was Cooper ditching school?

The man pulled a badge from his pocket, and said, "Detective Longworth. I'm following up on a complaint about identity theft, filed by, um, Robin…."

Alice by then had opened the door, and said, "Come in. Please have a seat." She led the officer to the living room, and dropped her stuff on a cabinet, saying, "I can make some coffee if you'd like, or tea. Or would you like a soda?"

"Is Cooper Briarwood here?" he asked again.

"Let me run upstairs and check," said Alice as calmly as she could manage. She dashed up the stairs, hoping to warn Cooper before he had to confront this detective, who obviously wasn't one of his cop buddies. He was at the desk in Robin's study, which now was mostly empty of anything of Robin's, and seemed to be video chatting with one of his buddies.

"Coop, get off the computer," Alice said so seriously that he instantly obeyed. Lowering her voice, she said, "There's a detective here to see you about that identity theft stuff of Robin's." Cooper briefly looked worried, so Alice said, "I really hope you haven't done anything you shouldn't have." Cooper hugged her quickly, then sauntered down the stairs.

Alice didn't want to leave her nephew alone with a detective, so she joined them in the living room. Cooper walked right over to the detective, and offered him a handshake, which made Alice feel only marginally safer. "What do you need," he said boldly.

"Geez, you're a kid," said Longworth, as Cooper smiled and shrugged. The detective pulled some papers from a briefcase, and handed them to Cooper. "Mackenzie suggested I talk to you. Said this reminded him of some of the work you did for Parakkat in recovering money from deadbeat dads."

"No kidding," said Cooper nonchalantly, glancing at the papers.

Longworth looked at his notes, then turned to Alice, saying, "And you and he are a couple?"

"Were," said Alice, as coolly as she could manage.

Cooper smiled as though he hadn't a care in the world, saying, "We were all relieved when she came to her senses."

Longworth scanned both of their faces for an instant, then asked Cooper, "Any idea what could have happened here?"

"It just looks like some money might have been hidden offshore," said Cooper, running his finger along the border of one of the documents passed to him by the detective.

"That sounds like Robin," said Alice.

"If he stashed the money, why would he report identity theft?" asked Longworth.

"Not sure," said Cooper. "But sometimes people with gambling problems report this sort of thing, in the hopes of getting some money back. They figure, well who knows what they figure, poor schnooks. But, I do consult for Mackenzie, so did you want me to look into this on the tech side, see if I can find anything?"

The detective took a long glance at Cooper, then smiled and said, "Sure, that would be great. I'll leave these with you."

"Have any of his credit cards been used fraudulently?" asked Cooper.

Longworth shook his head. "Now you mention it, nothing like that. This could be banking fraud and grand theft, but it doesn't seem like identity theft."

Cooper laughed. "Maybe the culprit met Robin, and realized no way would they want to be him." He rose, offered his hand to the detective, and together they walked to the door.

"Thanks for your help, kid."

"No prob," said Cooper.

After the detective had gone, Alice and Cooper sat back down in the living room. "He didn't exactly seem like a dummy, you know," said Alice.

"Who said he did?" asked Cooper.

"I could have fainted like twenty times during that inquisition," said Alice, putting her hand on her heart, and looking toward the ceiling.

"You worry too much."

"I think you should just put back Robin's money. I know it's not identity theft or whatever else. It's one good hearted, wiseass boy."

"Listen to me, Aunt Ally, he was living here rent free all my life. Do you know how much one K a month is for what was it—fifteen, sixteen years?"

"Okay I know it's wrong and it's a lot and I was stupid, so what like fifteen thousand dollars, yes it's a lot of money, but that doesn't make stealing right."

Cooper sighed. "It's not fifteen thousand, it's close to a quarter million. You've been thinking in teaspoons way too long."

Alice let out a huge sigh. "Still," she said lamely. "They could come after us, after me, take my home."

"Get real. Have you seen any of Robin's money?"

"No...."

"So don't worry about it. This has nothing to do with you. No connection to you."

"I'm picturing you in the slammer Cooper. Not a picture I want in my head."

Cooper laughed. "Erase that picture. I'm fine, you're fine, we're all fine. And we're going to stay that way."

Alice sighed as she listened to Misty tell yet another person about how she lost on *You're Cooked*. If it weren't such a sore subject, she'd be laughing by now, for with each retelling, Misty amplified the story, forcing Alice to contradict her and say no, nobody had gotten food poisoning, no, nobody's false teeth had cracked and fallen out into her dish, no, nobody had broken out in hives or had to be rushed to a hospital, no Alice had not fainted. With each bizarre conversation, Alice wished over and over that she'd not confided to these people that she was about to appear on that show, for now she would never live it down. She began to wonder, did this mean her confidence was at some inexplicable all time high? Had she actually believed that she would win the contest? Alice stopped to ponder, and she didn't find an answer. When in the past had she believed that anything actually would work out perfectly? She knew the answer to that question.

"And all this time, Ally here has been acting like some superior cooking know-it-all, and she goes on this TV show and tried to feed some chef live eels—a *real* chef," said Misty to a lighting guy, who was holding a meter in front of Misty's face and reading it, not really listening to what was being said. "I think all his hair fell out when one shocked him."

"No kidding," he replied distractedly.

"There were no eels, sheesh," said Alice. "You're killing me."

The guy clicked his meter again, saying, "That so…."

"Eel sushi," said Misty, giving Alice what she thought was a companionable little shove, "When do you ever see that on a menu? They'd squiggle right off the rice." Misty shivered in disgust.

"They do have eel sushi," said Alice, "Unagi. But I wasn't serving it."

"Ou-nag-you!" said Misty jovially, making a head-snapping gesture of a futile attempt to eat something that kept moving. "Must be how the fish feel with the worm on the line!"

"So are you ready to do this?" said Alice, trying not to sound as annoyed as she felt.

"Long as you don't electrocute me," said Misty.

If only, thought Alice. "So what we're doing here is doctoring a bunch of stuff from a market." She poured some white bean dip into a bowl, drizzled some olive oil on it and chopped a few pine nuts to toss on top. "This already comes with an oil drizzle and pine nuts on top."

"We have to do something to it to personalize it," said Misty.

"This is really easy to make from scratch," said Alice. All you do is whirl some canned beans in a Cuisinart. We could add some herbs, some garlic, and some pine nuts and it would actually be homemade."

"One more time, Ally. Company coming in fifteen minutes. Unexpected. Have to make a spread fast."

Alice sighed. "You can make little appy snacks pretty fast, and this way you don't have to constantly buy prefab food that expires in a week or so. What will you do with this stuff if company doesn't come? What will your viewers do?"

"Oh my God, there you go again—always trying to sabotage me—after all I've done for you. The maid can take the leftovers, okay? Her kids will wolf it all down."

"I just don't think the maid should be your go-to solution for every practical problem. Most people don't have maids."

"Life is simple," glowered Misty, "Either you have a maid or you are a maid."

Alice's eyes opened wide. She could just picture a sorority of bored, lazy, and useless women, with their battalions of maids, watching raptly as Misty served takeout food on television. "Okay. And we're actually making the cocktail dipping sauce for the defrosted, pre-cooked shrimp?"

"You said it's only ketchup and horseradish. But couldn't you just buy a jar of the stuff?" Misty asked, as Alice reached out among the bunches of containers, and selected a jar, then Misty smiled as though it were a trophy, and said, "Perfect. Another time saver. These are busy, important women who watch my show. They don't have time for horseradish."

After several hours of this, Misty managed to do her first moderately credible take, if dumping packaged foods into crystal bowls could be considered cooking, and then they all took a break. Alice stood in the prep kitchen creating a list of more items they could potentially use, as an older woman who looked a great deal like Misty peeped in.

"Hi there, I'm Rain," she said, smiling.

Was this Misty's mom, Alice wondered, expecting some sort of nightmare, not the beautiful woman in front of her. "Hello," she answered. "Are you looking for Misty?"

Rain burst into tears, and said, "No, Tom. Is he around?"

Alice grabbed a clean towel, which she handed to the now sobbing woman, and asked, "Are you okay," which seemed a preposterous question considering the river of tears.

"Buster has to be put to sleep," she said, each word punctuated by huge sobs. "I need Tom."

Alice put her arm gently around the woman's shoulder, thinking how much more genuine she seemed than Misty. How could this woman be Misty's mother? "Come on this way," said Alice, leading Rain to Tom's office. When they got to the door, Tom saw Rain, leapt up from his desk and dashed over to her, wrapping his arms around her.

Rain continued sobbing, lifting her head back now and then from inside Tom's close embrace, and she mumbled as she had before, "Buster has to be put to sleep."

"Oh no," said Tom, a tear running down his cheek, as Alice watched, amazed. "He seemed fine last week."

More sobs came from Rain, as she said, "His luck's run out."

Feeling like she was intruding, Alice backed out of the door, and Tom closed it behind her, never letting go of Misty's mom. Wow, they were unusually close, Alice thought as she walked back toward the prep kitchen.

Moments later, Misty appeared in the doorway, and snarled, "You bitch, you total, back-stabbing bitch."

Alice looked up from her notes. "What?"

"You brought that psycho twat here? And closed the door, and left Tom alone with her?"

Alice's eyes opened widely as she caught her breath. What had she done now? "Do you mean your mom?"

Misty walked over to Alice and gave her a shove, an actual shove, not one in jest.

"Hey," said Alice. "What's wrong with you?"

"Nobody's safe with her around. She snaps her fingers, and Tom comes running. You just did this to get back at me for teasing you about losing that game show. As if you ever had a chance."

"Your mom came in, was crying, and asked for Tom. I don't know what you're freaking out about. And I'll have you know I came in second."

"You've seen my mom. She's short and fat, a brunette. Old. Stop jerking me around."

"Okay so who was that? She looks like you, so I thought she was your mom, who by the way I've never met. She asked for Tom, began sobbing, and I just took her to his office. What was I supposed to do?"

"You weren't supposed to lock Tom in his office with his ex-wife, that's for sure. You oughta know he can't resist her. He's married her like three times."

"What? How was I supposed to know any of this? I'm not your security guard. Or Tom's therapist. All I knew was he was married before, and now he's trying his best to make you happy. And she came in crying about some pet being put to sleep, and asking for Tom. Anyone would have done the same thing."

"Yeah, bitch, keep pretending you don't even know what this means," said Misty, stomping up and down on one foot, then another.

"That she loved her pet, and Tom loves it too? I don't see the harm," answered Alice, staring at Misty, who grew more and more enraged.

"I'll tell you what it means. She's killing off some mangy mongrel because she wants Tom back. This is her way back in."

"That's insane," said Alice. "Nobody would do that."

Misty sneered at Alice. "You act so naive. I know better. I give and I give and you constantly, you constantly… you… you bitch. That's all it is—once a bitch always a bitch."

Alice thought ain't that the truth, but said only, "Look, if you're worried about Tom, go to his office. Stop taking your crap out on me."

Misty got up and shoved past Alice, saying, "You'll get yours."

Alice watched Misty march off, simultaneously conveying a sense of righteous outrage and deep despair, but she didn't spend too much time considering whether or not Misty's comments made any sense, because it all seemed too preposterous. The day ended not long afterwards, so Alice was free to go see Itch and Aunt Kitty.

She walked down the long corridor toward Itch's room, but before she could enter, she heard his voice and the therapist, Frankie's.

"I just want him to understand my feelings," said Frankie.

Itch laughed and said, "Guys get that girls are all about feelings. We'd just rather not have them inflicted on us, if you know what I mean." Alice imagined Frankie had made some facial gesture but said nothing, because Itch continued talking. "It was like me and Ally. I coulda been with a lotta girls, lemme tell you that, for sure. But Ally was more of a challenge. She made it more interesting. The others, they just said ok, football hero, whatever you want. Ally said no."

"You were just kids in school," Frankie said wisely. "At that age, all girls want to say no."

Itch laughed for quite a while. "Did we go to school in different countries?" he asked, then continued, "She said no, and she said no, and she said no. For months. Kissing yes, the good stuff no. Months. And months."

Alice leaned back against the side of the doorway, her hand on her heart, which was thundering in her chest.

"I couldn't take it any more. There's only so much a guy can do. So she was in the hallway at school, and she looked cute with her freckles, and I walked up to her, sort of fast and urgent, like some guy in a movie, or that's how it felt to me."

Alice sighed quietly, remembering the scene being described.

"And I walked right up to her, and she smiled like she always did, and I pressed her back to the locker, and leaned in against her, and I kissed her. Like the best kiss of all time, the kind of kiss that girls talk about to each other." Itch laughed again. "And then I leaned even closer, and whispered in her ear, 'I want to marry you, Ally.'"

Alice's eyes fluttered shut, as she was transported back in time to that intense moment, the one moment in her life which was a touchstone of what love felt like, of what passion felt like, of what it was to be with your destiny, your true love. But his voice lacked the sentiment the moment deserved, his telling of it was taunting and sarcastic. It didn't seem like Itch at all.

"Of course I didn't want to marry anyone. I wanted to be a football player or a rock star. I wanted sex, to get laid, to have this girl I'd dated for months and months and months finally just say yes. I would've said anything."

"And did she?" asked Frankie, breathlessly.

Itch laughed again. "Yeah, well the joke was on me. She said yes, we had sex, and she got pregnant. When everyone knows the first time is a free pass. Virgins don't get pregnant. Made me wonder who else she'd been with."

Alice gasped, pressing her hand over her mouth so as not to be discovered.

Frankie laughed. "They don't teach kids anything about biology. You can definitely get pregnant the first or any other time. Virgin or not."

"Says you," answered Itch. "So I was trapped. And my mom woulda killed me if I didn't marry her, but I kept hoping something would happen to let me off the hook, that her ball buster mom would send her to Swissland or wherever, or make her get rid of it. That's why I got my buddy to send away for that minister license from some newspaper, to buy time. But nope— she stayed pregnant, and the license came. So we got married. And I figured okay she's a nice girl, a girl I like a lot, a pretty girl, and she'd be okay with staying home when my band is on tour or I'm playing pro ball, so it didn't matter, I wouldn't be *so* very trapped, if you know what I mean. And it was my kid, well probably, so what'cha gonna do?"

Alice felt the tears rolling down her cheeks. She didn't even recognize the person speaking. He sounded like one of those sleazy high school boys from whom she always had tried to protect Skye, not like Itch, who was her one and only true love. She stumbled along, trying to brush away the tears so she didn't look like an idiot, until she reached Aunt Kitty's room, but Kitty was in the bathroom, because Alice could hear the water running, so she sat down on the loveseat and sobbed as quietly as possible, hoping she could stop and dry her eyes before Kitty came out, so that her aunt wouldn't have to worry about her.

Alice heard the water turn off, and she hastily brushed the tears from her eyes and tried to restore her breath, but she still seemed to be gasping, and her eyes were all itchy. Could she cite allergies? Maybe, although she didn't actually have allergies. This thought made her smile, and Alice felt marginally better until she saw the door open and he came out of it.

"You!" she said, leaping up and glaring at Johnny Badass, who inexplicably was in her aunt's bathroom. "What? You tracked me down to here? For what? You want to taunt me some more? You want to insult me some more? Or are you trying to scam some dentist money out of me? Good luck with that."

He flashed a smile, one that appeared to contain a full shark's mouthful of gleaming teeth, and said seemingly happily, "Well, hi, you *are* here." He walked closer to her and put his hand on her arm, as Alice attempted to take a step back, but there was little room and she was jammed against the loveseat, so in stepping back she ended up plopping down, which inspired him to sit down next to her and take hold of her hand, which Alice promptly snatched away.

"Are you insane?" she asked.

"It's crazy for sure. I see you on the show, feel like we had a moment, several moments, nothing I'd felt in a long, long time, and then I remember your name and all those letters, very beguiling letters I might add, and I knew I had to come see you." Once again he smiled at her. "You're the chef here, and you live here?" He glanced around bewilderedly, then gazed back into Alice's eyes with a dazzled grin.

Letters, Alice thought, instantly knowing what had happened. "What kind of moment should we have had with you torturing me on the show? What an egomaniac—you thought I went on the show to meet you? And then you slammed my food. And now you're here to shove it in my face?"

"Doll, your food is awesome, more than awesome. I fought like crazy for you to win, even though that nut did break my crown."

He seemed insane, Alice knew that, but he also sounded sincere, so she asked, "Then why were you such a prick?"

"Every show needs a tough guy — producer's decision. I was filling in for Kevin, and he's always tough on everyone. Sorry, really. I brought you these. Had them flown in from home."

Alice glanced at the coffee table, where next to a pile of letters tied in a blue ribbon was a box of candy. "Pecan pralines? You're some comedian."

Johnny smiled, saying, "You seem like a gal with a good sense of humor."

Alice shook her head. "I hate to disappoint you, but I didn't write these letters. Someone close to me did. She lives here." Alice observed a flicker of regret cross Johnny's dark eyes, as it was replaced with curiosity. "And she's absolutely crazy about you. Watches your TV show daily."

"I can't even believe that show is still on. I haven't done any new ones in years."

"Yes, I noticed how much older you appeared when I saw you on the show," said Alice, smiling for the first time.

"Hit a guy where it hurts, why don't you? Guess we're even now."

Alice opened the box of candy and offered it to Johnny. "Have some, please. Unless your dentures are too fragile?" Johnny laughed, and Alice had to admit that he didn't seem a terrible sort. "I can just imagine you and the author of these letters together as a couple. It will be wonderful to see her happy again. A nice wedding at home. I'll bake the cake."

Johnny laughed again. "Sounds like a dream come true," he said, in a tone that sounded oddly wistful rather than ironic. Then he reached in a pocket, withdrew a handkerchief, and dabbed at Alice's eyes. "Feel better now, sugar? Can't be as bad as it sounded from the bathroom."

Alice blushed, but before she could comment, she heard Kitty at the door, and whispered, "Here comes your blushing bride now."

"Thanks Reymundo," Kitty said, and the door opened. Reymundo, thought Alice, how amusing. There must be someone here she calls that, the person she was mentioning last time — it wasn't just a fantasy. Then Kitty was in the room, and before she could hug Alice, she spotted Johnny, and said, "My goodness, I just left you outside and you're back in here? How did you do that?"

Alice's heart sank. Her aunt now couldn't tell one man from another? If so, she was worse, not better. "Kitty this is chef Johnny from the TV, remember. He came to thank you for all your letters."

"John Badeaux," he said, extending his hand and smiling, "Not that anyone outside New Orleans can say the second one. That's how I got my nickname."

"Reymundo!" Kitty crowed, flinging herself into Johnny's arms, and he held her tightly until she stepped back.

"My darlin'," he said, "I'm so happy to see you."

"See," she said to Alice, "He's back, and now you'll get some help with P3. Well, sit, sit down." Kitty gestured, settling herself in the easy chair, forcing Alice to remain next to Johnny on the loveseat. "What took you so long to get back here?" Kitty asked.

For some reason, Johnny knew how to talk to her, and although nothing he said made sense to Alice, it seemed to make perfect sense to Kitty. "You know my dear Mama," he said, "She can be a trial, and I haven't been as firm as I should have. That whole engagement to demented Delphene was just 'cause Mama and Lurleen have been friends since grade school. Finally I got the hell outta there. Mama said do what you have to do, and here I am."

Alice sat there wondering if he were telling some tale at the expense of this Delphene the way Itch had just done, but to Kitty it did make sense. "Arranged marriages never work," said Kitty. "We're in modern times for goodness sake."

"I can tell you this, I've been holding my breath. For ages I expected to see demented Delphene appear at my hotel door. She's three pickles shy of a quart. Probably claim to be twenty-three months pregnant and the kid is mine."

Kitty laughed. "I guess if you haven't seen her for a couple years, you're probably safe."

"I come from N'Awlins. Shotgun weddin's and Voodoo. It's powerful stuff."

"Good God," interrupted Alice, "What are you, forty-five? If you're gay, be gay, don't whine about shotgun weddings. You're old enough to make your own choices."

"Ally!" said Kitty.

"Your older sister is a caution, isn't she," said Johnny, winking at Kitty, who beamed at him. "I'm thirty-nine, by the way."

"That's what hard living will do to you," said Alice.

Kitty made a placating gesture with her hands, then said, "So you're here, that's what's important. And you're going to work with Ally at P3."

"P3 burned down, remember," said Alice, hoping it wouldn't upset Kitty all over again. "He's on *You're Cooked*—he's the new judge. Remember that show?"

Kitty nodded, "Yup. Well at least we can get him out of that hotel. Long as I'm at this resort, you go stay in my place. Don't think Henry would mind, do you Ally?"

"I don't know," said Alice, clenching her teeth.

"Oh no, I couldn't presume," said Johnny.

Kitty rose from her chair, causing Johnny to rise as well, so naturally Alice got up too, and Kitty said, "You can and you will. I'd be insulted if you didn't. I just hope it's not too dusty. We've been on this vacation a very long time."

Alice tried to signal her aunt with her eyes, but she just continued, "Okay, on with you two, go get settled." Kitty hugged Alice and Johnny, and Alice found herself being forced to walk out with him.

They strolled quietly toward the parking lot, until Johnny said, "So what were you crying about? Not the show I hope."

Alice sighed. "I overheard something that sounded different from the way I remembered it. So I was thinking about someone I love, how I lost my virginity at the prom, what a cliché it all is."

"Nobody assumes you'll be with your high school sweetheart forever. They all say it'll blow over, you'll grow up, be different people. Maybe. I say maybe. I lived with mine until five years ago—she got uterine cancer. Died. So you never know. My mother's best friend said it was destiny, that I was meant to be with her Delphene."

Alice grimaced in sympathy, imaging how horrible it would be to hear such a thing after having lost the person you loved. "Oh, I'm so sorry," she said. "And you sold your restaurant, came all the way out here to avoid this Delphene? Seems extreme."

"Just wanted a completely new start, I guess."

Alice stopped beside her car. "I see. I'm really sorry it was so hard for you."

"Thanks for being so nice after everything. I could buy you dinner, maybe? Pick your brain about California cuisine?"

For a moment Alice's mind went a little fuzzy. She couldn't quite believe what she was saying, but there it was, words coming out of her mouth, "Aunt Kitty offered, so you know, c'mon and stay at her place if you like while you're here. It's better than some hotel, and there's a kitchen, a small one, but better than nothing." Alice watched Johnny and something crossed his eyes, and she expected him to say no, of course not, he couldn't, but that look crossed his eyes again, and then he spoke.

"All right. But I'll have to pay you rent."

Alice wrote down her address, and handed it to Johnny. "I'm in the house. The apartments are out back. I guess you want to check out of your hotel first, then come over?"

"I can stop, pick up some grub, cook us both dinner."

What was wrong with Alice? She was stunned to hear herself continue, "Well my nephew is with me now, and my daughter, and sometimes her sort of boyfriend and sometimes her sort of fiancé. But I have plenty of food at home, so you can join us if you like."

"I'll still bring the grub. Then you can rag on my cooking. Pay me back for real."

Alice laughed and Johnny laughed, and then they both drove off in their cars.

Alice found herself seething as she drove toward home. Her mind whirled and raged. That smarmy little Cajun. Was he a Cajun? He wasn't little. Maybe he was a Creole. That smarmy big Creole! Was everyone from

New Orleans a Cajun or a Creole? How had he manipulated her like this? Now here she was, stuck with another freeloader, another pain in the neck, some jerk who'd wormed his way into her life, and worse into Kitty's apartment. How had she allowed this to happen? The closer to home she drove, the angrier she grew. What a nerve. The nerve of this man, this big jerky jerk. When she heard herself call him a jerky jerk, Alice paused for a moment. Well, so what if her thoughts weren't elegantly phrased. He was a jerky jerk. He was a jerky jerked chicken, that's what he was, the Cajun Jamaican her mad. Alice laughed, and then she seethed some more.

She began to formulate an out for this situation, a way to extricate herself from the promise she'd made, under some bizarre version of mind-warping duress, to allow him to stay in her aunt's apartment. He'd manipulated her. And he called her doll. How vulgar. He was a thug! And he'd lied about wanting to marry her; it was just a ruse.

With that thought, Alice's eyes opened wide, and she pulled the car over to the side of the road, and just sat there, as more tears poured from her eyes. Her chest heaved as long-buried sobs hurled their way out of her. Johnny, that pig, she thought. He'd lied.

She sobbed for what seemed like a very long time, and then a quiet thought penetrated. It wasn't Johnny she was mad at—he hadn't manipulated her. She was angry at Itch. Alice gasped, tried to right her breath, but continued sobbing. She *was* angry at Itch, but then her heart clenched and the sobs stopped. The tears dried up, and they were replaced with something else: guilt. After all he'd been through, she wasn't allowed to be angry at him. Maybe he did say something childish and mean, but he hadn't grown up yet. A person in a coma didn't move forward. She'd had her life, she'd had the chance to grow up, but Itch was denied that chance. So was it worse that he manipulated her into having sex, or that he'd lost half his life because of her? Alice knew which was worse, and she knew that no matter what, she'd have to forgive him. The greater fault was her own.

Alice glanced at the dashboard clock, then turned the car around and headed back to the hospital. She had to see Itch, to look into his eyes and just feel him. But he wasn't in his room, and she didn't have time to wait for very long, because despite regretting her inexplicable offer, she couldn't just keep someone waiting outside her door with bags of food that could spoil. Alice turned to walk out the door and back to her car, when she saw Itch tottering down the corridor.

"Ally!" he said, not in the least confused, marching up to her as though he'd been walking for the last twenty years, and wrapping his arms around her tightly.

Alice leaned into the hug, and squeezed him back. "Fantastic job," she said sincerely.

"Whew," Itch answered, slumping down against Alice, "Tougher than it looks. Lemme sit down a bit. I walked the whole corridor up and back today a bunch of times." He leaned on Alice, and together they walked into his room, where he flopped down onto his bed, turning a radiant grin on Alice. "I'm Mr. Mobility now. Soon I'll be walking out of this place. No cane, no crutches."

"Of course you will."

"They actually said so. Only a few more weeks."

Alice grasped Itch's hand, and smiled. "That's wonderful."

"Stan said I could stay with him. Parents in that tiny condo now, you know."

Alice tensed. "Is that what you want to do?"

"Not like I can stay with you at your mom's. She hates me."

Alice laughed. "I don't live with my mom. I have Kitty's old house. I thought you knew that."

Itch moved in the bed as though he were uncomfortable. "Does Kitty hate me?"

"Kitty lives here now actually. Dementia."

Itch glanced up toward the ceiling, pondering this information. "Do I know what that is? Did I forget that? It sounds bad."

"It is bad," sighed Alice.

"So you live in a whole house, just like a grownup?"

Before Alice could reply, a nurse entered with a dinner tray, causing Alice to leap up. "Goodness, it's getting late. Okay hon, I'll see you tomorrow. Keep up the good work."

"You too," said Itch, then for some reason he said "Me too," and laughed.

Alice leaned down and kissed him, and as she did he squeezed her hand. "So you're not sorry?" she asked, and seeing his bewilderment, she added, "About us."

"Hasn't really been much of an us yet," he said, as the nurse placed his dinner on the wheeled table across his bed. "You got to do us without me."

Alice touched his face gently. How could she have been angry at him? He was dealing with so much. "I'm doing us with you right now."

Itch smiled, and Alice waved as she walked out the door.

This time the drive home was peaceful, and she felt all right about pretty much everything. Itch's comments were not erased, but pushed far back in her mind, overshadowed by the sweet moments they'd just shared. Now she could go home and just relax for a while, have something simple for dinner and take a long bath.

Everything would be all right. Alice sighed contentedly, then wondered if Skye or Cooper would be at home. If not, she'd just scramble an egg, which would be plenty.

She pulled into her driveway with this thought on her mind, but as she exited the car she could smell cooking aromas—fantastic, amazing, delicious scents. Johnny! He was there, cooking, of course. Alice shook her head—how had she forgotten him?

"Hello!" she called, walking into the house and back toward the kitchen. The grill outside was lit, and she could smell something inside frying. Was he making beignets? In her mind Alice could picture something typically New Orleans, a gumbo, red beans and rice, some of the many items she'd seen him cook, but she smelled none of those things. She smelled a sweet cake and a custard with a hint of lavender. And something frying, but it wasn't chicken. She smelled roasted vegetables, just the sort of nice fall smell anyone would enjoy in October, which is what it was.

Cooper was sitting at a stool in front of the island, which was covered with food, and on which lay a huge bouquet of mixed flowers, not the prefab kind from the market, but the kind someone took time to choose individually. Johnny stood behind the island, and when he saw her, he beamed and walked over to her, crushing her in a hug that was much too tight, and which she returned in a way that attempted kindness, but on some level felt merely polite.

"I thought you'd blown me off," said Johnny, grinning.

"No, I'm sorry, I had to run back to the hospital."

Cooper, with his mouth already full, took another morsel and shoved it between his teeth, saying, "This is fried alligator. And JB has the boots to match! Vintage, not the endangered kind."

Alice looked down at Johnny's feet and said, "What are you, Michael Douglas?"

Johnny laughed and said, "Yup, and I'm romancing the angry out of you instead of the stone." Then he handed her the bouquet.

Alice couldn't help but smile. "These are really beautiful and I thank you so much, but you do know I'm married?"

"Nobody's perfect," said Johnny, touching Alice lightly on the shoulder. He was such a touchy-feely kind of guy, Alice thought, stepping away slightly, then feeling badly as his eyes shaded because of it.

"I told him everything," said Cooper. "Man these stuffed peppers are good." He reached for a small pepper stuffed with crab and nibbled at it, knowing it was pretty spicy. "My mouth is on fire but in a good way, like when you kiss a trashy girl you shouldn't."

Alice and Johnny both laughed.

"What trashy girls have you been kissing?" asked Alice, with only a small degree of genuine concern.

"So is this it?" asked Johnny, in a way Alice knew was designed to help Cooper avoid her question. "Your little Skye let me in, and said to tell you she was going to New York with…um…Julie? Hard to picture you with such big kids. Thought little ones. That's why I didn't make my drunken bread pudding."

"New York?" Alice asked, as Cooper nodded.

"I told her to wait 'til you got here, but she's gonna call you later. He got an audition and said he couldn't do it without her," explained Cooper, as Alice shook her head.

"Um so yes, this is it. Looks like you made enough for twenty," said Alice, glancing at a beautifully arranged platter of greens, roasted vegetables, and grilled shrimp.

"You said nephew, boyfriends, I figured boys eat a lot. Though it seemed risky with fish, but I figured here in California kids have sophisticated palates."

"You didn't even see the barracuda," said Cooper.

"Wow," said Alice. "I'm so sorry. You really went to so much trouble and expense." She took a piece of the fried alligator out of a basket and tasted it, then grabbed her jaw. "Oh my God! Oh, oh, ouch! What's in here, a tooth? Some piece of a saw the gator swallowed? I think it's wedged into my gum." Alice stuck her finger into her mouth and wiggled it gingerly around, saying, "Oh wow, I'm bleeding, wait, here it is."

Johnny stood there looking at her with mock concern. "You have a lot of acting talent," he said drolly.

Alice sneered. "It's so bland I had to give it a back story. Maybe you needed some cumin."

Alice gazed at Johnny, keeping her expression stern and critical, and he gazed back at her, his dark eyes flashing. Something churned inside her, and it wasn't the alligator, so in an attempt to regain her balance, she looked away for a moment. Tentatively she glanced back, and it happened again. What was going on? Alice looked down at her feet, reached for the edge of the counter, then momentarily seated herself next to Cooper. Johnny had poured her a drink, a spiked fruity punch that wasn't the usual sangria, and she took a deep sip, but the alcohol hit her and her head began to spin.

"How much hooch would you have used if you thought I had grown kids?" Alice mumbled.

Johnny turned to stir the halved Jerusalem artichokes in the oven, then he walked to the door to grill the stuffed barracuda. "Or do you need the emergency room," he asked with exaggerated compassion, making Alice laugh.

"Ok, busted," she said, trying not to look into his eyes for too long. "It's all fantastic. Let me set the table."

"Done," he answered, and Alice looked in the dining room and it was all ready. "Wow," she whispered, mostly under her breath, "Nobody ever...."

"That's a shame," he said, winking, and out the door he went.

What was it with this guy? He seemed so nice, too nice Alice automatically thought.

"Do you think he's a serial killer?" Alice whispered to Cooper, who choked on his food, then spit out what he was chewing.

"He just really wants us to like him, nothing wrong with that," Cooper answered, coughing.

Alice found a depression glass pitcher and filled it with water for the flowers, which she carried to the table along with the salad platter, and leaned out the door. "Anything I can do to help?"

"Make sure all the knives are hidden, so you can't put up much of a fight when I murder you before dessert," Johnny answered.

"Before dessert? That would be more than murder, it would be cruel and unusual." Alice laughed, then added, "You certainly have an amazing sense of hearing. Sure you're not a werewolf or something? I watch *True Blood,* you know."

He walked over to Alice and leaned down, speaking softly, and said, "Don't worry. I won't bite your neck until you invite me to."

Alice sighed, growing nervous. The last thing she needed was some crazy cook coming onto her daily, while she allowed him to live in Kitty's apartment. "My husband's coming home in a few weeks," she said.

"What?" he answered with mock derision, "Friends can't bite friends' necks? They do it in Bon Temps all the time."

"That fish looks fantastic," Alice said, hoping the change of subject would reroute the conversation to something safe—dinner, food, anything but flirting. "I feel like I should invite some people, so it won't all go to waste."

Johnny was looking at her oddly, in a way he had before, a way that made her feel too revealed, too understood, which was a peculiar sensation, because normally those would be good things. "You'll be reopening your restaurant?" he asked.

"Waiting for the insurance to clear, been ages," she answered, "But yes, no choice, wouldn't want to let Kitty down. Though...."

"I'm doing a couple popups this month—come work for me. You can do all the pastry if you want. I'll bring the heat, you do the sweet. Hey—I like that. Hadn't chosen a name yet."

Alice stopped to think for a moment. Maybe she could do that, quit working with Misty, do Johnny's pastry. Then she thought of being around him daily, of these strange quivery sensations, feelings that produced extreme discomfort and guilt, not to mention the fact that he was a stranger, and someone whose trustworthiness was indeterminable, and she said, "Oh I don't know. I'm used to running things, not working for someone. Though...."

"Well, let's give it a go, and when I open a place for real we can be partners. I don't exactly rule with an iron fist."

Alice thought some more, and said, "I'm working on this insane TV show at the moment. It will probably never air. Kind of a vanity thing, my old high school nemesis."

"I'm only doing them on the weekends now. Just to test the market, the feel of it all. Help me out. I could use an ace like you." Johnny's voice was quiet, as though he were cooling it down a little, making a good offer, but not one that had any undertones at all, so that it did feel like a genuine business proposition.

"Well, what would you want me to bake?" Alice asked.

Johnny flipped the fish onto a clean plate and opened the door for Alice. "Let's eat. We'll discuss it during dinner."

Knowing it would be a very busy day and evening, Alice drove early toward the hospital. Her mind was on the events of the previous night, and how she had agreed to bake for Johnny for his popup the following evening. Was something going on with her? She kept saying yes against her better judgment, and now she had him living in her aunt's apartment, inches away from her door really, and she'd promised to be the sweet to his heat. Was her brain failing? Was she stricken with Kitty's dementia? What was it that caused her to say yes to him, when she knew she wanted to say no? Was she one of those girls who can't say n-n-n-n-no? It didn't seem so to Alice, yet something was deeply amiss, but what? Why was she taking all these risks when all her adult life she'd attempted so strenuously to avoid them?

Did she really want not to bake for a new restaurant? As Alice considered it, there was potential for it to be a good thing, for her to gain experience doing something that ultimately might be a better career move for her, at no risk at all. No, it wasn't the little bakery café she'd envisioned, but it also wasn't a bunch of screaming kids whose parents paid very little for the privilege of being served her party food.

What it came down to was chemistry, and that made Alice nervous. She hadn't had to deal with those feelings for a long time, and they were severely misplaced at this moment, when she was about to begin her real life, the life she'd always imagined living. So, she thought, what was there to worry about? Johnny was a congenial sort, and she liked him, but she wasn't about to go pounding on her aunt's door to hurl herself into his arms, not even if he did have some crazy little crush on her. Soon Itch would be home, she'd be living as a married woman, and Johnny would be just a friend, or maybe just a business associate. Everything would be fine.

Conceding that she worried too much, that she obsessed too much over minutia, Alice parked her car and began walking toward the door, as she spotted Emma waving to her. They stopped to hug and catch up for a moment. "We have to do better about getting together more often," Alice said, smiling.

"I was going to call you, but I only just found out. I'm in Itch's wing this week. I'll be taking care of your hubby."

"How wonderful," answered Alice. "He's due to be released in a couple weeks, and you'll be the one who ushers him out of here. Though maybe we'll need a nurse at home some of the time — they haven't told me any details yet."

Emma smiled. "I'm always here to help."

Alice put her arm around Emma's shoulder. "Well let's go in together, and I'll introduce you."

They walked slowly, talking and laughing, and Alice told Emma about Johnny and his offer.

"Of course you should do it," Emma said. "This is your chance to plan the rest of your life, instead of just stepping into someone else's shoes."

Alice nodded, "I know you're right. But there's something safe and comfy about those already-broken-in shoes."

"Well if you don't like it, you don't have to do it permanently, but if you do like it, it could be a great opportunity."

Alice sighed, "I know, I know." She heard Itch strumming on his guitar, and he sounded relaxed and happy, but the moment Alice and Emma entered the room, Itch glanced toward them, then began babbling hysterically.

"You ratted me out to Ally's mom?" Itch asked Emma. "And now what? You're gonna tell Ally?"

"It's me, Ally," Alice said softly.

But Itch clenched his jaw, and stared at Emma. "You bitch!"

"Itch, it's me, Ally. This is Emma, your new nurse. She's a good friend."

Itch started flailing around, pushing Alice away from him, saying, "Get off me, get off me." Alice stood back a bit, hoping he would calm down, when Emma walked closer and put her hand on Itch's arm.

"Calm down," said Emma seriously.

"You calm down, you bitch," answered Itch. "It wasn't supposed to mean anything—you knew it. Cause she wouldn't. You said no problem. Now here you are, you rotten bitch. Stan said don't think with your dick. Yeah, well."

"I'm Emma, your nurse," Emma said calmly. She poured a glass of water, handed it to Itch and said, "Drink this and take a deep breath."

Itch slapped the glass out of her hand, and said, "Shut up, Misty. Before I get up from here and toss your ass to the curb."

Alice gasped, reaching to steady herself on the frame of the bed. "You slept with Misty?" she asked.

"Why ask me what you already know," said Itch angrily.

"And you knew she was having your baby?" Alice asked.

"Mine and the rest of the football team's," he sneered.

Alice looked at Emma, who flinched. "Oh, honey," said Alice, hugging Emma.

"I'm okay," said Emma. "I just wanted my roots. Roots can be dirty, I guess. Not like there was ever any doubt I lucked out with the people who were my real parents. It was just about knowing, not getting new parents. Old parents. Whatever."

"Oh, honey," Alice said again, hugging Emma more tightly. They all took a beat as Itch seethed, Emma cringed, and Alice felt enraged. She'd faithfully waited for him for decades, and he'd been a cheater. But in her mind the image of Robin appeared, and she had two thoughts. For decades he'd thought Skye was his daughter, and he'd loved her so much, but apparently he had no child at all. Emma and Skye were sisters. Or they might be, unless some other switched baby was Misty's. And then she thought about the faithfully waiting part, and no that wasn't true. Her heart had waited, wished, and sighed, but her life had moved on. To some extent, she hastily added, remembering all the nights spent alone on her uncle's couch, knowing her heart had always been Itch's, and knowing she'd vowed to forgive him anything, because of all he'd lost as a result of her youthful stupidity.

Alice dug around in her purse and pulled out one of the swab kits she'd sent for, saying, "I've had this in my bag for months, never made sense. Well now we'll finally know."

She walked toward Itch, and said, "Open your mouth for a second, please. It won't hurt." But Itch pushed her away, saying "Get off me, Principal Catson. You always hated me. Now you'll make Ally hate me too. Happy now, you old witch? Yeah go ahead, give me detention. Well, I won't go. You can't make me."

"Oh don't worry," said Alice shrewdly, "You're not getting detention. You already graduated. We just need to swab your cheek, so you can be discharged from this place. You want to leave here, don't you?"

Itch's eyes opened widely. "This is the nurse's office? But I thought...."

"Here you go," said Alice, briefly tickling Itch's cheek so he would open his mouth, which finally he did. "Now we'll get the complete truth."

"Please don't tell Ally," Itch said, "She'd be so hurt and it was all nothing. Tell her Misty, tell her it was just a mistake."

Emma turned to leave the room, saying, "I'm going to ask to be reassigned."

Alice nodded, and said, "Wait. I've had this for weeks as well." She removed a Ziploc bag containing a spoon, and another one with a few strands of hair. "These are her samples. I know I should have just given this to you, but she'd said no, and I didn't want to overstep. Well, it's time we all had answers."

Emma smiled softly, "Thanks, Ally."

"You know...you and Skye are probably sisters...maybe. At least that's something nice."

Emma nodded. "Look, don't feel bad. I knew when I went searching, I might not like what I'd find."

Alice nodded. "I'm still sorry. It can't feel good."

Emma hugged Alice and said, "I'll call you. Or do you need to talk? Can't feel good to you either."

Alice paused for a moment, thinking of all she'd just learned, and said, "Yeah, probably to a world-class therapist for many years." Emma laughed, and Alice smiled, saying, "There, that's better."

Alice readied to leave the room with Emma, but first turned back toward Itch, saying, "And you—think about what you've done."

Itch's voice was plaintive and melancholy as he responded, "That's all I do."

Alice walked sadly down the corridor. Had she always been a fool? What if she had learned this long ago, when her life was her own, and she was young and in love? What would she have done? Are there some choices people make which can't be ignored, to which action is the only correct response? Would she have walked away? Would she have left Itch? Would she have had Skye? Alice felt a cloud of misery envelope her, and she sped up her pace and walked rapidly to her car, where she could have a measure of privacy. Then she sat and thought and thought.

For decades she had wished for a do-over, for Itch to be returned to her, so the interrupted life she'd endured could be made right. And it had happened. Against all possible odds and in the rarest of situations, it had happened. She was getting her chance to have the happy life she'd always envisioned, and with this guy who could always crawl up into her heart. He'd been a jerk, yes, but was that even true? He'd been a kid. A teenager. A boy like Cooper, not much older than Cooper, a kid who compared eating crab stuffed peppers to kissing trashy girls. That's what boys do, Alice thought, because they're kids, and they don't know anything about life.

She hadn't even told Itch about Robin, about how she'd tried so hard to move on with her life, because she didn't know how he'd respond. Would he act like a boy and accuse her of cheating on him, even though he was asleep and not expected to recover? Would it mean anything that she chose a guy she didn't love because her daughter did? Would it mean anything that never did she yearn for him, and always she'd yearned for Itch? Alice didn't know.

Alice pulled the car out of the lot, and as she drove to the studio, a calm settled over her. In her heart she'd decided. She would forgive Itch for a stupid, childish choice. And they'd have their future.

She walked into the studio thinking about Misty, and how their paths kept crossing. Briefly Alice wondered about the peculiarity of life, and the people who are tossed in front of us all. She allowed herself the imaginary pleasure of driving right over Misty on that symbolic path, and as she walked, the angrier she grew. She envisioned herself striding over to Tom and telling him she was quitting, because Misty had slept with her husband. How shocked he would be, particularly if she never mentioned when it had happened. Alice smiled, and then pictured more mischief she could play. Wouldn't it all just be worth it—but then she pictured Tom and the pain in his eyes, and she knew there would be no reason to make him the victim in her war with Misty.

Some things do have consequences, however, and Alice knew that despite the little voice in her head nagging her about money, she couldn't keep working with Misty. Perhaps her heart insisted on forgiving Itch, but where Misty was concerned, the right choice was to part, not to hang on and be miserable. So in she marched to Tom's office, and tapped lightly on his door.

"Got a minute," she asked softly. He waved her in, and she took a seat opposite his desk. "I'm sorry to tell you, but I'm quitting the show. Immediately. I really hope this doesn't leave you in the lurch."

Tom's eyes opened widely, but instead of concern, there was a shadowing of relief in them. He smiled wanly at Alice and said, "I was going to talk to you today, anyway. I feel badly that I got you into this in the first place. I know you never thought it was a project with the slightest merit." Alice just looked into Tom's eyes, and she said nothing as he continued. "Something big has happened, my wife, well you met her, Renata, well we're…."

"Renata?" Alice asked. "I didn't meet a Renata."

"Oh right," Tom answered, "Rain — her stage name. I've known her since before that. In college when she was Renata. Anyway she's always been the love of my life, and we have unfinished…um…well it's not business, but stuff. So Misty and I are divorcing." Alice gasped, as he continued. "I just thought I'd be frank with you since you've always been so nice."

"Wow," said Alice, thinking she hoped he had a prenup.

"But listen, Ally, I'm going to pay you for two months' work, it just seems fair. And if you or other chefs you know want to pitch me a real cooking show, I'll certainly listen."

"Wow," said Alice again, "That's so nice of you. I'm sure it's a very stressful time for you, and I appreciate so much you stopping to think of me in all this turmoil."

Tom grinned. "Renata and I have what they call a checkered past." He laughed and continued, "But you know I always love playing checkers with her."

Alice smiled. "I might actually know a real chef, with TV experience, who might want to do a show. We're doing some popups together starting tomorrow night, then maybe a restaurant. I'll tell him about you, and if he's interested you can meet."

"Fantastic." Tom rose, and Alice did so as well, shaking his hand. "Oh, wait," he said, opening his desk, and withdrawing an envelope, which he handed to Alice. "Don't forget the loot. You've been great to work with, and if you need a reference, please use me."

Alice tried to hold back a laugh. Where would a reference from this project ever come in handy, she wondered. But she smiled and said, "Thanks, Tom, and I wish you all the best, and so much happiness."

"When true love clobbers you, you gotta give in."

Alice walked out of Tom's office and toward her dressing room, where she had only a few personal things to gather, but there was Misty, pacing back and forth. "You!" she accused, like a heroine in an old-timey melodrama.

"Don't even speak to me," answered Alice.

Misty approached Alice and attempted to shove her, but this time Alice raised her hands, looked threateningly into Misty's eyes, and said, "Don't even think about it." She tossed her items into the tote bag on her arm, and turned to leave. "No decent guy will ever want you for long. Or for more than the obvious."

Misty gasped, and lunged toward Alice. "You'll get yours. I'll see to that."

"What's important is that you already got yours." Alice turned to walk away, and she didn't look back. She knew she was walking away from something, this woman she'd hated since they were girls, and a ridiculous job that anyone else would have quit in the first fifteen minutes, but there was also the sense that she was walking toward something that was more than a car ride home. Tomorrow she'd be a pastry chef, and then during the week she'd finally see that attorney Cooper knew about the absurd delays in the insurance payouts. Tonight she'd bake alligator-shaped cookies for the popup, and she'd sleep, and tomorrow she'd bake elegant desserts. And then she would make some decisions about her future. It seemed like a century since she'd started on this path, but now there were so many new roads ahead. Normally she'd be terrified. What if she messed it up? That's what she'd usually ask herself. What if some of her crazy or wild or irresponsible instincts caused her to take a chance that was risky, far too risky? Alice shivered at the thought. It hung over her for a moment, but she knew it was time, time to put her fears aside, time to take a risk, time to hope for the best. At least she wouldn't be motorcycling down any docks in an earthquake.

Alice had dressed carefully in her perfectly ironed chef whites—no old fashioned aprons. She knew that she'd be leaving before any of the clients arrived to dine, but it never hurt to be doubly prepared, so a hanger held a change of uniform. Johnny had given her a tour of the temporary spot and a key, and Alice expected to be there alone for at least three hours, and then to be there with prep cooks for several more, while she finished the desserts. Pastry chefs work early in the day, which was the flip side of her life at P3. Alice had quipped that she'd probably get jet lag, but instead she had an overabundance of adrenalin, and it was that which fueled her courage.

The supplies were ready, the walk-in stocked with everything for the evening's adventure, and Alice had only to begin, which she did efficiently, and she kept working until more than two hundred desserts had been made. They were serving a limited menu, including the dessert course, so it wasn't terribly difficult to produce chocolate cakes with a salted caramel drizzle, coconut cakes with various curds as fillings, tarts made of several assorted fruits, batter for molten lava cakes in chocolate and caramel, brownies, and cheesecakes with passion fruit topping. She worked in a corner of the kitchen reserved for pastry, and by the time she took a breath and looked up, some rag-tag looking prep cooks were simmering stocks, chopping vegetables, and cleaning lettuce and herbs.

Johnny arrived by ten, carrying two large bags filled with artisanal breads. He was wearing some raggedy gray shorts and one of the wacky t-shirts sold on Venice beach.

Alice glanced at him and then off to the other side of the kitchen, and said, "You don't really work dressed like that, do you? No wonder everyone else looks like refugees."

"Hiya, doll," he said, hugging Alice and grinning, as he surveyed all she'd accomplished. "Wow, no flies on you!"

"You really will be changing, right? What if someone wants to see the chef?"

Johnny laughed, and looked down at his sneakers. "I'm a casual guy. If the food's good, nobody cares what I look like."

"Nobody wants to eat at a fine dining place where the workers look sloppy and unclean. Don't you want everything to be perfect?"

Johnny laughed. "Gee you're channeling my third grade teacher, Miss Wretched. Maybe with fewer chin hairs." He paused then asked, "Where you at with all this?"

Alice scowled for a moment, but then decided to let it all pass. "Just have to frost the cakes and make some fruit sauces. Unless you think we need more?"

"Over a thousand bucks profit right here," he answered so quickly that Alice was impressed. He paused a moment, then added, "I hate to ask you this, but my seafood guy is down with the flu. Could you stick around and help me with some prep? I'll probably run his station later so you could maybe expedite? Ah geez, that's too long a day. Forget it, I'll swap some people around."

"Don't be silly," she answered, "Of course I'll stay. Might as well get the full experience."

"I know CPR," he said, "Just in case."

Alice nodded. "I guess I can relax then. You won't be defibrillating me or anything, will you?"

"Only if absolutely necessary." Johnny laughed, stuck a spoon into the buttercream and scooped up a nice sized blob, which he inserted into his mouth, closing his eyes and sighing. "My God," he said, "Oh my God, this is good."

Alice nodded. "Will I have to defibrillate you?"

"At least three times a week," he answered, "But more often at first." Then he laughed so hard and so much that Alice stopped worrying about the passes he might make, and joined in.

By two, they'd portioned and scaled some beautiful fish, cooked a dozen lobsters and removed the meat for a pasta, peeled pounds of shrimp and made stocks from the shells. Meat bones were roasting, peppers were being seared and peeled, crab cakes were made and chilled.

Johnny walked through the kitchen, checking on his cooks, all of whom had worked for him before and knew what to do. "What was I thinking," he said to Alice. "You've been here eight hours already. And you haven't even had lunch. C'mon."

Alice followed him into a small office off the kitchen, and sat as directed on the couch. Johnny reached down, grabbed her feet, and put them up in front of her, swiveling her around sideways. "I'll be right back with some lunch. Rest."

Alice took a deep breath, realizing that yes she was both tired and hungry, but she wasn't exhausted. It was exhilarating working so intently with such focus. She didn't do any of the cooking at P3, because there really wasn't any reason to. The food was good but it was simple, nothing like the menu being prepared tonight. This was real cuisine, and it was impressive. People didn't realize what it took to produce this level of food, night after night. Before she could ponder any further, Johnny arrived with two beautiful salads containing a medley of baby greens glistening with a lemony dressing. Alice expected him to serve her something fancy, some of the seafood they'd just prepared, but to the side of the salads were oozy grilled cheese sandwiches.

Alice just looked at him. Very softly she said, "This is exactly what I wanted."

Johnny nodded, opened a bottle of wine, and poured them both a glass. "To a wonderful night, good food, and a new partnership," he said sincerely.

They sat eating and talking casually for a few minutes, until Alice's phone rang. She answered, listening quietly, a pall coming over her. "All right," she said, "Soon as I can." Then turning to Johnny, she said, "My aunt is much worse. Apparently her favorite orderly took another job and it sort of sent her into a stupor."

"Oh, sugar," he answered, "Go on, go and check on her. Don't worry about tonight. I'll handle it."

"I can probably be back in a few hours. Maybe if I spend some time with her, she'll snap out of it."

"You just go take care of my fiancée." Then he smiled kindly, and Alice smiled too. As Alice walked toward the door, Johnny said, "Wait, here give me your phone." Alice handed him her iPhone and he clicked the camera and set it to video. Then he smiled into the phone and began talking. "Hello, my sweet darling. I just wanted to send you a big kiss and a hug," and here he made a big smacking sound with hand to lips, and continued talking, "I hear you're down in the dumps, well I sure hope you'll be up and at 'em soon. We all need you to feel just fine. So you get well, and I'll come see you soon." He made another kissing gesture, and clicked the phone off. Looking at Alice, he shrugged and said, "Well it's worth a try."

She nodded and said, "Gosh, thanks. Couldn't hurt."

Alice dashed to her car, and arrived at the Wellman Center in minutes. Apprehensively she walked toward her aunt's room, her heart aching. She'd known this would happen eventually, but of course she'd hoped it wouldn't. Not a day had passed since Kitty had moved into the nursing home had Alice not felt guilty, and daily she'd wondered was a mistake being made. Would Kitty have been better off at home; could they have been more vigilant, allowing her to remain at home? Alice sighed, remembering the kitchen on fire, remembering P3 on fire, remembering Kitty going missing. It wasn't about the property, but about the safety of her aunt. Even a right decision can feel wrong, Alice knew that, and it was that which weighed on her at this moment.

"Kitty," she called softly, entering the room. Her aunt was slumped in a chair, her hands clenched together, her head down. Alice walked over and kissed her lightly. "Hi Kitty," she said warmly. "How are you today?" Alice sat next to her aunt's chair, reaching for Kitty's hand, and grasping it tightly. "I'm here. Look at me Kitty, everything is ok."

Her aunt raised her eyes momentarily, glancing at Alice with what could best be described as confusion, then she lowered her gaze once more. She opened her mouth to speak or so it seemed, but all that came out was a quiet hum.

"Know who I was just with, someone who loves you," Alice said, pulling her phone from her pocket. "He sent you a message." Alice played Johnny's video for Kitty, and just as it was about to end, Kitty briefly raised her hand, then let it drop back down. "Here, want to see it again?" Alice clicked the button, and the message played again, but Kitty remained downcast and unresponsive.

"Oh Kitty, Kitty, snap out of it," said Alice desperately. Then she snapped her fingers in front of Kitty's face, and thought for a moment that the shadow in her eyes dispersed and focus almost returned, but then there was nothing. Alice tried singing, "If you're happy and you know it, clap your hands," and she clapped her own hands in front of her aunt, then took Kitty's hands and clapped them together. With each new attempt Alice scrutinized her aunt, but nothing seemed to help.

"Oh Kitty," Alice sighed, then began speaking in a quiet voice. "Do you even know how much you mean to me, how much I love you, how much I've always loved you?" Alice clutched her aunt's hand tightly and kept speaking, hoping that something she said would get through. For more than two hours she tried, patiently and quietly speaking words of love, gazing at her aunt, but nothing penetrated.

"Maybe tomorrow," Alice said. "Tomorrow you'll feel better, and I'll visit and we'll talk some more. You just rest tonight." Alice hugged Kitty tightly, then left the room in search of someone who could offer more information, but what the young doctor on call had to say was of little comfort. Sometimes it happened like this, a sudden valley, rather than a gradual fading. Tests would be run, nurses would attend, Kitty would be cared for. She might need to be moved to another room, a more serious care room. It was all so disheartening, and Alice felt herself stumbling, as she walked through the door and back to her car.

What she wanted was to go home and just lie on her bed and rest and not think at all. She sat behind the wheel of her car, feeling herself slumped as much as Kitty had been. It was all so overwhelming, everything, not just this. Here she was, about to begin a new life, and Kitty was slipping over a cliff. Her marriage was about to begin in a real way at last, and yet Alice was foolishly entangled with some psycho slob with an inexplicable but clearly crazy crush on her. Why did it all have to be so insane? Couldn't she just have a normal, dull life? That was all she wanted, all she'd wished for since the accident.

She looked at the dashboard clock. It was nearly five, and soon the restaurant would be full of people. Well, maybe it would. Alice didn't really know. Do people come to popups, and how do they even know they're there? This was not a question she bothered to ponder. Maybe there was a little time, maybe there was time for a shower, so Alice drove home, took a quick shower, ate an apple, and sat down in a quiet, empty room for ten minutes. What she needed was more like ten hours, but even the ten minutes produced irrational guilt. Alice had made a promise, so back to the restaurant she went.

There was a line in front of door! Alice let herself in with a key, and searched for Johnny to let him know people were gathering, although she felt a little silly, for even if he was a bit crazy, he seemed totally rational about work; he knew they were there. She found him giving a pep talk to the waiters and to a girl Skye's age, who apparently was the hostess, and Alice noticed the gleam in the girl's eye when she looked at Johnny, a gleam she was sure he also recognized, because his New Orleans accent seemed more overblown than usual.

"Okay," he drawled, "Open the doors, and let's have a good night." Then he turned toward Alice and reached out to wrap his arms around her. "Oh sugar," he said, "That bad?"

Instead of being grateful for his astuteness, Alice somehow grew enraged. Look at him—he was still in his ratty attire, and now he was wearing an old and stained apron over the clothes. She pushed him back and said, "Are you kidding me? You really didn't change. This is the most unprofessional display of disregard for... for... everything." She stopped speaking, knowing that if she attempted to utter one more word, the slim margin of composure she'd maintained would completely evaporate. Instead, she imagined him acting like Ramsay and yelling, 'Get out, get out," in an infuriated falsetto. Just the thought of that calmed her immensely, for then she could leave; she could end this night, and this irrational association. Alice pictured him shoving her out the door, then later disappearing from her aunt's apartment and never bothering her again—what a relief that would be. She waited, steeling her spine for the assault, clenching her fists, in case he decided to manhandle her out the door. And she waited. But there he was looking in her eyes, not with anger but with sympathy.

"I'm gonna get you a punching bag so you can release some of this stress," he said softly. "Before it wrecks your colon." He rubbed his hand along her arm for a second, until she wrenched it away. "You've had a long hard day. Maybe..."

Before he could continue, Alice said sharply, "Look, just tell me what you want me to do. This is work, not tea and sympathy."

"I'm a little hesitant," he said frankly. "I was going to ask you to run the pass, but these guys have been with me since I got here, and I don't want you snapping anyone's head off. Firm yes, Miss Wretched, no."

Alice was about to shrug, and tell him to have it his own way, when the little hostess girl came back, saying some people were looking for her.

"For me?" Alice asked. "Who even knows I'm here?" She followed the girl to the front of the restaurant, and Johnny followed her. "My goodness, hello!" said Alice to Tom Angelico and his other wife, the one with two names. Regina? No, Renata. Or Rain. Was she Mrs. Angelico, or did she too have another spouse being discarded in the wings? "How on earth did you know I was here?"

Tom laughed. "There was an ad in the paper with your name and picture. And this fellow here." Tom pointed toward Johnny, who shook his hand.

"John Badeaux," he said.

"My goodness," said Alice again. "Johnny, this is Tom Angelico. He's a producer. I told him you might be interested in doing another show, but I didn't have time to ask you if you were."

Johnny shrugged. "You never know. Be happy to talk with you about it later, but now I have a mob of people to feed. Please—stay, have dinner. On me." Then he motioned toward the hostess, who seated them at a table, as Johnny winked and disappeared back into the kitchen.

"I'll try to come back out later," said Alice. "Hope you enjoy the meal."

What followed was a blur of exhausting yet exhilarating frenzy. Plate after plate left the kitchen, each one aromatic and beautiful. Alice felt like the conductor of a symphony, and the cooks her orchestra. After the first hour, Johnny took over and Alice plated her desserts, which was artistically fun and far more relaxing. By the end of the evening, the only ones left in the dining room were Tom and Rain, and some brunette in a big hat at another table.

Johnny grabbed a bottle of champagne and some glasses, signaled to Alice to bring some of the alligator-shaped sugar cookies she'd made to be given to the clients with the check, and together they walked out to talk to Tom's table. "Everything all right?" he asked, flashing a grin.

"Amazing," said Rain, her blue eyes twinkling, her cheeks flushed.

Alice looked toward the solitary diner in the big hat, but she couldn't see the woman's face. She sat there, nursing a glass of wine, an untouched dessert in front of her, in what Alice assumed was some new form of kinky masochism.

Johnny poured champagne for all four of them, and he and Alice sat down with Tom and Rain.

"So now," said Tom, "This place is only open tonight? I never heard of such a thing. Isn't it a lot of work for such a short time?"

"It's a way to experiment and test the waters," answered Johnny.

"Look at these cookies. How adorable," said Rain, nibbling the tail off the alligator.

"Ally made those," said Johnny. "Lagniappe."

"I noticed everyone got some with the check. Very classy," said Tom. "And you'll be opening a regular restaurant together then?"

Johnny nodded, "That's my plan."

"And all this time you never said a word," Tom said to Alice.

"We only just met," she said sheepishly, not wanting him to think she had been planning to ditch him or their project for a long time. "Nothing's been decided at all."

"Really?" asked Rain, "You seem like you've known each other forever."

"Ya see," Johnny said to Alice, then he winked at Rain and continued, "She just thinks I'm some kind of crazy masher."

"I hate to sound like a dummy," said Tom, "But what kind of cooking show did you do in the past? This is all new for me. I'm mainly an infomercial guy."

Johnny grinned and said, "Well if ever I get my own line of like-every-other-chef-cookware, I'll know who to go to, to make it sound special and worth buying."

Tom laughed. "That sums it up."

"Johnny did a great cooking show, New Orleans favorites. Beautiful food," said Alice, munching on one of her own cookies.

"Not sure I'd want to do that again," Johnny said, "But it's nice to hear you sounding like a fan." Briefly he pressed his hand on Alice's shoulder, she stiffened, he lowered it and continued, "I was thinking maybe Ally and I could do something to go with our new restaurant. Like we cook in the restaurant kitchen, or some set made to look like it. A little prep, some info, some banter. She can be a tough cookie you know."

Tom laughed. "Our little Ally? No way. She has the patience of a saint." He looked around the room. "You fully funded for the new place? Maybe I could invest? Then we could always get a table."

Johnny squinted a moment, saying "And a chair, what's the line about the chair?" Alice laughed, and they said simultaneously, "*The Big Chill.*" But Tom and Rain just looked bewildered.

"Okay," said Johnny, "Give us a few days to think about it all. I have most of the numbers, but I'd have to think about the investor part, and discuss it with Ally, and maybe about the show too. It's been a long day, longer for her than for me, so why don't we touch base mid-week?"

Tom nodded, and he rose from his chair, helped Rain into her coat, and shook Johnny's hand. Tom hugged Alice and she saw them to the door, then turned back to the solitary diner. "Anything else we can get you?"

"Get me? Get me? I like that. First you shove my husband into a closed room with his ex, then you steal my idea for a cooking show with some bum. I like your nerve."

Alice's jaw hung open, then she looked closely at the brunette. "Misty? Holy crap, what are you doing here?"

"Keeping track of what's mine, what do you think? You're just lucky I didn't make a scene."

"You dyed your hair to spy on Tom?"

Misty laughed. "Dumb as always. Is wig too big a word for your pea brain?"

"Enough's enough," said Alice. "It's time for you to go."

"Yeah, when it's time, I'll say so." Then Misty took the plate of untouched cake and hurled it across the empty room.

Johnny stepped up to Misty's table, and said, "That's enough. Up." Grasping Misty by the arm, he easily maneuvered her to the door. "Out." He opened the door, and it was as though she were nothing more than a twig being propelled through it.

"Ha!" she said with a bizarre note of triumph, "Jokes on you, slobby, I didn't pay the check."

"Use the money to pay for therapy," he said without a second glance, leaving her at the curb and returning to the restaurant, where one of the bus boys had already cleaned up the mess.

Alice stood dumbstruck. "Wow," was all she could say.

"And you thought I was some kind of pansy," he joked. "Sugar, I can be a son of a bitch without even a qualm. Just not to sweet little gals in trouble like you."

Alice didn't know whether to be touched or annoyed, so she followed him into the kitchen, where everything had mostly been taken care of. "Leftovers?" she asked, once again changing the subject to the practical.

"You plan right, and ain't nothin' left, all sold," he said, flashing her his most wicked grin. "But maybe enough for a midnight snack. C'mon, let's go home. Wish you didn't have to drive yourself. Want me to get one of the guys to bring my car, and I'll drive you?"

Alice laughed. "That much of a damsel in distress I'm not."

He nodded, "Okay then, see you at home."

At home, thought Alice. It sounded so odd.

They drove off separately, but arrived at the same moment, and after parking his car on the street, Johnny walked over to Alice. "I really want to thank you. I never had a partner before, just a crew, and you were a tremendous asset. Even exhausted and under pressure."

Alice looked at him and smiled. "Thanks. I always had to do it all myself too. But this was a much different experience than what I'm used to. And it was the first time I really…." Her voice trailed off before she could finish the thought, which was that it was the first time she really loved what she did, the first time it felt like her choice, not something she had fallen into.

Johnny looked at his watch. "No chance you're up for a movie now, I guess. I know you got up really early. I'm always so wired after closing, it's how I wind down."

"I know," she answered, "Usually I come in and want to collapse, but there's all this residual energy. But no, you go to the movies without me. Think I'll just have a cup of cocoa." Johnny looked so hopeful that Alice couldn't just leave him standing there in the street, so she said, "Would you want some?"

He smiled, and for a moment Alice forgot how crazy he seemed, and was reminded of all the nights she'd dozed off to the sound of his voice, and she observed again for the millionth time how handsome he was. Then, automatically, she stood more erect, and was less at ease. She expected him to plow his way in her door, but then she noticed that he was watching her in the way he always did, seeing through her so disconcertingly.

"You know, I'd love that," he said, "But why don't you just go have some time for yourself. Have brunch with me tomorrow, somewhere we can go and let other people do the work, and we can discuss business stuff, and then I'll come see your aunt with you. If you want me to, that is, if you think it would help."

Alice was flooded with appreciation and then guilt, although she knew she'd never really been mean to him, except maybe about his clothes. He'd been so exceptionally nice, and she'd done everything to alienate him. It was so unkind, and really nothing like her, except that she was so uncomfortable in his presence, which wasn't his fault, not even the part about the show. "All right," she said softly, and then as he was turning to go to her aunt's, she heard herself speaking, almost without intent. "Hey, c'mon and have some cocoa. I can put on one of my zillion DVDs if you want to unwind to a movie. Some scrambled eggs maybe?"

His smile was like the sun coming out of the clouds, and he said, "Aww, thanks. That would be fantastic." Johnny followed Alice into the house, carrying the bag containing the few leftovers from the dinner service.

"I just want to change," said Alice, looking down at her still-pristine chef whites. "Two minutes."

Alice was up and down the stairs in what seemed like a blur, now wearing comfortable jeans and a simple shirt, but he'd already toasted some of the leftover bread, sliced some persimmons, and put the cocoa on. Alice laughed. "You're like a super hero with a whisk. Warp speed, whatever that is. Let me make the eggs at least. I feel guilty."

"Whisk away," he said, laughing.

Alice made her favorite scrambled eggs with blobs of cream cheese and some chives, and they filled two plates and walked into the living room, carrying the food and their mugs of hot cocoa. "Anything special you want to watch?" Then for the second time, they both spoke simultaneously, "*The Big Chill.*"

He laughed, "I couldn't remember the line about the table…"

"And the chair," she said, getting up to pull the DVD from her collection of movies. "Oh," she mused, "Popcorn? Candy? I do have chocolate chip cookies."

"Plenty," he said, motioning toward the couch, so she sat down next to him with a reasonable distance between them, and took a big sip from her mug.

They watched in silence for a while, laughing at the comedy, and falling into a lull. A long day had ended, and they both needed the quiet. Alice remembered Mary Kay Place talking about the rigors of dating, then she was looking out the window, and there was Aunt Kitty on a brown horse riding off into the distance. Alice yelled to her aunt, but Kitty galloped along, getting smaller and smaller. She turned and Itch was there, with his old motorcycle, except that it was as shiny as it once had been, and she asked him to chase after her aunt, to bring Kitty back, so he hopped on the bike and sped off, waving to Alice, which made her terribly apprehensive. Then for some reason, Itch had a gun, and he was shooting at Alice, forcing her to dart back and forth, ducking and jumping and dodging, as the bullets sped beyond her. "Don't shoot at me," she yelled, "Are you nuts? Get Kitty, and bring her back." But Itch rode off into the distance, and then she couldn't see either of them. She turned around, and there was nothing left in the room, nothing all around her; she was in completely empty space, as though she'd landed on an unoccupied planet, one with no buildings or people. She looked in every direction, and it was nothing but a void, and although Alice expected there to be a door, there was no door, no gate, no grass, nothing but clean, empty, blankness. She grew more and more terrified as she dashed about, trying to find something, anything. As she was about to yell for help, some music began playing, some weird song that seemed so familiar, but it sounded faint, and she didn't know from where.

Finally there was a familiar voice, a comforting voice, saying, "Sugar, sugar, wake up."

Alice opened her eyes and jumped. Her head was on Johnny's leg, and he was shaking her shoulder. Alice wrenched herself awake and turned to get up from the couch, but ended up tumbling onto the floor. "What are you still doing here?" she asked, trying to rise without looking even more stupid.

"I think I fell asleep. Then you were talking and moaning, and woke me up. That was some dream. And your phone was ringing." Johnny got up from the couch and stretched, then he reached down to pat Alice on the back. "You okay?"

She shuddered, then walked to the cabinet where she'd tossed her purse, and pulled out her phone. Cooper had called her three times in a row. And she'd nodded off on Johnny's leg, when the one thing she wanted was to keep her distance? She'd had a nightmare, she knew that, but she couldn't remember, except maybe it was about cowboys and Indians? Her phone beeped again, and this time Coop had sent her a text asking her to call him urgently, and saying he needed to see her at P3.

"Hmm," she said softly, "Cooper wants me at P3." Johnny, who had turned to go out the back to Kitty's apartment, stopped and waited, as Alice dialed the phone. Cooper answered immediately, and Alice listened as he spoke. "Okay" she said, "Thirty minutes, okay?"

Alice finished the conversation, and said to Johnny, "I have to shower and run out to my restaurant. Some breakthrough or something about the fire."

"Need me to come along?" he asked. "Then we could have our brunch and see your aunt—if you still want to."

"Um," she mumbled, thinking. Did she want him along? "I hate to take up your time," she answered honestly. Alice was less afraid now, for even if they'd found evidence indicting Kitty, nothing could be done. They'd never prosecute Kitty in her current state. But would the insurance pay out? "You might know some stuff about insurance in disasters, though this might actually have been arson."

Johnny nodded decisively. "I'll come. You go shower and change, and I'll be back here in ten minutes."

"Thanks." Alice watched him walk to the back door, then she ran up the stairs, almost relieved that she would have him with her. At the least, he could vouch that Kitty was very ill, and maybe he would be an asset regarding the insurance—if it came to that.

She showered quickly, dressed and raced back down the stairs, to find him standing there with a glass of fresh tangerine juice. "Drink this," he said, "Better than coffee," so Alice downed the juice, and then they were off in his car, quickly arriving, and finding several police cars in the P3 lot. Alice identified herself to a cop at the entrance of the lot, and they were allowed to drive in close to the building.

"This was a big place," said Johnny.

"My uncle built it a long time ago, when land was cheaper." By then they'd parked, and Alice got out of the car and walked over to where Cooper was standing next to that detective who'd been to the house, what was his name? Longfellow or something like that.

"What's going on?" Alice asked Cooper.

"Detective Longworth," said the officer, shaking Alice's hand. "We met a little while back." Alice nodded, and he continued, "I owed your nephew after he solved my case for me."

Alice looked at Cooper again.

The detective flipped through the pages of a little notebook, and asked Alice, "You know your boyfriend was doing so much online gambling?"

"Robin?" asked Alice, thinking that he wouldn't waste a dime in a quarter slot machine.

Hearing the word boyfriend, Johnny looked at Alice for a moment, then turned his attention back to the detective, who continued. "Well, Cooper here recovered as much of his money as was left, twenty something thousand, and we closed the case. Couldn't really arrest anyone because it's offshore, way offshore, but at least some money was recovered, and the case was closed."

"That is good news," said Alice, continuing to look at Cooper, who smiled innocently.

"So when he asked me to look into your fire, I was glad to oblige. And this is what I discovered." From his pocket, the detective pulled out a ziploc bag containing what looked like some strips of stained, partially burned red fabric. "Any thoughts about this? It was under a dumpster. Must have been there all these weeks."

Alice reached for the bag and looked at it carefully, then realizing what it was, gasped and took a step back.

"Julian," whispered Alice. "That night I said he couldn't perform the show he wanted to do. The scarves that were supposed to simulate blood. Oh my...."

"I already told him," said Cooper.

"We'll definitely be bringing him in for questioning," said Longworth, "But this is pretty strong evidence."

Alice's mouth hung open. "My God," she said, thinking of Skye and how she would feel.

"And now the insurance will pay out, right?" said Cooper, as the detective nodded.

"Shouldn't be a problem, even though he is sort of connected to your family," answered the detective. "I'll speak to the arson investigation team immediately."

"My daughter will be so upset," sighed Alice.

Cooper said, "And then she'll snap out of it. Don't think you'll have to worry about conjugal visits."

"Geez," whispered Alice. "Can I call Skye and let her know?"

Longworth raised his hand. "Please wait until we have the boy in custody and back here. Should be picked up momentarily—again thanks to Cooper here and his phone tracking. You know—I think this young man would be a great cop."

Alice cringed, but tried not to let her feelings show. The last thing any of them needed would be to worry about Cooper, out in the world with bullets flying all around him. Bullets flying around, was there something familiar about that? She squinted a moment, trying to picture it, but nothing came through.

Finally she spoke, saying, "He seems all grown up, but please, he's just a kid in school, and then he has college, so let's not plan his future yet."

Cooper smiled at Alice in a goofy way, showing that he knew exactly what she was thinking.

"All right, Ma'am, we'll call you when the boy is in custody. Then you can call your daughter, and arrange for her to come home. Or she might be calling you."

"Thank you very much. This is just so unreal, but I appreciate all your hard work. Otherwise we might never have known or had any sense of resolution or closure," said Alice, shaking Longworth's hand.

"We coulda had a wedding and little clown babies," said Cooper, grinning.

"Thanks Coop," said Alice, hugging him. "Need a ride home?"

"Got my car," he said.

"Could we take a walk around before we leave?" asked Johnny.

"Just don't go inside," said Longworth. "Unsafe."

Alice walked around the building with Johnny, answering questions about P3 and its setup, how she'd come to work there, and what the business had been like. He nodded and said, "Like a blast from the past."

"Yes," said Alice, "Exactly."

"And now you'll go back to this exactly as it was?" he asked, clearly worried that his plans for their partnership were just a fantasy.

Alice took a moment to think, recalling her certainty that there was no choice but to reopen P3 just as it had been, and recognizing that her frequent desire to quit wasn't a whim but something genuine, and she said, "I'd sort of felt I had to, but I don't know. After last night...."

"When you find your true calling, you can't go back to an imitation, no matter how easy it might be. Plus there's way more profit in a restaurant for adults, not kids. Same work, better return."

True calling, he'd said. Alice stopped a moment. "True calling," she repeated.

"Exactly."

"Well, we'll see."

"And the boyfriend?" Johnny asked. So as they entered the car and drove toward the Wellman Center, Alice told him all about her life and about Robin. He listened carefully, and as they arrived and began walking in the door, he said, "Well, doll, I'd say you've used up your quota of misery for this lifetime. Time to turn things in a better direction."

Before Alice could respond, she saw Itch in the corridor, and he waved to her and said, "Ally, great news. Wednesday!"

Alice and Johnny walked toward Itch, and then all three stopped and waited. Itch threw his arms around Alice, and said "Did you hear me, Wednesday I get sprung."

"Wow! Only three days!" said Alice, smiling and sinking into his hug. "Itch, this is Johnny. He's maybe going to be my business partner."

The two men shook hands, then Johnny said, "I'll go see Kitty, leave you two to visit a while."

Alice looked gratefully into his eyes. "Thanks," she said softly, and she followed Itch into his room.

It was still dark out when Skye called. "Mom, Mom, thank God you're there!"

"Where else would I be," answered Alice sleepily, "It's five in the morning."

"Oh geez, I totally forgot about the time difference. Sorry. But Mom, they arrested Julian. I don't have the money to post bail."

"Bail? Bail? Really?" asked Alice, growing more agitated with each word. "He burned down P3. All this time we suspected Kitty, but no, it was Julian. They have actual evidence, which I saw."

"That can't be true."

"Skye, I've had it with you. Snap out of it. Julian got all pissy when I said he couldn't do his blood and guts show with those stupid scarves, had some sort of meltdown—literally—and he burned down P3—our family business, not just some random target. He's either going to jail or a mental institution. And you're talking to me about bail money?" Alice heard herself as she was speaking and the rage in her voice increased with each additional word.

Skye burst into tears. "You're being so harsh."

"I saw the evidence. He used those stupid red scarves to burn the place down."

"But you don't even know they were his."

"Okay," said Alice, her patience snapping. "I've had enough of this. I've been more than tolerant with you during this whole personal crisis of yours, but I will not listen to another word. Forget about this guy. He's nuts. What he did could have ruined all our lives. Or don't. You're an adult. Do what you want. Goodbye."

Alice heard Skye wail, "But Mom," and then she hung up the phone. Alice lay in bed, her heart thundering, and she tried to quiet her breath. There was time to sleep a bit more and she knew she needed the rest, but she just felt so agitated that she rose and began the chores that would precede her going to the hospital to pick up Itch. She worked steadily and with concentration, hoping to put the nonsense with Skye out of her mind, but how was she to erase the worry? Could she rely on her daughter to come to her senses, and what if she didn't? Could Cooper's quip about conjugal visits turn into reality? Alice shuddered. If Skye stood by Julian, wouldn't the police begin to suspect her, and wouldn't that impinge on the insurance? Alice sighed and kept scrubbing and vacuuming, as though she could wash away her angst.

When the phone rang again, Alice was tempted not to answer it, but she couldn't be that mean, so she took a deep breath, and said, "Hi. Have you come to your senses?"

Skye was sobbing. "Oh Mom, I'm so sorry. He actually signed a confession. So it's all true. And it's all my fault."

"How is it your fault?" Alice asked. "You didn't tell him to set that fire."

Skye took a deep, rasping breath, then said, "No, but I brought him into our lives. Otherwise none of this would have happened. I'm so sorry."

"Crazy clown or not, there's no way you could've known all this might happen. Look hon, come on home, for goodness sake, put this behind you and move forward."

Skye sniffled like she used to when she was a little girl, and said, "That's what I'm calling to tell you. I'm on a flight tomorrow. I'll see you tomorrow night."

"That's great. You know your dad will be home tonight. Finally."

"You mean Robin?"

"You know I don't."

"Well I'm happy for you both." Skye sniffled a few more times, blew her nose with a very loud honk, then said, "I'm really sorry, and Mom?"

"I'm going to break up with Greg. I'm taking my apartment back and going to college like you said."

"Well, well," said Alice, "Maybe P3 being burned down was a good thing. I'm glad to hear you're snapping out of it. Must be that New York water they're always bragging about."

"But, Mom," asked Skye, "Would you think it was so terrible if I went to dental school? I really do like dentistry."

Alice chuckled, thinking that Robin got the last laugh, except he never urged Skye to be a dentist because that was his role; he'd expected her to be an assistant. "Well, well," she said again, "I think that would be just great."

"Really?"

"Sure. Why not? Be Doctor Skye, and slay all those cavities. Remember the year you went as a tooth for Halloween?"

Skye chuckled, then asked, "Anything you want me to bring home from New York?"

"Just yourself. Need a ride from the airport?"

"Nope, my car is there."

They talked a few minutes more, and Alice felt a huge weight drain from her heart. Skye was going to be all right. All those years of dentist talk had apparently sunk in, and it wasn't such a bad thing; they'd have a dentist in the family after all.

When the doorbell rang, Alice glanced at her watch. She had cleaned all morning, was now showered, dressed and ready to pick up Itch. She didn't have time for a neighbor or a tenant. Twice more she glanced at her watch as she ran down the stairs. Her stomach was fluttering in anticipation of all that was to come. She peered through the glass in the front door and then opened it. "Hello!" she said, stepping back so her insurance agent could enter. She walked into the living room and he followed her, taking a seat as she did.

"I really want to apologize," he said. "I know it's taken a very long time, and normally we pride ourselves on taking good care of our customers. But considering how it all worked out, you can understand our delays."

Alice looked at him with little expression. Her intention was to find a new insurance company. "That may be," she said coolly, "But it certainly hasn't felt like it."

Reaching into his pocket, the man withdrew an envelope and handed it to Alice. "We have to take allegations of arson seriously," he said, "But after speaking to that detective, Long-something-or-other, we knew you were in the clear, so I'm happy and relieved to present you with this."

Alice looked in the envelope and saw a check for the full amount of the policy. "Thank you," she said, standing up.

"I was hoping we could talk about your policies as long as I'm here," he countered rather lamely.

"Sorry," said Alice, "I have somewhere to be like five minutes ago."

"All right then." He offered Alice his hand, she shook it, then escorted him to the door. When he was safely down the driveway, Alice walked back in the house and collapsed in a chair. It was finally resolved, but it didn't feel resolved, because she had a huge decision to make and needed to talk to someone, but the person whose advice she most wanted was unreachable.

Every day this week, she'd spent hours talking with Kitty, coaxing Kitty, cajoling Kitty, but her eyes simply grew more dull, and her responses even more minimal, if that were possible. Alice's heart ached, and that pain marred the joy she felt about Itch's homecoming. It didn't matter how much she hoped or prayed — it was likely that Kitty wouldn't be having a turn for the better, rather that she was mired in a black hole out of which she'd never emerge. Seeing her aunt in this dark cloud was more than Alice could bear, for Kitty was such a fun person, so sparkling and humorous, always so full of life.

Every time Alice thought of Kitty, her tender heart felt a little more tattered. Losing someone old and beloved through death was deeply painful, but losing her this way while she was still alive tugged at Alice's heart even more — it was just such a terrible waste. What time they might yet have had was so tragically diminished, and there was poor Kitty enduring it all alone in a way, walled off from life and unable to be comforted by those who loved her. Alice allowed herself a few moments to mourn for her aunt, trapped in a death-in-life, and to feel the pain of the situation. Then for the last time she glanced at her watch, rose from the chair, freshened up and drove to pick up her husband.

Beyond all rational probability, miraculously their life together was beginning. It all felt so odd, but so wonderful, and then odd again. Soon it would feel normal, wouldn't it, and she would have a chance to live that ordinary, dull life which for so long she'd yearned. As Alice walked toward Itch's room for the last time, those special but yet unlived images floated through her mind like a slide show in slow motion, a montage of hoped-for eventualities, the small moments, the sweet moments, the bits and pieces that together made up a happy life. They were the memories she'd created without having lived them, and now there was the likelihood that some or even all of them would become real. In a flicker, his room would be her room, and together they would build a future.

She heard his laugh as she entered the doorway, and a familiar voice. Misty was in the room with Itch—and they were laughing together. He smiled at her and said, "Do you know Ally, my girlfriend?"

Misty snorted, and turned on the edge of the bed, saying "Unfortunately so."

"What are you doing here?" asked Alice.

"I have a right to visit an old friend, don't I?" Misty leaned down and kissed Itch, not on the cheek but on the mouth, her hand trailing along his thigh.

"Hey," said Alice, watching as Itch recoiled from the kiss. She walked toward them, and only then did Misty lean away from Itch and rise from the bed.

"Don't worry, I'll be around. We don't have to lose touch again," she said.

"Get out," said Alice.

Misty sauntered toward the door with an exaggerated wiggle, stopping to bend over as she exited, as though she were in a comic book version of a trashy movie. Then she turned back around and blew Itch a kiss. "I still love you," she said.

"Nobody gives the smallest little crap," said Alice. "Do I need to call security?"

"Why don't you just get your boyfriend to manhandle me again. I'm seeing a lawyer about that you know."

Itch looked perplexed when he heard the word *boyfriend*, and he said, "Lawyer? About me?"

"Not you, sexy pants," said Misty. "Her other boyfriend. One of them anyway. She's a total slut you know."

Alice strode toward Misty, who then quickened her pace and exited the room. Then she turned back to Itch, who still looked confused.

"Who was that lady?" he asked, then lowering his voice to a whisper, said, "She showed me her boobs! I didn't ask, really I didn't."

"Of course you didn't," said Alice. "Ready to go home?"

"Will your other boyfriend be there?"

Alice laughed. "I don't have another boyfriend." Then she took a deep breath, paused for a moment, and began telling Itch about Robin.

"Whoa, that dental dude Misty dates?" Alice watched him as his mind processed all the information she shared. "And you live with him and have sex with him and he sees you naked?"

It sounded so simplistic to Alice, but it also was honest, so she said, "You were assumed practically dead, never to recover. Skye needed a dad."

"Maybe. But he won't be there when we get there, will he? I don't know if I could punch someone out. Maybe I could." Itch grabbed a pillow and gave it a practice punch.

"As soon as you woke up, I made him leave. It's just you and me, now and forever."

"Wow, forever. That's a little scary."

Alice smiled. "Not scary, good. Happy. Finally." She touched Itch on the back of the hand, and he dropped the pillow he was clutching and squeezed her hand in return.

After the discharge papers were signed, and Itch was wheeled out to the parking lot, he walked on his own with Alice to her car. "Do I have any clothes?" he asked.

Alice smiled. "I got you a bunch of things. Can't have you wrapped just in a towel every day."

"And your mom won't be there?"

Alice shook her head. "Not 'til Thanksgiving. She'll come over then. Along with Totsie and Mitchell and Cooper. Remember them? Wait, of course you don't. You never met Mitchell. Well, you will."

"Whew. It's better to meet people than to feel bad you don't remember them."

Alice reached out to rest her hand on the back of Itch's neck, and he relaxed a little as she drove toward home. "Hon, could I ask your advice?" she said.

"Me? My advice?" Itch looked very nervous, but then said, "Sure, I guess, just don't expect too much." He began drumming his fingers on his thigh, almost as though he were playing an imaginary piano.

"You remember P3, right? Well, it burned down, you knew that, right?"

Itch nodded, gaining confidence that the advice being requested was about something he actually knew, although the rapid finger movements didn't cease until Alice took his hand in hers and paused a moment to let them both take a breath.

"So I have to decide if I should rebuild it with the insurance money. It's a really hard business, and I have an offer to open a different kind of restaurant, which is way more fulfilling, but if I just let P3 go, it would feel like I was letting my aunt and uncle down. They entrusted it to me."

"Wait a sec," Itch said, "You got a lot of money from the insurance? Then why work at all? We can go cross country like I said. This is a super nice car. We could drive. Think they'd give me a license?"

Alice sighed. "Maybe you can get a license, yes, once you're totally recovered, but I can't just go off on an adventure and squander insurance money. I have to work, pay bills, be a grown up."

"So really you don't want my advice? My advice is have fun. Don't worry about dead people or nearly dead people. Not like they're in a coma about to wake up."

Alice sighed again. "It was their legacy and it meant a lot to them. They did so much for me, and I always want to…um…not let them down. Uphold all their faith in me."

"Just cause somebody told you not to have fun doesn't mean you have to be their slave when you're old. It's like you want to be their age, not teenagers like us, well ok we're not teenagers, I guess. But we could still have fun." Itch glanced around as Alice pulled into the driveway. "Hey I remember this place. I can set up my band in the garage or out back. That'll be totally cool."

"Hmm, maybe." Alice walked around to help Itch out, but he seemed fine getting out on his own. "I just don't think that any of those guys are still making music. They all have jobs. Or maybe they moved away. Families, kids, responsibilities."

"Whoa. This is like a science fiction movie—the land that fun forgot. You make it all sound so gross and miserable, like everyone's a robot." Itch starting walking, swinging his arms, making quirky head gestures, and stiffening his legs. "Look at me, I'm a grownup robot. I have responsibilities. Fun? No fun, not now not ever. Tick tock I'm old, old, old."

Alice watched Itch walk in the house, still doing his robot impersonation. Then he followed her upstairs to see the clothes she'd bought for him.

"So this is my room?" he asked, noticing that Alice's clothes were on one side of the closet and his on the other.

"Our room."

"Oh, no," he said, "Your mom will put me in jail. She threatened to. You know that, right?"

Alice laughed. "We're all grown up. Nobody can put us in jail for living in the same room."

"And like being naked, and having sex anytime we want? In here, not in the car, right? No way."

Alice laughed again.

Itch looked down for a moment, "I'm not sure...."

Alice patted his cheek gently, "Don't worry about all that now, hon. It's a lot to adjust to, I know. Let's just take it easy. If you want to sleep in Skye's room, that's okay. Whatever makes you comfortable."

"Could I have a glass of milk?"

Alice smiled. "Sure and some cookies too if you want. Let's go downstairs and relax. You're home now. Soon enough that will sink in."

"You think my folks have my sports stuff somewhere?"

"Maybe."

Itch sat at the counter drinking his milk and eating cookies until Cooper came in.

"You," said Itch, "Are you Ally's other boyfriend?"

Cooper laughed. "Uncle Harvey, it's me, Cooper. Ally's my aunt. What an imagination." Cooper slid the cookie jar toward himself and shoved his usual two cookies into his mouth, as Alice poured him a glass of milk.

Itch continued to look suspicious for a while. "But you live here? Up there?" He pointed out toward the staircase. "In Ally's room?"

Cooper laughed again. "Sheesh. I'm here cause my parents are nuts. I sleep in the little room upstairs. Who sleeps with their aunt?"

Itch squinted at the boy for a moment, paused to think, then asked, "You play football?" When Cooper shook his head, Itch continued, looking even more suspicious, "You play basketball?" As Cooper shrugged, Itch grew a bit agitated. "You're a kid, right? You one of those no-fun robots?" Itch began jerking his head around again, and raising and lowering his arms in his robot imitation, but his hand caught the edge of his milk glass, and it flew off the counter and shattered on the floor. Alice bent to pick up the pieces, and carefully tossed them in the trash, mopping up the spill with some paper towels.

"I'm sorry. I'm sorry. Oh wow. My fault. I'm sorry," said Itch.

"Don't worry about it, hon," said Alice calmly. "We have plenty of glasses. But no robots." Then she grinned at him.

Itch pointed at Cooper, saying, "You, you're a kid right, not like you're an old man of thirty or something? What kind of a kid doesn't do any sports? You in a band?"

Cooper laughed. "Nobody wants to hear me be musical. Trust me."

"I may have been napping a while, but you trust *me*, kids are supposed to be out playing basketball. Isn't there a hoop outside? Like over the garage? They always have those on TV shows. I mean you gotta have a basketball or a football — or both."

"I'm a techno guy," explained Cooper. "I have computers. Here, check this out." Cooper reached in his backpack and pulled out an iPad.

"I've seen that picture screen before," said Itch, still sounding suspicious.

Cooper tapped the iPad and began playing a video basketball game, as Itch watched with fascination. "No way, super cool," he said, sounding happy again. Cooper handed the device to Itch, who needed some coaxing, but managed to play it fairly successfully after a bit. By the time he'd advanced several levels, it became more difficult, and he quickly grew frustrated. He began squeezing his left hand into a fist repeatedly as he tapped the screen with his right. "Broken, it's broken, this doesn't really work," he said agitatedly, shoving the device across the counter.

Cooper quickly grabbed it, saying calmly, "No, no Uncle Harvey, don't slam it, it'll break. These are fragile. Can't knock them around. Gotta be careful."

Itch snorted, saying, "It's stupid anyway. Get a real basketball. Hey gimme the phone, willya? I want to call some of the guys. They have basketballs."

Alice looked sympathetically toward Itch—it was all so hard for him. "Who did you want to call?"

"Do I have to tell you everything?" Itch asked.

"Sorry hon, but I don't think anybody's at their old numbers is all. We'll have to look them up, if they're even still here."

"Okay, well gimme the phone book."

Cooper laughed. "Does anyone have a phone book any more?" As Itch glared at him, Cooper said more kindly, "Okay Uncle Harvey, tell me their names, and I'll look them up here."

Itch glared at Cooper. "You butthead. You know what Miss Pac-man, never mind. I'll just go walk around the block. That ok with you?"

"Honey," said Alice, "I don't think you should go walking off alone. You're not used to everything yet, and you could get tired or lost. You've only been out of the hospital like five minutes. Maybe take it easy today? Or if you want, I could come with you a little ways. Or hey, want to sit right outside here?" Alice opened the kitchen door and looked out into the courtyard. "It's still sunny out. We could grill some burgers later if you want."

"Will my dad be here?"

"I think your parents'll stop by tomorrow. Not tonight though. Is that okay?"

"You said grill burgers. Dad's the one who does the grilling is all."

"That's okay," said Alice, "I can do it. I do it all the time." She touched Itch's arm gently, and said, "Come on, let's sit outside for a bit. It's still kind of early for dinner. Tomorrow your folks will visit, and Skye will be home, and you'll feel more settled in."

"All right, but I'm taking my guitar out there." As Alice turned to get the guitar, Itch said, "I'll get it. I can do it." Alice watched him walk toward the stairs, and she took a deep breath.

"Whoa," said Cooper, opening his eyes widely to convey his dismay about what Alice would likely be going through. "Hey," he said, "Insurance guy come over with a check? Longworth promised to close that investigation."

"Yes, just this morning," said Alice. "Hey, Coop?" As Cooper turned his attention toward her, she asked, "Do you think I would be a terrible person if I didn't rebuild P3, and just opened a new restaurant with Johnny? I don't want to let Kitty down, especially now."

"I think more than anything Kitty wants you to be safe and happy. Besides a new restaurant isn't that different from an old restaurant is it? I mean you're not opening a skating rink or a bowling alley, right? Or a clown supply store?" Cooper chuckled, then said, "You have a right to your own life. Everyone has that, don't they? Not like you'd tell me or Skye we gotta work at P3 forever, right?"

"No I'd never do that, but well, I don't know."

Itch returned with the guitar slung over his back, and said, "Bowling alley for clowns? Let's go there. I want to see clowns bowling."

"Nobody in this family likes clowns any more," said Cooper, grabbing his backpack and heading toward the stairs. "Homework," he said quietly, but Alice suspected he just wanted to get away from Itch.

"Harsh. Super serious and harsh," answered Itch. Then he followed Alice out the door and sat down next to her, his hands flicking the strings of the guitar as she sat silently thinking.

After what seemed like a short while for her to ponder her future and whether she could abandon the legacy entrusted to her, Alice rose to start the grill and get the burgers going. Itch continued to strum his guitar, in what to Alice sounded like a melancholy fashion. She touched him lightly on the back of his neck and whispered, "Don't worry honey, it'll all be all right soon enough. Don't be sad." Itch looked at her with surprise and just nodded, seemingly deeply engrossed in his guitar. Now and then he'd look up and out into the courtyard, surveying his surroundings.

As Alice was about to set the burgers on the flame, Johnny walked over. He smiled brightly, and was about to greet her with his usual *sugar* or *doll*, but something in Alice's eyes must have caught his attention, so a simple, "Hey there," was all he said.

"You," said Itch, rising from his seat and looking combative, "You. You Ally's other boyfriend?"

Something flickered across Johnny's eyes, he glanced toward Alice, who was about to step forward and remind

Itch who he was, when Johnny extended a hand to Itch and said, "Hi, John Badeaux. We met the other day."

Itch scowled and refused to shake his hand. "I said you—you Ally's other boyfriend?"

Alice put her hand on Itch's arm, and said softly, "You know Chef Johnny. We worked together the other night. I told you all about it, remember?"

Itch's voice halted, then seemed to stumble, then grew irritated as he continued, "Yeah well maybe I was asleep a long time, but I guess I know when a question is answered and when it isn't."

Alice was grateful to see the look of sympathy cross Johnny's face, as he spoke softly and calmly. "I asked her to be my girlfriend, but she told me she was married. That enough of an answer for you?"

"Maybe," said Itch, glaring at Johnny.

"Mind if I talk about some work stuff with your wife?" Johnny asked, as Itch shrugged. "Doing one last popup this weekend. You in?"

"Then what?" she asked.

"I've been looking at locations for the permanent place. Time to commit."

Alice nodded. "Maybe you're not the right person to ask, but I've been obsessing about this constantly. Do you think I'd be letting Kitty and Henry down if I didn't rebuild P3?"

"Hang on a second," said Johnny, turning and walking back into Kitty's apartment.

"He lives here?" asked Itch. "At least not in the house with us, right?" His grip on the guitar tightened, and his other hand repeatedly made and released a fist.

"My aunt invited him to stay here. She always watches him on TV. You know—cooking on TV."

Itch laughed. "Cooking on TV? Like who does that other than that giant English lady with the squeaky voice?"

Alice smiled. "Julia Child was American, though she cooked French food. Lots of people cook on TV now."

Itch emitted a loud guffaw, and said, "Who'd ever watch that."

Johnny returned with the opened packet of Kitty's letters. "I looked over these again and wanted to show you this one." He handed Alice one of the letters.

"Hey," said Itch, jumping up again, "Those look like love letters."

Johnny's voice stayed calm as he said, "Ally's aunt sent them to me." Itch squinted at Johnny again, then sat down and continued playing his guitar.

Alice glanced over the note her aunt had written. Much of it was praise for Johnny's food and his show, but some was about herself. "Oh my," said Alice softly. She began reading aloud from the letter, *"We had this kids' party place forever, and Henry and I talked about retiring and selling it, but he never wanted to, then he died and I thought all right, I can sell it now and have some kind of life, but my little Alice loved that place so much and it made her so happy to work there that I figured okay no reason to sell, let the younger generation enjoy it the way I never did."*

"I thought maybe you didn't know she felt that way," said Johnny.

"I had no idea," answered Alice. Then she sighed, and said, "She sounded so coherent…."

"So now you just have to decide what actually does make you happy. You know I want you for a partner. That's for sure."

"Hmm," she answered, "Not as though we could use P3 for a new place. Pretty sure it has to be razed."

Johnny paused only a moment, then said, "Maybe we could lease a place for a while, and build something on the location you already have. Then we could either move or have two locations. And meanwhile we'd have the income from the first place."

"Maybe," said Alice. "Guess I can get some engineers in there for an actual report."

"You think about it. We have to let your friend know about investing, and just make these decisions. Once it's all decided, it gets easier. We can talk more about it Saturday night."

When he heard the word *Saturday*, Itch began strumming even more loudly on his guitar and he glared at Johnny.

"I'd better get these burgers on," said Alice. "Want to stay for dinner? Really simple—I have potato salad and coleslaw, nothing fancy."

"No, no, you go have a family dinner," said Johnny. "We'll talk more on the weekend."

Alice looked at him with gratitude. "Thank you so much. I'm so glad you kept those letters."

"Me too," he answered, about to reach out and touch Alice on the arm, but then he stopped himself. "Night," he said simply.

As Johnny walked away, Itch said, "You're going out with him Saturday night? So he is your boyfriend."

"Honey, listen to me. I don't have a boyfriend. I'm working with him. In a restaurant. People go out to eat on the weekend. So chefs work on the weekend. It's a work thing."

"All you think about is work. What am I supposed to do? You won't let me go anywhere or call anyone. Is this home or jail?"

"Skye will be here, or Cooper. You can hang out with them, can't you? Or we can call Stan or your parents.

There are plenty of people who want to spend time with you. I can't just not work. It takes money to live. Do you understand?" Alice sat back down next to Itch, and looked into his eyes. She grasped his hand tightly, trying to make him feel safe, secure, and loved. "Besides," she said softly, "It's only one night of work right now, then all next week we'll spend every day together, and we'll have fun, doing whatever you want, and it'll be wonderful, just you and me."

After dinner was over, Alice and Itch sat inside on the couch, looking at their yearbook from high school. She'd provided a pad of sticky notes, and asked Itch to put one on each person he wanted to call. Slowly he turned the pages, commenting now and then about the images. "Ha—that was the shirt we filled with red ants.... Thirteen to twelve, closest game of the season.... My old motorcycle, you think my parents have...oh yeah, right.... Look at Misty in that sweater, oh sorry...."

Alice sat quietly, watching Itch make his comments. To him all this was yesterday, not like yesterday but actually yesterday, and it was as though she floated back in time with him for an instant. Then, inexplicably, she burst into tears.

Itch glowered at her, "What, what did I do now? I didn't ask for sex. What'cha crying about now?"

Alice turned her face toward him, tears flooding down her cheeks. "It's just that I pictured this, or something like it, so many times over the years. You and me on the couch, watching TV, babies upstairs, family portraits, trips to the mall, all of us around a table. And it never happened, but I kept picturing it, as though I were actually living the life in my dreams, the life with you that I never got to live." She paused, sniffled, and took a deep breath, then said, "And now here we are. It's happening."

Itch frowned. "Couch and television, that's what you pictured? Were we still breathing or were we like ninety-two?"

Alice smiled. "I just wanted a normal, simple life."

"That's so sad. Who wants fantasies duller than reality?"

Me," said Alice, sniffling once more.

Itch raised his eyebrows, glanced up at the ceiling, looked back at Alice as though he didn't quite recognize her, and continued turning pages, stopping now and then to post a sticky note on a face. "Now what?" he asked, "That wise guy upstairs gonna do something else to make me look stupid, like say none of this really happened, and these guys don't exist?"

"Oh honey," said Alice, "Coop is a great kid, and I'm sure he'll be happy to toss a ball around with you once we get you one. Please be nice to him."

Itch raised his hand in a salute and said, "Yes, sir, coach." Then he rose from the couch and said, "So where should I sleep?"

Alice looked at him, spotting his hesitation, and said, "Well you can sleep in Skye's bed instead of mine if you'd rather."

"Will she be in there too?"

Alice smiled. "No, of course not. Not tonight anyway. We'll see about tomorrow when we get there."

"I just don't want to get into any more trouble," said Itch. "Learned that lesson the hard way."

"What lesson?" asked Alice.

"Nothing. Maybe I could shower? You got some pj's up there for me? Can't walk around in my shorts with a kid and a girl in the house."

"A girl? You mean me?" Alice laughed.

"Yeah, I'm a riot." Itch glowered at her, then walked toward the stairs and went up, turning back toward Alice to add, "I don't need any help."

Wanting to give Itch his space, Alice sat on the couch, now and then flipping through the yearbook, but mostly daydreaming about the future, about the moment when Itch would catch up to her and be an adult with grownup desires and expectations. After just a few minutes, Cooper crept down the stairs.

"Hey, Coop?" asked Alice.

"Hold that thought," said Cooper, disappearing into the kitchen for some cookies, then returning with a handful balanced on top of a soda can.

"I'd hate to think you felt you had to hide out upstairs," said Alice softly.

"Don't worry, I'm fine," he answered, flopping down on the couch beside Alice. "He's asleep in Skye's room, snoring pretty loud." Cooper sniggered, then he scrutinized Alice for a moment and added, "You okay?"

"Sure, fine, why not?" Alice smiled as Cooper's eyes widened. "You think you could get phone numbers for these old classmates?" Alice handed Cooper the yearbook.

"Wow, ancient history," said Cooper.

"Hey, watch it, mister."

Cooper chucked and said, "Sure, I can find them, a number, a web address, a Facebook account. Probably by tomorrow."

"Fantastic. This way he won't feel so hemmed in and alone. Though I don't know if it'll be better once he talks with these guys and learns nobody is in the same place they were."

"He's gotta grow up sometime, right? Not like you want a teenage husband, do you?" Cooper scrutinized Alice's face one more time.

"If there's something you want to tell me, just say it," said Alice, sighing.

"Do they say his brain is okay? The doctors I mean." Cooper said this nervously, then tipped the soda can up and swallowed most of the contents in a single gulp.

"I think so. I know it's a lot to adjust to, for him, for you."

"But what about for you?"

Alice paused a moment, then hesitantly told Cooper about the night of the accident, about how it was her fault it all happened, and how she had so much to make up to Itch.

Cooper shook his head, stuffed the remainder of the cookies in his mouth, and just looked at Alice. "I wonder about the way your mind works. It's like you have the Girl Scout curse on you. First you can't have your own career and own life, and now you say you're responsible because of an earthquake? Cause you were a girl who wanted a romantic moment? Well, duh, even lesbians want romance. It's a girl thing."

Alice laughed. "Girl Scout curse? Where do you get this stuff! And what do you know about lesbians anyway?"

"I watched *The L Word*. Okay?"

Alice laughed again and shook her head. "Well I guess lesbians aren't really the issue."

"You won't live forever you know, that's all I'm saying."

"Maybe you should be a guru, ever think of that?"

Cooper scowled in mock annoyance, and said, "Yeah I can be a life coach like some goocher we both know."

"Oh honey, don't say bad things about your mom."

Before Cooper could answer, there was a faint knock at the door, and Alice glanced at her watch. It felt so late, but it was only nine o'clock. She shrugged and started to go answer it, when Cooper leapt up and beat her to it. "Hi!" he said, his eyes shining as Emma walked in the door.

"I hope I'm not disturbing you," she said.

"It's really nice to see you again," said Cooper, impressing Alice with his increased poise, after having been so tongue tied around Emma the last time.

Alice rose from the couch and put her arm around Emma's shoulders. "Come on in the kitchen. I'll make us some tea." Emma walked alongside Alice, and Cooper trailed closely behind them.

Emma smiled wanly. "You may not want to drink tea with me any more."

Knowing instantly what she was about to hear, Alice's heart clenched, but she didn't want Emma to feel responsible for something so clearly not her fault, so she smiled brightly and said, "That would never happen. So—Itch and Misty, huh?"

Emma nodded miserably. "I'm really sorry."

"What?" said Cooper, "Catch me up."

"You know about the baby switching letter?" Emma asked as Cooper nodded. Pulling a lab report from her purse, Emma handed it to Cooper.

"Wow," he said, "But that doesn't make you and me related."

Emma and Alice both laughed, then Emma turned serious again and said, "I'm really sorry."

"Oh hon, none of this is your fault. And at least you and Skye are sisters, which is something really nice. So you're in our family now. And I'm sure Itch will be thrilled once he gets to know you."

Emma's eyes opened widely, as she recalled his outburst in the hospital room. "Oh I don't know...." Her voice trailed off, then she accepted a cup of tea from Alice, and sat down opposite her in the kitchen booth.

"I'm sorry you're so sad," said Cooper kindly, easing his way into the booth beside Emma. "Is there any way I can help you?"

"Aw, thanks Coop," said Emma, patting him on the shoulder, and causing his whole face to turn a shade of raspberry. "Nothing to be done. I went looking for answers when I should have left well enough alone."

"So I guess I took the right baby home, and you got the right parents — the good parents you deserved." Alice reached across the table and squeezed Emma's hand.

"I lucked out, yes," said Emma.

Cooper said, "Hey you bet you did. You should meet mine. Both wackadoodle. Wasn't for Ally here, I'm off joining the army or living on the streets."

Alice snorted. "Knowing you, you'd be living in a cabaña at the Beverly Hills Hotel."

"What?" said Cooper. "Then what the hell am I here for? They have room service. Maybe even hookers." Then Cooper blushed some more and slapped his hand over his mouth, as the two women laughed again.

"You guys are so great," said Emma. "I really didn't want to tell you this. I thought about just tossing the results and hoping you wouldn't ask me, but at least now it's all out in the open, and you don't hate me after all."

Alice shook her head. "Oh, honey, don't ever think like that. You know we all love you."

"I definitely love you," said Cooper, blushing again.

Emma reached out and hugged Cooper, saying, "You're such a great kid. I wish I had a little brother just like you. Skye is lucky to have such a great cousin."

"Little brother," said Cooper, looking downcast.

"Okay a cousin then, that better?" asked Emma, but Cooper didn't respond. Alice could see the wheels turning in his head as he searched for a way to seem older, to seem more in Emma's league, and she half expected him to leap up and make them all martinis, but he just sat, silently morose.

"So, what should we do now?" Emma asked softly.

"I know a place with some pretty epic music, though I don't imagine Ally wants to leave Uncle Harvey, but we could go," said Cooper brightly, beaming toward Emma.

Alice covered his hand with hers and said, "I think she means about telling Itch and Misty."

Emma nodded. "I'd guess you'd want to tell Skye's dad, but maybe we can just leave Misty out of this, since she's not interested in knowing me or about me."

"Oh honey, she's the one who's missing out, you know that don't you," said Alice.

Emma nodded, but she looked rather dejected. "You just don't really think that someone who gave birth to you would rather pretend you don't exist, but who am I kidding. People who want kids don't give them away, do they? Besides, from what you've told me she's a horrible person, and I probably wouldn't like her, would I?"

Alice didn't know how to respond to this, so she took a moment to refill their cups with tea from her old china pot, and then she got up to grab the cookie jar and set it on the table between them. "I guess no amount of cookies could cheer you up as long as you assume that's true. But honey, some people aren't meant to be moms is all, so at least she knew it and did right by you."

"I know, I know," said Emma, sipping her tea.

"I'll tell Itch tomorrow, and I'm sure he'll love you to pieces once he understands who you are. Even if you weren't his daughter he would love you, because you're just so lovable," said Alice.

"Aw, Ally, you're the best," said Emma.

"Well, she's right," said Cooper, attempting to hold Emma's hand, which she allowed for a moment, then she made a big show of taking and eating some cookies, although she did smile sweetly at Cooper. Alice smiled at both of them, feeling sorry for her nephew with his crush on this girl who was so beyond him, at least for the moment. No adult would date a boy his age, no matter how smart and accomplished. She would have to discuss it with him in a way that would let him down easily — poor kids with their improbable crushes. People had to line up somehow, Alice knew that; there had to be some level of simpatico and a sense that they matched and were at the same place in their lives. But how hurt Cooper would be to be ruled out as a candidate simply because of his age. Alice hoped she could make him see the sense of it all.

Alice leaned toward Emma and said, "I have Itch's parents coming tomorrow and they'll be here for dinner, then Friday I have to prepare and Saturday do the popup, but why don't you plan on dinner here on Sunday? Then maybe you can start getting to know each other, plus of course Skye is home tomorrow, so you'll have her support, I'm sure."

Emma nodded. "Okay, unless you think he'll have another meltdown. I don't want to cause you any problems. It's not like I'm looking for a new dad. I just wanted answers, and I got answers. I could just go back home to San Diego now. I do have aunts and uncles and cousins there."

"No way," insisted Cooper, "Not as good as us."

Emma smiled, "Of course not. You're a very special boy." At the word boy Cooper sat up taller and straighter, and once again Alice expected some exaggerated gesture designed to impress his maturity on Emma, but he remained silent.

Emma rose, forcing Cooper to exit the booth to let her out, and so Alice stepped out as well, and wrapped her arms around Emma, saying, "Don't worry, honey, it all will be okay." Then she remembered saying the same thing earlier to Itch. Well, it would all be okay, wouldn't it. Of course it would. They'd all be fine.

After Emma had left, and they were back in the living room, Alice said, "Hey, Coop, sit with me a minute. You okay?"

Cooper flopped back down on the couch beside Alice and said, "Yeah, why wouldn't I be?"

Alice just looked at him. "Well I know you want Emma to see you as a boyfriend, not a little kid. But you do understand that the age difference is a big deal, right?"

"Only right now. What is it, five years, six years—it's nothing. It won't take long for her to see that. I mean you can understand that better than anyone, can't you?"

"Me?" Alice cocked her head as she listed to her nephew.

"You're with a guy who is basically twenty years younger. And you don't even know he'll ever grow up—leastways not fast enough to catch up with you. But for sure I will. And it won't be all that long, either." Cooper rose then and walked to the stairs, carrying the yearbook with the sticky notes and smiling at Alice. "Hey don't worry, Ally, I'm just a kid—what do I know. By next week I could be madly in love with some cheerleader." And then he laughed and just kept laughing as he climbed the stairs.

It was time for bed, not exactly the romantic homecoming she'd envisioned, but time none the less, but Alice just sat on the couch for a while, not thinking, but muddled in a raw state of emotion. Little flashes of memory floated up in her mind, Itch's meltdown when he first met Emma, along with moments from the past, all just blurring together, scene after scene, and Alice made no sense of any of it. She just let it wash over her. She knew something was wrong, and wondered was this overwhelming sense of sadness because of Emma's news. Surely something from that long ago couldn't matter that much, could it? But the truth was, everything was from that long ago. Nothing was current. The present was yet to be created, and so far it was nothing like the way she'd envisioned it in her many fantasies over the years. But only a day had passed, less than twenty-four hours, so there was no reason to grow disheartened. It was going to be a learning process for them all, and then they'd all be fine, just as she'd told both Itch and Emma. Everyone had to create the future day by day in the present, via the ordinary moments that clicked together like bricks. That's what they'd do together, and she was willing to be flexible in how they came together, for that was life, wasn't it? It was, Alice knew that, and all she had to do was relax a little and life would happen.

So up the stairs Alice went, and into her empty room, and she put on a big comfy t-shirt, not any of the pretty lingerie she'd bought in anticipation of romance, and she slipped into her bed, and she tossed and turned, finding it difficult to nod off. Alice was supposed to be wrapped in Itch's arms, drifting into a peaceful, joyful sleep but instead she awakened every hour or so, glanced at the bedside clock, groaned, turned over, and fell back into her fitful slumber. After what felt like no sleep at all, a hammering sound from outside wakened her. Again she glanced at the clock. It was ten in the morning. She'd slept badly but late.

Wrapping herself in a robe, Alice walked to the back of the house. Out in the courtyard were some men with heavy duty equipment pulverizing some of the cement in the back and digging a hole. What on earth? Alice raced down the stairs and out the back door, saying, "What are you doing?"

One of the workmen walked over, glancing up and down at her form, and causing Alice to wrap her robe even more tightly around her body. "What are you doing?" she repeated sternly.

"Installing a basketball hoop," he said, in a much too surly manner, handing Alice a work order. She examined it and saw Itch's signature.

"Good heavens," she said. "Wait, just wait." She held up her hand in the universal gesture of stop, then walked into the house. "Itch," she called several times, but there was no answer. She heard a noise from outside, a peculiar rat-tat-tat, so she walked outside into the garage, where a bunch of musical equipment had been set up, and Itch was seated behind some very expensive looking drums, attempting to play them.

"Honey! What's going on here?"

Itch smiled. "Got some band equipment today. Finally gonna learn the drums, and the guys are here installing the hoop. Some of us don't sleep all day."

"You ordered all this stuff?" asked Alice. "But how did you pay for it?"

"Used one of those credit cards in your wallet. So cool. How did you get all those? I made the calls, they said okay, and now it's all happening. Even if there's no phone books, you can still call 4-1-1."

Alice's eyes opened wide. "But how much was all this?"

Itch shrugged. "I didn't really ask for the total. I mean if you don't wanna pay, just don't pay. Not like they can do anything to you."

"Of course they could—they could sue me or ruin my credit rating. You have to pay your bills."

Itch looked crestfallen and said, "So it all has to go back, and I won't have my band or my hoop?"

He was so downcast that Alice said, "No, we'll keep it all, but honey please don't just order stuff with credit cards again. Talk to me first."

"You sound just like my mom," he said, banging loudly on the drums.

"It's still pretty early, so try to keep it a little more quiet, okay? The neighbors will all be screaming."

"Not when they hear how cool it sounds. And when I play gigs, they can all come."

"Okay honey, okay," said Alice, turning to go back into the house and out to the courtyard to speak to the workmen, all the while wondering if she needed a permit for construction this minor.

By the time she walked back outside, Johnny was out there talking to the guys and examining their plans. "Look," he said, don't dig a giant hole in the middle of this courtyard. Put your hoop over there." He pointed to the edge of the property, which actually made much more sense. "And you're going to repair all this concrete? I didn't see a mixer outside."

"It's a small job, we got equipment in the truck," said the surly guy, this time far more respectfully.

"You should have waited for the owner before starting," said Johnny. "And I don't want to see a lumpy repair job on the concrete. It has to be perfect."

"Hey bud, not our fault if some retard told us to dig here."

Johnny took a step closer to the man, and although they were both tall and roughly the same size, he seemed to tower over the worker, perhaps because he was in such good shape, while the guy was doughy with a squishy looking donut of fat all the way around his middle. Johnny took hold of his shirt and pulled him closer, saying quietly but in a voice best described as scary, "You watch your mouth. That is if you want to be able to continue chewing with it."

"Yes, sir," the guy mumbled.

Alice by this time stood close by, watching this intimidation. He wasn't kidding when he said he could be tough, and she was thankful to have him there. Johnny smiled at her. "Okay with you if they put the hoop over there? It would look better and also be better for playing."

"Absolutely," said Alice. "I'm glad you were here."

"Always," he said. "You go on inside and dress. I'll keep an eye on these guys." Then he grinned and said, "You're far too beguiling in your bunny slippers."

Alice looked down at her pathetic attire and chuckled. "Thanks so much," she answered. "Want to come in for waffles in a bit?" As she smiled and made this offer, Johnny glanced casually at her, and on his face Alice read relief about her appearance, that she wasn't wearing something more suited to the wedding night she'd envisioned. Then she felt silly, for it was absurd to attribute to him feelings that were really more her own, although relief was not what she was feeling at all.

"You eat without me. I should make sure they dig deeply enough to support this pole. You don't want it crashing into anything or anyone."

"Oh my God! What a thought," she said, her eyes widening. "Okay then, I'll bring you a plate."

He shook his head. "They don't need to think I'm picnicking out here instead of seriously watching them. It's better if they think I could decapitate them at any moment."

Alice laughed. "Maybe only as a plan B."

Although Alice had made a nice breakfast, Itch was impatient and ate little, wanting to be outside with his basketball court. She'd told him several times that the workmen had said he had to wait for the concrete to dry for at least a day, but he just scowled and grimaced, saying, "You know, you're more of a goody-goody now than ever."

"Thanks for that," said Alice softly.

After another short interval, and although there were still some wooden boards securing the goal post in its bed of still-damp cement, Itch managed to go outside and spend some time shooting hoops, which seemed to mellow him a bit. Alice watched from the window, noticing that of course he was less adroit than before, but still able to play reasonably well, even after all he'd endured. At least she hadn't taken that from him; he was still an athlete. He did look warm, though, and it was a typical fall day in Los Angeles, hot and dry, so she made some lemonade and took two glasses outside, hoping they could have a talk before his parents arrived.

Itch sat willingly beside her this time, the glass in one hand, and the basketball bouncing up and down in his other hand, making a slapity-slap-slap sound against the ground.

Feeling nervous and apprehensive, Alice steeled herself. What if he reacted as violently as he had before? Would she be able to handle him? Would he have some sort of turnaround as a result of hearing what she had to say? She wished there were a way to ease him into the information, but really, ultimately it was something he needed to know. "I have something serious to tell you," said Alice. "Could you stop for a bit?"

Itch turned to the side, still bouncing the ball hard against the ground. "Think you can make me?" he asked playfully.

Alice stood up and tried to take the ball from him, but he kept turning this way and that, always dribbling, making it very difficult. She darted to one side and the other, attempting to be part of his playfulness, because he was smiling, and jostling against her, but he was too fast, too strong, and too tall. Finally she gave up and just sat back down, saying quietly, "Please put the ball down for a moment."

"Kill joy," he answered, holding tightly onto the ball and sitting on the edge of his chair.

"Did you ever study DNA in school?" she asked.

Itch shrugged.

"DNA is this stuff inside us, like the recipe for our individual bodies, and it's unique, different for everyone."

Itch snorted loudly. "First you're my jailer and now you're my teacher? You interrupted my game to talk about science? Who are you, anyway?" He rose from the chair and started bouncing the ball again.

"Stop it," said Alice, hearing the irritation in her own voice. "Sit down a minute, please."

Itch refused to sit, but at least he stopped bouncing the ball for a moment, so Alice continued. "Remember that girl who was going to be your nurse? You thought she was Misty?"

"Oh for God's sake. I told you it didn't mean anything. You're going to bust my chops about her again?"

Alice sighed. "The girl you met wasn't Misty, she was Emma. And she's your daughter — with Misty. Misty had her the same time I had Skye. You have two daughters. That's what I'm trying to tell you. Emma is a very nice girl, and I'm sure you'll like her once you get to know her."

"Look, no way do I believe this. I told you—coulda been anyone. Only one who didn't screw Misty was Misty." He paused for a moment to consider this idea, then chuckled, and finally sat down so he could face Alice.

"That's why I was trying to tell you about DNA. They have these tests now that can prove who someone's parents are, no doubt at all, a hundred percent accurate. There's no question—you're Emma's dad and Misty is her mother. Well her birth mother. Emma had very nice adopted parents, but they're dead now."

Itch held his hand up to his head. "So what—you're saying I gotta marry Misty now? Maybe she's like all those guys you said moved away."

Alice reached out and touched Itch lightly on the arm, but he shook her hand off and glared at her. Alice smiled gently and said, "Misty's the one who came to see you, who flashed her boobs at you."

Itch squinted for a moment, looked perturbed, then determined, and said, "No way. They didn't look anything like Misty's boobs."

Alice was astonished to feel herself leap up and angrily say, "Well, pardon me. I didn't know you were such an expert on Misty's boobs." Then she grabbed the two glasses and marched in the house, thinking *what a jerk, what a jerk*. She stood at the island, her hands gripping the edges of the counter, her heart pounding, and she wondered how many times he actually had been with Misty, what other things he'd lied about, and suddenly a little voice crept in, and asked had she been wrong about him all this time. Alice pressed her hand to her heart. Her thoughts were some kind of mutiny, and apparently she was more upset about Emma than she had let on. Well of course she was upset. Being cheated on is upsetting. Being one of two women simultaneously giving birth to the same guy's child is upsetting. What about this whole situation wasn't upsetting? And then the same little voice intruded and said, *at least he's awake now. At least he's in your life now.*

Alice looked around. She was alone in the empty kitchen after having stormed off in her jealous rage. But it wasn't the jealousy or mistrust, it was the storming off. She'd stormed off, and what was supposed to happen? Itch was supposed to chase after her, and be humbly conciliatory and apologetic. That's what boyfriends did. That's what husbands did. Alice went to the back door and looked out. Itch was shooting hoops again, and Cooper had come home and was playing with Itch. She smiled for a moment. Maybe Itch would be good for Cooper, and help him be more of a typical boy. After all, he'd been raised by a much older dad, so maybe he just missed out on the sports that guys learn from their dads.

She watched casually for a moment, but the play grew less mellow, and they were bumping against each other in a way that looked too rough to Alice, and Itch crashed against Cooper, taking the ball and shooting it as Cooper backed off a bit. "C'mon Miss Pac-man, defend your turf," shouted Itch derisively, as he caught the ball and tossed it in the hoop. Then Itch darted around Cooper, who wasn't exactly engaging in combat, and grabbed the ball again, his shoulder slamming against the pole, causing the wooden struts steadying it to come tumbling down, as the post wobbled in the now enlarged hole.

Cooper had seen the danger and shouted, "Back off, look!" But Itch ignored him and slammed the ball against the backboard, causing the pole to veer dangerously back and forth in the widening hole.

Alice ran out the door, shouting, "Get back from there," just as the pole careened down, and would have fallen on top of Itch, had Cooper not shoved him aside, tripping in the process, causing Itch to land on top of him, as the pole slammed to the ground far to the side of both of them. "Thank God!" she said, running to stand beside them.

Itch jumped up, off of Cooper as the boy groaned, "My wrist's broken."

"Don't be such a girl. You're fine. Shake it off," said Itch.

Alice looked at Itch and said softly but sternly, "Be quiet. He just saved your life." She reached down, not knowing what to do. "Can you get up? Should you get up?" She held up her hand toward Cooper, saying, "Wait, let me see if Johnny is here." Then she ran to his door and pounded on it, but there was no answer. Alice ran back, saying, "Phone in your backpack?" Cooper reached in his jeans pocket and pulled out the shattered iPhone, shaking his head with disgust. "Just sit there," said Alice, running in her own door to grab her phone. "Let me look at you," she said, "Is your head and neck okay? Don't try to move if it hurts." Alice walked around Cooper, looking everywhere to see if he had any visible injuries.

"Don't treat him like such a baby," said Itch.

"Oh I wish Johnny were here," she said softly.

Cooper started to rise, but Alice could see the pain on his face. Alice ran in again for something to use as a sling, then returned with a small flowered tablecloth, causing Cooper to laugh then grimace. "Really?" he asked as she shrugged.

Once his arm was inside the sling, he could rise more easily, so Alice got him up and into the house, as she dialed her sister's number.

"Oh hells to the no," said Cooper, "Don't call the 'rents."

"They may have a doctor they want you to see," said Alice. "They have to be called, you know that." Cooper nodded glumly as she made the call, and the hysterical voice of Totsie echoed out through the phone, even though it was pressed to the side of Alice's face.

"Okay," said Alice, "Meet you there."

"This day just gets better and better," said Cooper, then more softly, "Ten pounds of shit in a five pound bag."

When Itch heard this slang, he began laughing and repeating it over and over.

"Can I trust you to stay here by yourself?" Alice asked Itch. "Your parents will be here in a little while, so let them in, and sit down in the living room until we return, okay?"

Itch shrugged his shoulders and said, "Five pounds of shit in a ten pound bag."

A nurse escorted Cooper to have his wrist x-rayed as Alice agonized outside in the orthopedist's waiting room. Thankfully, Totsie knew a doctor who did this sort of thing routinely, so that Cooper wouldn't have to sit and wait for hours in an emergency room, but it was quite possible he would need surgery, and the poor kid would deal with this injury for some time. The image of what had happened played over and over in Alice's mind as she waited, but then Totsie raced in like a tornado, and there was more to deal with than just his injury.

"You!" Totsie said in a rage, "You're harboring my son against my will, and he ends up maimed and broken—on your watch, Ally, your watch."

"I know," Alice said miserably, knowing there was no excuse at all.

"Exactly how did you let my son's wrist get fractured?"

Alice quietly described the event, leaving most of the details intact, without making Itch sound quite as derisive as he had been, and emphasizing Cooper's heroics. Still, her voice trembled and her heart ached.

"Well, well, Itch, of course. You know Mom was right about him. I remember the day she said it too."

Alice tightened up, inside and out, waiting for some critical remark from her mother to be repeated, as her sister stared fiercely at her.

"Instrument of rebellion, that's what she called him. Your instrument of rebellion. She said you were just using him to get back at her, because no way would a big dumb jock be of interest to you otherwise. Well I hope you're happy now. My baby is paying the price for your rebellion."

Alice thought about the words she'd just heard, *instrument of rebellion*. She had no memory of her mother saying that to her at all. She only remembered her own wild side, and the sense that she and Itch belonged together, that together life would be exciting and wonderful.

Alice pondered that information, as Totsie continued, "A nice, simple, straightforward, serious girl, that's what she said. That you were using him to pretend to be someone else."

Alice felt the sting of those words. She'd been serious for a long time because she had to be, but did that mean she was boring and dull? Was that what her mother thought of her? What difference did it make now, she wondered, but somehow it still mattered. Alice didn't have more time to contemplate these comments, because a nurse summoned them to an exam room, so she and Totsie jumped up to go see Cooper.

The doctor showed them the x-ray, explained the damage, and how the cast would solve the problem. "So he doesn't need surgery?" Alice asked.

"Nope," he said, "This should do the trick."

Totsie almost hurled herself into Cooper's arms, but Alice and Cooper both said, "Careful," so she held back. The cast took only minutes to apply, and Cooper made some jokes as it was being done, because his arm had been numbed enough so that he was no longer in pain.

"So does this rad black cast make me cool, or just a dork?" he asked.

"Cool," everyone said hopefully, although nobody had any real clue.

After the cast was applied, the wrist was x-rayed again, and they were walking out, Totsie said, "Want to go for ice cream?"

Cooper laughed and shook his head. "Geez, this isn't like when I was five and toppled out of my little red wagon."

"Yes it is," said his mother. "I hope now you'll realize you belong at home. You're safe at home. I want you to come home. And I'll make it worth your while."

Alice and Cooper just looked at Totsie, then they exchanged a glance without appearing to be too obviously critical.

"Once I get my share of the insurance money on P3, I'll buy you a brand new car. A convertible even."

Alice didn't want to start an argument while Cooper was injured, but she said softly, "You don't get a share of the insurance. It wasn't your business. That's money for the business, not a windfall."

"You see how she treats me?" said Totsie to Cooper. "And you're choosing her over me? Come with me immediately, and let's go home."

"I'll talk with you another day," said Cooper. "I'm going home with Ally." He reached down and kissed his mother on the cheek, saying, "I'm tired and tingly. Your car's over there." He pointed toward Totsie's car with his cast and touched Alice with his other hand, indicating they should walk in the opposite direction toward her car.

"This isn't the end of any of this," said Totsie. "We were partners you know. Partners. I just wonder if being a thief is part of your rebellion. Is it Ally, is it?"

"What was it, like ten minutes it took her to make my broken wrist about her?" Cooper asked Alice as they drove home.

"You okay?" she asked Cooper. "Driving's not jostling your arm is it? I can try to go slower."

"Nah, I'm fine. That's what the cast is for. And you'll notice the macho sling—nothing like the girly one you foisted on me." Then he offered an impish smile and continued, "Though not as useful for a picnic, it's true."

Alice laughed. "I'm glad you're Mr. GQ and back to your usual self."

It didn't take terribly long to return home, and Alice saw Skye's car parked on the street behind Itch's parents' car. When she opened the door, Skye hugged her then asked, "Where's Itch?"

Alice hugged the Itzkins before answering. "What? He's supposed to be here. Didn't you see him?" Everyone shook their heads, so Alice walked out back, to see if somehow he was sitting outside playing the guitar and unaware they'd arrived, but the courtyard was empty.

After grilling everyone about how long they'd been there, Alice sat down on the couch. Each pair of eyes glanced back and forth at the next, the communal worry increasing as the minutes ticked away.

Alice got up, helplessly served a platter of cheese, crackers and crudités, nervously opened a bottle of wine, which nobody touched, and tensely made a carafe of mulled cider, which almost nobody touched. "Who could we call?" she asked, expecting Itch's nice, sweet parents to turn on her for losing their son the way Totsie had done about Cooper's wrist.

"The other day he said he wanted to go for a walk," said Cooper. "Do you think he's out strolling around?"

"Could he be lost?" asked Alice, causing the ambient worry level to increase.

Skye said, "We could all go cruise around in our cars, looking for him. Maybe Coop, you stay home in case he comes back? He doesn't have a phone yet, does he?"

Alice shook her head, "Not yet."

Skye's plan seemed reasonable to everyone, so ensemble they headed out the door to their three vehicles, when Cooper looked after them and said, "Whoa, wait a sec. My car is gone. I parked it right there where Skye's car is now. The keys were in my backpack." Everyone followed Cooper back into the house, and watched as he pawed one-handed through his backpack, his jaw clenched. "He stole my car." When he saw the horrified look on Alice's face, he quickly amended his comment to "Borrowed. He borrowed my car."

"Oh God," said Alice, "This is dangerous."

"I can call some cop buddies, they can send out an APB, bring him back, don't think they'd arrest him. Might be faster and safer than all of you out there searching."

Alice was about to nod that Cooper should do that, when she heard the sound of a motorcycle a block away, so she stepped out the door and looked in the direction of the sound, anguishing during the moments before she could see, and then there was Itch, pulling up into the driveway and dismounting the cycle, with a huge grin on his face.

"Cool, right," he said, hugging Alice, then walking into the house and hugging both his parents. "Got my bike back," he said. "Well, a replacement."

"Where's my car?" demanded Cooper.

"Keep your wig on, Miss Pac-man. Gotta pick it up at the parking lot, you know, where that big market is."

Cooper was obviously about to say some harsh words, but Alice was relieved that he restrained himself in front of Itch's parents.

"You bought this motorcycle?" asked Itch's dad. "With what money?"

"Don't worry, don't worry," said Itch. "Ally already told me not to just use all those million credit cards she has stashed in her wallet. So I just took a check from the desk. She owes me a new bike I figure."

"But you can't just sign Ally's name on one of her checks. That's illegal." Itch's dad sounded patient but stern.

"No worries, Dad, the guy didn't say a word. He took the check and drove off with some chick."

Alice sighed, then said, "Coop, think you can drive? Skye can take you to get your car now. Or I can do it. No I can't—I can't drive that stick you have."

"I'll go, I'm fine."

So Alice watched Skye and Cooper go out the door then she went into the kitchen to make dinner, as she heard Itch's dad giving him a stern lecture. Tomorrow she'd get a safe, or a lock for one of the desk drawers, and she'd make sure he couldn't do anything like this again. But would he even be allowed to drive a motorcycle? Should he? Alice was terrified.

After what seemed to be a relatively uneventful remainder of the evening, in which they ate dinner and both Alice and Mr. Itzkin spent time impressing upon Itch the fact that he could drive neither a car nor a motorcycle without a license, Itch's parents left, Skye went over to have her discussion with Greg, Cooper went upstairs, and Alice cleaned up the kitchen, then began making many batches of cookie dough for the alligator freebees—what had Johnny called them? Lagniappe. What she craved was absolute silence, nothing but the freedom to concentrate on making sugar cookie dough, which would be refrigerated and cut out the following day. For some reason she'd set an appointment with an engineer to inspect P3, which really shouldn't take much time, so there was no reason to delay another week. Last week it had taken her only a few hours to bake the cookies, so there should be plenty of time, but so much had happened in the short span between this Friday and last, and it seemed every single day had been littered with chaos, so Alice decided to take no chances.

There was a comforting peace in the whirring sound of the Cuisinart, as batch after batch of cookie dough emerged from it, and was spread out in a flat sheet and wrapped for the fridge. Once Alice had timed herself and was amazed to learn she could make a batch of dough in under a couple of minutes. Tonight, though, the silence Alice craved eluded her, for Itch stood in the kitchen by the wall phone repeatedly calling his doctor and leaving urgent messages.

"Honey!" said Alice as calmly as she could manage, "Don't leave more than one message. He'll get back to you. Really he will."

"I need to get this cleared up right away. The DMV will be open soon, and Dad said I have to have doctor's permission to get my license."

"The doctor will probably want to do some tests on you. You've only been out of the hospital a couple of days. And you can't just walk into the DMV and get a license. You haven't driven in twenty years. You'll have to take tests, written and probably a driving test."

"I just took that test in driver's ed." Ignoring Alice, Itch dialed the doctor's exchange yet again, and assured the answering service that it was in fact an emergency.

Alice felt herself wishing that he'd just stop, that he'd go into another room and leave her alone for a while. Her head began to pound, but she kept measuring ingredients and adding them to the Cuisinart, batch by batch, with Itch's voice rising above the sound of the motor.

"Hey!" he said angrily, "She said I should stop calling. She said he would call me back."

"So, stop calling," said Alice. "He can't call you back if you're on the phone, can he?" Alice knew this was technically untrue because the call waiting would beep, but for all she knew it had been beeping, and Itch had ignored it.

Itch shrugged and took a seat at the counter, repeatedly glancing from the clock on the wall to his wrist, although he was wearing no watch. Alice tried to focus on what she was doing, and the flat sheets of wrapped cookie dough mounted up. Once they opened the restaurant, she would get a sheeter and that would cut this work down to practically nothing. Alice paused a moment to consider her thought. She'd just made plans as though opening the new restaurant had been decided. Was it really that simple?

Skye had been gone only a few minutes, when she crept back through the opened kitchen door. "I actually did it. It's done. He says he'll be out on the weekend. But holy bejeezus, that place is a toxic pit. I don't think there's enough bleach on the earth."

"And you're feeling okay?" Alice asked.

"I guess I was making too much of this all along. I should have done this when I met Julian. What was I thinking?"

"I can't tell you how many times I asked that same question," said Alice, grinning at her daughter.

"Well thanks for hanging in by my side," said Skye, reaching for a piece of raw dough.

"Hey!" said Itch, "Don't eat that—it's raw dough. It can blow up in your stomach and kill you."

Alice laughed, "That's just an old wives' tale they use to scare kids, so they don't eat all the dough before their moms can make the cookies."

Itch looked a bit suspicious, but then noting Skye eating some and Alice eating some, he said, "Well then, gimme some. What'cha waiting for." Alice offered him a cookie sized chunk, but then the phone rang, and he leapt off the stool and grabbed it.

"Yeah, doctor?" Itch said. "Do I need your permission to drive a car or a motorcycle?"

Alice and Skye were quiet, hearing only Itch's half of the conversation.

"Oh well, sorry, but this is important to me…. Yeah I remember that…. No I didn't realize that…. I drove today…. Yeah I knew that…. Okay see you…."

Alice hoped that the doctor was saying that under no circumstances could Itch drive immediately, but after he hung up the phone, Itch said, "I already took those motor skills tests. But there wasn't a car there, so how motor skills could it be? But I'm good to go."

Alice's heart sank. Now she'd be worried on a constant basis that he was out, who knew where. "He said that for sure? He said it's okay for you to drive? In those words?" she asked. "And don't forget you'll also need insurance. Can't drive without that."

"What time does the DMV open?" Itch asked. "Never mind, I'm going to bed now so I can be ready. See ya."

Skye stayed in the kitchen with Alice for quite a while, and they shared some peaceful conversation, Skye's plans and Emma's news. Cooper came down for a snack, and then both kids disappeared up the stairs, Skye to Alice's room where she would share her mother's bed for a couple of nights.

At last it was peaceful in her house. Nobody was talking to her or at her or to anyone else. Alice did the final clean up in the kitchen, then she walked with a mug of tea into her living room, where she sat down without even turning on the lights. Her mind whirled. She felt exhausted, but Alice suspected that she wouldn't easily fall asleep. She could go soak in a bubble bath for a while, and maybe she would do that in a bit. For now, her head was pounding and it was filled with the echoes of the past. Her mother considered her a boring poseur. Her sister thought she was a thief. She finally had her husband and the chance to live with someone she'd always believed was her one true love, and if she were honest with herself, everything he did annoyed her. So she was a boring poseur, thief, and clearly the world's most shallow, impatient person. She didn't have the self-control to be kind to someone who was nearly killed because of her, who'd lost so much of his life. Of course it was easy to love someone who was in a coma; nothing he could do would annoy her at all. It was like being one of those widows whose dead husbands could do no wrong. Didn't they have a line in some movie saying the dead make very few mistakes?

Had she been wrong about everything? Was she cheating her sister? Alice thought back. Had there ever been a moment when her aunt and uncle discussed giving Totsie half of their business? No, never. She'd agreed to work there only now and then, in-between her various forays into dilettantism. As Alice considered this, she felt mean even having the thought. Was she angry at Totsie? Her sister was the most truly free, utterly self-absorbed person Alice had ever met. She had no responsibilities at all. Well, she'd been a mother for a while, and Cooper was a great kid, so Totsie hadn't done everything wrong, but that wasn't the issue, was it. Alice had worked herself into exhaustion for years, and at this moment she was mired in doubt and anguish over a decision about her future, a decision about her Uncle's legacy. And here was Totsie with her hand out, wanting more money to squander, just as she did on a constant basis with any money she had. And she always had plenty. Maybe Alice had missed something along the way. Maybe she'd missed the life lesson that would allow her to be fancy free and a lighthearted spendthrift, permanently absolved from the necessity to deal with life's annoying practicalities. That was the day she wanted to do over.

Sighing, and feeling guilty that after only two days of marriage she was miserable, Alice trudged up the stairs, changed into nightclothes, and silently slipped beneath the covers on her side of the bed. Skye's breathing was quiet and regular, and Alice didn't want to waken her, so she lay rigid and wooden, clenching her eyes shut and willing sleep to overcome her.

Alice was certain she checked her bedside clock hourly, and it seemed she hadn't slept at all, but suddenly her eyes snapped open, indicating that indeed she had been asleep, and in blurrily searching for the clock, she spotted a hulking figure standing over her. Alice gasped, clasping her hand to her throat, as Itch said, "It's me. Time to go to the DMV."

This time Alice could see the numerals on the clock. "It's six in the morning," she whispered, "They're not open for hours. Go back to sleep."

"Can't we just go now and sit outside and wait?"

Alice was about to say *are you nuts,* but she stopped herself and said only, "The parking lot is locked at night. They don't allow that." If this were true she had no idea, but it sounded plausible and she hoped it would make sense to Itch. "Go back to sleep. We'll go after ten in the morning, okay? And...um...get you a cell phone too. Then I have a meeting and I have to work. So could you let me sleep now, please?"

"Yeah, whatever," he said grumpily, and Alice was relieved to see him pad out of her room.

Once again Alice closed her eyes, and in her mind she revisited her days as a babysitter for little Glen... Glen... Glen... something or other. What was his name? She always thought of him as Glen, the worst boy in the world. Of all the children she babysat, he was the most annoying, the sort of kid who could do something hugely problematic during ten seconds in which she'd turned her head. Once she'd made a phone call to Itch, and then turned around to see a pile of food in the middle of the floor, which Glen had dumped from the fridge. Eventually she'd gracefully stopped being his babysitter, citing college pressures, but she suspected his mother knew, because she always had problems getting sitters. Glen was like the boy in *The Ransom of Red Chief*, which Alice remembered reading in school. Not even hardened kidnappers could tolerate him.

Her mind grew fuzzy and her thoughts became unclear. Why was she thinking of babysitting anyway? Why was she not asleep? And then she knew why. And then she was asleep.

Three hours of fitful sleep felt more like three minutes, but at nine Alice roused herself and showered, dressed, and walked down the stairs, expecting Itch to be there drumming his fingers on the counter in determined impatience. But he wasn't downstairs, or outside, or up in Skye's room, or in a bathroom. Not again, Alice thought, then she looked outside, and offered a rare prayer of thanks when she realized all the cars were untouched and still present. But what about the motorcycle? She couldn't see it from the front window, so Alice walked into the garage and there it was. Apparently Itch had remembered that he couldn't drive yet. Maybe there was hope. Maybe he was growing up a little. Maybe he wasn't Glen. What, she thought. Glen, who was Glen?

Alice's mind was fuzzy, and no amount of coffee helped her to feel coherent. She could only imagine the disasters that would ensue tomorrow at the popup if she didn't sleep soon. She'd be putting chopped liver in the desserts.

Assuming it logical that Itch had decided to walk to the DMV, Alice grabbed her car keys and went in search of him. She drove slowly and carefully, scanning the sidewalks on either side of the street, but there was no sign of him. She drove all around the parking lot, but also, nothing. So Alice parked her car and went inside. The place was mobbed as usual, and people sat and waited, and those who had no chairs stood. Life seemed to move in slow motion, but that didn't bother Alice. She walked around the office, looking everywhere for Itch, but nothing. Then she went to the information desk and asked had he signed in. His name was on the list, the first name on the list in fact, so for all she knew, he'd walked there at six after she'd finally fallen asleep.

Alice had him paged, and several times the loud speaker called his name; finally he appeared from a men's room.

"Thank goodness," said Alice. "Have you been here all this time?" she asked Itch.

"This place is a pit," he said angrily. "They say I failed the test."

Alice reached out to pat him comfortingly on the arm, but he wrenched away from her. "That written test is hard," she said.

"No not that test. I passed that test. I told you I just took it in driver's ed."

"What, when you were sixteen?"

"Whatever," he said.

"So you failed the driving test? But how could you even take it without a car?"

"That's what they said, they said I needed a car, but I said I couldn't bring a car 'cause my dad wouldn't allow me to drive. So they said I could come back and take that test."

"Then you didn't fail," said Alice, feeling guilty that she was growing impatient.

Itch took his index finger and rapped it repeatedly against his cheekbone, pointing to his eye. "Eye test, Ally, eye test. I failed the eye test. Whenever did we take an eye test before? Nobody told me about that."

"Look," said Alice calmly, "We'll get you to an eye doctor. If you need glasses, you'll get them. Then you'll pass the eye test. And then you can take the driving test, okay? But I really wish you'd slow down a little. All this frenzy can't be good for you. You're supposed to be recovering, not driving yourself crazy over driving."

"Oh so now I'm crazy. Thanks a lot."

"It's just going to take a little time. That's all I'm saying. I'm saying slow down, calm down, take it easy."

"So where's this eye doctor?" Itch asked. "They got one here?"

Alice looked at her watch. "I have a meeting at noon. We'd have to make an appointment with an eye doctor. You can't just go. We can do it on Monday or Tuesday."

"Maybe I should just go back to sleep for another five years, that work for you?"

Alice glanced at her watch one more time, then pulled out her phone and did a search for opticians. She motioned to Itch to step outside where they could hear, and she began calling. The first four were booked, but one had a cancellation, so she made the appointment.

"See," said Itch grumpily, "How hard was that?"

"Well just prepare yourself. If you do need glasses it takes a week or more for them to be made at a lab."

"No part of this doesn't suck."

"Okay, okay, I can try to find a twenty-four hour lab. If possible. But let's not get ahead of ourselves. Let's see what the doctor says."

The optician turned out to possess superhuman patience, and calmly and repeatedly asked Itch whether the various changes were better or worse, as Itch said, "Just hurry up and gimme the glasses."

Alice maintained her own patience, despite frequent glances at her watch, as her meeting with the engineer grew closer. Finally she called him and asked to postpone it by two hours, which amazingly he allowed, then she called Johnny, who was to meet her at P3, and informed him of the change as well.

The doctor had settled on what seemed to be a good correction, and then handed Itch a document to read aloud.

"This isn't about driving," Itch complained, but then he read it credibly.

"And he'll need these for close up and long distance?" Alice asked.

"I can do bi-focals," said the doctor calmly.

Alice accepted the prescription, and then drove quickly to the lab, saying, "Even if these are ready tomorrow, I won't be able to take you to get them. I'll be working from before they're open until late at night."

"Who works that many hours," said Itch.

"Chefs," said Alice. "Besides, the DMV isn't open tomorrow afternoon, only in the morning, no wait that was the old days. Now they're only open during the week. So it can't be before Monday anyway."

"Look, Ally, I'm not gonna run out on you. We got married, I accepted it. So stop trying to hold me back by making stuff up. You can't make me a prisoner."

After she parked the car, Alice pulled up the DMV site on her phone and showed it to Itch. "See—see the hours listed. Not open on weekends. I'm not making stuff up."

"Okay, okay."

It took less time to choose the eyeglass frames than Alice had expected, leaving them time enough to stop off and get Itch a cell phone, which he played with on the drive home. "Don't go anywhere, okay," Alice asked, and content with his nod, she drove to her meeting, hoping all the while that he wouldn't do anything crazy while she was gone.

There were heavy chains preventing anyone from entering the parking lot at P3 and danger signs clearly posted. Alice knew that a decision would have to be made, because this was what television attorneys called an attractive nuisance, a dangerous situation that inspired kids to explore and potentially injure themselves. She parked on the street, exited her car and walked toward the front of the restaurant, where Johnny was already waiting. Alice glanced at her watch. The engineer wasn't due for a few more minutes.

"Hiya, doll," said Johnny, flashing a grin.

"Sorry about the delay," she said quietly. "Nonstop emergencies."

He scrutinized her face silently for a moment, then gently rubbed his hand across her back. "I saw the hoop on the ground."

"Don't ask," she said.

"This is a mighty big spot," Johnny said, and as she listened, Alice knew he was letting her off the hook, not asking her to talk about something she didn't want to articulate. She assumed he knew what she was feeling, because he always seemed to know. "Huge parking lot."

"It's not exactly a place for a little bistro, I know. Even when Spago was in the hills, their lot wasn't this big. Nor Chasen's. A developer would probably put a strip mall here. Or a Target." She flashed Johnny a grin, relaxing a little.

They both looked toward the driveway, where a tall, lanky guy was straddling the heavy chains and walking toward them. He shook their hands and said, "Okay, now, let's take a look-see." Alice and Johnny walked behind him as he circled the building, examining this and that more closely. Normally Alice would have asked questions as they proceeded, but she was tired and decided just to allow him to do his job. He took out a small camera and recorded various images, she assumed for a report. Then he asked them to wait while he disappeared inside.

"Anything I can do?" Johnny asked.

Alice shook her head.

"Could I just ask you something?"

Alice looked at him, hoping it was a question about the restaurant, but instead he said, "Does he seem as you remember, or is his behavior changed due to the injury?"

Alice stopped to think for a moment, and what she yearned for was a slide show of positive memories, for surely there had been many of them, or else what was it that she had been holding on to all these years? Hadn't he said that she was the bread to his peanut butter and Skye would be the jelly? Or had she said that? She remembered the flirty games they'd played, and hadn't he initiated some of them? More than anything she recalled how she felt when she looked into his eyes. She was in love, that she remembered, because the love she felt as a girl had lasted all this time, had remained in her heart even when he wasn't in her life.

When she snapped back out of her reverie, Johnny was there, still scrutinizing her face, but just looking into his eyes caused her to burst into tears, the flood of emotion she'd been holding back since Cooper's injury. "Oh, sugar, sugar," he said, wrapping his arms around Alice, tightly holding her, letting her cry all over his chest. "Let it all out," he said softly after a moment, when she was attempting to straighten up and control herself. So let it out she did, and it seemed as though she was sobbing for an hour, although of course it wasn't that long and when the engineer reappeared, she had to straighten up and brush the tears away.

"My goodness," the man said, "I'm sure it's all very emotional. But I have good news. I'd like to investigate a little more, take a little more time, but I feel fairly certain that the exterior structure is sound. You'd have to redo the inside of course, the electrical and plumbing, but you won't have to demolish completely. I'll send you a written report in a few days."

Alice sniffled in a way she knew was completely unappealing, and then she shook the man's hand and thanked him.

"So," asked Johnny, "Does that make it simpler or more complicated?"

Alice shrugged.

"Well, I'll take it easy on you tomorrow. After you do the desserts, go on home. You won't have to do a killer day like last week."

"I was actually looking forward to being there, to not being home," she said, then immediately felt ashamed of herself.

"Doll, all I can say is being in a time warp is complicated."

"Time warp," she repeated.

As Alice drove home, she thought about the time warp. Was Itch exactly as he had been, and was that the problem? Was he the same wild teen she once adored, but now she was a dull, middle-aged woman and immune to his charms? *I'm far from that old,* Alice repeated to herself a few times, for it was true. She was only forty. Itch too was forty and he was an attractive man. Alice still found him attractive, although at this moment, she had no desire to follow through on her plans for the romantic wedding night, the series of romantic wedding nights she'd so long envisioned.

Or was Itch somehow changed? He'd been through a trauma, so maybe he wasn't himself. In fact, trauma was far too bland a word to describe what he'd endured, and in a way his recovery was more than remarkable, it was miraculous. He'd regained the use of his mind, his limbs, and he was determined to resume living his life. He had courage, and Alice had to admire that. She did admire it, but she didn't particularly enjoy being around Itch.

And the question she asked then, the thing that had been on her mind since all this happened, was the most difficult to confront. Had it all worked out, had they not gone on that pier, had the pier not collapsed, had the accident not happened, would they have been happy? Would they have grown up, hand in hand, or would they have started in love and ended embattled?

Who could answer questions such as these without the help of a wizard? Alice knew there was no hope of an answer, because it was all conjecture, and where in the evidence of the current moment lay the seeds of that answer?

Alice walked back into her kitchen, content to begin making cookies, because it was a task that required concentration, and one which once begun led to a positive conclusion. She knew precisely what to do and what the outcome would be, which was a blessed relief compared to all the other matters weighing on her mind, including the most difficult one, the fate of P3.

She gazed out the door, and saw Itch sitting quietly on one of the chairs, his phone in his hand. He was calm, and seemed to be operating it without frustration, which by any standards was impressive for someone new to technology; maybe she'd been too hard on him. Alice stepped outside for a moment and smiled at him. He looked up at her, and she gazed into his eyes, those green eyes that always produced such a compelling reaction in her. "Enjoying the new phone?" she asked. "Did you figure out how to download some games onto it?"

"Yup, cool toy," he said.

Impulsively Alice walked over to him and stepped between his legs, then leaned down and kissed him deeply. She felt him tense, but she kept kissing him, her hand trailing along his shoulder and the back of his neck. She tried to lose herself in the kiss, as she had so many times before, on so many kisses bestowed while he slept. He softened a bit and began returning the kiss, and it did feel nice.

When he leaned away from her, Alice stepped back and took a seat beside Itch. "Could I ask you something," she said.

"I already gave you my advice," he answered. "Stop being a drag, and have fun."

"What I was going to ask was what did you picture after we decided to get married. Did you picture anything like this?"

Itch began to laugh. "Who pictures taking a twenty year nap, and waking up an old man with an old wife?"

Alice's heart cringed. "We're not old," she said sadly. "I meant back then. What did you picture regarding us?"

"Hell, Ally, I don't know. I was a kid. I wanted to play ball or be in a band. Instead I was in a coma. Now I'm in a cement back yard. Far as I can tell, it's the *Twilight Zone*."

She reached out and squeezed his hand. "I'm sorry I've been so hard on you. I know it's tough. Any thought now about what you might like to do at this point in your life?"

Itch jumped up from the chair, almost dropping his phone, but catching it in time, and said, "You know what I want. I want to be able to drive, so I can get a little piece of myself back. I know you want me to come up with some new forty year old dream, but how am I supposed to do that when I haven't got to live my teen dreams yet?

All I want is myself back first. At least you got to live the last twenty years. You weren't asleep."

"Oh honey, I'm so sorry," she said sincerely. And then something in her opened up and she whispered, "My heart was asleep. My heart was in suspended animation. I was in a coma as much as you were."

"Get over yourself," he said, looking at her as though she were insane. "I'm gonna make a call on my phone now, okay?"

Alice rose from her seat and walked in the house, still thinking about the confession she'd just uttered. She might have been physically alive all this time, but emotionally she was inert, as much in a coma as Itch, even if he found that absurd. No wonder she hadn't pursued any dreams of her own. She'd not allowed herself to have any. No wonder she'd clung so hard to the dream of Itch, for no other dream was permitted to penetrate. "What a fool I've been," she whispered. Then she walked to a cabinet in her living room and rummaged around in a drawer. Surprised to locate it, Alice withdrew the card from that real estate agent she'd tortured the night she deliberately got tipsy. Wouldn't he be shocked to hear from her—assuming he'd take her call. Alice grabbed the phone, and in moments she'd agreed to let him represent her in the sale of P3. Kitty would applaud her decision, of that Alice was certain, if only she were in a position to do so. And Henry would have been just as proud to see the new place as he was when she'd graduated from cooking school. Alice paused a moment, casting her mind back in time. What else might she have chosen, had she stopped long enough to ponder a completely original future? No inspirations emerged, and she felt a kinship with Itch, whose poignant comments about his state of cluelessness elicited more of a response from her than anything which had happened over the last few days.

The real estate guy would drop around in an hour or two with a contract for her to sign, and the property would be sold. It would move into the future without her, and sadly without her aunt and uncle. She would open the restaurant with Johnny—but first she would pay off her mortgage, pay for Skye's college, and use some of the proceeds to set up a trust for Skye, Cooper and Totsie. That way her sister couldn't squander the money, and Alice couldn't be accused of being a thief. In some corner of her mind, Alice knew that she would get so much money from the sale of the land, that if she managed it correctly, she wouldn't actually have to work, but then what? She didn't want to drive around the country just spending money. She didn't want to sit around doing nothing. She wanted to open a restaurant with Johnny.

Alice stopped to catch her breath. It felt so odd to make so many decisions so quickly and without qualms. It also felt great. Yes, she was nervous, for restaurants sometimes failed, and then perhaps she'd be left with nothing but whatever nest egg remained after she did the trust and invested in the restaurant, but if that happened, she'd get a job. In the meantime, she'd do everything possible to make a success of the business she and Johnny would start.

Pulling her apron off its hook, Alice began rolling out the dough and cutting out all the many alligator cookies that were needed for tomorrow's clients. She established a rhythm and pan after pan of cookies entered and exited the ovens. Rack after rack held the cooling cookies. Eventually a big plastic bin was filled with the pristine, glistening cookies, and then the doorbell rang.

Alice walked to the door and opened it, allowing the astonished real estate guy to enter the house. "You sober?" he asked.

Alice smiled and said, "First, please let me apologize about the last time we met. That was far from my usual conduct." She watched the man's eyebrows rise, then said, just to amuse herself, wondering what was it about this real estate guy that made her want to torture him, "Can I get you a drink?"

Hastily he took a seat in the living room, saying, "No, no, no, let's not go there."

Alice laughed and sat opposite him, saying, "Let's see your contract."

She read over the document, wondering did she need an attorney to examine it, but that seemed unlikely, as people engaged real estate brokers all the time. "Pen?" she asked, and held back her smile as he tried to control the stunned look on his face. Obviously he thought he was on a fool's errand, but he came anyway. Alice took the pen and signed the contract, then she stood up. "Okay, then," she said, "Get out there and sell that property."

He rose and shook her hand. "Wow. I really want to thank you."

"Well," she answered, "After what I put you through, it seemed only fair to give you the business.

He smiled with a preposterous level of joy, and shook her hand again. "Your faith in me will be justified. You'll see."

"Excellent," she said, walking toward the door, with him practically prancing behind her. "I'm looking forward to getting some big, big offers."

After he had gone, there was one thing on her mind. She dialed her phone and Johnny answered. "You home?" she asked.

"In the car, just pulling up."

"Have time to talk with me?"

"Always," he said, and Alice could picture his grin.

"Okay, I'll knock on your door in a sec." Alice walked outside, where Itch still sat, and said to him, "I need to go talk to Johnny about some work stuff, okay? Then we could order some pizza—would you like that?"

Itch nodded, and seemed to want to remain silent, but after a moment's pause, he said, "I know about you and cooker man. I saw you today. You said he wasn't your boyfriend, but I could see he is."

Alice sat down beside Itch. "What are you talking about?"

"I saw you. I took my bike out. I didn't want you to know, what with the whole license thing, but I saw you. In his arms, like a real couple, a grown up couple."

"Oh! I was crying, okay? It's all been so complicated, and Totsie screamed at me, and I had all this P3 stuff weighing on me, and you broke Cooper's wrist, and it's not like we feel like a couple, and I was crying. And he just let me cry. That's all you saw."

"You could just tell me the truth. I'm not stupid or blind. He's your boyfriend."

"Enough. For the gazillionth time, I don't have a boyfriend. Are you my boyfriend? It sure doesn't feel like it. Nobody is my boyfriend. Nobody is my husband. I'm just some idiot who didn't live her life for twenty years. At least you had an excuse. Now I'm going to talk about the new restaurant, then come back here and order pizza. If that's okay with you."

"I might be busy tonight."

Alice stood up and flapped her hand at Itch. "Fine, whatever. When I get back here, I'll order pizza. Either you'll eat it or you won't."

Before she even tapped, Johnny answered the door, a worried look on his face. Alice smiled at him, and he took a breath. "Oh," he said quietly, "I thought you wanted to tell me it was all off."

Alice shook her head, and followed him inside. They both sat down, and for a moment Alice had to chuckle. "Boy, do you look out of place in here."

"No way. I could add some flowers, a little more chintz, maybe one of those girly aprons you favor. You can't see me in one of those aprons?"

Alice laughed. "I'd love to see you in one of my old fashioned aprons. Think maybe we found the true you."

"So," he said in a voice filled with double entendre even Alice could comprehend, "You finally figured out I'm your destiny. And here you are, ready to..."

"In a way, yes," she said, interrupting him. Then she explained all the decisions she'd just made. "So maybe we could go over the numbers, so I know what I'm in for."

"Oh," he said, pausing just long enough, "The restaurant. Numbers are tentative, but I've done this before, so it's all a matter of how big and how fancy. And if we want investors."

"I was thinking about that. I just wonder if the more people we have to answer to, the less freedom we have. Though I'm pretty sure Tom would be a silent partner. I just worry about the other people in his life. Don't want other people complicating our work situation. Or messing with our chance to make everything perfect."

"Sounds like you made a decision about that too. I'm really impressed with you. Did you have a colonic or something this afternoon?"

Alice groaned and said, "Eww. But if you want to do the show, and don't want to alienate Tom, maybe we could give him a small chunk. What do you really think?"

Johnny reached out and clasped Alice's hand in his. "I think as long as it's you and me, it's going to be perfect. In every way. Investors or no investors. Show or no show. Okay, let's start here," he said, pulling a sheaf of papers from his briefcase. And bit by bit he took her through it. She listened and asked questions, all of which he could answer.

"I hate to say it, but it all makes sense. Seems like we'll be in good shape." Suddenly Alice looked outside and noticed how dark it was, then she glanced at her watch. "My goodness, it's been hours. I said I'd order pizza." She leapt up and then cocked her head. Someone was playing really bad music really loudly. "What is that noise?" she asked.

"Go on, take care of everything," he said softly. "See you tomorrow."

"Tomorrow," she answered, walking out the door and following the sound to her garage. There with Itch were a bunch of people she knew, people she could recognize, guys who looked the same but older. And women who were probably their wives. There were opened boxes of pizza, bags of empty soda cans and beer bottles, her dining chairs in which nobody was seated, and the bin of cookies she'd made, most of which had been eaten.

"My goodness," she said softly, looking for Itch, but he was having what appeared to be a contentious exchange with his former best friend, Brian, the boy who'd performed their wedding. Misty pulled away from one of the women, someone who'd been part of her posse in the old days, and she took her place behind a microphone, which Alice hadn't even realized Itch had bought along with all of the musical equipment, and then they performed a number which sounded pretty bad, not just to Alice, for many of the wives grimaced as well, as Alice glanced nervously at her watch. The neighbors on her left were old and they would very likely be in bed already, and she didn't want to see them padding across the lawn in their robes and slippers.

After they finished the song, Alice spoke up. "I'm really sorry to be a kill joy, but I have old neighbors who go to bed early, and it's already pretty late. Please come inside and enjoy the reunion, but we can't play any more music tonight."

"You live in this dump," said Misty. "No wonder you, well no wonder everything."

After hearing Misty's remarks, the women who didn't know Alice walked over to her to introduce themselves, and the guys she remembered gave her a hug. Then everyone went inside, and they all reminisced about way back when. It was so odd to be back with the old group, and Alice found herself laughing at their jokes and enjoying the casual social atmosphere, something she hadn't had much of in a very long time.

By eleven, only Misty and Brian remained with Itch, and they seemed to be having a serious conversation, and although Alice wanted Misty out of her house, she couldn't really evict her with anyone else there, so she went into the kitchen and began making cookies. By two in the morning the cookies were made again and stored in the bin, which Alice locked in her car.

Then she crept back into the living room, and found Itch, Misty and Brian smoking some pot. "Are you kidding me? Itch is recovering from a brain injury. The last thing he needs is drugs. Look—enough is enough. Could we call it a night, please."

Misty giggled, stood and adjusted her cleavage while staring pointedly at Itch. Brian rose, saying, "Oops, sorry Principal."

"That's not funny at all," said Alice. "Are you sober enough to drive, or do I have to call you taxis?"

"I'm sober enough," said Brian, "But they took away my license after the last run in. Lousy cops."

"You too?" said Itch, almost in slow motion.

"Come on," said Misty, "I'll drive you. Can't get out of this dump soon enough."

Alice saw them to the door, then said to Itch, "You okay?"

He laughed and said, "Better than that I hope."

Alice put her arm around his waist and helped him up the stairs, hearing bits and pieces of his mumbles. "I know what's on your mind—but you can't fool me twice." Then after she tucked him into Skye's bed, he said, "Don't worry, Ally, I won't let Brian take you away from me."

Alice laughed. "No chance of that."

Itch mumbled, "Even if you do get pregnant on purpose to trap me."

Alice allowed herself to drift into a bubble of serenity while baking the desserts for the popup. Hours passed in silence as she created a symphony of sweetness. Gradually the empty counter in front of her was filled with beautiful cakes, pies, and mousses. As she worked, Alice sighed happily, crumb coating, frosting in big, luscious swirls, or filling ramekins and parfait glasses. Nobody would leave the restaurant unsatisfied, and neither would she.

As she was almost finished, Johnny arrived with the breads, setting them on an empty counter, and saying, "You know, we should discuss the lagniappe. People love the cookies, but I'm thinking with the permanent place, we shouldn't do it. We'll have regular customers, and people won't bother ordering desserts if they think they're getting free cookies. Good hospitality, bad business."

Alice wanted to smile and agree, but there he was in a pair of cut off shorts and another bizarre t-shirt with a wacky cartoon on it. The lack of respect it showed just irked her, and she scowled at him and said, "Again? Really? What's it going to take for me to get you to appear in proper attire? That's what I want to know."

Johnny made a mockery of her comments, holding a hand to his eyes and peering off into the distance like a sailor scanning the horizon. "Gracious me, Miss

Wretched, what happened to Ally? Did you kidnap my dream girl?"

"Stop it," said Alice sternly. "A lot is riding on this new place and I don't want to make any mistakes It all has to be perfect."

Johnny laughed. "Putting soap in the whipped cream is a mistake. Me dressing like this just makes me quirky."

"No, it makes you a slob."

Johnny laughed again, walked over very close to Alice, put his arm around her shoulder, reached down and kissed her soundly on the cheek, and said, "Good mornin' to you too, sugar lump."

Alice raised her hand, planning to push him away, but all she actually did was rest it gently on his chest for a second, and as she did, she felt her knees buckle a bit, just as they had when she first encountered him on the show. Johnny said nothing, and he stepped back after the kiss, but Alice saw him scrutinizing her the way he always did. She took a deep breath, regained her composure, and pursed her lips for just a second. "You think you're just so… so… so… well everyone isn't going to fall at your feet, mister, that's all I'm saying. So don't think you can distract me with innocent kisses."

"Okay then, I'll keep that in mind. When I want to distract you I'll stick to kisses of the far less innocent variety."

Alice's mind was still fuzzy, which was completely his fault, so she mumbled harshly, "See that you do," but then she realized that wasn't what she meant, that wasn't what she should have said, so she retreated back into her unyielding self and said, "So, what next?"

He laughed, and when she scowled he laughed even more, but finally he grew serious, and they started on the fish. Alice worked side by side with Johnny for a while, talking here and there about menus for the new place and other details, until he said, "I'd miss this. But how can you be expected to work these hours daily? I know I said you'd do sweet, I'd do heat, but is that what you want? We could hire a pastry chef to work under your direction, then your hours would match mine. It's still a killer day. Or if the new place is big enough, maybe you could start later."

Alice thought about Johnny and how kind he always was, how concerned about her welfare, how nurturing. "This *is* a comfy part of the day," she agreed. Then she squinted at him and pointed a finger, saying, "Except for your getup. Very hard not to be distracted by all that…"

"Hunkiness?" he asked, grinning.

"We *will* have proper attire in the new place. You, me, the cooks. It can be something simple, doesn't have to be whites. I don't want to just fantasize about this — it has to happen." Alice liked the no-nonsense tone she employed and she was certain her point was made and accepted. Or it should have been. She turned to him, expecting to see a conciliatory nod.

Johnny was boning a large fish with elegance and grace, but it didn't distract him from nudging Alice. "Overalls like Lil' Abner, I'm thinking. You, of course, could dress like Daisy Mae. In fact, you do that, and I'll get my whites out of my trunk and have them starched."

Alice continued peeling shrimp, but said quietly, "Who do I speak to about sexual harassment, that's what I wonder."

Johnny held up the head of the fish with his hand inside, moving the mouth up and down like a puppet, and said in a goofy voice, "Don't harass me please, all my good parts are gone."

"Oh Johnny, how sad for you," said Alice with mock concern. "Was it a tragic war injury? A deep fryer melt down? Naked knife juggling gone horribly awry?"

"Most people would be suspicious of your motives, what with you leaping instantly to the image of me naked, but I'm not like most people, and I don't blame you at all." He made a sweeping gesture, implying who could resist all of this, and he smiled the way he always did, with his irresistible, megawatt grin.

Alice steeled her knees, and she almost felt stable, as she said, "Good thing I'm used to you now, and we're friends and all. A week ago, this lack of decorum, and I'm running in the opposite direction."

Johnny leaned toward Alice and bumped his shoulder against hers playfully. "Maybe a week from now you're running toward me."

Alice cocked her head at him, and quietly said, "Married. Still married."

"I'd offer you an ice and quote *Body Heat*, but I'm not that mean a guy."

Alice sighed. "Maybe I should have been less forthcoming and more professional myself, then you couldn't remind me that I might as well have said *'how happy I am is my business'* like Kathleen Turner did."

"The day your happiness isn't my business, well we won't see that day coming—I can promise you that."

"You're just too nice," Alice sighed, wishing somehow he were less giving, less warm, less likeable. "Sometimes I just wish…."

He wiped his hands on a towel and turned toward Alice, his hands on her shoulders, and he drew her close to him and asked softly, "What? What do you wish?"

Alice looked into his sparkling brown eyes, and was tempted to say much more, but instead she said something she knew would take the sparkle away. "Sometimes I wish… that you…weren't so nice."

Johnny winced for a moment, then he winked and said, "Just keep remembering that I'm too good to be true. Restaurant opens, and women'll be lining up, slipping me their numbers, asking for autographs. On their tongues!"

"Eww!" Then her voice grew soft and Alice said, "I'm sure they will."

He stared at her briefly, his eyes all fiery, and said, "Life's a buffet, doll, you don't want to miss out."

Alice turned away from his glance briefly and said quietly, "Full plate."

"C'mon, it's two o'clock. Let's take a break and have lunch in the office."

Alice sat as before, sideways on the old leather couch, her feet up, and soon she and Johnny were eating steaming bowls of soup with thick buttered bread topped with cucumber slices and flaked salmon.

"You can go if you need to," he said kindly. "You've done more than a full day already. Plate one of each dessert, and I'll have someone match them."

"It's been a good day," she answered, thinking a better day than she'd had in a week.

"Okay then, not gonna force the best partner on earth outta here, but lie down a while, take a nap. It's all going like clockwork out there."

"Too much adrenalin," she answered, but after he'd turned out the light and left the room, her eyes closed and she drifted at last into peaceful slumber. When she wakened and glanced at the dial on her watch, Alice leapt up. It was six o'clock. She'd been complaining constantly about lack of professionalism at work, and then she allowed herself a four hour nap—Alice was mortified. She swished some wine around in her mouth, crept out to the ladies' room, then went into the kitchen to find Johnny.

"Sleeping beauty!" he said.

Alice was about to apologize, when she noticed what he and all the cooks were wearing—matching black tuxedo t-shirts. He must have sent someone to pick them up. She began to laugh and couldn't seem to stop, but finally she caught her breath, and said, "Thank you. I know you did this to rib me, but I still want to say thanks. It's not exactly my fantasy, but even as a joke, it's an improvement. "

"I wanted to get tutus but the guys outvoted me."

The evening commenced and continued in a blur of hard work, with no surprise guests of the friendly or psychotic variety. Everything went perfectly, and the diners offered nothing but raves. Eventually it grew late, the last client left, the crew cleaned and departed, and Alice sat with Johnny at one of the tables, drinking wine and relaxing.

She said, "It's been an amazing week, what with all that's happened." Alice thought about last time, about feeling tempted, about ending up asleep next to Johnny on the couch. Tonight she had a husband at home, and no clue what she would find when she got there.

He smiled at her, and saying nothing, placed his hand quietly on top of hers. Alice took a peaceful breath and said nothing either, but then there was a loud noise from outside, the rush of a motorcycle, and she glanced out the door and was certain she saw Itch blaze away on his bike, with Misty on the back.

Alice stood up and said, "I should go."

"I'll come up with a schedule so we can visit locations, supply places, and so on next week. If we choose a place that doesn't require too much in the way of renovations, we could be open in a few weeks."

"Wow," she said, "Imagine that."

"That's all it takes, imagining it and doing it."

Alice laughed. "Oh you're so wise, oh visionary guru of food."

Johnny laughed too, and he stepped toward Alice to hug her, which she knew was a bad idea, but rejecting his innocent hug would be unkind, so into his circle she moved, unwittingly becoming lost inside his embrace, her arms wrapping tightly around his back, her eyes closing, as they stood there for what seemed like an endless stretch of time. Losing track of all good sense, Alice rested her cheek against Johnny's chest as his hand lay tenderly on the back of her head. *Oh*, she thought, *oh*, and some intense emotions rose inside her, and there was this sense of steam, and she remembered feeling those sensations when watching his show. She knew what she wanted, but then Alice thought *what am I doing*, and she stepped back out of the hug, looking down at her feet, unwilling to let Johnny gaze into her eyes.

"No," he said, his voice rather gruff, and without hesitation, he gripped her arms and pulled her against him, limb crushed to limb, then pressed his mouth against hers in the most intense kiss she'd ever experienced. Alice knew she should want to push him back, but instead her arms wrapped around his neck, her mouth opened and she melted into him and the kiss. Her heart thundered, and for a laughable instant Alice grew fearful that she was having a terrifying cardiac episode, but somehow she recognized that this was not health related, and that her mind had stopped working; all she knew was that this was the greatest kiss of her life. Alice expected to snap to her senses, to regain her composure, to be some version of proper again, but absent of determination, she could merely stand there, supported by his arms, her mouth lost in his.

Just as she thought her knees really would buckle, Johnny stepped back and indifferently pushed her away from him. Puzzled, and unaccustomed in the extreme to what had just happened, Alice looked quizzically at him. She knew she should be relieved, but all she could think in the static that was her brain, was why had he stopped.

"I decided it was time to stop being so nice," he said, looking at her in such a way that Alice felt as though her eyes were being seared.

She opened her mouth to speak, but the words wouldn't come out. Once, twice, three times, Alice attempted to say something, anything, so that he would better understand, and really so he wouldn't be hurt, but she was like some cartoon animal, suddenly struck mute.

Johnny ran his finger along her jawbone for a second, and said, "Doll, don't worry about it. Next time this happens, you'll be asking me. Now, git, go on home."

Alice was glad for the chill in the night air, and she drove home with the window open, the icy blast against her cheek restoring her ability to think rationally, although thinking was something she actually preferred to avoid at this moment. Alice didn't want to hear the voice in her mind, or to worry that she was heading down a path that would capsize her life. She knew absolutely that Johnny wouldn't make her do something she didn't choose to do, but that realization was of little comfort because where he was concerned, Alice now understood that her choices could be very suspect indeed. For so long, she'd been in control of her out-of-control urges and now, without her permission, everything had been turned around and upside down. She didn't know from one day to the next what might happen, or what her reaction would be. Inside, Alice felt like that wild girl she once had been, and it terrified her. What if again she made bad choices and tragedy struck? The one thing Alice knew for sure was how easily such catastrophes came to pass.

But what was it about Johnny that allowed him to provoke those feelings in her? Was she some sort of crazy groupie? Had all this happened because she felt something unusual when watching him on television? Alice realized that such an assumption was truly insane, but what was the alternative rationale? She didn't know.

At least she'd made it home safely, and Alice locked the car and entered her house, which was oddly quiet, and she felt instantly relieved. Thankfully there was no loud party, or music that could wake the neighbors — or the dead. Tossing her keys and purse on the hall cabinet, Alice climbed the stairs, saying softly, "Hello? Anyone home?"

There was no sign of either Skye or Cooper, and as Alice peeked into Skye's room, she saw Itch in bed, sleeping peacefully. She must have imagined that he was on his bike outside the restaurant. Walking softly to the back of the house, Alice peered out into the courtyard. The lights were on in her aunt's apartment. He was home. Alice thought about Johnny, about what had just happened. For a second she worried about whether there would be a repeat of this evening's events and how she might handle it, but only for a second. Afterwards, she mulled over the likelihood that it wouldn't happen again, admitting to herself how much she wanted to feel those intense sensations again, for in her heart she knew that absolutely she shouldn't.

Alice slept erratically, dreaming intermittently that she was being tossed back and forth between Itch and Johnny. Each said to the other, "You take her," then they'd hurl her away like a volley ball. Then she and Johnny were working, and the women were lined up outside, just as he'd said. She miserably watched him head out the door toward one of them — and they all looked like Misty — and her heart ached as he waved callously, then embraced his femme du jour. She and Itch were still married but very old, and he kept saying that when he was ready to grow up he'd let her know. Every now and then, Alice would wake, look at the clock, then sink back, exhausted, into the web of her dreams.

When it was finally morning, she awoke and her first thought was of Johnny. She lay there, repeatedly replaying in her mind the images of the previous night and the small but shattering moments they'd shared. Then she would sink into a pit of guilt, only to repeat the whole cycle. Briefly, she thought of Robin and how uncomplicated it had been, being with him. There was no temptation and no guilt, and no matter how she'd tried to build a life with him, the allegiance in her heart was never in question, at least not to her. Now she felt like a clueless fool. If only she could have a moment of awareness as she'd done about work. But even then, what if her epiphany led her in the wrong direction? She couldn't possibly choose other than Itch. She owed him her loyalty; there was no other option.

So Alice lay there, attempting to envision a happy future with Itch, which in fact she'd had years of practice doing. In some corner of her heart, Alice knew such a future could be possible, if she were patient, kind, and loving, which is the least he deserved from her. That was her one and only alternative, and although she would work with Johnny, she couldn't find herself melting into his arms, for that was a very perilous, and deeply wrong choice.

Dressing quickly in some jeans, Alice walked downstairs thinking of breakfast, and then she remembered there would be a family dinner in a few hours, and Itch would get to know Emma, and she would get to know him. It was the right thing to do, she thought, and that comforted her, for if you did the right thing, nothing could go wrong.

Itch sat at the counter in the kitchen, drinking a glass of juice and playing a game on his phone. Alice walked up to him and kissed him gently on the cheek. "Morning," she said. "Remember what's happening tonight?"

"Will you be off holding hands with cooker man, and pretending he's not your boyfriend?" he asked.

"Dinner with Emma and the kids," she said softly, determined not to argue. "But hey would you like to go out for a while? We could take a drive to the beach, have breakfast on the pier, ride the merry-go-round. Gee, if it's open. Not sure if they close it down in the autumn."

Itch looked at her. "Will it be falling down?"

"Oh honey, no, of course not. It's a very sturdy pier, with an amusement park on it—thought you might like that. Games and rides. But we could just stroll around a little or drive, if you don't feel like walking. Eat anywhere you'd like."

"You totally forgot about my glasses," he said accusingly.

"Oh my gosh, I'm sorry. We can go right now and get them."

Itch pointed toward his glasses, right there on the counter. "Good thing I still have some friends around here."

"Misty," said Alice. "Look Itch, she's really not who you think she is. And I definitely don't want her in my home."

"I'm not some appliance you know. You can't just turn me off when you go out. Sorry if I'm a super inconvenience to you, but I have friends, okay? Now are we going out or not?"

"Let's go. And honey, tomorrow I promise we'll go to the DMV and you'll get your license."

The day seemed pleasant but odd, as though they were two former friends, reconvening after a very long absence and willing to be congenial, but unable to pass beyond a sort of tentativeness. They walked haltingly through the farmer's market, buying an assortment of produce, played games on the pier, rode the carousel several times, and ate at a couple of the food stands.

"I wonder if I could surf again," Itch said, as they were walking back to the car.

"Long as you have someone with you when you try," said Alice.

"So what do you suppose this Emma will want me to do?" Itch asked suddenly.

Alice pressed her hand against his arm, saying kindly, "Nothing really. She just wants to know you a little. She doesn't expect anything. So don't worry. It'll be a really nice evening, I promise, okay?"

"Then later maybe you and I can sit and talk," he said softly.

Thinking that perhaps they were making strides, Alice smiled and said, "Sure, we can sit, talk, hang out, just you and me. I really do want you to be happy, I hope you know that. And spending time together is very important to me."

"Okay."

Later, Emma arrived, carrying a tin of her homemade cookies.

"Oh," sighed Alice, "How déjà-vu!"

Emma and Itch sat at the counter, and as Alice cooked, they exchanged a few casual comments. It all seemed to be going fairly well, when there was a loud knock at the door.

Alice walked to the hallway and peered through the glass in the door, surprised to see Robin, with two small but burly guys behind him. A truck was parked at the street, and they wore those belts designed to protect their backs.

Alice opened the door, saying immediately, "This is not a good time."

"Well that's your problem," answered Robin. "I'm here to get my bed. I paid all that money for it, and you didn't really think I was going to leave it here with you, did you?"

Itch had walked over behind Alice, and he said, "Bed?" Then his voice grew strained as he said, "Are you Ally's boyfriend?"

Being inches shorter than Itch, Robin stood more erect in an attempt to make himself look more formidable, saying in the deepest voice he could manage, "Matter of fact, yes I am. She is—was—my wife—if you really want to know. I'm the father of her daughter."

Itch looked confused for a moment, saying to Alice, "Which daughter is he the father of?"

"Neither," said Alice.

"You sleazy bum," said Itch, striding forward and punching Robin on the jaw, causing him to tumble to the ground like a rock sinking in a pool. The two small guys behind him looked at each other, then toward Itch, who might as well have been a giant, and they tiptoed toward the truck at the curb and drove away.

"Frankenstein," said Robin. "Think what you want, but Skye is my daughter. And Ally was my wife 'til you came back from the dead."

Itch took another step toward Robin, who cowered on the ground, wriggling backwards, but not attempting to get up.

Alice held her hand up, indicating that Itch should do nothing further, and saying, "Look, Robin, I'm sorry. We had tests done. I didn't want you to find out like this, but Skye is Itch's daughter. And so is Emma. Apparently you tried to switch them, but you didn't succeed, and it wouldn't have mattered because Misty lied to you. I'm sorry."

Itch glowered at Alice. "You're sorry? You want him to be their dad, not me?"

"Sorry he's hurt, I meant," Alice answered.

Robin sat up and raised his fists, thus appearing more comical than menacing, and groused, "Yeah well no matter what you say, Skye is my daughter. Ask her. And I want my bed back."

Skye, who had been cleaning her apartment, appeared for dinner from the back door, and hearing the noise, walked in, saying, "What's going on here?" Emma leaned in and whispered to her, explaining what had happened.

Skye burst past her mother and Itch, saying, "Maybe he did make a mistake, but that's no reason to clobber him." She reached down and helped Robin up, scowling at Alice.

"No more hitting," said Alice, as Itch kept moving closer toward Robin, who appeared to be inching behind Skye.

At that point, Misty roared up in her Mercedes, parked in front of the house, and sauntered up the pathway. "What in blazes? Itch, are you hurt?"

"What are you doing here?" Alice asked Misty. "I really don't want you here."

"I figured she had a right to be here," said Itch.

Robin turned toward Misty, saying, "You lying bitch. You trashy, dimwitted, useless, lying bitch."

Unaffected by all the insults, Misty turned toward him and said, "Nice to see you too." Then, without a qualm, she walked in the door, reached out and crushed Emma in a hug. "You must be Emma. I'm thrilled to meet you. I'm your mommy."

Emma's arms stretched out to the side and her hands flapped awkwardly, in evidence of her unwillingness to be hugged, then quickly she stepped back and said, "Hello. Nice to meet you."

"You're beautiful," said Misty. "The daughter I've always wanted, don't you think so, Itch."

Itch nodded, saying, "Yes, she's very pretty."

Skye let go of Robin then, and walked through the door, saying, "What about me?"

"You're pretty too?" answered Itch.

Misty clenched her arm tightly around Emma's shoulder, causing the girl to wince in actual pain, then said, "You'll move in with me of course. I have a beautiful house. Nothing like this dump."

"Actually, I was going to tell you," said Emma, looking at Alice, "I've decided to go home to San Diego. So this is sort of a farewell dinner."

"Oh no," said Misty, "That's just tragic, now that I've found you, to lose you again right away. My heart is breaking." She looked down at her blouse, which was so low cut it was barely a suggestion of a garment, and adjusted the neckline, as though more breast baring would cure her heartbreak. Stroking her cleavage suggestively, she said, "Itch, whatever will we do without her?"

Alice was about to speak up, when her phone rang. Pulling it from her apron pocket, she said "Hello," and then all the blood drained from her face. "Kitty had a stroke."

It seemed so odd that there was a measure of comfort sitting beside Kitty, her lifeless but not yet cold hand in Alice's. The family had raced there in an assortment of cars, and everyone had cried and said goodbyes, but Alice had remained, wanting some time alone with her aunt. Kitty lay there, inert, and Alice could clearly see that her aunt was gone. The body was there but all of her aunt that ever existed had vanished. Although it was sad, therein lay the comfort, for in the sense that Kitty was gone, resided the hope that she had gone somewhere else. Alice spent no time at all in her daily life pondering philosophical or religious issues; in fact she preferred to avoid them. Heaven or hell, it did not weigh on her mind, but at this moment she hoped there was something, somewhere, and wherever this afterlife place was, not hell of course, but some form of positive existence, that Kitty was there, back with Henry at last, no longer lamenting that he was off somewhere without her.

"Oh, Kitty," Alice sighed now and then. For a moment she bowed her head and rested her forehead on the hand that held Kitty's. Then she just sat, thinking of her aunt and hoping that she was now better off. For certainly the state of life she most recently inhabited was difficult to define as an improvement over death, that muddle of silence and unawareness, that shroud of death in life that had claimed her. Alice hated to see her aunt in decline, but she also knew that it could have been worse, could have lasted longer, and in a way there was some relief that no longer could Kitty descend into the sludge that was muddling her brain and robbing her of any form of meaningful reality.

Alice's mind raced over all the things she would have to attend to in the coming week. People would call at the house, for days possibly. The family was at home now, she knew that, and in a moment she would join them; they needed her now. Alice squeezed her aunt's hand one more time, and felt her aunt's hand in hers for what would likely be the last time. She knew there would be tears later and for a long time to come, but for now, Alice got up and went out to speak to the nurses, and then she left the Wellman Center forever. How odd it felt to know that after decades of visiting this place under dire and hopeless circumstances, no longer would she be walking its halls. Now she would go home to her family.

Emma had finished cooking the dinner, and set it up as a buffet, so anyone who was hungry could eat. By the time Alice pulled up, everyone was in the living room, talking about Great Aunt Kitty.

"She got me my first bike," said Cooper.

"Me too," said Skye. "And she helped me with cheerleading. She could jump high for an old lady."

Everyone laughed then.

Alice sat on the couch between Skye and Cooper, and both automatically took her hand.

"Will we have to go to undertakers and stuff?" asked Skye.

"The plans were made years ago by Henry," said Alice. "They were discussing it, and he said they should be cremated, and she said no way, she didn't want to end up like a burned pizza, and then he laughed and nudged her the way he always did, and asked did she think he was planning for them to be shoved into the ovens at P3 on a giant pizza peel." Alice smiled, thinking back to all the memories of Kitty and Henry. "They were so funny."

"Henry's in a cemetery near Santa Monica College, isn't he?" asked Cooper.

Alice nodded. "He said he wanted to go to Forest Lawn, but Kitty said it was too hot there. They argued for a while, and he got exasperated and said dead people don't get hot, and she laughed and said he missed too much Sunday school. Then he asked if she was saying he was going to hell, and she said no but she wasn't going to Forest Lawn, where it was too hot. Not after living on the West Side for so long."

Everyone laughed again, and Alice smiled. There were so many stories about her aunt and uncle. Alice wondered if there would be any about her, or would everyone say, *Oh Ally, all she did was work.* Maybe Itch was right; maybe she was a drag.

"So we'll have a funeral, and people will come?" asked Skye. "I mean did she have any friends who're still alive?"

"There are people, friends, yes, people who used to work at P3, there will be people. Maybe not too many," answered Alice.

"I called Mom and Gram," said Cooper.

Alice squeezed his hand. "Thanks, hon."

Time passed as they talked and shared memories of Kitty, and then Emma rose, saying, "I should really go. I was supposed to leave on Wednesday, but I'll wait for the funeral before I go home. When will it be?"

"Gosh, I don't know," said Alice. "We'll decide that tomorrow, and I'll call you."

Cooper leapt up, "Home?" he gasped, "You don't mean home, do you? I thought we decided this was to be your home."

Emma walked over to him and hugged him. "I know you don't understand it now, but I got what I came for, some kind of closure maybe. So now I have to go back to my home, my real life."

"No, don't go," he said so plaintively that Alice ached for him. "Honey," she said comfortingly, "Emma will come and see us again, won't you Emma? She has to do what makes sense to her."

"No, she does not," Cooper insisted. "Because this makes no sense at all."

"Well, I'll stay through the end of next weekend, okay?" Emma patted Cooper on the back as she said it.

"Not okay," insisted Cooper. "You're making a huge mistake."

"Take it easy, Coop," said Skye. "You're sounding crazy."

Emma reached up and kissed Cooper on the cheek, but he only looked more miserable, and as Alice was walking her to the door, he ran up the stairs. "He has a huge crush on you," Alice whispered.

Emma nodded. "He'll forget me in a week."

Alice hugged Emma, then said, "Don't know about that."

"I'm here for you, Ally, just call. I'll come help you with anything you need this week."

Alice hugged Emma again and said, "Thanks hon, I know you will. We'll all really miss you. And I do hope you'll come back often. We're your family."

After closing the front door, Alice followed Skye into the laundry room, where she was busy folding some of many items she'd been washing, and asked, "Your apartment de-germified now?"

"I've been running both the washers in the tenants' laundry room and this one all day. Everything's been bleached except the walls. I can't believe a dentist could be such a pig," Skye answered.

Alice laughed. "We can repaint if you want."

"Good idea. Do you need me here tonight, or is it okay if I sleep in my place?"

"I'll be fine, you go on home. I might need you tomorrow to run errands for or with me though, okay?"

Skye nodded, and walked out the back to her apartment with a bundle of slipcovers in her arms.

Alice returned to the living room, where Itch sat alone playing his guitar, and joined him, her heart aching. "I'm sorry we messed up your dinner with Emma," she said. "But you and I can still hang out and talk like you wanted. I'm here now."

Itch continued strumming on the guitar, and said, "Nah, don't worry about it. I know you're super sad. Our talk can wait a while. It's late. Okay if I go to bed?"

Alice rose from the couch, saying, "Sure, get some rest. It's going to be a little chaotic for a few days. But oh, don't worry, we can still go to the DMV tomorrow. I didn't forget."

Itch patted Alice on the back, rather like someone might do to a big dog, and said, "No, no, you have too much to do. Don't worry about it. I got it covered."

Alice sighed as he walked up the stairs, knowing precisely what that meant. Itch wasn't her child, so she couldn't order him not to see Misty. He didn't feel like a husband, for if he were, she could insist he stop seeing her, and a husband would have to stop. When might he actually be a husband, she wondered, or what in fact was he, there sleeping alone in Skye's room.

She walked into the kitchen and peered out the back. What she wanted was to go see Johnny, for he had a way of making her feel better, but Alice also knew that considering all she was feeling at this moment, that was probably a very bad idea; yet he would want to know about Kitty, and also he had a right to be informed that this week she might not be available to do everything he expected regarding making decisions about the new restaurant. Couldn't she just tap on his door for a moment? Would that be so wrong?

Instead, Alice locked the back door, turned on the dishwasher, and walked up the stairs. After showering, she slipped into bed and reached for the phone.

"Hiya, doll," he said, and Alice could envision his smile.

"Hi," she said quietly, pausing for a moment.

"Oh no," he said.

"Aunt Kitty. A stroke."

"Oh, sugar, I'm so sorry. What can I do? I'll come right over there."

"No, no, I'm okay. In bed actually. Long day, going to be another one tomorrow. I just wanted to let you know because of everything, well you know. And 'cause I won't be free this week."

"Oh, sweetheart, don't worry. Take all the time you need. You sure you don't need me to come over?"

Alice remained silent. She did need him to come over, yes, but there was no way to make that happen. Even hearing his voice made her feel better, but how was she going to say that? How could she say that he was the person she counted on now? Or that he was her best friend? None of that could be said, and it could never be said, so it was better that it shouldn't be said.

"Just wanted to let you know. I would have called sooner but...."

"I'm here, whatever you need, I'm here."

"I know," she said, then quickly mumbled, "I'll let you know about the funeral." And then they both hung up the phone, and Alice turned on her side and buried her face in the pillow, sobbing until it was soaked.

In the days that followed, there was the chore of arranging the funeral and everything that went with it, the sadness of attending the funeral, the work of receiving people at home and cleaning up afterwards, but what Alice felt most strongly was the down time, the moments in which there was nothing to do but sit and think about Kitty, and feel the pain of her absence.

By Sunday morning, the week was over, and nobody was there but Itch and the kids, and Alice felt a bit calmer. They sat in the booth in the kitchen, eating waffles Skye had made, and talking softly.

"End of an era," said Alice.

"Emma's gone," said Cooper.

Skye sounded disgusted as she said, "Geez, Coop, get over yourself. This crush is beyond insane. She's like old enough to be your mom, well your young aunt."

Cooper sneered at Skye. "So what does that make you, my grandmother? She's only a few years older, nothing really."

Itch sat, typing into his phone and growing frustrated. "Even with these glasses, it's hard to see the teeny little words. Why is it so small!"

"What are you trying to find?" asked Alice.

"Recording studio. We need to make a demo so we can get a contract and sell CD's."

Cooper laughed. "Nobody buys CD's any more. We download the songs we like."

Itch gave Cooper a look implying he was just a kid who knew nothing at all, then said, "Michael Jackson is like the richest guy on the planet, isn't he?"

Cooper shook his head, "What with him being dead and all, that doesn't seem to be of much relevance now."

As Itch registered shock, Alice said, "But Cooper could do a recording for you, like a demo, couldn't you Coop?"

"Wouldn't be professional, but I could make an okay one, just for a demo, I guess. Have to rent some mikes," answered Cooper.

"That sounds nice, doesn't it? You guys could bond while recording," said Alice. "And then it could go on your phone, and any time you wanted to hear it, you could play it on the phone. Even hook the phone up to speakers like I do sometimes in here." Alice pointed to the little iPhone dock she had on a counter as Itch nodded.

"Cool," he said. "So maybe we could record the group doing a few songs and me by myself on the guitar? Okay with that, Miss Pac—uh Cooper?"

"Sure, whatever. Give me something else to think about, I guess," Cooper said glumly.

"Just not past nine at night," cautioned Alice. She rose to examine the contents of her overflowing fridge, which was filled with many half-eaten casseroles, offered along with condolences. When the doorbell rang, Alice grimaced. She prayed it wasn't someone else coming calling; they were all exhausted from the strain of exchanging pleasantries.

Alice walked to the door, also hoping Robin hadn't returned to attempt again to claim the bed, something she considered unlikely after his altercation with Itch. But no, it was Totsie, carrying an assortment of empty boxes.

She smiled bravely, dropped the boxes, and hugged Alice tightly. "It's just us now. Well, and Mom of course. And the kids. Well, and Mitchell."

Alice laughed, and said, "So what's your point?"

"Don't joke," said Totsie, "It's unseemly."

"Joking is what gets everyone through times like these, don't you know that? So—what's with all the boxes?"

"I told you yesterday, you don't remember? I'm here to help you clean out Kitty's place."

"Wow, I didn't know you meant today or so soon. My partner is living there. We can't just invade his space."

"What kind of guy wants to live in a place filled with an old lady's stuff? He's an odd duck that one," said Totsie. "Let's just go over there and see if he's okay with us cleaning some stuff away. This is important, it's how you get closure, don't you know that? People think it's icky 'till they do it, then they feel better. When's the reading of the will, anyway?"

Alice laughed. "Kitty had no will. I own this place and P3. Nothing was in her name for years. There might be some money in her bank account, but I haven't had a chance to look."

"Where do you get off," groused Totsie. "And what, no life insurance? Who doesn't have that?"

"Actually, I think she did have a policy. I'll have to check on that. You will certainly get a fourth of that."

"And what, you get the other two-thirds? Ally, I'm shocked at you and your greed. First you trick an old lady with mental problems into giving you all her assets, then you steal everything else. And now you don't even want me to have my share of her jewelry and knickknacks. I don't even know you any more." Totsie snatched up the boxes, and walked to the back of the house, calling Cooper.

Alice followed her, saying, "Of course you can have some of Kitty's things, but do you have to be such a vulture about it?"

Totsie sneered and kept walking faster until she reached the kitchen, and once again dropped the boxes to rush over and smother Cooper with hugs.

"Mom, Mom," Cooper protested, "You're acting like King Kong. Watch out for my cast." He waved his arm in front of her to make his point.

"I blame you for all of this," said Totsie, scowling at her sister. "I used to be able to hug my son without being called a reptile."

Alice pulled her phone from her pocket and dialed Johnny, explaining what Totsie wanted. She turned toward Totsie and said, "He's out at the gym, but he said sure go take whatever you want. Okay? You happy now?" Alice observed the sympathetic glances of the kids and said, "You guys want to help us clean out Kitty's apartment? Not the furniture of course, but the closets and so on. We'll have to donate her clothes. I mean you don't want her clothes do you?"

Totsie rumpled up her nose.

"Want to help us?" Alice asked Itch.

He shook his head, saying, "Think I'll just go for a ride on my bike, if that's ok with everyone."

Alice followed her sister and the kids out back and into her aunt's apartment, saying "This feels like such an invasion."

"What do you mean, he said he was fine with it," insisted Totsie.

"No, I mean of Kitty. It's like we haven't waited long enough," said Alice, gazing around sadly.

"She won't get any deader," said Totsie.

"Mom!" said Cooper.

Skye grew exasperated and said, "We don't have to do this now."

"I told your mother, this is how people get closure," said Totsie, walking into the kitchen. "I'm taking this toaster oven."

"Don't you have that brand new Cuisinart steam oven?" asked Alice. "Why do you want a toaster from the 1980's? Look, let's start in the bedroom, deal with the clothes. You can look at her jewelry, which is actually personal, and a real memento."

"Assuming she didn't *give* it all to you already," sneered Totsie, making big air quotes.

"You suck!" said Skye, glaring at her aunt. "Henry gave Mom the business when I was little, and Mom took care of Kitty for all these years, and where were you? At some mall. And she ran that business night and day, and where were you? Starting and quitting like twenty jobs. Why are we even here?" Skye turned to Alice and made a gesture with her thumb as though they should leave and kick Totsie out. "It's not like you and Kitty were ever close. Even your own son…"

Before Skye could finish her sentence, Alice kissed her and said, "Thanks for defending me, but it's okay. Let's just go deal with the clothes and look at the jewelry. Then we can look at all the whatever knickknacks in the cabinet in the living room, okay?"

"You should learn some manners," Totsie said to Skye, huffing, as she walked into the bedroom and flung open the closet doors.

"Ditto," said Skye.

Cooper laughed. "This is like something outta the WWE. Thanks, girls I needed that. Will there be any hair pulling?"

All the women turned toward him and said, "What?" simultaneously.

"Wrestling," he answered. "Lady wrestlers. Well the word lady is stretching it."

"Look at this," said Totsie, ignoring Cooper. "Some of these dresses are vintage."

Skye laughed and said, "That's a polite word for old."

"I have a client who goes to thrift shops, buys stuff like this and sells it on Ebay. She makes a bundle."

"I thought you quit the real estate business," said Skye absently. "Or is she someone who buys your make up? Or waterless cookers?" She moved some clothes aside, then said, "Oh look, it's my old cheerleader costume. I thought she was holding that stuff for me in the second bedroom. Geez, it's all dirty."

"What, you never told her I'm a life coach," said Totsie, causing both Skye and Cooper to guffaw.

Skye removed the cheerleader outfit, and said derisively, "Glad you finally found the perfect vehicle for your talents."

Cooper sat down on the bed, indicating his complete disinterest in anything happening except the harsh words, then looked at the nightstand. "Hey, look, mail."

Alice took the mail from his hands, assuming it was old mail of Kitty's.

"Did you know JB has another address?" Cooper asked.

"What?" said Alice, glancing at the mail. She was about to say oh, this isn't Kitty's, but then she actually read the address. "How odd. It's addressed to a residence, not that far from here."

Totsie grabbed the envelopes from Alice, saying, "Let me see that. You see? What did I just say—you don't know squat about this guy. He's obviously a con artist. Nobody with muscles like that is a chef. Chefs cook, eat, get fat."

Alice laughed, "Well thanks for that. Maybe I better get my own gym membership."

"You're not catching on here, Ally," said her sister. "You're tossing all my insurance money into a new restaurant—supposedly—but you don't even know this guy. He's probably a scammer and gonna take your money and run."

Cooper typed the address into his phone and pulled up an image from Google Earth. "Recognize this place?" he asked.

"Nope," said Alice, "But I think I know a decent guy and a great chef when I meet one." She began folding the items Totsie nixed and placing them into the big plastic bags she'd brought. "Oh, this is so sad." Alice sighed and slumped down on the bed. "It's just too soon."

"Power through," insisted Totsie. "Once we finish, it will be like we had a visit with her. I read all about this on a coping with death website."

As Totsie and Skye sorted through the clothing in closets and dressers, Alice sat on the bed, occasionally making a comment about having seen Kitty in the various garments. Sometimes there were anecdotes and laughter, and surprisingly, she began to feel better, just as Totsie had said.

Eventually Totsie pulled the old leather jewelry case from the top of the closet and dumped out the contents. "It's all here, isn't it? I mean other than the stuff she—air quotes—put in your name—air quotes."

"Nobody *says* air quotes. You *do* air quotes," said Skye.

Alice laughed. "I do have her diamond engagement ring, but you or Skye can have it. They gave it to me at the Wellman Center after she died."

"Hey, if I offered that to Emma, you think she'd snap out of it and be my girl?" asked Cooper.

"What!" said Totsie. "Of course you are not to get engaged. What has happened to you? Ally did you hear this? My baby is being molested."

"I wish," said Cooper.

It took a while, but eventually most of Kitty's personal items were either packed for donation or selected as a memento. Alice glanced into the closet. It stood there empty, as though nobody had ever used it. As everyone finished loading Totsie's car, Alice quickly stepped back into the bedroom and took a picture of one of the envelopes so she'd remember the address.

After Totsie drove away and Skye returned to her apartment, Cooper said he would go rent a few mikes for the recording project, so Alice decided to go check out the address. After what they went through with Julian, it didn't hurt to be a little cautious, and Johnny had said he was in a hotel, which was why Kitty had offered him her place. At the very least it was suspicious.

As she drove, Alice felt a bit disloyal. But why would he make up a story about a hotel? She knew it was malicious to assume he was a con artist, because he was definitely a chef, but they weren't mutually exclusive, were they? Nobody had said a word about contracts or lawyers, although it was assumed they'd both contribute equal amounts of money. But a con man would have wanted Tom to invest, wouldn't he? Certainly he would, thought Alice. It was just too silly.

She arrived at a nicely maintained house in Santa Monica, and there in the driveway was a bike. It was tossed down the way kids did when they were in a hurry to do something else, and was the sort of thing dads universally groused about—after they'd run over the bike. Dads. Alice heard the word inside her head. Dads. He was married! Maybe he was separated and that was the reason for the hotel, but still, he must be married.

Alice grew enraged. All that talk about her being his dream girl. All those *dolls* and *sugars*. The hugs, the tender back pats and hand holding, the sympathy and understanding. She was right about him from the start! He was a thug—a married thug. A sweetly nurturing, married thug. Alice felt like marching up to the door and ringing the bell, but that made no sense. What was she going to tell his wife? *Your husband has a crush on me but I told him no*? Then what, the wife says, *good to know* and *beat it*?

Alice drove absently, and soon found herself at the beach, where she pulled into an empty space and stepped out of the car, gazing at the Pacific. Life was so odd, but often it was so miserable, and there were so many opportunities for dreams to get washed away. She stood there for quite a while, hoping the sea air would clear her mind and provide some rationale she could accept that would help her deal with this betrayal, for what other way could she possibly regard it? He'd lied and manipulated her. He'd tried to seduce her. The only thing he hadn't done was poison her tea. Over and over she replayed the moments they'd shared and the way he'd behaved. The sky turned from sunny to dusk and still she stood, gazing at the sunset, still in a blur of bewilderment.

As she drove home, Alice's mind reviewed many of their exchanges. Just the other day she'd invited him for Thanksgiving, and he'd beamed and said of course he would come. How could he do that to his family, she wondered. Then she recalled that kiss, that perfect, amazing, wonderful kiss. He probably learned how to kiss like that by cheating on his wife with all those Misty-looking bimbos who wanted his autograph at the restaurant door. The more she drove, the more she seethed. He had led her on—and for what—for sport of course. Just like… just like… her mind spun as she deliberated, and then she pulled into her driveway and it filled in the blank… Itch, just like Itch.

Alice became even more enraged. Itch was her husband, even if he hadn't wanted to marry her. And there he was hiding out alone in their daughter's room, whining about driver's licenses and recording music. Husbands, she thought, useless creatures all of them. They finally buy a bed, and they want it back just 'cause you kicked them out. Freeloaders, she thought, useless freeloaders who can't wash a dish.

She had a husband, didn't she? Alice wondered why had she bothered all those years. She called his name and there was no answer, but she could hear the sound of music being played on a device. Had she really been gone long enough for Cooper to make a recording? She ran up the stairs and there was Itch, lying on Skye's bed with his phone in his hand, as though he hadn't a care in the world. Well, did he have a care? Alice knew that was an unreasonable assessment, because if anyone were burdened with cares, it was Itch, but in her current state of rage, she didn't care.

"You know," she said, angrily, "We got married. That's supposed to mean something." Itch seemed bewildered as Alice glared at him, then he leaned far back as she flung herself into the bed with him and began kissing him. "This," she said, "This is what it's supposed to mean. Love, passion, togetherness. Help, kindness, consideration. What a joke."

"Whoa," said Itch, appearing rather nervous, but Alice was unconcerned. She continued kissing him, then began touching him in a way that was nothing like what he remembered, nothing like her tentative caresses as that young virginal girl after the prom.

"Wow," he said, flipping Alice over and onto her back as he leaned onto her, returning her ardor for once, actually participating. Alice's arms wrapped around his neck, and she continued kissing him. He leaned up then and looked into her eyes, grasping her hands in his, then pressing back down, causing Alice's arms to lie flat next to her head.

"Just a second," he mumbled, reaching toward the nightstand, as Alice's arm inched back beneath the pillow. She felt something odd, then grasped it and pulled it loose: a red lace bra. Instantly she knew whose it was.

Alice leapt up, shoving the bra toward Itch in her tightened fist. "Are you freaking kidding me," she said.

"Oops," he replied, turning back toward her with a condom in his hand.

"Are you kidding me," she said again, reaching out violently and slapping the condom away, as he turned and watched it fly across the room.

Itch paused, looked up and down at Alice, then took a breath. "Maybe we should have that talk," he said. "First off let me say, I didn't know anything about this 'til Brian confessed. He shoulda told you, for sure. And I told him that."

"What?" said Alice, "What does Brian have to do with you screwing Misty in my house?"

"We were kids, you're always saying we were just kids, right?"

Alice tossed the bra into a wastebasket next to Skye's desk, and said, "So? You'd better say something that makes sense pretty quick."

"He screwed up the marriage papers. Something not filled out or not mailed in, I'm not exactly sure. But we're not actually married. He's not actually legal to marry people, did you know that?"

"Are you kidding me," said Alice a third time, her voice rising, "Of course I didn't know that. How would I know? I was a kid. He said it was legal. You said you loved me and Skye would be the jelly."

Itch walked around the bed toward Alice, who instinctively raised her hand to stop him from getting any closer. "It was a long time ago, Ally. That's what you keep saying."

"Yeah."

"Those were nice kisses just then, for sure. I wanted to...."

"Yeah."

"But the thing is, do you really see us together? I mean really? I mean now?" Itch looked down at Alice, his face sincere, some small shadow of pain on it that neutralized her anger, and caused her to look at him openly.

"I saw us together for years, while you were sleeping. Then you came home, and it all seemed so different. But I owed it to you to make it work," she said simply.

"That's not love," he said softly. "That's a debt, and consider that debt cancelled."

"I see," said Alice, her stomach churning.

"I really did love you," he said, opening his arms as if to hug her, but when she took a step back, he lowered them again. "I just can't seem to catch up with you now."

Alice's heart ached, feeling that she'd failed him somehow, that she'd been too demanding. "I should have tried harder," she whispered.

"You did everything, more than everything. I'm alive because of you. I'll always be grateful. But I just don't think we love each other any more. Or," he paused, trying to think, "It isn't even that, because I do love you, love the memory of you and being with you. It's just, just, too big a gap maybe. I need to go find my own life, not be some kind of sideshow in yours."

"So?"

"I'm gonna go. I'm sorry Ally, but I know you won't really be sad. You'll be relieved."

"That's just so mean," she said.

"It's not cause I think you're a slut or anything like that, even with all the boyfriends. I just want you to know that."

Alice looked toward the ceiling, feeling she should defend herself, but realizing there was no real point in doing so.

He stood tentatively for a moment, then said, "Could we hug goodbye at least?"

Alice stepped into Itch's arms and let him hug her, and she hugged him back, her mind spinning. All she'd done her entire life was try to do what was right. And not a single thing turned out as it should. He was the living embodiment of a dream she'd held onto, yet in his arms she felt wooden and strange. It was so much easier to love him when he lay inert in the hospital. Surely that wasn't as it should be. Itch was right, Alice realized, and she relaxed into the hug for a moment, feeling sad for the past, which was where that hug belonged.

Itch stepped back and said, "I really thank you for everything. And if you ever need a favor or anything, you call me on my phone. I have it right here."

"Okay," she said.

Then Itch tossed some clothes into a brown supermarket bag, which apparently he'd brought upstairs for just that reason, and he followed Alice down the stairs, and walked out the door. "You can send back that stuff to the music store," he said. "Miss Pac-man made a practice recording of us. We sounded like crap. Gotta get a new dream."

"Why don't you take it," Alice said, "Sell it maybe? Always need money."

He kissed her on the cheek and said "Thanks. And I can keep my bike?"

She smiled briefly. "Of course. I owed it to you, remember?"

"I would have gone out on that pier even if you didn't say to. You know that, right?"

Alice cocked her head, looked toward the sky, and said nothing. Then she stood silently and watched as he rode away. There was something familiar about the scene but she couldn't quite recall what. Alice turned back toward her house, almost expecting to see it vaporized with nothing left but emptiness, but why? She sat down in the silent room, which she could clearly see had not changed, and pictured a void, but why? Then it came back to her, the dream of Kitty riding away on a horse and Itch supposedly chasing her but actually leaving, and shooting at Alice as she dodged his bullets. Alice laughed then, out loud in that empty room, all alone. Itch's leaving meant she'd dodged a bullet. In her mind, she could hear his voice saying she would be relieved, and it still made her sad, but he had known what she'd refused to admit—their time together was over before it began.

Alice glanced around the room, which was not empty, which was filled with the artifacts of life, her life, even if it began as her aunt and uncle's. She'd filled her life with what was theirs, but now they were gone, Itch was gone, her dreams, such as they were, they too were gone. Her attempt to circumvent those dreams and build a life on something else with Robin, well it was all gone. But there was no void and no emptiness.

"I'm here," she said, to nobody but herself. "And now it's my turn."

Alice had struck a balance between bland professionalism and casual friendship with Johnny, and she was pleased to feel in control. No longer was she the damsel in distress, not even in his eyes, for she projected an inner calm and an outer poise which created a unbreachable barrier between them more effectively than had all her protests about being married. He was her business partner, nothing more. She allowed him to continue living in her aunt's apartment and didn't inquire about his marital status, for what was there to ask? He was married, and if it were happily or unhappily, Alice refused to make it her business. She observed him scrutinizing her now and then but she didn't worry about it; that was his choice. Nothing had been said about Itch's departure, and for all she knew, he believed Itch remained and that they were at last making the marriage a happy one. If so, that was fine with Alice. They would work together, hopefully successfully and for a long time, and it was better this way.

The first task was to find the location, and for several days they looked at empty restaurants all over town. Doing so gave Alice a sense of hope, for it meant that soon their business would be up and running, and the next phase of her life would begin, but it also produced a feeling of sadness and uneasiness. If the restaurants were empty, it meant that someone's business had failed. Success was not guaranteed.

"All these lost hopes and dreams," she whispered.

"Don't feel that way," Johnny said. "Businesses don't just fail on their own. People make mistakes. Restaurants aren't magic. They take commitment, expertise, and work. With those ingredients, restaurants don't fail."

Alice smiled. She appreciated the encouragement but didn't really need it; she felt committed to the project and its success. "It's funny how you describe everything as a recipe, some sort of fool-proof soufflé."

"I yam what I yam," he said, making a face that looked like Popeye.

They'd ended up in Culver City, in a large restaurant that featured a dance floor. "We'd get the studio business here, all those bottomless expense accounts," he said.

"Except on the weekend," she answered.

"We could have bands come in or a crooner doing old timey stuff. Dancing." He began humming, and swept Alice into his arms, twirling around with her.

Briefly she relaxed in his arms, feeling those old sensations returning, but her knees remained solid as she allowed him to dance her around for a bit. Alice lay her hand on his shoulder, but when she became tempted to press it against the back of his neck, she stopped moving and stepped back, out of his arms.

"Stoves look old," she said, all business again.

"Place in the promenade? We'd get non-stop foot traffic there, but it didn't feel like…"

"Us." She answered.

"Yeah, that's not the spot for fine dining. I liked the place in Malibu, but getting there daily, killer. PCH gets crammed, clients cancel."

"Beverly Hills?" she asked, shaking her head. He responded similarly.

Then in unison they said, "I like the little place off Wilshire by the beach. With the garden." They both smiled at each other.

Johnny said, "Okay, let's sign that lease and go buy some tables and chairs."

"Uniforms," she said seriously.

"Oyy," he said equally seriously.

"How about a simple T and some stretchy shorts or slacks, seasonally. Black or Gray."

Johnny looked down at his attire. "I wore decent clothes today thinking I'd distract you from this. I like to cook comfortable."

"I'm the one who's compromising here, you know. I've given up on the fantasy of seeing you in your chef whites. I said a simple T, not chef whites. How uncomfortable would it be? It wouldn't be different, just neat, and everyone would match and look presentable. And maybe we could get a logo drawn and get aprons made, and if they're cute, sell them. Maybe."

"Maybe," he said.

"If I spend all my time worrying about what you're wearing, I can't think about the food," she said.

"Still fantasizing about getting me naked I see, well can't blame you there."

Alice took a step away from him and said, "No, I'm not."

Johnny winced for a moment, then shrugged and attempted to put his arm around Alice's shoulder to lead her to the door, but she stepped forward and began walking, so he followed her outside to where the real estate agent quickly ended a call.

After signing the lease, they drove around town, buying or ordering everything they needed. Alice tried not to keep a running total in her head of all the money that so rapidly was being spent, because it might terrify her, but she knew it was all written down, in advance on the plans Johnny had showed her, and today in the margins with actual figures after the fact, evidence of her money disappearing.

"Like buying a very expensive car," she murmured.

Johnny laughed. "It's always scary at the beginning, everything flowing out, nothing flowing in. But that'll change quick enough."

"We're keeping the banquettes already there, right?" she asked. "I love sitting on them."

"Me too, but the guy never gets to. You gals always assert your entitlement."

Gals, he'd said, and Alice's mind pictured whatever gal lived in the house with the bike out front, and whatever other gals he might be recalling, probably too many to list. Unconsciously, she leaned away from him in the car, pressing her shoulder against the door.

"Hey," he said, "Your pal Tom been calling you? He's called me several times."

This was it! Alice pictured all the money they'd just spent being flushed down a toilet the size of Niagara Falls. Totsie was right, for once in her life. This was the con, the big con, or the long con, or whatever Redford and Newman called it in *The Sting*. Alice's eyes blazed as she spoke, "Tom? How much money did you take from him? What did you promise him?"

Johnny automatically reached out toward Alice and squeezed her hand, which she wrenched away from him, prompting him to exclaim only partly in jest, "Sugar! Are you all right? Did a bee fly in here and sting you?"

Alice's voice was icy as she said, "I asked you a question."

"I didn't take any money yet, still negotiating. But I'm thinking maybe we should do it, be good for the restaurant."

How dare he! Alice began to reconsider her choice to partner with this man, but what good did second thoughts do now, after all the money had been spent? Well, she reasoned, much of it was on chairs and tables, dishes and silverware, pots and pans, thousands of dollars worth of items, all of which could be cancelled. And maybe the lease could be broken.

"That lease has an out clause, doesn't it," she asked seriously, causing him to look at her for a shade too long.

"Road," she yelled, "Road—eyes on the road." But they were in no danger, and he continued driving.

"What's the matter with you?" he asked.

"I don't like broken agreements. I'm not some bimbo you can push around is all."

Johnny laughed. "Sugar, trust me, nobody thinks that about you. And what agreement am I breaking? I said okay to the precious little outfits you insisted on—didn't I?"

Alice glared at him. "Outfits? What was I thinking. This is a huge mistake."

Johnny turned the car down a side street and parked, then he turned toward Alice, reaching out his hand, hesitating, then quickly taking it back. "Suddenly you're jumpy as a long tailed cat in a room full of rocking chairs. Why?"

"I ask about Tom, and you give me the run around. Then you pretend it's about attire. Not exactly feeling confident about you here."

"Whoa, glory be, save me Jesus!" he said, his drawl extremely pronounced.

"We agreed, didn't we—no investors. Now you're wooing Tom behind my back."

"Tom's been calling me about the show. Remember? I already told him no about the restaurant—you knew that. I'm thinking we should do the show together. Just like I said before. That kind of thing fills the seats in restaurants."

"The show," she said softly. "Oh."

"Sometimes I wonder about you," he said. "Just that I had a talk with my agent, who's been negotiating with a big guy at the network about me doing more episodes of *You're Cooked,* and of course she wants me to say yes to Tom, more money for her, and good for me, and she mentioned to him about the show, and he remembered you and said we had good chemistry, so he's already interested. And my agent'll represent you too, unless you want someone else."

"Wow," she said.

He paused for a second and just sat quietly, looking at Alice. "Feeling better now?"

Alice nodded. It didn't seem like a con, not as far as she could discern today anyway.

"So I'm thinking why not, we tape one, two shows, we see how it goes. I know it's a lot to handle now with the new place and all, but Tom keeps asking, and he has a good idea for the show. We'd get paid, I'll see to that. And we'll keep at least part of the rights, and if the show goes, well it's good money, and believe me it helps business."

"But you have an audience already. Why do you want me in it? All those women drooling over you won't like it."

Johnny laughed. "That's their problem. Plus they will like it—they'll pretend they're you." This time he didn't hesitate. He reached out and squeezed her hand.

Alice sat still, his hand on hers. She didn't snatch it away or grimace, but she felt very uncomfortable. He was just too easy to like, too easy to trust. What if she felt this way for years to come? How would she be able to work with him, with a constant burden of awkwardness between them? Alice took a deep breath. "Don't we have somewhere to be?" she asked.

"You don't want to know Tom's idea?"

"What is it?"

"He comes to the new place with a crew, we're there, getting the place ready step by step, and trying recipes. Each episode, another detail has been decided, the place looks better, and the menu is more developed. Then we're up and running, and each one is about us running the place, planning and testing menus, cooking together."

"I thought that was your idea."

He laughed. "See, it's your snappy comebacks that'll make it a hit."

"Heaven help us," she said. "And when is all this to happen?"

"Next week?"

"Getting ready, and Thanksgiving, and now taping a couple shows? Well, I won't have to worry about the grand opening, because I'll be in my grave."

He laughed. "No you won't, a spring chicken like you. We'll have to be there anyway, the kitchen is clean, so we can cook there while painters paint. We'll select chairs, talk about colors, meet with the upholstery guy."

"We just did all that."

"So—see it'll be easy to recreate on camera. All day Monday, Tuesday, Wednesday. If it clicks, we'll have a decent pilot and two or more shows, and the place will be in good shape. Thursday cook, Friday…."

"Be in traction?"

"I'll be in traction way before you. I've seen you work."

"Sounds like you've got it all figured out. And you didn't even tell me."

He shrugged. "It just came together right now in my head. I could see it. When that happens, I know it'll be fine, so I just go with it." Johnny pulled into the lot behind their new place and stopped the car, but seemed in no hurry to exit it.

"At least I won't have to teach you to boil water like I did with Misty."

"Nope, I'm sizzling hot—water just boils when I look at it."

"Oh there's an old song about that, tea and stir it up," Alice said.

"Bob Marley," he said and began humming the tune.

"No, something Kitty used to play from like the 1940's. Before our time." Alice sighed, thinking of her aunt and the old stereo she played so often. "Hmm, how did that go? Oh wait, not hot, sweet. It's so sweet when you stir it up? What is that song? I'm so bad at lyrics."

Johnny gazed at Alice and began to sing softly, "Don't buy sugar; you just have to touch my cup. You're my sugar—it's sweet when you stir it up."

Alice almost relaxed, and she smiled. "Yes, that's it. You're a good singer."

Johnny laughed, saying, "Only in the car with you."

"What's the name of it? Oh I wish Kitty were here. She knew all the songs, old and new. Well, she did, she used to." Alice sighed softly, remembering her aunt from years past rather than more recent times.

Johnny looked at her sympathetically, then smiled and kept singing, a glint in his eye, "When I'm taking sips from your tasty lips, seems the honey fairly drips, you're confection, goodness knows, you're my honeysuckle rose." He clasped her hand then, and she looked into his eyes, forgetting everything but the way they sparkled.

"Honeysuckle Rose!" she said, "That's it."

"I was raised on those old tunes," he said. "Folks dance in the living room every Saturday night, just them."

"Wow, romantic. All their life? Really? And still?"

He nodded. "True love and old music, that was my childhood. Don't know what one parent would do without the other. Hope I don't have to find out any time soon."

"Ahh, that's so nice. So nice." Alice was touched. She smiled at Johnny briefly, thinking how amazing it must have been to have witnessed such a romantic marriage at home, and as the moment lingered, she felt him leaning toward her, then she snapped out of it, and opened the car door.

Alice knew she should be exhausted, but every night she came home exhilarated. Taping the show was actually fun, and even when they had to redo little gaffes, it wasn't hard to make it work. They taped all the details of getting the place ready, details which happened much more quickly than would appear on the show, assuming it actually aired, because the restaurant had to be made ready to open, and the genesis would be harder to recreate for the camera after the fact. Johnny had introduced Tom to some people, and they provided the expertise Tom lacked and some of the scripting it needed. Alice was pleased and proud to be working on this production, and it seemed to her that they were creating something people might like and want to watch, which was a vastly different experience than she'd had before with Tom and Misty.

By the night before Thanksgiving, she stood in her own kitchen, making a couple of different versions of cranberry sauce, as Cooper moped on a stool at the counter. Alice looked at her nephew; his broken heart was hard to witness, and she felt badly for him.

"I thought about going down there for the weekend," he said.

Knowing instantly what he was talking about, she said, "No, hon, I'm sorry, you can't do that, and I can't allow you to. You never know what's going to happen in the future, and maybe if she's the soulmate you think she is, something could magically bring you together. But now you can't go chasing her, plus no way would I let you drive so far at your age."

"I know. Knowing doesn't help, you know that, right?"

Alice laughed, then said, "Sorry hon, just sounded funny. I saved a movie for you on the DVR. Want to watch it with me in a bit? Might cheer you up."

Cooper shook his head. "I don't see video therapy as all that valid at this moment. I just have to know I'm gonna feel crappy until I stop feeling crappy."

"And you have to know you're the one who made me feel that way," said Alice.

"What?"

"From *Tootsie*," said Alice, smiling. "Anyway, ever see it—*Crazy, Stupid Love*? Steve Carell."

Cooper said, "Gosling. Yeah, I saw it. So what, you now think I'm the dopey kid with the crush on a babysitter? Thanks so much for that."

Alice dissolved some gelatin in water and stirred it, then gazed at Cooper. "Maybe you should see it again. Point was, he wasn't a dopey kid, not at all. He was a boy whose heart was more mature than his years. And yes, he does remind me of you, not because he's dopey, but because he's deep."

Cooper peered around at the ingredients on the counter. "What's the point of me being miserable in the kitchen if I'm not tasting stuff as you cook it?"

"Oh geez, I'm sorry," said Alice, gazing toward the fridge. "I know I've been eating out every night. Figured you'd heat something up for yourself. Johnny says we need to eat at many of the local places before opening, get a feel. Not like I've not eaten there before of course. You hungry? I can make you something—anything you want—the broken heart special. Just name it."

"Hmm," he mused, a devilish glint in his eye. "Have I ever had a cheese soufflé? Or maybe a seafood bisque. I know—meatloaf and mashed potatoes and some of those roasted baby carrots. With gravy."

"Meatloaf? Sure, why not," Alice said, worried that Cooper hadn't been eating properly, and she'd been neglectful. She glanced toward the clock on the wall. Even if she defrosted some beef in the microwave, it would still take more than an hour, and that would be pretty late for him to be eating such heavy food.

Watching the wheels in her brain spin, Cooper made a sputtering sound then laughed. "You're an easy mark. A soft touch. Of course I ate. You think I can't cook, I'm such a baby?"

Alice laughed. "Okay, tell me what you cooked."

"You know, the Spanish Inquisition started just like this."

"Of course it did. And they had frozen molten lava cakes too, so downhearted boys could cheer up. Want one?"

"Ack. Food isn't the answer to everything. You know that, right?"

Alice nodded, as Cooper waved his hand toward the fridge, indicating that even if it wasn't the answer, a molten lava cake never hurt. She pulled the packet of her homemade molten lava cakes from the freezer and turned, saying, "You'll be fine, you know that, right?"

"Yes, I'll dance at your wedding."

Alice sighed. "More like I'll dance at yours."

"Now you're talking."

Johnny had ordered an heirloom turkey, and he arrived with it early, and for the first time, Alice didn't cook Thanksgiving by herself. He attended to the turkey and the stuffing, which he called dressing, of course, as all Southerners do, as Alice made dough for rolls and baked several pies. He began a cream of mushroom and root vegetable soup, as Alice trimmed green beans.

"You make those sweet potatoes with the pecan topping?" he asked her.

Alice laughed. "Nope, but I've seen Emeril do it."

He turned the heat down on the giblets and turkey bits simmering in broth for gravy, and said, "I'll do it. Unless you want them another way?"

"Will you now be cracking one of my teeth? Do I need to worry?"

Johnny laughed. "I'm the injured party, and somehow I never get to live it down. Where's the justice?"

Alice walked across the kitchen to grab a bowl of sweet potatoes, which she set on the counter. Then she removed a bag of perfectly shelled pecans from the freezer and set it next to them. "Do you also want mashed potatoes? Cooper mentioned them last night, but I think he was teasing me."

"Doll, it's your family. Make it if they expect it. Otherwise, I'm the interloper who screwed up Thanksgiving."

"My mother would hang you out to dry," Alice said, only partially joking. "She hasn't cooked a holiday meal since I was sixteen, but she still has unreachable expectations."

Johnny mock grimaced. "Oh an old lady, full of piss and vinegar, whatever will I do?" Then he just looked at her, as if to say there was no old lady on the planet who was now or ever would be immune to his charms.

"Full of ourself today as ever, I see," she said, bumping her shoulder against his arm, and it felt as it used to, good company and plenty of humor. Alice smiled at Johnny and looked him up and down. He had turned up in a new-looking pair of jeans and a proper shirt, rolled up at the wrists, not at all unreasonable for someone cooking a big meal.

Noticing her glance, he actually blushed, and said, "I didn't know what getup to put on, couldn't really see me coming over in a suit carrying a turkey like I was its undertaker, not its chef."

Alice laughed. "Turkey undertaker huh? Sounds like Tim Burton territory." She paused again and said, "You look very nice, and I really do appreciate the effort."

"Apps, munchies, crudités?" he asked.

"Ack. I know it's nice, and people sit and talk—other people's families anyway—but I figure they eat all that and then are full, and the dinner goes to waste."

"Well, I made a platter of shrimp and crab claws with a simple dipping sauce, so you think that's too much?"

Alice glanced around. "You did? I didn't even see it."

"In the fridge. How did you not see it?"

Alice opened the refrigerator, and on the bottom shelf sat the shellfish, beautifully arranged on one of her aunt's platters. "Oh," she sighed, "That was the plate Kitty always put cupcakes on for Skye's birthday parties. She said when they were all gone, seeing the rose in the middle was the surprise. Year after year she said that, even though we all knew it was there."

Alice sighed as she thought of her aunt, absent for the first time from a holiday meal. "Oh thank you. Thank you so much for that," she said.

"Well, you know what a chintz-loving guy I am," he answered, smiling, and that was enough to cheer Alice up for the moment. They worked jovially for a few hours, and soon the fragrant turkey lay tented on a platter, and the ovens were filled with everything else, as pies glistened on the counter.

Skye arrived first, with a tall chocolate cake.

"Beautiful!" exclaimed Alice.

"We need to put her to work in the new place," said Johnny. "You want to be assistant pastry chef?"

"She's going to college and then dental school," said Alice, before Skye could answer. "But maybe in the summer and during holidays?" she asked, turning toward Skye, who shrugged and smiled, happy her cake met with approval.

Cooper, who'd been in and out of the kitchen for hours, ducked back in to grab a roll, hot from the oven, just as the doorbell rang.

Alice walked to the door to welcome her mother, Totsie and Mitchell, who, as always, dumped their coats on a chair and walked back toward the kitchen. Alice paused a moment to hang them up and then joined the family.

"Stanley, you seem to have changed completely," said Pauline Catson, sounding bewildered and delighted at the same time.

Johnny offered her his hand, saying, "John Badeaux. A pleasure to meet you, ma'am."

Alice watched her mother take Johnny's hand, and it almost seemed she was about to lose her balance, but he put a hand on her elbow and steadied her.

"Who are you?" she asked softly.

"Mom, this is my partner, Johnny. We're opening a restaurant together. You knew that."

"Maybe," Pauline answered. "And where's Harvey? Didn't they tell me he was out of the hospital? Can he walk yet?"

Alice didn't really want to answer her mother, because she knew doing so would lead to many more questions, so she just said, "Yes fully recovered, but Itch won't be here today, sorry. I know you wanted to see him."

Alice could feel Johnny staring at her, and she suspected he knew what had happened, but prayed he wouldn't say anything, for it would be just so awkward, but before either of them could prod Alice, Mitchell offered Johnny his hand and began speaking.

"New restaurant, huh? I want to invest. C'mon let's go sit over here and discuss it."

"Why don't we go relax for a moment in the living room," said Totsie. "No business or money talk today, Mitch, not a word, not a single word, I'm warning you."

"Not as though you wouldn't give up turkey day to be out shopping," he said sourly. "Only thing stopping you is the stores are all closed." He turned toward his son and said, "Those little fingers were busy as usual on the way over here — what with Ebay being on her speed dial, or whatever it's called. She probably bid on another husband, so she can have twice the loot to throw away."

"And we're back," said Cooper, grabbing another roll and heading toward the hallway to retreat upstairs.

"Wait," said Alice, desperately reaching inside the refrigerator. "Look at this beautiful shellfish platter

Johnny made. Let's have a glass of champagne and enjoy it, and then we'll eat, okay?"

"Even me?" said Cooper.

Alice patted his shoulder. "Even you. We'll pretend we're French."

Pauline turned to Johnny, smiling as though she were flirting, and said coyly, "Habitez vous ici depuis longtemps?" Then she smiled at Alice and added, "You said be French. Did you forget I used to teach French back in the day?"

Cooper cringed and said, "Yeah before they made you the muscle."

Johnny adeptly opened the bottle of champagne; the top popped with no loss of wine, and he turned smoothly toward Pauline and began pouring, saying, "J'ai déménagé à Los Angeles il y a deux ans."

"He speaks French!" said Totsie. "Oh, how sexy!"

Pauline turned from smiling at Johnny toward her daughter, and with pursed lips, said, "Tatiana, watch your mouth. There are children here. No four letter words, please."

"Sexy isn't a four letter word," insisted Totsie, as everyone else laughed, prompting her to scowl and say, "What!"

Alice smiled at Johnny, and as he handed each member of her family a champagne flute, she said, "Maybe we should just speak English. Mainly three or five letter words, okay everyone?"

Skye took the shellfish platter from Alice, saying, "Oh look — the cupcake surprise plate — my favorite — now it's like Kitty's here with us." She walked into the living room, as everyone followed, carrying their champagne flutes.

Johnny leaned in toward Alice, whispering, "So, don't *you* think my French is sexy?"

She looked at his sparkling eyes, his steamy grin, and what was she to answer? The answer was the simplest of all the three letter words, but Alice knew she shouldn't say it now, nor would she ever be able to say yes to Johnny.

"For all I know you said I miss my grungy t-shirt," she answered, walking away from him to glance into the dining room. It was ready, which she already knew.

Alice took a deep breath. It was all perfect and they were ready. Not only had they completed every step of the process, but they'd actually filmed it. *Heat and Sweet* was open, and to her it felt like the accomplishment of a lifetime. She stood outside the restaurant and just took it all in. For the first time, something belonged to her, an endeavor that represented her ideas and her visions, well, hers and Johnny's, but apart from the battle over uniforms, they'd agreed about everything. It was their vision, and it would be their livelihood for many years to come.

They'd decided on what was called a soft opening, no fanfare, just open the doors and anyone who came was welcomed and fed. It gave them the chance to ease into the process, to work through any kinks that might arise and make it all perfect in advance of the grand opening, which was to be tonight. The whole process had been remarkably fast and efficient. If they'd built a place, or even if they'd opted to rebuild P3 instead of selling it, they'd still be waiting, but choosing a location that formerly held a restaurant was a smart move.

Cooper had introduced them to a P.R. person, the wife of that lawyer who sometimes hired him, and Alice was amazed to learn that she was Tom's other daughter, not the prissy one who looked like Misty. Los Angeles is a big place, but sometimes it's a small world. She had set up interviews and they'd met several times to discuss ways to generate a buzz. It felt as though everything was in order.

Although Alice had no idea if the show they were taping would make it on the air, she didn't really care. Everything Johnny had said about it made sense, and it might be exciting to be a television chef. But even if it never materialized, Alice was content to have her business up and running, and she felt secure for the first time in a very long time. No longer was she overwhelmed with worries about money. She felt successful, and she didn't feel burdened at work because she wasn't alone in it. There was help, support, and someone else to pick up the slack.

Alice smiled as she gazed through the windows at the restaurant inside. The walls had been painted white but with a faint pink tint, making everyone glow a bit more sweetly. The banquettes were upholstered with what looked like antique leather, and the chairs were all whitewashed, so it had a comfortably beachy but elegant feel. Several candles twinkled on every table, and against the faint pink of the tablecloths, it was a very romantic setting. They'd arranged with a local gallery to provide art on a rotating basis, and of course there were lush flower arrangements.

Clients could walk through the restaurant and down a small hallway, and out French doors to the garden beyond. There were heaters, and people had already requested to be seated outside, even on chilly nights. From a center pole, dozens of strings of lights extended to the fences on every side, making a canopy that gleamed softly. A gardener had been engaged, and from the fences had hung pots filled with seasonal flowers and trailing vines. Against the far wall flowed a fountain, making a nice gurgle of sound.

Alice glowed as she walked through the restaurant and out back, appreciating everything, and breathing in what they had created. Even if she didn't own it, she would love to eat there. She could imagine small weddings and other celebrations taking place in the garden. There was no dance floor, but they actually could remove some of the chairs and tables, if requested, and install one in the middle of the outdoor space. It had a magical quality, at least in her mind.

She glanced at her watch. It was five in the evening. Soon the tables would hopefully be filled, and they'd be on their way. Alice walked into the kitchen, where pots were bubbling, and everything smelled beautifully fragrant. The cooks were neatly attired in the uniforms they'd chosen, which to Alice's mind were basically workout clothes, so who could complain.

"Doll," said Johnny, "Come taste this." He turned, and he too was properly attired.

Alice beamed. "My fantasies have been realized," she said, teasing him as she often did. "Every day I come in here worried you've reverted to your old ways, and here you are...."

"The man of your dreams?" he asked, bowing as though he were on stage.

Alice laughed, and accepted the spoon from him. "Whoa," she said, "Pickle my tongue why don'tya?"

Johnny shook his head and yelled toward the crew, "Paul, did you hear that? Do we want to pickle ladies' tongues?"

"Sorry, chefs," came the sheepish reply.

"I told you an hour ago this wasn't right. Dump this and start over, and please pay attention to the salt. Even if you did get engaged last night, you can't float along in a fog."

"Sorry, chefs, will do."

The moments clicked by quickly, as they attended to all the details, large and small. Soon the restaurant was filled to capacity, and plates flowed out of the kitchen, each one perfect, filled with delicious food. If someone asked to speak to Alice, it was always to gush and offer compliments. After ten in the evening, the diners in the final seating were finishing up, and Johnny sent out complementary glasses of champagne to everyone, as he and Alice walked into the dining room to make a toast.

"I want to thank you all for sharing our opening night," he said.

"It's been wonderful having you here," said Alice, "And we hope to see you back again, and often."

They raised their glasses, and everyone followed suit. Then people began trickling out, tables were emptied and the kitchen was cleaned, ready for tomorrow. Alice walked to the front of the house once more, as she often did, just to appreciate it all, when she noticed a woman opening the door, someone who wasn't at all familiar, yet instantly she had a sense of who it was.

"Hello," the woman said, "Is Johnny here?"

It was his wife; Alice just knew it. "He's in the back — I'll get him for you," she said, wanting to flee as quickly as possible.

"I'm Delphene. You're Alice?"

Alice took a step back. Johnny's wife knew who she was. Alice imagined how she must feel, what she must be assuming, and although it wasn't technically true, there had been a great deal of flirting. Could she find a way to tell this woman that no, she hadn't been having an affair with her husband, and she never would? In the few seconds it took Alice to consider the situation, suddenly she realized something. Delphene, she'd said Delphene. This was the woman he'd mentioned the day he tracked her down to Kitty's room. Demented Delphene—the girl his mother had expected him to marry.

"I'm Alice, yes," she said coolly, thinking Johnny wouldn't be happy about this at all.

Delphene reached out and crushed Alice in a hug, planting air kisses on each side of her face. "Johnny's mama told me lots about you."

Alice stepped back and tried not to register too great a shock, but said quietly, "Oh, really?"

Delphene nodded. "I was in town, some big doings, so I had to stop by and see Johnny, give him a hot, wet kiss."

"You do know he's married, right?"

"What? No way. Nobody told me that."

Alice nodded. "Yes, for quite a while now."

Alice looked up and saw Johnny slowly walking toward them. "Well, hell's bells," he said, "I can't believe what I'm seeing."

"Johnny!" said Delphene, hurling herself into his arms. "You're still hotter than a two dollar pistol, and with double the fire power."

Johnny hugged her briefly, then managed to extricate himself. "I can't believe you're here."

"Come on, now, you knew I always wanted to see the ocean. Well here it is and here I am."

Johnny sounded incredulous as he murmured, "The ocean?"

Oblivious, Delphene continued, "Alice here told me your news. Congratulations. I'm happy for you. Guess I lost out for good when you came west, even if nobody believed you'd stay. Hmm. Smells right good in here."

Johnny looked at Alice, and she saw frustration in his eyes, overshadowed by good manners, and heard him say, "We're closed for the night already, but I can fix you something easy and quick."

"Well thank you kindly, that'd make me happier than a dead hog in the sunshine. And then we can catch up, and I can hear all about you being married, and you can hear all about the home folks," said Delphene.

Johnny looked toward Alice, who attempted to rescue him by saying, "You won't be too long, will you? We have to do all that—er—stuff."

Delphene quickly interjected, "Oh no, I'm sorry to hijack your night without any warning. I promise not keep him too long, but you go get started with all that—um—stuff—if that would help."

Alice cocked her head for a moment, wondering if she were being mocked, but she couldn't really discern any plausible undertone, so she just nodded and headed for the door.

Johnny sighed, then said, "I'll see you in a bit. After I tell Miss D all about being married."

Alice nodded, and soon found herself driving home. He seemed to react oddly to the mention of his marriage, didn't he? Certainly he did, but why wouldn't he, as he'd failed to reveal it. Alice wondered how long this Delphene would be in town. She seemed like someone who undoubtedly could cause trouble, and Johnny wasn't pleased to see her at all. Maybe he'd led her on, obviously he had, because he'd said they'd been engaged, and only fleeing New Orleans had allowed him to break her hold on him. Now what? Would she be there daily, disrupting the restaurant? Alice fervently hoped that Johnny wouldn't give Delphene a job.

Alice showered and dressed, then made a cup of tea and sat on the couch with her feet propped up, thinking about this new development for nearly an hour, until she heard a tap at the back door.

Johnny smiled and said, "My little genius! Telling Delphene we were married was brilliant! Now she'll see the ocean, go back home, and that'll be that. I should've thought of that years ago." He stepped very close and scooped Alice into his arms, crushing her to him, until she pushed against his chest and stepped back, out of his hold.

She said, "I told her you were married, not that we were married. Look, enough is enough, I know everything. Okay?"

Johnny appeared perplexed, and asked, "What all everything do you know?"

"I know you're married and have a house not too far from here. When we cleaned out Kitty's place, I saw your mail with that address, and I drove by there and saw the bike in the driveway. Married with kids. It's okay, we're just partners, but you should've told me. People get separated, I get it, but I don't see why it was such a big secret. Or why when we met, you said you were at a hotel."

Johnny's dark eyes flashed, and for the first time ever, he appeared to be angry at Alice. "I see. So you snooped through my things, and you didn't think it was worth it just to ask me about what you thought you found, because it was so much easier to go cruising around, spying on my life?"

"I didn't ask you what you hadn't told me. Not that complicated."

Johnny squinted at her, and began speaking in a deep drawl, "Tell me somethin', Ally. We been playing Scrabble here ever'day, you'n'me?"

"What? We never played Scrabble."

"Well then, you got a Parcheesi game out somewhere? We been hot'n'heavy at Parcheesi? Or maybe Backgammon?"

Alice shook her head with frustration. "What are you talking about? We don't sit around playing board games."

"Exactly. And we don't play any other kind of games, either. I told your aunt I was afraid Delphene would show up at my hotel, but I meant when I was at the hotel. I've been in Los Angeles two years, as I told your mother when she asked me. Who lives in a hotel for two years? Do I seem like Howard Hughes to you?"

Alice shook her head.

"I thought you knew me, knew who I was. Do I seem like a cheating husband?"

Alice shook her head.

"You know my history. When was there time for me to be married long enough to have a kid big enough to ride a bike?"

Alice shrugged. "I figured a divorcee with a kid, I don't know."

Johnny's eyes flashed and he looked disgusted, and Alice cringed a bit to have so much of his anger directed at her, when she was accustomed to being treated with only kindness and concern.

"When you said come on and stay at your aunt's place, I did it for only one reason—to be near you. Because I told you—we had a moment, and I felt things I hadn't felt for a long time. I thought you were the one, but you hated me, so I wanted you to get to know me. I was as upfront as a man can be—I was so upfront I was boring—maybe that was the problem. Obviously I was nuts. I'll go back to my house tomorrow—where I have no wife. No kids. Just a neighbor boy who likes to swim in my pool."

Alice's mouth hung open, as Johnny rose and walked toward the door. She rose too, but he held up his hand, "Don't trouble yourself. I can see myself out."

Alice watched Johnny walk out the door, her heart pounding, thinking what a fool she'd been. She should have known better, should have trusted him, or at least just asked him. Why hadn't she? Alice paused for a moment to think about the choices she'd made, and the answer came readily: she was afraid of making another mistake. Suddenly her mind opened, and it all seemed so preposterous. She was a grown woman now, not some silly teenager. She could make good choices, professionally and personally.

It was as though a weight Alice didn't even know existed had fallen away. No wonder he was so determined to be near her, for he'd known, he'd said, he'd made it clear so many times, even in good natured jest, that they belonged together. And he was right.

Alice's heart felt open and clear, and she knew exactly what she wanted, and at last there was no reason to hesitate. She barely had to tap on the door before he opened it, grinning at her as though he knew precisely what was on her mind, without her having to say a single word.

She smiled, looked down at her feet, looked back up into his twinkling eyes, and smiled again. "I'd like to see you out of your chef whites," she said, blushing.

Johnny swiftly reached out, swept her into his arms, and kicked the door closed with his foot.

"Ohh," Alice's breath whooshed out of her mouth.

His arms encircled her tightly, and he reached down and whispered in her ear, "You mean like in a three piece suit?"

As Alice laughed and said, "Maybe," his lips grazed across her neck.

"Some kind of jeans and an oxford cloth shirt?" he asked, sliding his hand up along her back, and with one easy motion, unhooking her bra.

"Ohh," Alice said, feeling the steam rise inside her. "Could be nice."

"Maybe one of those teeny tiny thong bathing suits?" he asked, slowly unbuttoning her blouse.

Alice laughed, "Er no, probably not."

Johnny laughed too, and then he kissed her in an easy, slow, and comfortable way. He kissed her in a way that promised he knew exactly how to do it, how to do it again and again for a long time to come. He kissed her in a way that was just what she needed. And then he kissed her again.

Alice reached up and touched his face, smiling into his eyes. She ran her fingers along his neck and the curve of his shoulder. She opened her mouth, and he kissed her again, several more, heart thumping, knee weakening times.

Alice's arms tightened around Johnny's neck, as he swept her up off the floor, strode into the bedroom, and tossed her on the bed.

"Oh my," she said. She could feel him leaning in, knowing that at any moment they would finally be together, that at last her life really would be starting.

Alice pressed her hand to the back of his neck, and pulled him toward her. She opened her mouth and closed her eyes, yearning for more kisses, but he pulled up and away again.

"Are you trying to torture me to retaliate for all the times I said no?" she gasped.

"Torture you?" There was a glint in his eye that implied he knew many ways to torture her that she might like very much, but he kept moving away from the bed.

"You're going in the wrong direction," she whispered, barely able to speak the words. She watched him as he moved, and everything seemed to be in slow motion, everything except her heart, which was pounding.

She took another breath and said, "You can resist all this?" And imitating the many times he'd taunted her playfully, she gestured down the length of her own form, blushing again.

Suddenly she realized he was standing by the closet door, and had flung it open. There inside her aunt's formerly empty closet, Alice spied a collection of decent looking clothing, along with at least half a dozen nicely ironed sets of chef whites.

"Just in case you want to fantasize," he said, flashing her his wickedest grin, and then he was in the bed with her, his hands tugging at her clothes, her hands tugging at his.

Alice felt her mind grow fuzzy in that intoxicating way, the heat of his skin against her hands, the weight of him on top of her, the sweetness of his mouth, and softly she moaned, "At last."

He leaned up for only a second, saying, "Oh, it'll last."

And then they didn't talk any more, and everything was perfect.

ABOUT THE AUTHOR

Nancy Frederick was born in Brooklyn, New York, raised in New Jersey and Florida and has been an uneasy California transplant for the last couple of decades. She's an internationally acclaimed astrologer who is the author of thousands of articles and six New Age books. When she's not doing readings for clients across the globe, she's writing novels, of which this is her sixth. She enjoys strolling outside in the beautiful California sunshine, going to movies, and cooking. She's @NancySussan on Twitter.